THE GIFTS THAT BIND US

CAROLINE O'DONOGHUE

WALKER BOOKS

Copyright © 2022 by Caroline O'Donoghue
Illustrations copyright © 2022 by Stefanie Caponi

First US edition 2022

Library of Congress Catalog Card Number 2021947459
ISBN 978-1-5362-2222-7

22 23 24 25 26 27 LBM 10 9 8 7 6 5 4 3 2 1

Printed in Melrose Park, IL, USA

This book was typeset in Warnock Pro.

Walker Books US
a division of
Candlewick Press
99 Dover Street
Somerville, Massachusetts 02144

www.walkerbooksus.com

TO MY SISTER JILL,
WHO TAUGHT ME ABOUT BOOKS,
TELEVISION, AND SURVIVAL

bind

verb

 to tie something or someone tightly

noun

 a difficult situation in which none of the choices
  available are good

Cambridge English Dictionary

1

I SUPPOSE I'LL ALWAYS REMEMBER THIS AS the summer that Roe learned to drive and that I learned to read minds.

He got his license in June, was promptly insured on his mum's car, and since then, the car has been a part of him. A part of us. They're always interviewing TV actors who say things like "Really, New York City was the fifth character on the show," and I suppose you could apply the same logic to Mrs. O'Callaghan's Nissan Micra. Roe calls her Linda. My mum calls it "the galloping maggot."

"Maeve," she calls up the stairs. "The galloping maggot is outside."

I bounce down into the hallway heavily, not having quite broken in my Doc Martens, the new leather rubbing away at the skin. Mum is giving the dog his eye drops, trying to hold his head steady, her fingers prying open an eyelid. I take my little drawstring handbag from the coatrack in the hall.

"Take your coat."

"I don't need it," I reply. "It's balmy."

"Hmm?"

I realize then that my mother didn't say that out loud, and that I am responding to a coat request that was only thought, never uttered. She looks at me oddly.

Roe may have taken to driving quickly, but telepathy is a gift that comes slowly, strangely, and, ideally, with a lot of eye contact. You should really know when someone's mouth is moving. I double back. Wary, tense.

"I thought I heard you say . . ."

Tutu wrestles his head free and tries to wander off. Mum snatches him back.

"It's not that warm."

"It's August!"

"It's Ireland."

I shrug and head for the door. Her voice again.

"Do you need . . . money?"

I stall. "No, Nuala paid me yesterday. I'm grand."

I've been doing shifts at Divination, the occult shop in town, since school finished. Nuala can't afford to pay me much, but given that all I seem to buy is tarot cards and McDonald's, it generally lasts me.

Another pause. "There's a tenner in my bag, if you want to take it."

"I'm fine, Mum."

"Just . . ." The dog is free now, each drop having been ineffectively applied to the outer rims of his eyes, Mum giving up on holding him still.

"Take it," she says. "Just in case."

Everyone still thinks the ritual was a suicide attempt.

Oh, Fiona lied all right. She played the part of silly drama student trying to construct a stabbing scene with her friends so well that we were convinced everyone believed us, not realizing that they were merely humoring us, waiting for the moment when things had calmed down and they could find out what *really* happened. It's made my telepathy very useful.

When I concentrate, I can see the light in people. I find my

2

mother's light—a sort of lilac tinged with silver—and I follow it straight to her until I know exactly what she wants to hear. I know when to reassure her, when to be elusive, when to imply that there is more information to disclose and that I *will* tell her, but just not today.

It has been five months since the ritual. Five months since Lily O'Callaghan disappeared for all of February. Since a spell and a struggle with a knife almost killed me and Roe. Since she climbed out of the river, dripping wet and angry. She's not interested in lying, like the rest of us are. Her answer is clear every time. "I was the river," she says, a touch of mourning in her voice. "And the river was me."

The most common thought my mother has is worry, which is not surprising, but the shape of the worry is. She is constantly thinking that I have gone to a place beyond her, a place where I am sure to meet danger. She wants, very badly, for me to need her. So she tries to give me money, and when I take it, she feels happier.

"OK," I say, taking it out of her bag. I kiss her on the cheek. "Thanks."

And the lilac light glows.

Fiona is in the front seat and, seeing me emerge from the house, gets out to join Lily in the back. It's very pleasing, this little car hierarchy. I'm the girlfriend, and therefore I sit in the front. I've always admired those girls in school in long-term relationships: the sort of elder-stateswoman energy they give off, the First Lady air of dignity. I never thought I would be one of them. And now that I'm firmly that kind of girl—a girlfriend girl—I can't help but feel older. More legitimate somehow.

Roe likes to use gender-neutral phrases where he can, but he and I haven't found a word that fully replaces *boyfriend* yet. We've Googled it. *Lover* is icky and technically incorrect. *Partner* is too

3

dull, too grown-up. After that you start falling into terms like *my sweetheart,* and the idea of saying that in front of people is nauseating to both of us. Sometimes I say *joyfriend,* as a joke, but mostly I just say *Roe.*

"All right, Chambers," Fiona says as she flicks the front seat forward, ready to climb into the back. "Docs still giving you trouble?"

I grimace down at my feet, my heels still bleeding despite the two pairs of socks I'm wearing. "How can you tell?"

"You're walking like a duck on Prozac."

"Can you sort me out?"

"Cost you a milkshake."

"Done."

"Go on, take off your shoes in the car, then."

We climb into the car, and I kiss Roe on the cheek, his long earrings brushing my nose. I bought him these, for his birthday, back in June. Long seed pearls on a golden chain, the kind he fell in love with when we watched *Shakespeare in Love* together. He's into a kind of Elizabethan look at the moment. He's trying to track down a ruff to wear onstage.

"Hey, you," he says, putting his arm around me. "How are the shoes?"

"You could tell, too?"

"You walked out of the house like you've only just achieved sentience."

Lily, in the back, says nothing. She has no suggestions of what I might look like when I walk, and it's not because she wants to preserve my feelings. When we were kids and Lily's hearing aid wasn't as good as the one she has now, she would find group conversations hard. She would lose track and eventually zone out, and people would think she was being deliberately rude. That's not what's happening here.

4

If you were to see the four of us out together, you'd probably think we were four best friends, and that the best-friendship held an equilibrium that shot in all directions. But if you looked closer, really watched us, you'd see that Lily rarely speaks directly to me, and often looks out the car window when I'm speaking. My heart sinks a little when I catch her blank expression in the rearview mirror. *Please*, I think. *Please make fun of me.*

"Fiona," she says instead. "Can you help me tomorrow with my math stuff?"

"Math," I say. "In summer?"

Silence. Then, Fiona: "Lily is doing Leaving Cert prep, aren't you, Lil?"

"Yes," she answers bluntly.

Even the mention of the Leaving Cert has me swaying with nerves. No one expected much from me toward the end of last year. Everyone assumed I was too traumatized by Lily's sudden disappearance and my odd role in it. A tarot reading, a strange card, a public fight, and then—poof—girl gone. Then she turns up on the same day that I'm hospitalized with wrist wounds? It was all too odd for anyone to compute. I was frequently checked up on, which I hated, and then I was ignored, which I loved. There's nothing that annoys me more than an *Is she OK?* look, closely rivaled by an *Aren't you brave* head tilt.

It's not going to be the same this year. Teachers won't just leave me alone. It's our exam year, after all.

"I don't know what I'm going to do," I say grimly.

"You'll be fine," Roe says. "It's not as bad as everyone says. They love making a big drama out of exams."

"Easy for you to say, you're basically a genius."

He pulls down his mirror and starts doing his eyeliner, black ringing around his eyes. My heart thumps a little, a sucker for eyes that smolder like burning coal, even if it is via a Rimmel pencil. The steering wheel moves effortlessly as he does his makeup, the gear stick shifting without his touching it. No wonder he learned to drive so quickly, when he can talk to the car without putting his hands on the wheel.

"I'm not a genius. I'm just good at taking tests," he replies. It's what he always says whenever I talk about the huge gap between our school careers. "Anyway, results aren't for days."

His tone is breezy. Roe's problems aren't so much about his results but the way in which he plans to throw his results away. Everyone's expecting him to get at least 550 points, which is enough to get into some of the best schools in Ireland as well as the UK. Roe, however, has already decided that he wants to go to Kilbeg University, which is nowhere near a top university. His band, Small Private Ceremony, is starting to get some recognition, and he feels like breaking up the band for a different county at this point would be stupid. His parents, unsurprisingly, feel the opposite.

"You taking those torture devices off, Maeve, or what?"

"Yeah, OK, then."

I take off my boots and socks, but then deal with the problem of getting my feet to Fiona. I curl into a ball and roll my body around, sticking my legs through the space between the driver's and passenger's seats.

"What are you *doing*?" Roe says, his face almost colliding with my foot.

"My heels are in agony," I say. "Fiona's going to heal them." Then I laugh, because I hadn't realized that both words sound exactly the same. "She's going to fix them, I mean."

"Can't you wait until . . . ?"

Fiona holds my feet.

"Jesus, Maeve, you know there *is* such a thing as polish remover? I mean, you don't have to wait until it just *erodes* off your toes."

"I have a job, Fi. I'm a *career* woman."

"Right," she says, and I feel her small, warm hands wrap around my ankles as I'm upside-down in the passenger seat.

I feel the heat under her hands, and there's an odd sensation of tightness in my legs, of skin building and knitting together. It's still incredible to me that she can do this, even though she has done everything from banishing period cramps to making stitches dissolve.

"You're incredible," I say. "Thanks, babe."

I then try to slide my feet back and, in the process, kick Roe in the head. The car swerves slightly, and we all yelp. Within half a second, it's fine, and he's regained control again, but he's annoyed.

"*Maeve*," he says snappishly, "you couldn't have waited?"

"Waited until what?" I reply. "We don't *have* anywhere except here."

This is a problem for us. Our gifts are starting to grow, from little kittens in cardboard boxes to full-grown tomcats. We need our own space. It's not like we can risk normal people seeing us. People think we're weird enough already. But it's hard: Fiona's house is out because her cousin Jos is there during the day. The O'Callaghans are too jumpy, and Mr. O'Callaghan works from home. My mum is on summer break from college. All that's left is the car. Linda.

Lily clears her throat. "I've been practicing," she says.

Fiona and I look at her. Roe looks in the rearview mirror, scrutinizing his sister.

"Where?" We all ask it, a choir of voices.

"School."

2

ST. BERNADETTE'S IS A SCHOOL THAT
should have never been a school. It's two Victorian town houses on
the top of a hill in Kilbeg city center, and it has almost no facilities
to speak of. There's no PE because there's nowhere to do sports. The
music room has just an out-of-tune piano, and Lily has to do all her
cello lessons at the School of Music on the other side of the river.
Having said that, whenever I meet girls from other schools, they
always say how lucky we are. Lucky that we're in the middle of town
and not in some austere building at the end of a suburb. For years,
St. Bernadette's was supposed to have this brilliant reputation for
educating girls to a college standard, back when sending your daughter to college was as rare as owning a racehorse. Now that everyone's
daughter is a racehorse, and every school competing to be a stable,
Bernie's has lost its sheen. It's now just a run-down old building
that people still inexplicably spend a few grand a year sending their
daughter to, when most of the free schools are probably just as good.

Roe drives to St. Bernadette's, the summer twilight settling into
night, the sky turning dark blue.

"When you say you've been practicing in school," Fiona says to
Lily, "what exactly . . ."

"Around the back," she says.

"It's only garbage around the back," I say, remembering the scrubby patches of grass where an old garden used to be. Now it's where the wheelie bins are.

"They've cleared all that," Lily responds, but looking at Roe, as if he had asked the question.

"*They?*"

"I go there for tutorials, and they've got builders in, doing stuff. Miss Harris says they're doing up the place."

"So, you hang around after and practice magic?" Roe cocks an eyebrow at his sister.

Lily shrugs. "No one notices. They've all gone home by then."

When we get to the school, the first thing we see is a dumpster in the car park, filled with pieces of wood and rubbish, old curtains and moldy wallpaper. Roe parks outside the grounds, in case they have cameras. We walk up, the whole building fresh with the chaotic air of a dancer with half her outfit on. The downstairs windows have been totally replaced; the heavy old Victorian windows that you need at least two people to pull up are now shining walls of new glass. The paint has been scraped off the old door, the wood naked and chipped, almost shivering in its desire for a new coat.

"Can we just . . ." Fiona begins, but Roe is already making his way up the steps. All summer long, he has been salivating at the idea of a locked door. But no one wants to risk breaking and entering.

"Wait," Lily says. She sidles up the steps, leaning on the iron guardrail, and then climbs onto the rail like a gymnast on a balance beam. My eye follows her, and I see what she's going toward: the security camera, angled above the school door. She's tall already, almost six foot, and with one hand on the old building for balance, she's able to reach the cord connecting the camera to the electrical system within the school. She holds on. She closes her eyes.

9

The air fizzes and pops. I stare at Lily, her eyes briefly meeting mine, and I swear I can see something flashing behind her pupils. A fevered yellow underscoring the gray green of her irises, like a fire in a forest.

"There," she says simply. "Roe?"

Roe goes quickly to the door. I follow him, fascinated by the way his gift manifests itself. With his right hand on the door handle and his left thumb on the keyhole, he cocks his ear. He listens. Listens for the four pins in the lock, listens for the soft rotating of the cuff, for the firm nod of a spring. I look at my watch. Thirty seconds. One minute. One minute thirty. No one says a word.

Just before the two-minute mark, the door opens.

It's funny being in your own school in the summertime. You realize that all the things that usually make it familiar are built around the people, not the place. The smell of perfume and deodorant and old sandwiches and books and toilet cleaner and bins—all that is gone. There is no real odor to speak of except for the light hum of drying paint. The only sound is my boots, hissing quietly off the new parquet floor.

"It looks *good* in here," Fiona says. "Where on earth are they finding the money?"

"What do you mean? They're loaded, aren't they? It costs enough to send us here."

"Not enough to pay for all this," Fiona replies, shaking her head. "And besides, half our year are gone. Ran into Michelle Breen. She's not coming back, either. People are starting to realize that Bernie's isn't worth the money."

"Plus," Lily calls, looking around. "No one wants to send their daughter to school with the head case."

10

She's not entirely wrong. The end of spring term last year was tense, and there were too many stories about Lily O'Callaghan to make most parents feel comfortable. Lightbulbs exploding near her. A small electrical fire in the bathroom. Her gift is wilder than the rest of ours, more dangerous. And even though Nuala is the only adult who knows what she can do, they all suspect something is off.

The hexagonal entry hall has Miss Harris's office on the left and Sister Assumpta's on the right. Roe examines the locked door of Sister Assumpta's, and I put my hand on his.

"Not this one," I say. "She wouldn't like it."

I feel oddly protective of the somewhat senile ex-nun who owns the school. She's so particular about her office. He nods and wanders off into one of the bigger classrooms.

"So where are they getting all this floor money?" Fiona says, squeaking her trainers on the shiny wood.

"Holy shit," says Roe from the classroom. "Where are they getting *tennis court* money?"

We follow his voice and see him at the back window, peering out. We join him, and Fiona lets out a sharp whistle.

"Jesus," she says. "I remember when this was all bins."

"They've obviously bought the land behind," I say, astonished. "God, it's huge."

And it is. I'm trying to remember what was here before. An old newsagent, a few anonymous apartments, something like that? Now the ground has been completely flattened, and there's a proper tennis court, the net not yet mounted. The beginnings of a changing room appear to be in the works, a tin structure that I shudder to think of actually using. Surely they won't make the sixth-years do exercise? Not this late in the game?

Tall privacy hedges have been installed around the court fence, bald and alien looking. It all looks too strange, like the school has been picked up and plopped on another planet.

"Let's have a look, then," Roe says.

We wander out through the back fire exit, back into the warm summer air, where the tennis court gates are open.

"You've been practicing here?" I ask Lily, and as usual, she doesn't bother answering me directly. She just takes her backpack off, unzips it, and produces a bottle of water.

It's starting to get dark now, as we inch closer to ten p.m. The sun sets two minutes earlier every day, summer slowly trickling away without our consent. I feel my stomach drop. I'm not ready for summer to be over. For Roe to start college, for me to start my exam year, for the daily, crushing inadequacies of school life to take over again. I like life how it is now. I like having my job, and my people, and my schedule.

Lily unscrews the cap of the water bottle and slowly walks to the other end of the court. The floodlights don't seem to be hooked up yet, so we can barely see her. All that is visible is the moon bouncing off her blond hair.

"Are you guys ready?" she calls.

"Yeah!" Fiona and Roe call back, while I murmur a soft *no* under my breath.

We hear her shake the bottle into the air, water spraying everywhere. And before you can say *That was it?* there's a crackling sound, and the whole court is illuminated in a split second of white light. In that moment, all you can see are Lily's hands up, pointing at the airborne water. The spray is conducting her sparks, lighting her like a strobe.

A moment later, we're in darkness again. We hear the spray of water and another crackle. White light fills the space, and Lily's face is in the middle of it. She does it again and again as the three of us stare at her, dumbfounded.

Darkness. Water. Crackle. Light. Lily.

Darkness. Water. Crackle. Light. Lily.

And we stand there, dazzled at this light show, these fireworks just for us.

·)) ● ((·

No one wants to feel like they've been outdone by Lily. So we all throw ourselves into practicing, showing up at the tennis court night after night, long after the builders have left for the day. If anyone has noticed that the security cameras are no longer working, they haven't done a thing.

This is our place now. For as long as there's a summer left, we have somewhere to be ourselves.

"Who wants to see a magic trick?" Fiona says on the second night, her voice full of mischief.

"Go on, then," I call back, lying on the sun-warmed rubber of the court. My head is on Roe's stomach. I can smell him, that special Roe smell, that combination of roses, jasmine, charcoal, and salt. Sure for Men and Chanel No. 5.

She takes an apple out of her bag. "Observe: the apple."

"All right, Steve Jobs."

She sticks her tongue out and produces a sharp kitchen knife.

"All right . . . Jack the Ripper."

She starts to peel it in front of us, the long strip of skin coming off in one curling layer. I peer at her, the sun still bright enough to see what she's doing. She's focusing hard, biting on the side of her lip in concentration. And I can see, as the peel gets longer, that the skin on the apple is growing back. By the time the strip has hit the floor, the apple is almost perfect again. Untouched.

"Jesus Christ!" I yelp, jumping up. "Fi, that's amazing!"

She takes a deep bow from the waist.

"So it's not just human skin you can heal? You can do other things, too?"

"Yeah! Loads more, I think. The other day I got a hole in my tights, and I sort of pinched it together and imagined the material like it was skin. And it came together."

"That's amazing," Lily says. "You're so good at magic, Fiona." She says it with such bald admiration that I feel a twinge of jealousy. She's very fond of Fiona. The two of them have formed a kind of separate friendship, independent of me and Roe. It seems like a natural thing to do for two people who hang around with a couple, but it makes me feel a bit left out nonetheless.

When Lily first came back from the river, she found adjusting to real life hard. It took a little while for her to get clothes right again. For weeks after the ritual, she struggled with buttons, zippers, laces. It was like she had completely forgotten how they worked. Once, she came down the stairs of the O'Callaghan house wearing her dad's work shirt backward, the buttons fastened halfway up her spine. No bra. "Fiona," she said plaintively. "This isn't right, is it?"

"No, babe," Fi had said softly. "It isn't."

The two of them disappeared up to Lily's room while Roe and I worried downstairs whether Lily had been the river for too long. Her magic was bizarrely strong. If we all gained more magic from simply accessing the world of the Housekeeper, how had it changed her, someone who had been soaking in it for weeks?

Fiona helped her develop a method for her clothes. If everything is the same color, then you can't get too confused. So Lily picked a color, and now everything is blue. If everything is blue, then nothing can clash or look strange. If everything is blue, then everything is OK.

I just wish I could have been the one to work it out with her.

"All right, Maeve," Roe says now. "Your turn."

I sigh. "Mine isn't cool like yours all are."

"Dude, you can read minds," Fiona responds dryly.

"I know, but it's very . . . internal, y'know? It's not theatrical, like electricity or machinery or healing. There's nothing to see. No dog and pony show."

"I'm thinking of a number," Fiona says. "Go on."

"It's really tiring," I protest.

"You'll never build the muscle if you don't work the muscle," she retorts, like she's a personal trainer.

"Try it, Maeve," Roe prods. "Do the Process."

Sometimes, with people I know well, random thoughts of theirs will slip into my ear like a whispered secret. But most of the time, I have to try really hard. There's a series of mental exercises I have to do before I can look properly into someone's brain. Roe started calling it "the Process" for a laugh. It was one of those things that we started saying ironically and now we just say it. The Process starts with me closing my eyes and clearing my mind.

"Clearing your mind" is one of those dumb things you always catch YouTubers saying when they decide they suddenly care about meditation, but it's the only way I can explain it. I visualize my brain like the desktop screen on my laptop, and I drag everything—my friends, my family, the country, the earth—into a recycle bin in the bottom right corner. When the screen is finally empty, the inside of my brain is tar black. That's when the lights come.

The lights are harder to explain. I tried to tell Fiona and Roe a million times what it looks like, until one day I saw a picture of the northern lights. The streaks and swirls of endless light, the explosion of color that seemed to be perfectly organized without being the remotest bit planned.

Breathe in. Breathe out.

That's the easy part. The pretty part. Now is when it gets complicated. Roe must feel my shoulders tense, because he starts to stroke the soft skin behind my ear with his thumb. I lean into it, feeling his touch reverberating through my spinal cord like a current through copper wire.

Focus, Maeve. Focus. Back to the lights.

I look for Fiona's light, trying to separate it from the countless others: the deep shimmering blue of Lily's, the crystal white of Roe's, the blips of brown and green that must represent every beating heart of each tiny, unseen life. The mosquitos, the roosting birds, the urban foxes in the bushes. There are bigger streaks just outside them, flecks of color standing for the countless sleeping humans in the city around us. I don't know how to follow them. I can't read the minds of strangers or animals or anyone that I'm not directly looking at. What seems like a gift of limitless potential is actually very limited: I can read the minds of people I know extremely well already, which sort of feels like a waste of time.

Fiona's light is a shimmering orange. It's important to find the tail, to grab on to it, and to follow it until you can feel yourself riding the wave like a surfer, crashing right into the frayed coastline of your best friend's brain. I explain it to myself like I'm writing a guide for future telepaths. I have no idea whether these people exist.

Then, I find it. At the end of the tail, there are two black digits, sitting at the front of Fiona's brain.

"Fiona."

"Maeve."

"Fifty-seven."

She sits up, stunned as ever.

"Have I ever told you that you're a genius?"

"Not nearly enough."

"How do you know? How does it *look*?"

"I told you."

"Like the northern lights?"

"Exactly."

"Wow." She lies back on the tennis court and stares at the stars, knowing that we're in the wrong country to see the northern lights, but peering for them anyway. "How's my color today?"

"A shade earthier, now that you mention it. Deeper. More clay than orange, like a plant pot."

"Oh, I *love* it. What do you think it means?"

"No idea," I say, biting a hangnail off my thumb. "I feel like everyone's colors are a bit deeper when we're at the tennis courts. Richer or something."

Roe sits up and stretches. "What about me, Mae? What am I thinking about?"

Now that my mind is settled, I can see into Roe easily. "Your gig tomorrow night," I say.

"Well, that's easy. You could have guessed that."

I root further. And then I grab something more specific, hold it like a squirming puppy in my hands.

If the Children of Brigid show up again, he thinks, *we're fucked.*

I sit up. "Why?"

"Why what?"

"Why are you worried about the Children of Brigid?"

For a little while after Lily came back, the Children were frighteningly active. There was an antiabortion rally in Dublin, a protest at a gay club in Cork. But whatever interest they had in Kilbeg in particular seemed to quell. They were horrifying. But it was all so far away from us, so beyond our pay grade, and frankly, we were tired. We had Lily to worry about. A religious group at the other side of the country doesn't seem as pressing as your best friend forgetting how to put clothes on.

"I saw him the other day," Roe says. "Aaron."

We're all silent. The air around us seems to chill.

"Where?" Fiona says eventually.

"He . . ." Roe is silent for a second. "I saw him at city hall. Just for a second. He was with people. He was wearing a suit. It looked like a business thing. But . . . I don't know. I was wearing my ModCloth skirt, and he . . . the way he looked at me. He knew exactly who I was."

"Of course he knows who you are," I say. "He crashed your gig. You crashed his meeting."

"No," Roe corrects me, then stops, because even he doesn't seem to know what he means. "I mean . . . like he could see inside me. Like he could see literally who I was. Remember, at his meeting, how he made all those people confess their weird non-sins to him? I felt like how they must have felt. Exposed or something. It was horrible."

I put my hand on the back of his neck, my arm falling down the length of his shoulder blade. "I'm sorry, babe."

If the girls weren't here, I would wrap my arms around him. If the girls weren't here, I'd tell him that there's not a single horrible thing about him. That he is calmer and kinder than anyone I've ever

18

met. That he has taken the best traits I typically associate with each gender and made a cocktail of them all. The deepest part of chivalry. The oldest kind of beauty.

But the girls are here, so instead I say, "Why were you at city hall, then?"

His face flushes.

"Oh," he says. "I was going to wait until . . ." He gestures around, subtly inferring the word *alone*. "But I'm changing my name. Legally, I mean."

"Roe!" we all gasp at once.

"That's *amazing*!"

"That's so *grown-up*!"

"Does Mum know?"

"No, Mum doesn't know," he says, answering Lily first. "But the thought of starting college, doing all that paperwork and class enrollment, I mean, and having Rory O'Callaghan on everything. Felt a bit. *Ugh*. Y'know?"

Back in February, when Lily first went missing, Roe was a secret name. Only a few people in the world knew it. Me, Miel, a couple of people Roe spoke to online. Now almost everyone knows him as Roe. His interest in a double life is limited. Which is, I suppose, something that happens when you come close to losing the one life you actually have.

"I was just getting the forms from city hall," he says, turning to me. "I'll have to go to Dublin to do it officially. Will you come with me?"

"Of course!" I say, pulling him into a hug. "Road trip!"

"This is a cause for celebration," Fi says, jumping up.

"McFlurries on me," I say, thinking of Mum's tenner.

And we all troop back to the car, congratulating Roe. We focus on the future. We count our blessings. Then we fall into quiet.

I don't need to read minds to know that we're all thinking about Aaron at city hall. Why is he back in Kilbeg?

"I've been thinking," Fiona suddenly says, breaking the silence, "that we've been given these gifts for a reason, y'know?"

"I survived the Housekeeper," Roe chirps, "and all I got was this lousy T-shirt."

"No, I mean . . ." She gazes out the window. "I mean, the Children are coming back, aren't they? To Kilbeg. We can't ignore them anymore."

Quiet again. "No," Roe says.

The whole time we're driving, I feel a dark bloom in my stomach and pressure behind my eyes. Like if I turned my head toward the window, I'd see the Housekeeper standing on the overpass. Like I might see Aaron standing in the road.

I lean my head on Roe's shoulder and close my eyes so I don't have to look at anything at all.

3

THE NEXT DAY I'M SCHEDULED FOR THE
early shift at Divination, so I have enough time to go home after work
and get ready for Roe's gig. He phones me in the morning as I'm getting dressed, already in a panic.

"Maeve," he says. "What time are you on today?"

"Nine thirty," I say, looking at my watch. It's just gone eight.
"Why?"

"Listen, I think one of my earrings fell out at the tennis courts
last night. I looked in the car and it's not there. Can you do me a mas-
sive favor and get it for me? Before your shift starts?"

"Ah, Jesus, Roe," I say, exasperated.

"I know, I know." He sighs apologetically. "I'm a dumb bitch."

"You *are* a dumb bitch."

"I'd go myself, but I have to drive out to the back of beyond to
pick up Liam's drum kit for tonight, and I'm terrified of losing the
earring. Pleeeease? You're in town, anyway."

"All right, then," I say, yawning. "But I *better* be on the guest list
for tonight. If I'm not on the guest list, the bouncer will try to ID me.
So don't forget." He forgot once, and it was a nightmare. Fiona and I
had to sit in the chipper until the set was over.

"You're a star," he says. "Thank you so much."

"Mmm. Love you, see you later."

"Love you, too. Oh, and . . ."

He trails off.

"What?"

"No, I've already asked you for too many favors today."

I sigh. "Go on."

"Will you sort of . . . put the word out, about the gig tonight?"

"Roe!" I splutter. "That's not really how the delicate shopkeeper/customer dynamic *works*."

"I know," he says. "Sorry, forget it. It's just, the headliner is coming down specially for this, she's not on tour or anything. Miel has been trying to get her to come to Kilbeg for ages."

I sigh again, realizing that I probably have to do this, too. Miel and Roe have been excited about Honor Own for months. And I get it. She's exciting. A few years ago, she was the lead singer in a band called Jason & the Aeronauts. She was Jason. They were huge, in an Irish kind of way: afternoon main stage at music festivals, on TV whenever there was an album out, the occasional song in a commercial. Then, suddenly, they announced a name change: they would just be the Aeronauts. No one thought much about it. Then Honor came out as a woman, and Ireland had its first trans rock star.

"Fine, I'll try my best."

"I love youuuuuu . . ."

"Yeah, yeah. You're taking advantage of my affections."

"I know," he says brightly. "Isn't it great?"

I tie my hair back, fuzzy from the static of the brush, and quickly finish getting dressed. Within five minutes, I'm out the door, bounding toward the bus, slightly resentful that I can't take my time this morning. But god, what a morning. Roe and Fiona are always

22

on about Dublin and London, but I don't understand why they can't see how beautiful Kilbeg is. The honeysuckle is in full bloom, and everything is green and sun-dappled, the heat of the day already settling in. A family of coots are gliding along the river, their black faces splashed with white, like a coating of Wite-Out.

Within forty minutes, I'm at school. By now, we've found a way into the tennis courts through an alleyway behind the school that completely avoids the main entrance.

I reach the tennis court gates, and the sun is so high now that I can see Roe's earring from five hundred yards away. The seed pearls are winking in the sunlight, the gold flashing. I jog toward the middle of the court and crouch down to pick it up delicately with my nails.

And suddenly, while I'm crouched on the ground, I hear whistling.

A tune I know.

A tune I will go on knowing forever, even if I live to Sister Assumpta's age.

I stop dead. I don't turn around. I close my eyes, but the whistling keeps going on.

That bluesy tune. Like something for a New Orleans porch, not a tennis court in the south of Ireland. It's amazing you can know a song so well despite never having properly heard it.

"*Stop* it," I say.

The answer is amused, immediate, American.

"I thought you liked that song."

I turn around. Aaron is standing there, hands in his hoodie pockets, box-fresh trainers on his feet. I haven't seen him in the flesh since March, but nothing has changed. Still easy and blond, the kind of person this tennis court was made for.

"I don't."

"Ladies, meet the Housekeeper card," Aaron sings. *"Now, she can be your downfall, or she can be your start."*

He cocks his head. Looks at me. "Which is it, Maeve? Downfall or start?"

"Why are you here?"

I try to keep my voice from trembling. Try to forget that the last time I saw him was in a dream, and he was stroking the House-keeper's hair, talking about death.

He ignores the question, paces around instead, inspects the court. "Look at that." He points. At first, I can't see what he's point-ing at. Then I notice a tiny green stalk shooting through the cracked rubber with the most delicate yellow petal sprouting forth from it.

Aaron crouches down—squats, really—his knees going out like a toad. Very gently, he plucks the little flower from the ground. "Hmm," he murmurs, and then opens his wallet and slides it into the leather folds.

"How did you know I was here?"

He straightens himself. "We're sensitives, Maeve," he says sim-ply. "If you're using your magic somewhere, I know about it."

He says it coolly, with perfect understanding, like he's telling me the capital city of France.

"That's not true," I say defensively. It can't be true. Can it? "If that were true, I could . . ."

What? Know what he was doing with his magic? Track his movements?

"You can," he responds. "If you knew what to look for, you'd be able to find me."

He's annoying me now. "Oh, for fuck's sake, Aaron," I say, exas-perated. "Since when do you talk in riddles?"

He grins, delighted at getting a rise out of me. "I'm not talking in riddles. I'm stating a fact. Why are you being so hostile? You've had a nice summer, haven't you?"

He says it like it was he who'd graciously allowed my summer to be good.

I actually laugh. A hollow, hard, brash little sound.

"The last time I saw you, you told me you wanted to kill me."

"No. Lies." He actually sounds offended. "I said it would be *interesting* if you lived."

"Why?"

"Because we're the same."

"We are *not* the same," I say fiercely, and I go to stomp out of the court, Roe's earring in my hand. I think I'm going to leave it at that, but I can't help myself. "For one thing, you're a Nazi. You've endangered the lives of the people I love, you attacked Roe, you sicced your dogs on my sister. And that's not even touching the people I don't know—that poor kid at the gig, the one you assaulted, the one whose face you washed."

The memories come back like food poisoning, a knot in my stomach, a gurgle of acid. The poor kid, who couldn't have been older than thirteen, and probably dealing with their own gender stuff. How much does an assault like that set you back?

He stands there looking mildly confused, as though I were a crossword puzzle. Tricky, but for leisure, so who cares.

"You and I are more alike," he begins softly, "than you and your friends."

I want to punch him in the face. I wish, for a brief second, that I were a boy, and huge. That things like this could be solved with fights. And then I remember why so few men do magic, compared to women. Why would you bother if the option to fight someone and win was always there?

"You don't know anything about me, or my friends."

"I know that you and I were born with what we have," he answers. "And that they got theirs a different way. Through spilled blood in a spell."

"So?"

"So it counts for less. They wouldn't be anything without you."

This makes me wonder whether Aaron has ever had a friend in his life. It's me who wouldn't be anything without them.

"Your magic will always be different from theirs. What they have is a party trick by comparison. Do you have any idea how special the thing we have actually *is*, Maeve? How deep, how old, how rare?"

He's talking like a wizard in a cartoon now, and I hate it. I want him to feel as stupid as he sounds. I cock my eyebrow then. I turn my back on him.

"This is a lot of bullshit for nine in the morning."

"You know, you can learn. Learn how to master your sensitivity."

I walk away, still not listening. He keeps talking.

"They can help you . . ." he calls. "The Children, I mean."

I start to run now.

From the alleyway, I hear his voice. Faintly shouting, an echo cascading around him.

"That's *one!*" he says. "Two more!"

"One what, though?" I ask Nuala. "One of what?"

I'm sitting on the floor of Divination an hour later, my takeaway coffee steaming next to me. I'm marking down a pile of books on numerology, trying to find a price that will make them better fated to sell. "This one says that six and eight are prosperity numbers, so maybe I'll make them all €6.80?"

"Sounds good," Nuala says, glasses on, examining a printout

of last month's sales. Owning an occult shop isn't exactly profitable work. "And tell me exactly what he said, and how he said it."

"He was on about my magic being different from Lily and Fiona and Roe's, and then he tried to get me to join the Children of Brigid."

"And then?"

"And then I left. Ran, really."

"And he said, 'That's one'?"

"Yes. And that I had two left. Is that a magic thing?"

"Hmmm. Not Wicca," she muses. "Some cultures, it's polite to deny someone three times. Like, an invite to dinner." She looks into the air for a moment, lost in thought. "Oh, *Christ*," she says in a moment of realization.

"What? What's wrong?"

"No, I mean, it's Christ. *Jesus* Christ. The apostle Peter denied Jesus three times."

I grimace. "I guess he sees himself as Jesus in this analogy?"

"I suppose so."

"My god. The *ego*."

"He's giving you three chances to come over to the good side. Or what he believes to be the good side."

"And then what? Eternal damnation?"

She frowns, looks worried. "It's probably something a bit more literal than that."

Nuala is the only adult in my life I can talk to about magic. It's funny, how our relationship instantly changed after the ritual. She went from being an ominous stranger to a mentor, almost a friend. She's the one who told me what a sensitive was. Now she's trying to teach me the basics of shop magics. Wicca, herbs, crystals, all the rest. She says that having supernatural power isn't enough. That I need to study, too.

I stand up, stretch my bones. "What are the Children up to, though? Why are they back in Kilbeg? And why do they want me?"

Nuala's face goes vacant for a minute, which I know to be a sign that she's thinking something she's not ready to share. I wonder, for a second, whether I should try looking into her mind, and then remember the pact we all made: Only at the tennis courts. Only when we're alone. Only to train.

"Have you ever thought about," she says at last, "how you work in all of this?"

Nuala can be so odd sometimes that I don't know if she means "this" as in magic, or "this" as in the shop and capitalism in general.

"Uh . . ."

"Sensitivity, I mean."

I shrug. Nuala has explained it to me before, in her typically vague way. About how being a sensitive means I have a special connection to magic and the earth. "You said not all sensitives are witches, but all great witches are sensitives."

"Yes, but . . ."

She pauses, presses a button on the till so that new receipt paper comes out of it, and grabs a Sharpie.

"That's me, is it?" I say, trying not to take the piss out of her. "Me and the triangle dress I always wear?"

"Shush, ciúnas," she replies irritably. She continues to draw.

"Right," she says. "So let's say there's a certain amount of magic that lives in Kilbeg. Like a fossil fuel. It's there, it's under the earth, and it's being used by everyone all the time."

"Everyone is using magic all the time?"

"If we think of magic as being, you know, free will, belief, choice, the inclination to draw a nice picture . . . All that is magic. Get it?"

"Wow, OK," I say uneasily, not quite getting it. Not quite believing it. I start to take the piss, which is how I usually process new information. "So when I *choose* to watch *Friends* reruns instead of actually watching something new, that is an act of profound magic?"

"It's also an act of intellectual laziness," Nuala huffs. "But it all comes from the same place. It's all about will. Being the mistress of yourself."

I can tell she's getting lost in the weeds here, because she goes back to the drawing.

"All those little dots are all the people using magic all the time without realizing. Every time they decide they want to wear red today because it makes them feel powerful—that's a tiny bit of magic. Now, *you*, Maeve." She taps her pen on the triangle girl. "You, as a

29

sensitive, have greater access to that magic. It has chosen you as its representative"

"Cool."

"So the magic goes up through the earth, into you, and to a smaller degree into everyone else. Then it goes back into the earth. You do a spell, it goes out into the air, into the trees, into the soil, back to the earth." She taps on the arrow very determinedly.

"OK, fine."

She draws three more figures wearing triangles. "And there's Lily, Roe, and Fiona. For whatever reason, when they went through that business with the Housekeeper, they all got dragged into the magic's supply chain. That's been my theory, anyway."

I try to think about this carefully, examining the crap diagram. "I suppose that makes sense. But what does it have to do with the Children?"

"I don't know exactly," she says uncertainly. "Just that . . . two sensitives. It can't be an accident. They must *want* sensitives."

"But . . . why?"

"I don't . . . I don't exactly know. But I know someone who does."

"Who?"

She taps her Sharpie to her nose, her way of saying, *End of discussion.*

Nuala is oddly silent for the rest of the morning. At about one, she disappears to the room behind the shop for a little while, and when she emerges, she's sealing an envelope.

"I'm going to the post office," she says. "Can you manage for half an hour?"

"Sure," I say, trying to sneak a look at the address on the letter. I have no doubt that it has something to do with magical supply chains and the person who knows all about them. Her thumb is covering the name. All I can see is *454 Rue Alexandre Parodi, Paris.*

"France?"

"Nosy," Nuala says, annoyed.

"Sorry," I reply bashfully. "I wish someone would write me a letter. I haven't had interesting post in years."

"Well," Nuala says, "you send a letter when you're not sure if someone will take your call."

She leaves, and I resume my work discounting the numerology books. It's funny, plenty of people love astrology and tarot, but no one seems to care much at all about numerology. Maybe it reminds them too much of school, all that adding up.

"Excuse me," a soft voice comes from behind me. "Do you work here?"

"Sorry!" I say, jumping to my feet. "Yes, I work here. Can I help you?"

Customers aren't exactly my strong suit. The minute I think I'm on the verge of becoming a great witch, someone comes in asking about past lives and Reiki, and I feel like a novice all over again.

"I'm looking for incense," the customer says. "Something to keep away mosquitos."

This, thankfully, is simple. "Citronella sticks are what you need," I say, leading her over to a shelf filled with long, rectangular packets. They look like boxes for a wand. I give her one, and her fingers brush my knuckles briefly, her hand strangely warm. It's such a surprise that I fumble a bit and look at her properly for the first time.

She's older than my sister Jo. Twenty-six, maybe. She's the kind of woman who dresses like I always *think* I would dress if I had money and knew how to put clothes together. She's wearing combat boots and a long wraparound skirt made of shining Indian-type material, with heavy silver rings on her fingers. Her hair is a kind of dark gold, curly, and loosely tied with a scarf.

"I'll take two boxes," she says, already wandering over to the tarot. She picks up a sample deck that we leave out for people to flick through. "Gosh, aren't these beautiful?"

"We have a really good selection," I reply proudly. "I help pick them."

"Can you read them?"

"Yep," I reply. Again, probably a little too proudly.

"Is it very hard?" She's gazing at the Ace of Wands.

"Not really. They have a kind of formula to them. The Major Arcana is easy to learn, they're all quite self-explanatory, and then the suits have a sort of numerical logic."

"You really know a lot," she replies. "Does your mother own the shop?"

"Nuala? No. Please." I laugh, trying to imagine Nuala with kids. "I just work here."

I take her citronella sticks over to the till and start ringing them up.

"It's good to know there's a shop like this," she says, nodding and looking around as if genuinely assured. "I wasn't sure what to expect. I've only lived here a week, and I don't know Kilbeg very well. I barely have friends in Ireland even. I've been abroad for ages."

Then I remember something. Something that might shore up my position as Girlfriend of the Year.

"Hey, um . . . if you don't know Kilbeg very well . . ." I stumble a bit, feeling awkward. She looks at me, bright eyes curious. "There's a gig tonight, at the Old Coal Market?"

She cocks her head.

"It's a venue," I clarify. "It's not actually a coal market. I mean, not anymore."

"Who's playing?"

"A local band, Small Private Ceremony," I reply, that old glimmer of pride back again. "And the headliner is a big deal, her name is Honor Own. She was on the cover of *Hot Press* last month."

"That sounds great. What time?"

"Doors are at eight."

She says she'll be there, and I instantly feel weird about inviting a stranger to hang out with me. But she's already taking her phone out, searching the location. "There," she says, pressing her thumb down to confirm a purchase. "Just bought my ticket."

"Roe will be thrilled," I say, and he will be.

"Are you together?"

I nod. "He's the singer."

"You have a great social life," she says admiringly. "I wish I had at your age."

I smile, feeling genuinely a bit flattered. Because I *do* have a great social life now, after all. Sometimes, when we're all at a gig together, I feel such a surge of luck and joy. I remember what loneliness feels like, and it's such a shock to not feel it anymore.

"Well, in the summer I do," I reply modestly. "But I'm starting my Leaving Cert this year, so that's about to change. My parents are going to be cracking down majorly."

I start bagging her items, conscious I've kept her talking too long.

"My school is only, like, five minutes from here, so I hope I'll still be able to pop in and do evening shifts."

She looks at me, astounded. "St. Bernadette's?"

"Yes."

"But *I'm* in St. Bernadette's."

"What?" I reply, confused. "Sorry, you look too . . ."

I almost say *old* and hold my tongue. She gives me a sly look, and we both start laughing at the faux pas I almost made.

"No, I'm *working* there."

"Oh." I feel a bit awkward now. A minute ago she was just a cool woman asking about tarot. Now she's a teacher. A teacher I have just invited to a gig. She seems to understand my sudden apprehension.

"Don't worry," she says. "I'm not a real teacher. Just a counselor."

"You've picked a good year," I say, nervous and jabbering. "They're doing the whole place up. We have a tennis court and everything now."

"Oh yes," she says, laughing a bit. "I've heard all about the tennis court. They're very proud of it."

"Yeah, well they would be. It was all bins back there before."

She pays for her incense. "I'm Heather," she says. "Or, I don't know, you'll probably have to call me Miss Banbury at school. But it's Heather."

"Hi, Heather. I'm Maeve."

She grins. "Good to have a friendly face on the first day. Between me and you, I'm pissing myself with nerves. I'll see you at the gig."

I laugh, thinking that maybe school won't be so grim after all now that we have at least one fun, young teacher.

ACE OF WANDS

4

FIONA AND LILY COME TO MY HOUSE TO GET
ready for the gig. Fiona with three outfit options, Lily wearing what
she's had on all day. As I'll end up wearing what Fiona decides she
doesn't want to wear, all my advice tends to be weighted.

"What about this?" she says, turning in a black velvet mini-
dress with a crescent moon embroidered on the thigh. Fiona's been
working this summer, too: in the mornings, at a speech and drama
camp for young kids. All her money has been plowed back into her
wardrobe.

"It's stunning," I say, mildly envious. It's not that I don't like
looking nice, it's just that I don't have the patience for shopping like
she does. I also have no imagination when it comes to putting clothes
together.

"But it doesn't go with these," she says, looking at her emerald
brogues. "And I love these."

"Well, then wear the shoes," I urge. "Build the outfit around the
shoes."

She wrestles the dress off over her head. "Don't think because
I can't read minds that I don't know exactly what you're doing." She
flings the dress to me, and I catch it in my hands.

"Thank you, dark mother."

Lily is lying on the floor, staring at her phone. "Fiona," she says. "My phone is on one percent."

Fiona zips on some black hot pants over her tights, and they look great with the brogues. She wanders over to Lily, pulling on a backless sequined top as she goes. I have the black dress on by now, but I already wish I looked like she does, so put together and chic.

She lies down on the floor next to Lily, and they both cradle Lily's old iPhone. I watch them from the mirror as I flick on my mascara.

"What are you doing?"

"*Shh*," Lily says, as if I'm annoying her. They both close their eyes, and there's a warmth in the room, the sense of magic around me. It feels weird, doing magic away from the courts. Not wrong, but unsettling.

"Fi, what're you doing?" I ask again. But they don't answer. Then a few seconds later, they open their eyes at the same time.

"There," Fi says, sitting up. "You're on one hundred percent now."

I gape at them. "Her phone, you mean?"

"Yeah." Fiona brushes herself down, wary of dust on her outfit. "We figured it out this afternoon. That our gifts can, like, work together?"

"You did? Where?"

"We were at the tennis courts."

The feeling of being left out solidifies, like a lump in sour milk. "You two went to the tennis courts today?"

"Yeah," Fiona says, and then, obviously feeling guilty: "You were working, so . . ."

This shouldn't bother me. If this were an ordinary kind of friendship group, this wouldn't bother me at all. However, the fact remains that Lily hates me, and so every fun interaction she has with someone else just feels like a reminder that she no longer has fun with me. She doesn't forgive me for dumping our friendship, she doesn't forgive me for the Housekeeper card reading, and she *hates* me for breaking the spell with the Housekeeper, the spell that made her the river.

I try to put a cheery face on, act all gung ho about it. "Well, let's try it with my gift, then. Fi, let's do something together."

She looks at me warily. "I don't know. I don't think your house is the right place to experiment. Your parents are downstairs. And we need to leave in, like, twenty minutes."

"Yeah, you're probably right," I say, trying not to sound put out. Then, I remember something. "I was at the tennis courts this morning. Roe asked me to go, to pick up his dropped earring," I say. "Aaron was there."

They both stare at me, dumbfounded. They exchange a look. A look that says, *And she's only bringing this up* now?

"Why was he there? At our place?"

"He said that he could tell where I was using magic. He said we were connected." I cringe at the thought. "He said he and I had more in common than me and you guys. That your magic wasn't . . ." I pause, trying to remember. "That you guys weren't born with it or something, so it counts for less."

"Oh, my god," says Fiona, tossing her hair. "That is so *him*. Leave it to Aaron to make magic racist. Next he'll be, like, taking out a tape measure and examining the width of our heads."

"He asked me to *join* them."

"Jesus," she says, furrowing her brow. "Gross."

Lily looks at me as if I were something she'd like to scrape off her shoe.

"Did you tell Nuala?" Fi asks.

"Yeah. She had all these theories for me. About how we're all part of a magical supply chain." I pause, trying to remember what she said. "I didn't really get it. Anyway," I say brightly, "we should start thinking about bus times."

But the atmosphere feels different all of a sudden. Like I've fallen out of lockstep with Fiona, and so far behind Lily that I can't even see her. Suddenly I feel like the third friend, the one on the outside. Like telling them about Aaron makes me even more connected to him. Like mentioning his offer for me to join the Children has only confirmed a suspicion that I might belong in their ranks.

No, Maeve, you're being stupid.

Fiona is rooting around in her makeup bag for highlighter.

But I better *check* if I'm being stupid.

"I'm just going to do my hair first," I say loudly, and I plug in the hair straightener. I wait for it to heat up, then wrap a length of my unruly hair tightly around the irons, trying to make a loose curl.

And while my hair steams with heat, I look for Fiona's light. Now that I've been practicing so much, it's easy to do. I can even keep the straightener going at the same time.

I wish Maeve wasn't so jealous. Like, you can't be in every single conversation all the time. Sometimes I think she thinks the world stops when she's not around.

I can feel tears build behind my eyes.

"You OK, Maeve?" Fi asks, catching my reflection in the mirror.

"Yeah," I sniff, releasing the straightener. "Burned my head a bit."

I look at Lily. I don't like to look inside Lily too often. It's a confusing place, still so full of water and currents. But I burrow. I find her light. I get there.

I'm so sick of her.

I drop the straightener, go to the bathroom, and have a small, stupid cry.

"Maeve," Dad calls up the stairs. "I can drop you and the girls into town, if you like."

"Thanks," I say, the word choking in my throat.

I feel so petty, so hurt, and so powerless. This is what telepathy is, really. Hearing awful things about yourself and not even being able to be mad at the people who thought them. Telepathy is the trouble you go looking for and have no one to blame afterward but yourself.

I don't say much in the car. Dad asks Fiona about her plans for college. My parents love Fiona. She's the kind of friend who parents always love.

"I'm hoping to do drama at Trinity, in Dublin," she says brightly. "That's where Ruth Negga went."

Fiona hasn't stopped talking about Trinity since the beginning of the summer. It is, according to her, the only place in Ireland where an aspiring actor can "catch a break."

I look out the window, still unmoored by my mind-reading, the bitchy thoughts from Lily and Fiona. Dad's eyes flicker to me.

"You know, Fiona, I was only reading the other day that Cillian Murphy went to UCC, in Cork. And he's done very well for himself, hasn't he? And Cork is much closer than Dublin."

Fiona scoffs. "Cork city is basically the same size as Kilbeg," she says. "And I'm sick of small towns."

"City," I say sharply. "Kilbeg is a city. It has a cathedral, so it's a city."

It's so annoying, the way she says it. Like she's some starlet from the 1940s whose hometown is just a post office and a pharmacy. I love her, but it completely pisses me off. I sink farther into my seat, saying nothing.

Seeming to sense a shift in atmosphere, Fiona keeps talking. "And Maeve is going to go to UCD, and we'll have a flat together, won't we, Maeve?"

This is a fiction that Fiona has been maintaining for some time now, and I've been humoring her. This notion of the two of us moving together, as if I'm ever going to have the grades to get into a Dublin college. Or any college. Dad, who had Stern Words with me two weeks ago about my report card, looks skeptical.

"Well, we'll see about that," he says. "And what about you, Lily?"

"Galway," she says. "I'm moving to Galway."

This is literally the first time I'm hearing about this. I turn all the way around in the passenger's seat.

"You're moving to *Galway*?"

"I am," she says coolly.

"What's in Galway?"

"The ocean."

"Ah," Dad says. "Nature girl."

"And that's why you're doing tutorials this summer? To get the points for NUI?"

I know that it's rude to sound this amazed, but I am. Roe and Fiona have always had big dreams, but I presumed that Lily, at the very least, was planning to stick around Kilbeg after school ends, not aim for such a good university.

"Yes."

"Well, girls," says Dad, pulling over. "This is where we part ways."

We all get out of the car, thank Dad, and walk down the street together. I can't get Galway out of my head. We cross the bridge, a fine mist coming off the Beg. Lily's head turns to look at it, like she's mournfully gazing at an old lover.

"So what are you hoping for, Lil?" I ask. "Points-wise, I mean?"

She turns her head back.

"Probably four hundred."

"Four *hundred*!" I exclaim. Mum totted up my report card and predicted that, at my current average, I would barely break three hundred. And I've always been slightly better than Lily at school. "You think you can get that?"

She says nothing. For some reason, I can't stop the anxiety rising in my throat. The idea that, at the end of next year, I will be the only one left in Kilbeg.

"And you need to pass Irish, math, and have a European language to get into a proper university, don't you?"

"Lily is working really hard," says Fi, a sharp edge to her voice. A *Leave it, Maeve* voice. "Aren't you, Lily?"

We fall silent as our shoes clack across the bridge. I can't stop myself. I don't want Lily to leave. I want her to stay here and learn to like me again. To change her inner monologue from *I'm so sick of her.*

"And languages aren't your strong suit, are they?"

Why am I doing this?

"Maeve," Fiona says warningly. "You're drinking dumb-bitch juice."

This is the gang's joke, for when someone is being insecure and stupid. I'm not in the mood for it today somehow.

Lily turns to me and smiles. She takes my hand, and for a second, I think she's trying to reassure me. And that's when it happens. The jolt. The white-hot flicker that bursts through my shoulder and shimmers down my body.

"Jesus *Christ!*" I yell, pushing away from her. "Lily!"

"What?" Fiona says, spinning around.

"Lily just shocked me."

"Lily, you didn't!" Fiona turns on Lily now, and I feel a flicker of satisfaction as the pain quickly ebbs away.

Lily just shrugs and picks up her pace. "We'll be late for the gig," she says, and walks ahead of us.

"Can you *believe* her?" I say to Fiona. "She used her power *against* me, Fi."

Fiona hesitates, then puts her peacekeeper face on. "You *were* goading her, dude . . ."

I can't believe this. "We promised we wouldn't use our powers like that," I say lamely. "Only in the tennis courts."

Fi cocks her head, looks at me.

"And you're sticking to that, too, are you?"

5

IT'S STILL AWKWARD WHEN WE GET TO THE
Old Coal Market, but it's the kind of awkwardness that swings in the
other direction. Everyone is acting too nice, too much like they want
to avoid a fight. This is somehow worse. We wait in line, shivering
outside, and make awkward chatter.

"I'm excited about Honor," I say, even though it's a boring thing
to say and we've said it three times already. Roe has been hyping us
for Honor all month. "I'm obsessed with her Instagram." I've looked
at it twice.

Fiona nods. "She's incredible, isn't she? I mean, the activism
stuff alone."

I nod back. Honor Own is trying to get the healthcare system to
change the way it acts around trans people. Roe's bass player, Miel, is
trying to get top surgery and has to pretend to have a mental illness.
"I'm not insane," they said. "I just don't want tits."

"Do you think we'll get to meet her?" asks Fiona.

"I don't know," I say, pulling out my phone. "I'll text Roe."

"This is taking forever," Lily says, stamping her feet.

We get to the front of the queue and see that everyone is getting
thorough bag checks, not just for alcohol but for weapons, or things
that could be used as weapons.

"I read that there was an incident at one of her gigs last month," Fiona says.

"COB?" I immediately ask.

"Could be." She shrugs. "Or just regular old transphobes."

We finally make it in, and Roe appears in a floor-length leopard-skin dress with a slit in the chest, his pale torso showing through. I fling my arms around him. "My god," I say. "You could hang a coat off those clavicles."

I can tell he's excited to play because he gives me a huge kiss in front of everyone. I laugh and take his earring from my pocket. "I love you so much," he says, taking it.

"Oh!" I say, remembering. "AND I got someone to buy a ticket."

"Really?" he asks brightly. "Who?"

"Heather," I answer, and everyone looks at me confused. "She's this new teacher up at school."

"*Our* school?" Lily says, mystified.

"You invited a *teacher*?" Fiona says. "Called *Heather*?"

"She's cool," I say, a little defensive. "She just moved here, she doesn't know Kilbeg at all, she seemed grateful for the tip. I didn't invite her as a teacher. I invited her as, like, a person. I didn't even know she was a teacher when I invited her."

They all look at me like I'm insane. Maybe I am?

"Imagine moving to Kilbeg," Fiona says. *"Willingly."*

"Wow, OK, Fiona," I say, not bothering to hide my hurt feelings. "Some of us like it here?"

Roe's eyes skitter between us, sensing tension. "*OK*, so, I have to go, but come back and meet Honor afterward? She's so cool, guys."

Roe leaves and Fiona turns to me. "So when is your teacher friend getting here?"

46

"She's not my teacher *friend*." I feel stupid now. "I'm getting a drink. Do you want anything?"

I stomp off, not waiting for the answer. I sit on the back bar stool, drink a beer, and watch people come in. Some guy approaches Fiona and starts chatting her up. Lily stands with her hands in her pockets. I watch them, wondering if Aaron was right and whether I have less in common with my best friends than I thought.

"Maeve," a cheerful voice says. "I'm so glad you're here."

It's Heather. I feel weird about talking to her since the "teacher friend" comment. "Oh, hey," I say uncertainly. "You came."

"Course I did. Eff-all else to do until school starts."

At the mention of school, I feel nervous about the drink in my hand. I'm still underage. Not that anyone really cares in Kilbeg, but she might.

She seems to read my mind. "Don't worry," she says, tapping her nose. "I was seventeen once."

I smile. "I'm actually not seventeen until November," I say furtively.

"Well, you seem very mature," Heather says kindly.

"No, I'm a baby," I reply, remembering the fact that I was crying in the bathroom an hour ago, all because my friends were *thinking mean thoughts*. A punky cover of "Fly Me to the Moon" comes on the sound system and we stand awkwardly with each other.

"I love this song," she says finally. "Actually, I think I love all songs about the moon."

"All of them?"

"They're all good. It's like—OK, I have this theory. The moon is the most beautiful thing in the world, right? The most beautiful thing we have. And if you're going to sing about the moon, you basically have to put your best clothes on. It's like you're going on a date with the moon, the most handsome boy in school."

I laugh. She's funny, and bizarre, and really not like a teacher at all. "'Dancing in the Moonlight,'" I volunteer. "Thin Lizzy, not Toploader. Oh, and 'The Whole of the Moon' by the Waterboys."

"Good one!" she says. She looks impressed. "Some vintage references there."

"I have a lot of older siblings. Everything is vintage."

The house lights go down, and Roe appears onstage in his leopard gown.

"We are Small Private Ceremony," he says. "And we're here to steal your dad's Barbie doll."

I laugh. He always says dumb stuff like this. *That's him*, I mouth at Heather. Roe starts to sing.

He's good, she mouths back.

After two songs, Fiona comes to find me. "Hey," she says, tugging on my sleeve. "Sorry I was being a bitch." She says it close, right in my ear. "There's nothing wrong with liking Kilbeg."

"It's fine," I say, and it is. I introduce her to Heather. They nod hello at each other, but then Fiona and I go and dance. I don't see Heather again. Fiona and I have one of those nights that you only have with your best friend after you've been a bit pissed off with each other but aren't anymore. We feel high, elated, like we're having a second honeymoon. Lily joins in the dancing, too, and seems to genuinely enjoy herself.

After the set, Roe comes out to the dance floor and puts his hands around my waist. "You look hot," he says, holding me tightly. I turn around, a bit drunk now, and kiss him deeply. I can feel him sweating through the cheap Lycra of the dress, the muscled curve of his arms even more defined under the thin material. Miel, Liam, and Dee come out, and Miel gives me a big hug. I was terrified Miel wouldn't like me at first, knowing how close Roe is to them.

"Mae Day!" Miel says, squeezing me. "That dress!"

"It's Fiona's."

"Even so, you look great. Give us a twirl."

I spin, giggling and feeling stupid. I ruffle their new pastel-pink pixie cut. "I love this."

Miel's hair changes with such astonishing frequency that every time we meet I end up considering dying my hair bright orange. I feel so stupidly conventional when we're together.

"Let me do yours. A nice witchy silver."

"My hair won't take bleach," I reply, pulling at the dark frizz. "But thanks anyway."

Honor Own comes on, and the room is immediately transfixed. She's six feet tall, with bright green eyes and cheekbones so wide they look like two polished piano keys placed carefully on top of her face. Her hair and makeup are styled in a kind of 1970s waves-and-winged-eyeliner look, something I know my hair is too thick and fuzzy to hold.

"Hey, everyone," she says, more low-key than Roe onstage. "How about it for Small Private Ceremony, huh?"

A roar of applause. The room is full now, nicely warmed from SPC's performance. "Now that," Honor continues, "is a *vocalist*. I never want to fight them for mirror space again."

Roe smiles, and I can't tell if he's just smiling at the shout-out, or smiling at Honor's use of *them*. We've talked about pronouns before. Roe has always said that *he* feels fine, although not exactly perfect, and that *they* didn't feel any more or less correct. I wonder if this is starting to shift, now that name changing is on the cards. Maybe Honor is just being polite, not wanting to presume a gender identity, being trans herself.

She launches into her set, and it's immediately clear why she was on the front cover of *Hot Press*. She's got a dazzling voice and great songs: smart but not too wordy, with lots of big rock choruses.

Roe introduces us to Honor after her set. We're all a bit lost for words around her, saying things like "Great set!" and "I love your outfit!" We sound like we're about thirteen.

"I've *got* to come back again," Honor says, zipping up her guitar. "You always think that outside of the big cities, no one's going to care, no one will have heard of you. But actually the opposite is true. Small cities are the best audiences, because everyone is just so grateful you came. The worst gigs I play are in London. Just a bunch of old men nodding."

"So what you're saying," I say loudly, so Fiona can hear, "is that Kilbeg is actually awesome?"

"Ha ha," Fi says. "I get it, Chambers."

Roe isn't drinking, so he's able to drive us all home after Honor's set. We're all a bit pissed and rowdy, playing Honor's CD in the car, fighting about where to get chips.

We order from the counter in Deasy's and eat them in the car.

"Roe," I say suddenly. "Hold my hand."

"But my hands are greasy."

I throw him the little wet-wipe packet. "Come on, I want to try something." I am thinking of Fiona and Lily and the phone. I've fallen behind with enough things in life without falling behind with magic, too.

"Ew," Fiona says.

"No, thank you." Lily.

But he wipes his hands and laces his fingers through mine.

"OK, so . . . concentrate on the car."

"But . . . we're parked?"

"Just do it."

He concentrates. I concentrate. I start the Process, find Roe's silver light, but I don't follow it into his head. I sort of wade in the energy coming out of him, and imagine the light stretching to the car.

Honor's music cuts out. There's a crackle and a buzz, and the feeling of something working. I hold my breath. Then, a man's voice from the car stereo.

"So that's two burgers, two chips, two curry sauce, one battered sausage, two cans of Diet Coke, yeah? Eighteen euros, love. For pickup, yeah? Lovely stuff."

"Oh, my god," I gasp. "Oh, my god."

"Is this someone's phone call?" Roe says, astounded.

"Not only is it someone's phone call," Fiona says. "It's very good value. Do you think they have a coupon?"

"Fiona!"

"I'm joking. This is amazing, though!"

It's the chipper man behind the counter at Deasy's. He hangs up and immediately takes another call about three orders of scampi.

"Not that this isn't fascinating, but can we get someone else?" Roe suggests.

"This feels illegal," Lily says with no intonation at all, as if the word *illegal* were a neutral term.

I hold tighter on Roe's hand, and I feel him grab back. There's a pulse of energy between our hands and the channel flips on the radio. After a short silence, we hear another voice.

"Cab to 63 Parnell Road? And where are you going?" A brief pause. "Lovely, will have someone up to you in ten minutes."

We gasp, staring at one another in total disbelief. We switch again. Someone is complaining about their babysitter not putting their kids to sleep. Switch. Someone is telling their boyfriend to come over. Switch. Someone is talking to their mother, asking if it's OK to softly bite off their baby's toenails because they're too afraid to use scissors. We howl with laughter, get greedy for information, switch on and on. We get a dozen snapshots of Kilbeg life on a Saturday night, and as the voices wrap around us, their accents so like ours, I feel a violent throb of love for the place. This home whose frequency I'm literally tuned in to. Why are my friends so desperate to leave? Why is being a stranger somewhere else so attractive to all three of them?

"I think I know who that last one was!" Roe says. "I think that was a guy in my old class. I recognize the voice."

"See?" I say, mostly just continuing my own thought out loud. "If you were in Dublin, you wouldn't know *who* that was."

Roe smiles at me fondly, but we're so connected that one of his thoughts swims into my head. *There she goes again, the Kilbeg tourist board.* I feel a flash of irritation and, still holding his hand, feel my muscles tense. The radio switches again.

"There's a decent argument for . . ." comes a voice. A familiar one. Then a pause, and I think I'm imagining it. An American accent. "No, I'm not saying I can't handle it. That's not what I'm saying at all."

"That's Aaron," I gasp. "That's his voice."

The others look skeptical. "Are you sure?" Roe asks.

"It's Aaron. There's not a doubt in my mind. I saw him this morning, his voice is fresh in my head. God, that's weird."

"Shhh, shh," Fiona hushes, turning the volume up. "Let's see what he says."

"I just think Kilbeg is a waste of time," he says. "What more do we have to do?"

We are all silent. No one moves. There's another pause while Aaron listens to the response. It's interesting, hearing the subordinate tone in his voice. Whoever he's talking to is more powerful than he is and deserving of deference.

"No, I get it," Aaron says. He sounds like he's annoyed and trying very hard to conceal it. "It's just that, you know, I was there when we did that gig. I did everything you asked me to, and I just . . . I think I've proved I can be trusted.

"I know it's not about proof," he says hurriedly. "I know it's about faith, you know I do. But I just . . . I could do more if I knew more. I could make things happen if I knew what things you wanted to happen."

Pause again.

"I know. I just . . . I want to do my best work. It's important to me, personally, spiritually. Whatever. You know that. So let me."

Pause again, longer. Aaron is begging here, really begging. But for what? And why?

The call ends. Roe turns off the radio.

"Wow," he says, raking his hands through his hair. "Wow, OK."

"How did you do that?" Lily asks, mystified. "How did you find him? Of all the people in Kilbeg?"

"I wasn't trying to *find* him," I say defensively. "He just happened. It was just a coincidence."

"Maybe the two of you *are* linked," Fiona offers. "Like he told you."

"What did he tell you?" Roe asks, alarmed. I fill him in on the tennis courts, the three chances.

"Well, in any case," Roe says when I finish, "we need to get our shit together. We have to use our gifts against the Children. It's clear they're not done with Kilbeg. And now that we can listen in on their phone conversations. This is huge."

"Even *he* doesn't know why they're back in Kilbeg," Fiona says ponderously. "*That's* what's huge."

We've always seen Aaron as a kind of ringleader, but maybe he's something more like a regional manager. That's the unsettling thing. If someone of Aaron's abilities is actually relatively junior, then how scary are the actual leaders of the organization?

"Nuala said that Kilbeg has a magical supply chain kind of thing. Maybe . . . maybe the Children are, like, trying to get in on it."

I try to get my head around this. We always assumed that Aaron was a magical person in a religious organization, not that the Children of Brigid *itself* was a magical organization.

I say this aloud. Fiona snorts.

"I mean, are they technically different things?" she asks. "Religion and magic are basically the same to most people, right?"

"Yes," Lily says coldly. "Except magic, as far as we've seen, is the one that's real."

Roe looks anxious, like he's aware of the political optics of this conversation. "I don't know if that's fair."

Lily shrugs. "Magic made me into the river. I know that for a fact. But I've never met Jesus. So."

Despite the fact that we're in the dwindling warm weeks of summer, I feel a chill come over us. A sense that the blood in our bodies is not moving as it should.

"It's almost September," Lily says, her eyes out the window. I don't know why she says it, except perhaps as a reminder of the longer nights, and the fact that everything might be darker from here on out.

6

SOMETHING CHANGES THEN.

Something in the air, something in the mood, something in us.

Roe starts getting ready for college and assembling documents for his name change. Lily keeps going to tutorials. Fiona's aunt Sylvia has to do some kind of new exam for her job, so Fi has to look after Jos even more in the afternoons. I pick up more lunchtime shifts for Nuala.

This is why we haven't seen one another in a week, when all summer we've been living in one another's pockets. This is what I tell myself.

But I also know there's something else. That Aaron's voice over the radio speaker shook all of us, and the reality of the Children of Brigid being back in Kilbeg starts to dawn on us all.

No one wants to face up to it. No one wants to talk about a battle plan. No one wants to risk their life again. Maybe we were all given our gifts for a reason, and maybe this is it. But who wants that kind of responsibility?

I ask Nuala what she thinks the Children's plan is. By her response, I realize she has thought of all of this already.

"It seems to me, judging by Aaron's invitation to you, that their focus on *young* people might be a way of recruiting talent," she says.

"I've been following them in the news. They're not so bothered about what adult sinners are doing. It's so much focus on the youth. 'Youth of today' this, 'youth of today' that. They have a sensitive, which is rare enough, and now they want you, a second sensitive. Which makes me wonder: What other witches do they have working for them?"

"Nuala . . ." I begin, shocked at myself for not asking this before. "How many witches *are* there?"

She ponders this, and I'm relieved to see that it is not a stupid question. "Wicca isn't really the kind of religion that is about keeping records," she says. "Which is part of why so many people like it."

"No, I mean . . ." I try to parse what I mean, exactly. Obviously, there are witches: the fact that I work in a shop that sells magical paraphernalia proves that. But there are witches and there are *witches*. People who believe in magic as opposed to people who possess it. "People like me and the lads. People who can . . . do stuff. Who are more connected to the supply chain thingy."

"Everyone has magic, Maeve. As I said. With the diagram."

"Yes, but you *know* what I mean."

"I do." She sighs. "And that's an even harder question to answer. Sensitives are rare, of course. One in one million, I would say. Perhaps less."

"That rare?" I ask, incredulous. "And you somehow know *three*, including Heaven?"

She blinks at me. You're not supposed to bring up her sister. She brings up Heaven with you. "Sorry," I say.

She nods. "Sensitives are indeed rare, but there are also people who are born with natural abilities, or tendencies toward certain elements. They say that the legends about witches who couldn't drown

56

were just about a certain kind of freshwater witch, born near lakes and rivers. And that great courtesans were witches of fire, crafting love spells."

This is all a bit wafty for me, so I try to bring Nuala back down to earth. "How many people can do what Roe can do? What Lily and Fiona can do? Real stuff. Electricity. Healing. Stuff like that."

She sighs. She hates when I get too specific. Not because she *likes* to be wafty, but because to Nuala, magic is so much more complicated than statistics.

"They exist," she says. "For different reasons, and with different methods, but they exist. They are rare but not unheard of."

·)) ● ((·

We meet that night at the tennis courts for the first time in a week.

"Results on Wednesday," Roe says, an air of hopelessness in his voice.

"Want me to come?"

"Mum and Dad are . . ."

"Meet you after?"

"Perfect."

There's a faint sound of an animal screeching somewhere in the distance, of a fox defending itself, or maybe two cats in a fight.

Fiona is quiet tonight. She's cutting cards, splitting the deck at random and looking at each result. The Wheel of Fortune. The Two of Swords. The Magician.

I nudge her. "You OK, little lady?"

"I'm just thinking," she says. "About monologues."

"For what?"

"Trinity auditions."

"They aren't even until next year! I don't think you need to worry."

She cuts the deck again. The Four of Pentacles.

"It's really competitive," she says. "Something like seventeen places every year."

I don't have the energy to reassure her, particularly when Fiona has gotten every part, every scholarship, and every test result she's ever wanted. "Oh, come on," I say. "You're Fiona Buttersfield. You're basically failure-proof."

"Don't say that," she says coolly.

"Why?"

"Because it's not true." She is picking at midge bites on her skin, digging her finger in aggressively, watching the skin heal even as the blood is breaking the surface.

"Don't do that," I say, a little grossed out.

"Don't tell me what to do," comes the immediate answer. She's so snappy that Roe looks up in alarm.

Silence. I feel like I've done something wrong, but I don't really know what it is. "Do you want me to read your tarot? Three-card spread?"

She nods.

"All right, shuffle, then," I say, and she does, the only sound the dim, slippery whisper of cards falling.

Suddenly, Lily speaks.

"New moon tonight," she says. "It was a new moon when you took me, wasn't it?"

"Took you?"

"From the river."

"When we saved you, yes. It was a new moon."

"Witches are supposed to be their most powerful then."

"I think the books just say it's a good time for the dark arts," Fiona corrects. "For our shadow selves."

Lily seems to take this as encouragement.

"I've got something," she says. She gets to her feet, taking her water bottle as she goes. We all sit up, balancing our weight on outstretched hands. Another light show. This should be good.

Lily walks to the end of the court. Fiona lays out her three cards. I flip the first one—the past card—over. It's the Sun.

"Joy," I say with a faint smile. "Feels appropriate, after the summer we've just had."

She flips over the next card, the present card. "Nine of Wands."

"Defensiveness," I say automatically, feeling as if this really requires no explanation.

"What is she doing?" Roe interrupts.

There's the choking sound of squeezed plastic, then the sound of droplets. We look up. We can't quite make out what Lily is doing. It's too dark and she's too far away.

Roe squints. "Is she . . . wetting the fence?"

And before I have time to confirm or deny that Lily has wet the wire court fence, there's a sharp, metallic *shing* noise.

"Lily," Fi calls. "What have you done?"

We each stand up gingerly, our limbs having started to fall asleep. There's another feeling of heat in the air, but it's not the sweating heat of magic working. It's something different. It smells of copper, in the way copper sometimes smells like blood.

"Have you charged the fence?" I call out. And across the court, I hear an excited laugh.

"Jesus," Roe murmurs. Then he calls out to her, his tone cautious: "OK, Lil, well done."

No response.

"I think it's time we go home," he calls again. We all look at one another, united in our disquiet.

"*Can* we go home?" I ask, fear creeping into my voice. "If we touch the fence, will we . . . ?"

There's a sudden flutter, then a loud, pained squawk. A thud of a muffled fall.

"What was that?" I don't know why I'm suddenly whispering.

There's a croaking noise, a ferocious high gulping, and the hot dry smell of something burning. Cooking. We move toward the sound. Lily meets us, her blond hair full of static.

It's a bird. A magpie, to be exact. It has flown into the fence that Lily charged, and has now fallen to the ground. It's trying to hobble around, away from us, terrified of what else we might do to it.

"What did you *do*, Lily?" Roe asks.

"Practicing," she says without remorse. "Like we're supposed to."

Fiona bends down and tries to scoop it up. It fluffs up its feathers, trying to make itself big and threatening while obviously terrified of her.

"Stay *still*, you idiot," she snaps. "I'm trying to *help* you."

You so rarely see a bird close-up like this. The shining beak, the beady eyes. They really are horrible, in their own way.

Fiona clamps her hands around the thing. "It's his wing," she says. "He's burned it on the fence."

I look to Lily, waiting for her to show some form of regret at the needless pain she has caused this random animal. Nothing. "So heal him," she says.

A few moments later, Fiona releases the bird and it flies off, a little lopsided and not in the least bit grateful.

"One for sorrow," Roe says, citing the old wives' tale. He salutes it.

"Two for joy," Fi says, finishing the verse. "Anyone see a second one?"

"No," I say weakly. And then: "Well done, Fi."

60

But we're all unnerved by what just happened. With how easily a bird could have been something bigger. A fox. A dog. A person.

A chilly breeze picks up, scattering the cards. We run to pick them up as they blow across the court, and whatever the final card was of Fiona's reading—the future card, as it were—is lost to the wind.

WHEEL OF FORTUNE

THE SUN

7

THE MOMENT WITH THE MAGPIE UNSET-
tles the three of us. We discuss it over the next few days, in our own
little bubbles: me and Roe, Roe and Fiona, me and Fiona. The brief
second where we all thought Lily was trapping us in the tennis courts;
the realization that she could; her utter lack of regret for the magpie
that tumbled out of the air.

What is Lily actually *capable* of? is the question we are all asking
but not asking. Not just magically but morally?

Roe gets his results the next day, and we decide to meet at
Bridey's Café after he's done with his parents. I buy two salted caramel éclairs and a huge pot of tea to celebrate with, and sit on the low
couch near the door. Waiting.

And waiting.

I check my phone a few times and start to get worried that
maybe he has had a disappointing result and doesn't want to see me.
I try to bring the excitement of my messages down a few octaves. I
delete my WhatsApp that says **Can't wait to celebrate!** and instead
say **Can't wait to see you!**

After twenty minutes, Bridey comes over to me.

"Sorry, pet," she says apologetically. She's old, at least eighty, and has always been very kind in the past. "We have the couch booked, would you mind moving to a smaller table?"

"Booked?" I ask, looking around. Bridey's is the cheapest café in Kilbeg. I'm surprised they even have a phone line with which to *book* parties.

I move to a two-seater table, the tea rapidly cooling. I pick the edges of the caramel icing with my finger. Then, the "party" comes in. I barely look up at first. Four guys, a few years older than me. I text Roe again. Then I hear my own name, and Aaron is suddenly sitting across from me.

"Is this for me?" he asks, pointing to the éclair.

"No," I say sharply. "Leave me alone."

"Have you thought about it?"

My instinct is to get up and leave, but I realize then that this could be an opportunity. The longer I keep Aaron talking, the more I can burrow into his mind and figure out what's going on.

"You want me to join the Children," I say. "Why?"

It's hard to read someone's mind and start the Process while they're looking right at you. I try to begin, making my thoughts as blank as possible.

"I think it would be good for you. I think you're very lonely."

He annoys me too much. My mind refuses to unclutter.

"That's big talk coming from someone with no friends."

"What do you call them?" He cocks his head to one side, motioning to the guys sitting on the couches.

"Minions."

"Does she still hate you?" he asks. "Lily, I mean."

I stare at him. "Yes."

"After everything you did? To get her back?" he says. "Seems a little rude."

68

"Why are you talking to me about this?"

He drums his fingers on the table. "There are things we can do to help, you know."

"To *help*? How could you possibly *help* me?"

Aaron gestures at the air. "Oh, I don't know. Love spells to keep Roe close. Friendship charms to make sure Fiona never leaves you. Something to make school easier. Something to make school irrelevant."

My spine arches like a cat's. I know that this is Aaron's gift at work. He knows where the holes are. I feel curiously naked for a second, my worst traits exposed.

"Oh, really?" I hiss. "And I suppose this is all free, is it?"

"You wouldn't have to get involved in any of the preaching stuff if you don't want to."

"Well, isn't that kind."

He picks a hair off his clothing. It's long and dark, and unmistakably mine. It must have come from my jacket, hanging over the chair he's sitting on, but it still disturbs me. Something of mine on something of his.

"Everything you did with Lily," he says again. "Whatever spells, charms, hexes . . ."

Then, something happens. It's like time slows down. What should be half a second, a fraction of an expression, something utterly undetectable to a normal person, becomes clear and blatantly obvious. His eyes slide across me, and a look of uncertainty comes into his face. *Spells, charms, hexes.* He's fishing.

Suddenly, it's like he's shown me his whole hand of cards.

I smile widely.

"You have no clue what we did, do you?" I say, trying to force as much power and glee into my voice as possible. "You're utterly dumbfounded by how we got Lily back. You're trying to figure it out. That's why you guys won't leave me alone."

He says nothing, seems to grope at the air for a second. This ability to see him so clearly, his motivations so obvious—is this the special kind of magic that sensitives have? *Are* we alike, like strange magical siblings?

"You don't have a clue, Aaron, do you?" I keep smiling the biggest shit-eating grin I can manage. "You have no idea why you're back in Kilbeg, no idea how we saved Lily . . . you're just some worthless henchman, aren't you?"

He settles back into his seat, the lost look disappearing into his face, now replaced by curious suspicion. I can see the abacus of his mind working. *How does she know that I don't know why we're here?*

"Bridey," I say as she passes. "Do you mind if I have a box to wrap these up? I'm going to take them to go." She nods in approval, probably a sign I've been here too long.

"The Children want magic, don't they?" I continue. I don't know where I'm getting these lines or this poise from. I sound like a person in a film. I need to leave soon, before I fluff it. "They're bored of whatever it is you have to offer. They're just using you as the chum to catch the big sharks."

I really hope that this is how sharks and chum works.

Bridey comes back with a white pastry box and I carefully transfer my cakes to it. I try to make every movement neat, precise, like *Tra-la-la, I'm so all-powerful that I can talk about this stuff while arranging a picnic.*

"You think I have something to learn from the Children," I say, wrapping the box up. "But I think that maybe you have something you want to learn from us?"

70

The cakes secure, I get to my feet and grab my jacket from his chair.

"That's two," he says smoothly.

"What happens after three, Aaron?" I hit back. "Or do you think you're negotiating with a toddler? Because I know nothing actually happens after Mummy counts to three."

I glance at the guys on the couch as I go, who have all been peering indiscreetly at our conversation. They are all, unsurprisingly, extremely good-looking. I am slightly revolted by how basic the Children actually are. This is what they've got? Hot twenty-year-olds and hate doctrine? Who cares?

There's a burst of sunshine on the street, blinding almost, and the minute I get out of the café I turn a corner, my back against the cold wall, my face in the shadows. The confidence and the power seep out of me, and, suddenly overwhelmed by my own weakness, I start to cry.

·)) ● ((·

When I do finally meet Roe, he's full of apologies. We sit in his car and eat the éclairs, the fresh cream already starting to sour in the heat of the day. We're near the river, in a little lay-by surrounded by trees where people park the car before taking their dog for a walk.

"Mum and Dad absolutely freaked out," he grumbles.

"But *why*?"

He shows me his transcript. "Jesus, Roe!" I say, almost shrieking. "It says here you got five ninety?"

The Leaving Cert is judged on your best six subjects, so the highest possible mark is six hundred.

"Yeah." He shrugs. "It's really good, isn't it?"

"Why are you sulking? This is amazing! You're a genius!" I stare at the transcript again. "Oh," I say. *"Ohhhh."*

"Yeah. Dad blew up at me for wanting to study English at KU. And then Mum cried."

"Why?"

"Because her dad always dreamed of having a doctor in the family? I don't know. It got weird." He sighs. "So then I told them the news. I decided to rip off . . . every Band-Aid at once."

My eyes widen. I thought I had been brave today by telling off Aaron, but it's nothing compared to Roe. "You told them about the name change?"

"Yeah." He shrugs again. "That bit they were actually less annoyed about."

He looks at his thumbs, and I realize that whatever news he told them, he is now gearing up to tell me, too.

"Roe . . . ?"

"I'm going on tour," he suddenly blurts. "With Honor."

He lets the information go with the recklessness of a child with a helium balloon. I watch it drift up into the rafters of our lives.

"W-when did this happen?"

"She got in touch a few days after the gig. Said she was planning a mini Irish tour in November. Two weeks."

"Well, that's good," I say, tugging on his sleeve, trying to avoid the knot in my stomach. "That's great. And you won't have to take too much time off college, will you? I mean, that's why you chose English, isn't it? Lots of essays you can do in your own time. Books you can read whenever."

He nods. "And," he continues, "if that goes well, she said . . . we could talk about my coming on her European tour, in April. But she loves Small Private Ceremony. She thinks we would have great chemistry on the road."

I swallow hard. Everyone's going to leave me.

He's looking at me warily, terrified of what I'm going to say, of how I'm going to react. No, Maeve. Don't ruin this for him.

"That's so great," I say, wrapping my arms around him. "That's so, so great. Wow. European tour!"

"She might not invite me," he says sheepishly. "It's so far off."

"It will come around quickly," I respond, and I can't keep the dismal tone out of my voice. Roe doesn't seem to notice it.

"And if the European tour goes well," he continues, "maybe I could defer my second year of college."

I run my hands through his hair and try not to be sick. "A genius *and* a rock star."

"It's so weird," Roe says. "That night when Aaron crashed our gig. That's the whole reason Honor heard of us in the first place. Why she reached out to Miel. Isn't that crazy? It all happened because of the Housekeeper."

"She can be your downfall." I smile. "Or she can be your start?"

As I hold Roe, Aaron's words come back to me: *You're very lonely.*

I know I'm not alone. That I have Roe in my arms, and friends who love me. Well. *Friend* who loves me. But the more they plan for their bright futures, their huge potential, their grand exits, the more I feel as if they're gone from me already. That I'll be the only one left in Kilbeg.

I start to kiss his neck, his ear, his mouth. I pull myself onto his lap. "I love you," I murmur. "I love you, and I'm proud of you."

But what I mean is *Don't leave me, don't leave me, don't leave me.*

8

DESPITE DREADING IT FOR WEEKS, SCHOOL
starting again feels like a terrible surprise.

We've spent so long mapping the small changes of St. Bernadette's over the last month that we feel a little smug, going in on our
first day. Everyone else is clearly surprised by the renovations. We
gather in the sixth-year classroom, shocked at how few of us are left.
Michelle Breen wasn't the only one to fly the coop. I do a quick head
count. There are about thirty-five of us left in the year; last year it was
fifty-two. We're allowed to wear our ordinary clothes now, a gift that
the school has always bestowed on sixth-years.

"Oh, my god," Fi says, looking at her phone. "Maeve, did you
know this?"

"Know what?" I say, dumping my bag on my desk.

"I've just seen on Small Private Ceremony's Instagram that
they're doing a national tour with Honor Own?"

"Oh, yeah," I say, taking out my things. "I thought I, uh, mentioned that."

She stares at me, dumbfounded. "No, you didn't! And neither
did Roe!" Fiona looks at the Instagram post again. "Why aren't we all
celebrating this? This is *huge!*"

"Mum and Dad are going ape," Lily says. "So he's trying to

downplay it. Like if he celebrates it too much they'll realize it's a big deal."

"But he shouldn't be downplaying it *to us*. We should be, like, dancing around the tennis court. He's only eighteen and he's touring with an actual rock star."

"Yes," I say very firmly and without much enthusiasm. "It's great."

Fiona cocks her head, confused by me. She looks like she's about to prod me more, but then Lily starts to make a noise. She is humming softly under her breath, a sort of tuneless, aimless sound that's more like a vibration beginning at the back of her throat. She sounds like a fridge motor.

"Hey, Lil . . ." I ask cautiously, motioning my eyes toward Fiona in an *Are you seeing this?* gesture. "You OK, pal?" She flashes me a smile, and for a few seconds, Lily's teeth are electric blue.

"Jesus!" I say, grabbing for Fi instinctively.

Lily presses her lips together, her teeth hidden once more.

"Lily, what was that?"

"Do you really want to know?"

"Yes."

"If I keep this little bit of spit gurgling at the back of my throat, I can create a current."

"*What?* How long have you known that?" Fi asks.

"Since this morning. I figured it out on the bus. Pretty cool, isn't it?"

"Lil . . ." Fiona says tentatively. "Maybe you shouldn't . . . be doing this so publicly. You'll get spotted."

"So." She shrugs. "Who cares? I don't see why I should be afraid of anyone."

Having seen what she can do, I don't see why she should be, either.

Miss Harris walks in, brown from the summer, and everyone takes their seats. Fiona, Lily, and I sit in a row, Fiona between me and Lily, of course.

"Good morning, girls," she says benevolently. "I assume you all had a lovely summer and are ready, at last, to become sixth-years?"

She goes on to talk about how our Leaving Cert year is bound to be stressful, but that if we study diligently and don't leave all our work to the final sprint, she's confident we'll all do fine. "There should be no reason that you won't all end up with the future you deserve."

The future you deserve. Not *want.* Deserve.

"Of course, you'll already have noticed that there are far fewer of you than in past years. Which means that we will have greater ability to give you individual attention, and in order to give you that kind of attention, we have to make some changes to the way you're taught."

Deserve. What kind of future does a middle-class telepath with crappy grades deserve?

"Some of you are already excellent students but will need some extra test prep to turn a five fifty into a five ninety," she says, and I can feel her eyes wandering to Fiona. "And some of you will be . . . struggling . . . and will need a different level of teaching in order to get through your exams. So that we can offer the best for everyone, after next week, we'll be splitting your year group into two."

Oh, god. Why didn't I see this coming? When I pictured my Leaving Cert year, I at least thought I would be spending it with Fiona.

"Group One will have their classes here in the attic," Miss Harris continues. "And Group Two will be in the basement."

"In *The Chokey*?" someone calls out.

"You're putting the thickos *underground*?" someone else says.

"There's been extensive building work done over the summer,"

Miss Harris corrects, her tone irritable. "The basement is now open plan, and it's wonderfully fitted. The Cho—the cupboard—has been extended into an office.

"On Monday we're going to do a few tests," Miss Harris continues, trying to keep her voice devoid of emotion. "Nothing to be worried about; we just want to gauge where everyone's capabilities are after the school holidays."

"Miss, *no*," one of the girls pipes up. "That's so unfair. We won't have any time to study. You can just sort us based on report cards, can't you?"

"I could," she says flatly. "But that wouldn't take into account the number of you who have been working over the summer. I trust some of you *have* been working."

Lily looks down and smiles. Did she know this was going to happen? Did she take lessons because she wanted to be in the same class as Fiona and leave me in the basement all alone? I'm furious at the prospect of the two of them up here, becoming best friends, when they only know each other because of me.

"This is bullshit," I tell Fiona as soon as Miss Harris leaves the room. "They're basically segregating us into smart and dumb."

"I'm sorry, pal," Fiona says, her brow furrowed. "This sucks. But we're still going to see loads of each other."

"Oh, great to see you have so much faith in me. We're not even going to pretend that I'm going to be in Group One."

"Maeve, you're being unfair. You're the one who has been saying all summer that you're never going to be good at school and you don't intend to try."

"I know," I say, raking my hand through my wiry hair. "I'm sorry. I'm just . . ."

"I know," she says, her hand on my shoulder. "I'm sorry."

I shouldn't have had my head in the sand all summer. I should have studied, or asked Fi and Roe for help. I shouldn't have just accepted things the way they are, or been so afraid of trying. Because that's what it was, really. Afraid that if I try, everyone will have to feel so awkward for me when I fail.

"Fi . . ."

"Yeah?"

"Will you . . . help me?"

She gives me a hug. "Maeve, of course. Come over for dinner tonight. We'll tackle whatever subjects you're weakest in."

Toward the end of the day, there's another announcement. And, like the tennis court, it's one the three of us are already prepared for. Heather Banbury is introduced to the class.

"Miss Banbury is our new guidance counselor and student liaison," Miss Harris says with Heather standing next to her. Heather's eyes wander over to me, and she gives me the tiniest nod. I smile back.

Fiona nudges me. "Oooh, Little Miss Teacher Friend."

"Shut *up*."

She starts giggling. "Say hi to your teacher friend."

It's as if Miss Harris has heard us, and her tone becomes short.

"Now, Miss Banbury is not a teacher. She's here to offer career guidance as well as regular mental health check-ins throughout the school year. Her office is in the basement. I know you must feel under a lot of pressure. No exam or college course is worth your health or happiness. Exam years can have serious strain on some people, and I want to make sure you girls always feel that you have someone impartial to speak to."

Heather steps forward. "Hello," she says, sounding a bit sheepish.

"I'm so looking forward to getting to know you all. And please, everything you tell me in our meetings will be held in the strictest confidence." She smiles at me again.

After school, I head straight over to Fi's house. She makes us sandwiches and spreads out her collection of past exam papers on the kitchen table.

"OK," she says evenly. "What's your weakest area?"

"Anger management."

"In *school*."

"I was *joking*," I say huffily. "Science. My elective is biology, and everyone said it would be easier than chemistry or physics, but . . ."

"I don't need your life story, Chambers."

So we go through it. Fiona talks about photosynthesis and plant cells and animal cells, and when she's done explaining something, she lightly quizzes me on what we've just been through. I try to be a good student, and to be fair to Fiona, she's an enthusiastic teacher.

But before long, it becomes astoundingly clear that we are putting up deck chairs on the *Titanic*. She will begin simply, talking about photosynthesis and how light and heat and oxygen are needed for plant cells to grow. Just at the moment when I'm thinking, *OK, this makes sense*, she starts heaping more information on me and things get too complicated and I just start blurting out random answers to get her off my back. She decides to leave plants alone and concentrate on human bodies instead. We talk about blood for what feels like hours.

"OK," she says patiently. "So, tell me, what's the difference between red blood cells and white blood cells?"

"Red blood cells are for . . . really bloody blood?"

"Red blood cells are for carrying the blood around the body, and white blood cells are for fighting infection."

My phone vibrates and I instinctively lunge for it, hoping it's Roe. He's starting college today. It's Mum. Fiona gets up to go to the cutlery drawer.

"Sorry," I say, putting the phone down. "You were saying?"

Fiona picks up a knife and, quickly and calmly, plunges it through her own hand.

"Jesus Christ, FIONA! Stop doing that!"

"You see, what's happening right now," she says evenly, unfurling some paper towels and daubing the blood, "albeit at a very accelerated rate, is the process of hemostasis. We talked about hemostasis; can you tell me what it is?"

She holds her bleeding hand up to me, the puncture slowly healing before my eyes. I want to be sick. Why would she do this? Does she not understand how disturbing it is?

"No, Fiona," I plead. "Just, put that away, will you? It makes me want to be sick."

"Hemostasis is blood clotting. After the blood clots, which is done with platelets, we enter the inflammation stage. Do you see the swelling around the wound? Quick, look, before it heals over completely."

I bat her hand away from me. "Fi, stop."

"I had to look at your blood, so now you have to look at mine," she says bitingly. "You stabbed yourself with a knife in front of me."

I look at her, my face frozen in shock. "Is that what this is about, Fi? Is this . . . payback, for what went down at the ritual?"

She shrugs. "Do you want to study or do you want to talk blood?"

"I want to know if there's something I should know." I focus my gaze on her. "We've talked about the ritual."

"*You've* talked," she says. "You and your big noble sacrifice and why you didn't want me to stop you. I know all about why my two best friends stabbed themselves in front of me, and the reasons are *extremely* compelling."

"Then why are you doing this?"

At that moment, the front door slams and Fiona's parents come into the kitchen. Fiona's dad is a hospital administrator so he works a regular nine-to-five, but her mum's a nurse and does all kinds of crazy shifts. It's rare to see them at the same time.

"Maeve! What a surprise." Marie pats my shoulder and looks at the exam papers spread around the kitchen table. "And you've been studying! Good girls. We had our union meeting so we both finished at the same time for once."

Marie starts bustling around the kitchen, filling the kettle to the top and switching it on. "We went for a very romantic autumn walk. You two should do the same. The light will change soon and you'll both get seasonal affective disorder."

"Um, I don't think Fiona and I need a *romantic* autumn walk."

Marie picks up the used towels, spattered with Fiona's blood from the wound that has already healed over. "Fifi, are you getting bloody noses again?"

Fiona's expression remains calm. "Yes."

"Cut a tampon in half," Marie says. "Stick it up there. And tell me if it keeps happening, OK?"

So, Fiona isn't doing this only when I'm around. This isn't just a lesson she's trying to teach me. This is a habit. This is something Fiona is doing *at home.*

"Maeve, are you staying for dinner?"

Fiona's face is inscrutable. I deliberately stall, waiting for her to tell me that I should stay. It never comes.

"I better get home, but thank you," I reply. I expect Fiona to come to the door with me and gently explain her behavior while I put my shoes on. She doesn't move.

"Thanks for your help, Fi. I think I really get hematosis now," I say limply as I leave.

"Hemostasis."

"OK. See you tomorrow, and . . . uh . . . mind those nosebleeds."

I leave her house, anxiety gnawing at the pit of my stomach. I wanted to stay, to get Fi alone and read her mind, to understand why she's doing what she's doing. But it would be impossible to do it in front of Fi without her knowing exactly what I was doing—the Process takes too much time, too much energy, too much quiet. I still need to close my eyes when I do it. She would know what I was up to right away.

Hey, I text Roe. **Can we talk?**

Just at practice, he writes back. **Call you tonight?**

I tell him that's fine, and he says he'll call around ten. Four hours away. I walk all the way home, the orange sunlight glowing in the early evening sky. Marie was right. It *is* beautiful out. It couldn't be more different from six months ago, when the citywide freeze that the Housekeeper left in her wake created snowstorms, power cuts, and road closures. We were all so afraid then, so constantly terrified for Lily, for the city, for ourselves. I lift my hand to my face, shielding my eyes from the glare of the sun, and try to remember if I felt as alone then as I do now.

9

FIONA DOESN'T OFFER TO TUTOR ME AGAIN.
Instead, I spend the week studying, trying desperately to cram years' worth of information into four days.

Roe starts college and immediately seems to love it. I don't see or hear a lot from him, and I try not to take it too personally. His band is playing at a few Freshers' Week parties, and he leaves me a few drunk text messages in the middle of the night.

Babe I cannot WAIT til next year when you're hear with me

Kesha is underrated!!! Also remember when she had a dollar sign in her name?

Whyyyyyy are you so pretty

Maybe should cover a Kesha song with the band? Wyt???

Lily seems to be studying as hard as I am, and it feels like we're both auditioning to be Fiona's best friend. It's as if someone has told us that there's only space for one of us in the higher-level classes, and the other has to die in the basement.

I go to the school's supervised study sessions one evening, partly because I think the studious environment might help, partly because I'm hoping to show Fiona how seriously I'm now taking school. It doesn't work. Everyone is so silent, and it feels unnatural to be in school this late and not practicing magic. It doesn't finish until nine, with a short dinner break at six. By the time we leave, it's getting dark out. I make my way to the bus, and at a certain point, notice that Aaron is walking in lockstep with me.

"Go away," I say, too exhausted to come up with anything more original.

"I'm just walking," he says. "I saw your . . . *partner* today."

"My *partner*?"

"Roe. He's at college now, isn't he? We were canvassing up there. Seems to have found himself a nice new crowd."

I feel my face going red in the half darkness. I hate that Aaron has seen Roe more recently than I have.

"I have questions," he says. "About you and him."

"Why on earth would I answer any of your questions? Especially about me and him?"

I notice then that our feet are falling at the exact same time, in the same precise rhythm. It sounds like one pair of feet walking, not two. I turn my face to the wall and notice that our shadows have merged into one form, the streetlamp casting a four-handed, four-legged, six-foot shape. I try to speed up, but I can't seem to break rhythm with him.

"I'll just ask them, anyway," he says brightly. "First of all, is there a future in it?"

I keep my head down, knowing he's trying to goad me.

"I know you think that I'm this maniac," he goes on to say. "But I'm just curious. His band is all about, you know, queer identity, isn't it?"

His voice is bright and soft, as if he weren't the person who showed up at a Small Private Ceremony gig to incite a riot.

"That wasn't the question," he continues. "I know that's basically a fact. It's on their social media. But how is . . . how is him having a girlfriend the basis of, you know, a queer identity?"

Don't respond, don't respond, don't respond. He's doing his thing, his Aaron thing, trying to worm into the little gaps in your resolve where your vulnerability lives. Don't give it to him, Maeve. This is a cheap trick.

"Because either he's sort of . . . *pretending* to have this queer identity to get gigs, which I don't think seems very like him, based on what I know of Roe."

"You don't know anything about Roe," I snap. I immediately know it's a mistake.

He smiles. He seems to think that he has scored a point and is recouping some kind of loss from our last conversation.

"Or," he continues. "Or he's not pretending, and he is bisexual, or pansexual, or whatever, in which case . . . well, he's only eighteen. You're his first partner, aren't you? That's not the question."

"What *is* the question?" I hiss.

"It's a math problem," he continues. "*One* young person exploring their sexual and gender identity plus *one* music tour, divided by *one* monogamous relationship with your childhood sweetheart . . . what does it all add up to, Maeve? To bring me back to my earlier question: Where's the future in it?"

I stop walking. Something about him just coming out and saying it stiffens my blood. My fingers clench and unclench as I feel a strange mix of hatred and release. Aaron can see your weakness. That's his gift. He can show you the things that you've even managed to hide from yourself. And here he is, exposing my deepest anxieties to the autumn air, and it has winded me. So why the release? He's pulled my guts out, but on the plus side, it means I don't have to carry them around anymore.

It feels, I think, like a kind of confession. Like he's the priest who is pulling it out of me.

"He loves me," I say. The words feel strong in my mouth, like a spell. "He loves me, more than anyone has ever loved you. That's why you don't understand it. Because you've never been loved."

He raises his eyebrows, like he's looking at a long bill and thinking: *Hmmm, not quite sure that adds up.*

"You're full of hate," I spit. "I guess it's the only thing you understand, so let me talk to you in those terms. I hate you, and you hate me and everyone I care about."

"I don't hate you," he says blithely.

"Yes, you do. You hate my sister, you hate her girlfriend, you hate Roe, you hate his fans. You hate anything that doesn't fit into your neo-Nazi white Christian worldview. And you know what the saddest thing is? It's not even original. You have all this power, obviously, and you can't think to do something properly crazy with it. You could be in some dictator's dream right now, convincing him not to kill thousands of people. But no. You're *here*. Here, in Kilbeg, with your idiotic bigotry from the Middle Ages."

He looks dumbfounded. It feels good to order my thoughts, to finally deliver the speech I've been composing in my head for months.

"Oh, I see what this is," he says finally. "You think I hate gay people."

"You're saying you *don't* hate gay people?" I let out a dry, hollow laugh.

"No," he says. "God does."

I imagine myself leaping like a wild animal and tearing out his throat with one bite. I know, in that moment, that I need to do something. To punch, or kick, or spit. To let him know that he can't talk to me like this and get away with it. That men, even the ones with magic, only really understand violence.

Then, I hear a light cough.

We both spin around. It's Heather Banbury, wearing a long coat and satchel, her eyes like stone.

"Maeve," she says. "Are you all right?"

I take a step toward her, desperately relieved at the presence of a grown-up in a position of authority. "No, actually," I say. "This guy won't leave me alone."

Aaron actually laughs.

"Oh, *this* is the play, is it?" Then he shrugs. "Maeve, can I assume this is three?"

"Yes," I say.

"Fantastic," he says, and he begins to walk away. "Enjoy Hell."

Despite his exit, I still feel a chill. What happens after three?

"Are you all right, Maeve?" Heather asks again. "Who was that?"

"Just some creep," I reply.

"Hmm," she says, and I can't help but wonder whether it's too much of a coincidence, her suddenly appearing. The wind picks up behind her hair, and for a second the smell of copper is in the air again. There's a feeling of struggle, of something hidden working hard.

"Which way are you going?" she asks.

"Bus station."

"Do you want me to walk you?"

"No, I'm fine. He's gone."

"Let me know if he bothers you again, OK?" she says, and it's the way she says *he* that makes me think that she knows Aaron is not any old creep outside a girls' school. But something different. Something she knows.

The copper smell passes. I feel like she was about to tell me something, something important, but at the last minute decided against it.

10

ENJOY HELL.

"Bit . . . *camp*, isn't it?"

It's Thursday night. On Monday, the tests start. We can't hang out at the tennis courts anymore with school back in session, so we're back in the galloping maggot. We're in the McDonald's car park.

"Heather showed up, and it was like . . . I don't know. There was a change in the atmosphere."

Roe wrinkles his brow. "Remind me. Heather?"

"Maeve's teacher friend," says Fiona. She clocks my expression. "*What?* I'm not even taking the piss. She is!"

"She's a counselor, not a teacher."

"What else did Aaron say?" Roe asks, stroking my hair. "Was there anything we could use? To take down the Children?"

He told me that we have no future, and I'm terrified that he's right. "Nothing. Nothing important." I hesitate. "He said he saw you. At college."

He blinks, bewildered. "I didn't see him."

"Maybe they're getting better at watching us. Observing us without our knowledge."

Lily dips her finger in the container of sweet-and-sour sauce and licks it. "I think I'm being followed."

We all turn to her, dumbfounded. "What?"

"I said, I think I'm being followed."

"Why? Why do you think that?"

She stops. Fidgets. Works out exactly what she means. Then: "A man followed me to school today."

"What man?" I reply.

"I don't know."

"Someone you've met before?" Fiona asks gently, knowing that Lily's facial recognition has not been great since the river. Lily shrugs in response. "Lil, this is kind of a big deal."

"Maybe for you guys," she says absently. "But I can just spark them if they try anything, so I'm not afraid."

Roe shifts uncomfortably and looks to me. "Maybe the two of you should start getting the same bus in the morning."

"What's Maeve going to do?" Lily asks before I have time to respond. "All she can do is read minds. And not even that well."

I want to dispute this, but she's not wrong. I still need so much concentration and focus to hack someone's brain—particularly a stranger—that it's hard to see how I could help her. But I agree that we should get the bus together.

"Do you think they're trying to suss out Lily? Talent scout her or something?" Fiona asks, sounding mildly offended that no one is attempting to talent scout her.

There's a special surprise assembly for all third-, fourth-, fifth-, and sixth-years. St. Bernadette's doesn't have a hall big enough to hold most of it so they stagger them throughout the day, starting with the youngest. All day you can hear snatches of gossip about what the assembly entails, but as sixth-years now, we don't deign to listen to any of it.

"It's just because they've brought lads in to talk to us," Fiona says, craning her neck as the fourth-years file into the double doors of the main hall. "You'd swear they were, like, famous. They're just *guys*."

Toward the end of the day it's our turn, and there are so few of us that we share the assembly with the fifth-years. You can already see everyone holding themselves apart, terrified someone's going to mistake one of *us* for one of *them*.

At the front of the room there are three boys, all in their early twenties. For an awkward moment, I'm afraid they're going to break into song. They are all standing in a way that suggests choreography, and their looks are so different that it's like they were selected to appeal to the collected fantasies of an all-girls school. One is broad and gentle looking, like someone who might build a log cabin and then carry you inside it. One is skinny and has pretty, puckered, bruised-looking features, like how Leonardo DiCaprio used to look in the nineties. One looks like a cartoon astronaut. They are all smiling at us. There's a strange mix of silence and giggling going on in the room, like the noise a beehive makes as you start to walk toward it.

"Afternoon, girls," says the cartoon astronaut. "Thanks so much for, uh, accepting the invitation."

A big laugh goes up, as if this is a real joke.

"I'm Ethan," says the astronaut.

"I'm Jeremy," says the pretty one.

"And I'm Tom!" the big one finishes with a sort of jazz-hands flourish.

Fiona leans over to my ear. "Kill me," she whispers.

"There's no un-awkward way to say this, frankly," Ethan says. "So I'm going to come out and say it, and you can hate me for it, or not. But you're all beautiful, intelligent girls with a bright future, and we've been asked to talk to you all so we can prevent . . . uh, the wrong guys screwing up those futures forever."

There's some mumbling in the crowd. Fiona, Lily, and I look confusedly at one another.

"Lord knows there are enough teen mothers in the world," laughs Jeremy.

More mumbling. Some uncertain laughter.

"Look," says Tom. "We're talking to you guys about sex and relationships."

What follows is the strangest forty minutes I have ever spent in St. Bernadette's, and I was once locked in a cupboard for an entire afternoon with a deck of cursed tarot cards.

They say they are going to talk about sex, but they don't really talk about sex at all. What they talk about is *not* having sex. They talk about how condoms fail, how the pill makes girls sick, how hormonal contraception is a multibillion-dollar industry not unlike the opioid crisis in America. Then there's role-play.

My god, is there role-play.

A fifth-year girl is taken to the front of the room. Her name, we are told, is Amelia. She reminds me a little of Lily, before the river: a bit gawky, a bit dreamy, a bit naive.

Ethan is holding a roll of tape, and I'm briefly worried he's going to use it to gag her. Instead he puts a long length of tape on her school jumper.

"Now, let's say Amelia meets a guy and falls in love with him and has sex with him," he says. At this, he rips the tape off. Amelia blushes. He smiles at her. The room ripples with laughter.

He puts the tape back on.

"And now, a few years later, Amelia goes to college and meets a new boyfriend, and she has sex with him."

The same length of tape is ripped off.

"And then, Amelia goes to a club, meets someone there, they get friendly, and *they* have sex."

Again with the tape. This is all so weird that the laughter has stopped, and everyone is just embarrassed and confused. The constant associating of poor, shy Amelia's name with *sex* is getting too strange.

"Then, *I* meet Amelia." Ethan smiles. "I fall in love with her, I want to marry her."

Amelia is now beet red, staring at Ethan's huge arms, trying not to be visibly pleased by this development in her apparently exciting future sex life.

He takes the tape off and puts his wrist alongside Amelia's. He tries to wrap the tape around their wrists, but it just waves around, the sticky underside covered in school jumper lint.

"See," he says. "It doesn't work."

"Use new tape!" someone yells.

"I can't," he says mournfully. "Amelia can only give her tape away once."

Afterward, Lily and I are confused. Fiona, though, is furious.

"How dare they?" she storms. "How did Miss Harris let that happen? That kind of insane, ridiculous, nonsensical slut-shaming belongs in the freaking fifties. The pill makes women sick? What the hell is that?"

"It was weird," I say, still dazzled. "Poor Amelia."

"This idea that virginity is some gift you can give a man. Give me a break. Only men are arrogant enough to think that they could put something in *us* and change the way *we* are."

I give this some thought. I feel weird about the word *virgin* and how it applies to me. I technically am one, although that differentiation is getting vanishingly smaller the longer Roe and I are together. We had a conversation about it a few months ago, during one of those rare moments where it simply seemed to make complete sense to have sex: an empty house, a long evening ahead, the fact that we were naked and on my bed already. But I just wasn't quite ready. Which he seemed surprised by, given that I tried to drag him into bed the night of the ritual.

The only thing I can compare it to is sleepovers. When Lily and I were about nine, there was a craze in our primary class for big group sleepovers, real *event* sleepovers, and I always found them oddly frightening. I dodged what few invitations I received, just because the idea of sleeping in a room with five other people felt weird to me. And then one day, it didn't make me anxious anymore. There was no explanation. My brain just got used to the idea, and I went to a sleepover, and it was fine. That's how I feel about sex. Like I'm waiting for my brain to catch up with it.

When I explained this to Roe, he thought it was funny, and true, and he also said that he wouldn't broach sex again until I was ready. Then I got awkward about the idea of just telling him I was ready, and he kissed me and said: "Just say the word *sleepover*."

"And what's even weirder," Fiona continues, still raging, "is that people in there were taken *in* by it. You could tell. Girls were just drinking it in."

"Younger girls," I correct. "No one from our year."

"I know, but that's even stranger. The younger years are usually even woker than us. Why were they going along with it?"

I shrug. We're always hearing about how the younger girls are apparently nicer to one another. We're the "problem" year, after all.

"It sounds like COB bullshit," I say. Then I stop. "Do you think it *was* COB bullshit?"

For a second, we're all silent.

"They're all like Aaron clones," I say, bile rising in my throat. And then I remember something. That day in the café, when Aaron came and sat with me. He had three guys with him, around my own age. I didn't really get a good look at them, but now I'm convinced that Ethan, Jeremy, and Tom were the boys on the couches that day.

My throat feels tight. I fumble at my collar, expecting to feel my old uniform tie there, instead just finding the flat cotton of my T-shirt. I tug at the air around my neck, touching nothing. The restricted feeling. The sense of tightening. They're in the school. *My* school. I run my fingers along my collarbone.

No, not a school tie. Something closer to a noose.

11

THE CHASTITY BROTHERS, AS WE HAVE
started calling them, have apparently been spreading their message
to every school in the city and there's a small faction of liberal parents who are so scandalized by it that they've started calling the local
radio station. That's when we find out that the talk really was spon-
sored by COB. We are almost proud of ourselves for guessing.

Of course, Aaron is dispatched to defend the Chastity Brothers.

"Word is, Aaron," the old radio host says slowly, clearly reading
off a sheet of paper, "that your organization is telling young girls that
contraception is dangerous and that condo—*prophylactics*—don't
work."

"The studies on the pill speak for themselves," Aaron says
smoothly. "Any adult woman you speak to will say the same thing.
That the pill causes weight gain, mood swings, and irregular bleeding. And the medical profession is ignoring it. You know, in twenty
years, we'll look back at this moment in women's health the way we
look at the opioid crisis."

The host is so shocked by the words *irregular bleeding* on a
morning show that he has a coughing fit, allowing Aaron to change
the subject.

"Of course, what we're really interested in tackling is the way young men and women are relating to one another online. The pornification of our society has completely eroded the way they relate to the opposite sex."

"Yes," the host agrees. "The internet. Terrible stuff. Whatever happened to finding an old magazine in a bush?"

"What we're showing young people," Aaron continues, "is that the only real *safe* sex there is, is what happens between a man and a woman in the covenant of marriage."

My toast falls on the floor, hoovered up quickly by Tutu.

"Mum," I say, squeezing my eyes shut. "Can you please turn that off."

"The radio?" she says, confused. "OK. What's up?"

"No, it's just . . . that guy."

"Awful, isn't he? They have him on all the time now. That's their idea of a 'balanced' debate. One scientist and one absolute nutter. Honestly, what do young people get out of that kind of nonsense?"

"God, Mum, you don't know the half of it. He genuinely believes that God hates gay people."

"Well, that's awfully sad for him." She doesn't seem particularly worried.

"But he has power, Mum," I press. "He's violent."

"Maeve." She sighs. "You don't raise a gay daughter without being completely and *viscerally* aware that there are violent, dangerous idiots in the world."

"So you admit that he's a dangerous idiot."

"I don't know him, but if you say he is, you're right. But . . . there will always be people like that. When Jo was a teenager, the thought of them used to keep me up at night. When she and Sarra came home bleeding back in February, I thought . . ." She massages her temples lightly and closes her eyes. "I don't know what I thought, but it helped to feel sorry for those dangerous idiots. To wonder how badly they were loved, or not loved at all. I suppose I tried to understand them."

I open my mouth to protest, but she doesn't let me get a word out.

"Note," she says, putting her finger up, "I said 'understand.' I did not say 'like.' I did not say 'agree with.' But if you want to change how someone thinks, you have to know *how* they think and *why* they think it."

I understand what she's trying to say, but it's hard to take it seriously when she doesn't understand what Aaron is capable of. Even I don't truly know what Aaron is capable of, but I know he's had longer to live with his gifts than any of us have. I don't know what he has that's currently lying dormant, and what the COB has in store.

"Go on," she says. "You'll miss your bus."

My books are open on my lap the whole journey to school. Today are the tests that will separate us into higher and lower, and I'm trying to cram as much information into my head as I can.

Fiona and Lily are already there when I get to our classroom. Or at least, *our* room until the end of today.

Miss Harris walks in, and the formal hush of test time falls on the room.

"OK, girls. One space between two."

Everyone spreads out, which is easy now that most of our year group is gone, and Miss Harris hands out the test papers. Everything starts off OK. The first paper is history, and I have to write three short essays based on a list of five questions. The first two I pick are fine: *What were the causes and effects of the Russian Revolution?* and *What events led to the American civil rights movement?*

I'm doing OK, I catch myself thinking. *This is all right.* I do the Russian essay in half an hour, but the entire time I'm writing about the civil rights movement, however, I'm thinking: *I don't have the faintest clue what to do for my third essay.* The only remaining options are about the history of trade unions, about which I know nothing, or Northern Ireland. Northern Ireland is hard because it's more recent, there are way too many dates, way too many bombings, and way too many sides of the story. I take a stab at it anyway, thinking I can bluff it.

The fight for peace in Northern Ireland, I begin, *has a long and complex history.*

And that's it. That's all I have. I desperately root around in my brain for more information, but I'm drawing a blank. I close my eyes and try to remember every conversation I've ever overheard my parents have about Northern Ireland.

Focus, Maeve. Focus. History is just stuff that has happened before you were born. All you ever hear about at home is stuff that happened before you were born.

The more I try to focus my brain, the more distracted I become. Over the summer I've trained my mind to go into telepathy mode whenever I start concentrating really hard. Automatically, it starts searching for lights that it recognizes, seizing on Fiona's bright, burning orange starburst.

The increased demand for emancipation, beginning in the 1950s when more and more Catholic students began attending third-level education, was largely nonviolent until the late 1960s . . .

Oh, my god. She knows everything. Fiona knows *everything.*

I tell myself that I will just take a couple of dates to get me started. Something that will trigger the rest of my memory into working properly. But now that I'm tuned in to Fiona's frequency, I can't get out of it. She's like a song I can't get out of my head. I start writing. I tell myself that I am not putting down exactly what she's thinking. I am changing words and phrases. Instead of *emancipation*, I write *freedom*.

This is cheating, Maeve. Cheating off your best friend's paper without her permission.

It's not as if she would care, anyway. She offered to tutor me, and this is the same thing. She's just sharing what she knows with me. It's the exact same thing. It's not hurting her or taking away from what she knows. And besides, I've done most of the paper by myself.

This is not a sentiment I am able to reassure myself with on the next test paper.

Or the one after that.

But like the knife through Fiona's hand, I know, deep down, that just because something isn't immediately a problem, it doesn't mean that it won't be eventually.

On Wednesday morning, we are both called into Miss Harris's office. Fiona isn't frightened so much as she is perplexed. I don't think she's ever been "called in" to an office before, unless it's to win some kind of award for penmanship.

Miss Harris makes us sit down in front of her, her hands folded like she's playing a president on TV.

"Girls," she says slowly. "I think you know why you're in here today."

We are silent. Fiona could not be more confused.

"I have in front of me," Harris says, "two very different girls."

Normally, these kind of teacherly melodramatics make me want to laugh. She sounds like she is judging a reality TV show. But panic has frozen me, and I'm gripping the corners of my chair in an attempt to stay upright.

"Maeve, we've been here. A lot. You've been in and out of this office since the day you started at this school. You've always been a troublemaker. But toward the end of last term, I thought that perhaps Fiona was having a positive influence on you. Your teachers all said your temperament was improving."

Your temperament was improving. Like I'm livestock.

"Now, Fiona," she muses, tilting her head. "You're one of our brightest girls. You've always been a pleasure to have in class, always been helpful to others. Never cliquey, never a bully. And all your after-school activities . . . the acting, the theater. We've noticed those, too. We pay very close attention to our scholarship girls, always hopeful that they achieve all they can. So it has been a delight, for the whole staff, to watch you flourish."

Fiona's mouth twitches. Harris has never said anything remotely as nice about me, but Fi is acting like she's being put on the rack.

"It's because of your sterling reputation, Fiona, that I'm going to give you a chance to confess."

Fi gazes around, as if looking for a hidden camera.

"Um, what?" she says, her tone indignant. "Miss, I have no idea what you're talking about. Are you going to accuse Maeve of stealing again?"

My heart breaks in that moment. We both remember last term, when the tarot cards kept sneaking their way back to me and Miss Harris gave me detention for allegedly breaking into her desk. Fiona was appalled, and has had a grudge against Harris ever since.

Miss Harris gives Fiona a sharp look. "I wouldn't lead with that tone if I were you, Fiona."

I've spent the last two nights tossing and turning, clutching some crystals Nuala gave me to prevent nightmares, waiting to be found out. During test day, I was able to convince myself that I was changing Fiona's test answers enough so that no one would notice. Every hour since has been agony. Of course they would notice. There are so few girls left in our year that they're bound to notice two identical papers.

"Miss," I say, my voice wobbling. "I know why we're here. And I want to take full responsibility."

"Maeve, *what*?" Fiona turns to me, deeply confused. "What is going *on*?"

I should have told her before now. I know that. If I had told her, we could have planned a way out together. But in my head, I thought that if I threw myself on my own sword in front of her and Miss Harris, she'd be so impressed by the noble gesture that she would forgive everything.

I now realize what an incredibly dumb idea that was.

"I cheated off Fiona's paper," I say, refusing to meet my friend's eye. "She knew nothing about it. I'm sorry. I just wanted to be in the same class as my friends. I didn't want to be put in the . . . the lower class. I'm really sorry, miss."

Fiona's mouth falls open, and I can see her starting to put the whole thing together. Her expression turns to fury.

"That's very noble, Maeve," Miss Harris says coldly. "But I'm afraid that won't fly. You still have a lot of explaining to do."

I don't understand. Surely this is all the explaining you could need? I'm bad, and Fi is good. Excuse her, punish me.

"I'm not sure what you want me to explain, miss."

"Well, for one thing, how. I supervised those tests, and you and Fiona weren't sitting anywhere near each other. You couldn't have simply looked at her paper. It would have been impossible."

Silence. Fiona's orange light is burning so hot that I can see it without having to focus; it's burning behind my eyelids like an allergic reaction.

"So tell me how you did it. How did you manage to collaborate?"

Fiona and I remain silent. I hadn't counted on this. I assumed she would be so mad at the *why* of my cheating that she would never think about the *how*.

"Girls, I can keep you here all day. You have to understand that you're in a *state* exam year. If there's a way of cheating that you two have figured out, you're likely to tell the other girls. And if St. Bernadette's gets caught up in a Leaving Cert cheating scandal, we'll lose our accreditation. This is very, very, *very* serious. If you tell me now, the punishment will be less severe."

I bite down on my cheek so hard I can taste blood. How could I be so stupid and not think of this? Are we really going to have to tell Miss Harris about our gifts?

Suddenly, Fiona starts to speak.

"Miss Harris, I'm so sorry for what we did," she says calmly. "Like Maeve said, we wanted to be in the same class together. I can tell you how we did it."

Fiona, *no.*

Miss Harris leans forward slightly in anticipation.

"When I was writing my answers, I leaned really heavily," Fiona says slowly. "And I had my notepad open underneath the test papers, so my writing would imprint on it. When I was done with part of the exam, I'd go to the bathroom and stash the paper behind the toilet tank, and then Maeve would go get it and shade the impression with a coloring pencil. The answers show up then."

Fiona isn't getting this from nowhere. I've seen people use this technique before, and it might work if the answer is one word long, but would take forever for an essay question.

Miss Harris looks suspicious, too. "That wouldn't give Maeve a lot of time to trace your answers."

"We practiced." She shrugs. "I'm sorry."

The three of us are silent as Miss Harris tries to decide whether or not she believes us. Finally, she speaks.

"Thank you for your honesty, Fiona. I must say, I'm extremely disappointed that you would get drawn into a scheme like this. I've never had a moment of trouble from you since the day you started here, and we still think that your future at St. Bernadette's will be very bright. I can see that this was a moment of weakness, of wanting to help a friend. Detention on Friday."

"Thank you, miss," Fiona says, her eyes shining with tears.

"Now, Maeve." She sighs. "This isn't the first time you have been here."

I don't say anything. I just hang my head like Tutu when he's pooed on the carpet.

"Honestly, Maeve, I don't know what to do with you. My *instinct* is that this is the final straw, because clearly St. Bernadette's is not the right place for you, and your influence is starting to have a negative effect on the other girls."

Oh, my god. Is she going to expel me? Am I going to be expelled? What . . . what would I do? What would my family say?

"Miss, please, I . . ."

She lifts her palm up, commanding silence.

"However," she says. "I want to take into consideration that last term was . . . extremely traumatic for you, and that you may need help readjusting. I can understand why the idea of being separated from Fiona was frightening, and you acted out of fear. Which is why you will have detention every Friday evening from now until half-term."

I nod mutely, flooded with relief that I'm not getting expelled.

"I will of course be writing to both sets of parents. Now. That's all, girls."

And suddenly, we're in the hallway, staring at each other.

"Fiona, I'm so sorry."

For a moment, I'm certain she's going to punch me. Instead, she just stares, as if seeing who I truly am for the first time. She looks like she's about to say something, but then the lunch bell sounds and breaks her concentration. Instead, she walks out the door and starts walking quickly away from school.

"Fi," I call after her, quickening my pace. "Fi, wait. I'm sorry. I'm really sorry."

She almost runs to get away from me, but is stopped short by the pedestrian crossing. She jams her finger on the button, the sign glowing WAIT at her, as if it's secretly on my side.

"Leave me alone, Maeve," she says flatly.

"Just talk to me, OK? Look, I know what I did was wrong but . . ."

"Do you, though?" she flares. "Do you really?"

"Yes!" I protest. "It was dishonest and terrible and a total betrayal of our friendship and . . ."

"Sure, Maeve. It was all those things. But did it not occur to you that Miss Harris could have taken my scholarship away over that?"

"What?" I say, my flow of words slowing. "N-no. She wouldn't have."

"What do you think all those hints were? All that bit about 'severe punishments' and my 'bright future' at St. Bernadette's. 'Keeping a close eye on scholarship girls.' She was going to take my scholarship away if I didn't come up with something, that dumb story about leaning too hard on my paper. Do you have any idea the amount of trouble you could have gotten me in? Maeve, you could have ruined my *life*."

"Come on," I plead desperately. "Come on, don't be so dramatic, that's not what would have happened."

"I *cost them money*, Maeve, do you get that? I cost them money, and you make them money. That's what scholarships are, at the end of the day. An expense."

How had I not thought of this? How had I managed, again, to both love Fiona and be completely unaware of the ways in which her life is different from mine?

"You know how hard I've worked. You know how badly I want to go to Trinity, to get out of Kilbeg. I can't believe you would put that at risk just to get into some stupid *class.*"

The disgust in her voice is rising like a wave. I stand there, ready to take the full crash of it, knowing that once she's said what she has to say, we'll go back to normal.

"And that . . . you have this epic cosmic gift, and that you would just . . . waste it on a dumb test? That is just so *you*, Maeve. You have all these chances and opportunities and privileges and you just waste them. Do you have any idea how frustrating that is?"

The pedestrian crossing beeps and she crosses the road, me trailing behind her. She finally stops walking at the bus stop.

"OK," I huff. "OK, I admit that I screwed up, but it's not like I do this all the time. It's a one-time thing."

"A one-time thing that is part of a many-time *trend.*"

I can feel my face getting hot. Why does Fiona have to expand this into some kind of psychological case study? How many times do I have to say I'm sorry?

Just swallow it, Maeve. Just accept what she has to say, and move on, and be friends again. But instead . . .

"OK, Fiona, as if I'm the *only* one who is using their gifts for less-than-ideal things."

There's a bunch of lads from the boys' school smoking cigarettes and watching us. They must have a half day. They start meowing desperately to indicate that we're in a cat fight. I hate them.

She swings around to face me. "What is that supposed to mean?"

"Getting a lot of *nosebleeds* lately?"

"Shut up," she snipes. "Don't talk to me about that."

I immediately regret my horrible tone and try to backpedal. "Look, I'm just worried about you, OK?"

She barks a short, dry laugh. "Oh, you're *worried* about me now, are you?"

"Why are you doing it, Fi? Why do you keep hurting yourself? We can talk about it. Properly, I mean. I won't judge you. I'm sure you have good reasons."

"Oh, you won't *judge* me? Wow, big of you."

The meowing is getting louder now. Some of the boys are shouting at us to kiss.

"I'm going home," she says through gritted teeth. "And I'm going to explain this shitshow to my mother before she hears it through Harris. Maybe if I do some damage control, she won't punish me *too* much."

The *for something I didn't do and had no part in* bit remains, thankfully, unsaid. Fiona walks away from me, and the boys finally quiet. Her bus is pulling up.

"I'll phone you tonight," I call after her as she starts to get on.

She turns around.

"Don't," she says as the bus door shutters.

12

I GO BACK TO SCHOOL AND MISS HARRIS has posted a list of the class groupings on the bulletin board. As predicted, I'm in the lower class. We'll have to move out of the third-floor classroom tomorrow. I'm so bleached through with shame that I don't linger at the wall to see who's with me. I just go straight to my old desk and look through the folder of test papers that have been dropped off at my desk.

Maeve—

The part of this exam that is <u>not plagiarized</u> is promising. Have more faith in yourself next time.

- H

The more I stare at Miss Harris's note, the less I notice the other girls in the room, the chatting, the noise. I'm so detached and miserable that I barely recognize the tears sliding onto the page as my own.

"Where's Fiona?"

I look up, and Lily is clearly not having a good day, either. Her face is red, and her hair is trying desperately to escape its tight plait.

"She . . . went home," I say, drying my face with my sleeve. It's not as if I need to. Lily clearly hasn't noticed that I've been crying. "She wasn't feeling well," I finish.

"I'm in the lower class," Lily says furiously. "With *you.*"

"Oh, Lil, I'm sorry. I know how hard you worked. And you can still go to Galway—"

"Stop," she says, and then sits down. "I don't want to hear it."

We are silent for the few minutes before class begins, the gap where Fiona usually sits yawning like a chasm between us.

A few hours later, we're walking down the hill together. The only sound is Lily's shoulder bag bumping off her leg.

"I should tell you something," I say limply. "About where Fiona went today."

"What?"

"I did something really bad," I begin.

"I know."

"No, I mean . . . to Fiona."

"OK."

"I used my gift to cheat off her in the exams. To read her mind while she was answering her papers. I knew it was a dumb thing to do, but I panicked. And then it was just so easy that I kept on doing it."

Lily listens and then nods. "OK."

"And . . . I didn't think. I didn't think about how that information wasn't mine to steal, and that Fiona had worked to put that stuff in her brain, y'know? It didn't just land there by accident. And when I got caught, Harris thought we were both in on it, and Fiona's getting detention, too."

"That's bad," Lily replies. "She shouldn't get punished."

"I know. I said sorry so many times, but she's just so mad at me. She said I jeopardized her scholarship, which I didn't even *think* about."

"She won't stay mad," Lily says. "Fiona's too busy to dwell on stuff like being mad."

To my utter shock, I realize that Lily is, in her own way, consoling me.

"Really?" I ask, hungry for kindness. "Do you think?"

"I do," she says evenly. She notices a fallen leaf stuck to her shoe, picks it up, and examines it. "I don't think it's such a big deal, what you did."

"No?"

She traces her finger along the vein of the leaf, following the stalk to the tip.

"The way people have set up the world . . . it isn't fair. Why should you only do well if you're good at taking tests? I tried all summer to be good at taking tests, I tried to play the game, and look where it got me. I still can't do it. I still can't keep all that stuff in my head."

She passes the leaf to me, as if I'm going to be equally as fascinated by it. I examine it, to be polite. It's still green, slightly yellowed at the edge. A sure sign that autumn is coming.

"They want *us* to do what *they* can do, but they can't do what we do. They don't know what it's like to be a river." She glares at the ground furiously, and I'm almost sure that I can see tears pricking at her eyes. I wonder how crying works with Lily now. How the water in her body reacts to the electrical currents, and whether she is being slightly fried alive at all times.

"Nuala thinks our gifts are meant to teach us something specific," I say as gently as I can. "What do you think the electricity is teaching you? And why do you think yours is so much more intense than ours?"

I've wondered this about Lily for a long time, but asking seems rude. Like asking a girl how her boobs got so big so suddenly. She's silent for a long moment.

"I don't know if it's teaching me anything," she says. "But . . . I think because of my ear. When I was the river . . . I was still me. I had my hearing aid in. This little battery. There was this buzzing, this heat. I think the water and the hearing aid fused together and made this current or something."

If I had a hundred years to think about it, I wouldn't have come up with this solution. I remember, in that second, why I fell in love with Lily when I was five. She thinks about things in a way no one else does. The fact that she can't do well on a test is just further proof of how stupid tests are.

"Do you miss the river, still?"

"Yes," she says flatly. "But I can accept that that part of my life is over now."

"That . . ." I'm at a loss for what to say, but I want to sound supportive. "That is very *adult*, I think."

We walk on. I am, for some reason, still holding the leaf.

"If I could do what you can do," she says, "I probably would have done the exact same thing. Fiona and Roe don't know what it's like. School comes easily to them. They think it's just about knuckling down, working hard, and concentrating. They have no solution for when you do all those things and it still doesn't work."

Lily is talking to me with something close to warmth. For the first time in almost two years, Lily O'Callaghan and I are having a real conversation. She doesn't seem like she hates me, either. She even uses playful air quotes on "knuckling down."

"So what are you going to do about Galway?" I ask. "You can still get four hundred points. Y'know, now that the class sizes are so small, maybe the teachers actually will be able to help us directly."

She raises an eyebrow. "You really think that?" she asks sarcastically. "Or are they going to put all their time into the girls who will make the school famous and look good?"

"I don't know," I say, and I try to hand the leaf back to her.

Slowly, Lily puts her thumb and her pointer finger into her mouth, like she's about to wolf whistle. Then she takes her fingers out and pinches the leaf between them. The whole thing sizzles, and I let go quickly as it falls to the ground. It burns, crumples, and folds in on itself.

"I'm done," Lily says simply. "And you look about done, too."

I can't even tell if she's talking to the leaf or to me.

I say goodbye to Lily and take a detour to Fiona's house. I don't go inside. I rip out a page from my homework journal and sit under her garden wall to write a note.

Fiona,

I'm sorry. There's no excuse for what I did and I won't try to find one. I was so afraid of seeming stupid that I acted like a real dumb bitch. I am now officially on a no-dumb-bitch-juice diet. I will sup the dumb bitch juice no longer.

Love you forever,

M xxxxxx

When I get home I take a big breath and walk into the kitchen. My parents are sitting with their chairs angled outward, like people on a talk show. The dog is lying on the ground, flattened by the tense atmosphere.

"Hello," I say weakly.

"Sit down," Mum says immediately. And I sit.

The next forty minutes are torture. About the cheating, the call from Miss Harris, the fact that I am on thin ice already, and, lastly, that I brought Fiona into it.

"Fiona," she says with affection and reverence, "who has such a big future planned."

I'm so browbeaten by the day that I can't help but fight back. "What? And I don't?"

Dad tries to be gentle. "We're not saying you don't have a big future. Just that you don't have one planned."

"We've hardly seen you in months because you spend so much time with your friends," Mum says, shaking her head. "The fact that you would jeopardize Fiona's exams is unbelievable, Maeve. What has happened to you?"

"Oh, my god." I can feel the anger rising in my voice. I know it's a bad idea, but I feel powerless to stop it. "Can't you accept that I'm in a system that is just not made for my type of brain, and that I got so sick of being lectured and patronized that I *did* something about it? I know what I did was wrong. I'm sorry. But I didn't, like, dump a drum of oil into the sea. I wasn't just randomly acting out. This is what people *do* when you set them up for failure."

There's a pause then, and for a second I think they understand me.

"Well," Mum says. "If you're quite finished with the melodramatic speeches."

I sink lower in my chair.

"The thing is, Mae," Dad says, "you didn't just do this to do better at school. You just wanted to stick close to Fiona, didn't you?"

I don't answer. I look at my feet instead. Why does Dad always have to sound like a hostage negotiator?

114

"We're so happy that you have such close bonds with your friends," he continues, all softly-softly, like I have a gun. "But perhaps you're a bit too bound up with them at the moment? I feel like it's all a bit too tight, too intense."

Again, I don't answer. Instead, I burrow into each of their minds, one by one.

Mum: *One more year. Just one more bloody year of school.*

Dad: *At least she's not so lonely anymore.*

Dad's thought is the one that kills me. I remember the loneliness of last year. No real friends, no gang, versus the endless joy of summer.

"You're grounded, obviously, for everything except school," Mum says. "And no more Divination on the weekends."

I nod. I sort of knew this was coming.

"Can I go now?"

"Yes."

I trudge upstairs and decide I'm going to cast a spell. There are witches and there are *witches*; there are spells and there are *spells*. Some spells are meant for changing the world and some spells are just to make you feel less miserable. Less helpless. I get on my knees in the bathroom and start concocting. I craft a spell to make myself less of an asshole. There's a little case that lives under my bed, essential oils and dried herbs and that kind of thing. I take out a bottle of sandalwood, for banishing negativity; some sprigs of thyme, for cleansing bad vibes; almond oil, for sweetness. I deal the Devil, the Seven of Swords, and the High Priestess and lay a piece of toilet paper on top of each one.

"Help me get rid of my bad habits." A drop of sandalwood for the Devil, the oil splashing on the tissue and making his face visible.

"Forgive me for deception." A sprig of thyme for the Seven of Swords.

A drop of almond oil for the Priestess. "Give me a little more foresight, please."

The candles burn down in the bathroom, and I put myself into what yoga people call a child's pose, my face resting on the floor. The tiles feel cool on my forehead and the room starts to feel spicy, like magic. Like forgiveness.

13

THE NEXT MORNING, EVERYONE WHO DID badly on the tests has to go downstairs to the basement classes. We never went down here when we were breaking in over the summer, so it's a surprise to see it now. The smell of mold is entirely gone. They've knocked down a wall so that there's just one big classroom now, airy and fresh and full of light. We have a new sixth-year break room, which we still share with the girls in Group One.

"You're still *very much* a year group," Harris says in a speech that sounds suspiciously rehearsed. "You'll still be relaxing and studying together, just like before."

A brand-new kettle and microwave sit on the kitchen counter, waiting for their maiden voyage. They were once so desperately longed for that their presence now feels almost mythical. There's even a bookcase and a few armchairs to hang out in. A screen door opens to a little patio outside, with steps leading to the street. "I wonder if we can smoke out there?" is the first thing Róisín O'Mara says when she walks in after me. Two minutes later, another girl shows up and says the same thing. I can already tell that a lot of this term will be spent debating whether or not we're allowed to smoke on the basement terrace, the debate intensifying as a few of the girls start turning eighteen. Upstairs, they're probably all talking about what kind of doctor they're going to be.

"The Chokey is gone," Lily says suddenly behind me. "It's an office now."

The classroom that The Chokey was part of has become part of the locker-lined hallway, and The Chokey itself has been extended into a small office. Lily and I saunter in, and for a moment, it's like we're back in first year again. Slipping away and exploring the school, always hopeful of mysteries.

The office is cozy and lined with books, the desk a heavy oak. It doesn't look particularly official; it looks like Mum's study, where she goes to mark papers.

"They've kept the shelves," I say, running my hand along the new book spines. "So it's still *kind of* The Chokey."

Lily is already behind the desk, glancing at papers with no attempt to maintain secrecy. "Heather Banbury," she reads slowly. "Guy-dance-counts-elor."

I try to hide my shock. Lily's grades have never been great, but she's always been a reader. She used to read big thick fantasy novels, sometimes several a month. Now she's struggling to read *guidance counselor*. The river gave things to Lily, but it also washed things away. It deteriorated part of her original mind, severed pathways that were once clear.

No wonder she hates me so much.

I walk around to her side of the table and see that HEATHER BANBURY, GUIDANCE COUNSELOR is plated in *brass*.

"What's with the engraved desk?" Lily asks.

"Maybe she brought it from home."

"Is that normal?"

"I don't know."

I put my hand against the back wall, where I can still feel the slight dampness of the foundations of the old house. There's a purplish line, running like creases through a palm, up from the skirting board and to the ceiling. Mold already breaking through the new paint.

"I talked to Fiona last night," Lily says. "She's still mad."

My stomach sinks. Fiona wouldn't even pick up the phone for me last night. I wait for Lily to deliver another robotic put-down, one of her icy observations of my character. It doesn't come.

"What did you say?" I prod.

She shrugs. "Nothing."

"Great, thanks."

There are eleven other girls in our class, which I'm surprised by. I always assume other people have it together. There are quite a few girls who look a bit lonely and adrift. No one has a gang anymore.

You can feel the prickling anxiety of the room, the sense that everyone knows they are low achievers in a school designed for high expectations. We've all known one another for years, but we are all suddenly embarrassed by one another. We're like those prisoners who all insist they're innocent, locked up for the wrong thing. This changes when our first class starts. For once, our English teacher, Miss March, isn't banging on endlessly about Sylvia Plath. Instead, she hands us old exam papers.

"The place where ninety percent of you go wrong in exams," she says, "is in the wording of the question."

We look at one another, startled by this switch in her tone.

"When an examiner asks you to *show evidence* of something, that's *all* you need to do. If you're going to get through your exams, you need to first understand exactly what's being asked of you, and exactly what's expected."

That's how all our classes go. They've given up on trying to make us fall in love with school. This is about rewiring our brains so that we're good at exams, and I can already tell that most of us are finding it a refreshing change.

At lunch, we wait for Fiona in the sixth-year break room. All the other girls come downstairs, but Fiona doesn't.

"I thought that was good," I say to Lily, stirring my instant hot chocolate. It's a bit gross, made with hot water, not milk, but it's still a bit of a thrill to make it in school. "The classes, I mean. More straightforward."

She shrugs and looks into her own mug of hot water.

"Are you going to put a tea bag in that, or . . . ?"

Her eyes flicker mischievously to me, inviting me to gaze into her cup. Inside she is creating a very small firework display. Tiny sparks the size of gnats dance across the surface of the water, the steam capturing them midhover. I catch my breath, astonished by the electric beauty made miniature.

"You shouldn't do that in school," I whisper. "You'll get caught."

She shrugs, and the sparks fall into the water, drowning instantly. Luckily, everyone seems too busy reuniting with their friends to notice.

"Hello, girls," comes a soft voice, and I jump, instinctively moving in front of Lily so she's not seen. It's Heather Banbury.

"Hey, er, Miss Banbury," I say. "How are you?"

It's quite weird to ask a teacher how they are, I realize. I have never asked Miss Harris how she is.

"Yeah, fine." She smiles gratefully. "Getting on, you know. I've been talking to the third-years all day, already stressing about their Junior Cert. It's so hard to tell them to relax without specifically saying 'This literally does not matter.'"

I laugh, remembering how serious everyone got during the Junior Cert, and how stupid that all seems now. "I hope the Leaving is like that. Like, as soon as it's done we'll all realize what an insane fuss over nothing it was."

"Believe me," she responds, leaning in conspiratorially. "You will. You know what I got in my Leaving?"

Lily and I look at each other, amazed that a teacher would talk like this to us. Well, not a teacher, but still. "What?" we both ask.

She bites her lip, lowers her head slightly to not attract the attention of the other girls. "Two twenty-five."

"Wow." I am genuinely shocked. I don't know anyone who has scored that low. But then again, all my siblings were in the five hundreds. "Could you get into college?"

"I did a technical course, which I actually really enjoyed, on jewelry design," she says happily. She starts fiddling with an opal ring on her finger.

"And did you become a jewelry designer?"

"No," she says, just as sunny. "But I got a really weird job cataloging estate sales—you know, calculating the worth of dead people's jewelry, writing little sales pitches for the auction house. It was fun! I met lots of, like, weird old eccentrics."

"Wow," I say again. And then feel embarrassed because I'm repeating myself. "I've never even heard of a job like that."

"Yeah." She shrugs. "I've had loads of those weird little jobs, to be honest. Then I was a buyer, trying to find unusual stones, so I lived in India for a few years."

This is utterly amazing to me. Quite frankly, I had no idea you could do so much with so few qualifications. "And what was that like?" I ask, unable to hide my curiosity.

"India? It was fun! I was traveling around a lot, so I sometimes got a bit lonely, but I did an online course in textiles and I met a lot of cool people along the way. Then I got into yoga while I was out there, and sort of meditation in general. Which led me into counseling. God." She stops, laughs at herself. "There's my life story for you, I guess."

The lunch bell goes. "Sorry," she says, looking a bit sheepish. "I shouldn't have taken up your lunch break, blithering on."

"No, no," I reply. "We were really interested. Weren't we, Lil?"

Lily has gone back to playing with her water, and is showing no interest whatsoever.

"I'd really love to learn more about, like . . . I don't know, how you find cool jobs like that."

"Luck, mostly," she laughs. "Well, listen, you've got detention this Friday, don't you? I'm supervising you. We can talk more then, if you like."

For the first time in days, I don't feel so heavy, so broken down with worry and hopelessness. Maybe it's the spell I did in the bathroom, or just talking to someone who doesn't treat education like the be-all and end-all, but I feel cheerful. Jolly. We say goodbye to her and head to our first class, and I feel so brave that I loop my arm through Lily's.

We walk into class with our arms linked, like we used to do a hundred years ago.

·)❭●❬(·

Fiona's mood does eventually thaw, partly because she's not the sort of person who can easily hold a grudge, and partly because school becomes so strange that she can't resist talking to us about it.

123

"Have you *seen* them?" she explodes one day when Lily and I are sitting in the break room. "The pins?"

I instantly know what she's talking about. I've noticed them, too, without necessarily thinking to question them. Some of the younger girls have started wearing tiny gold pins on their shirt collars, in the shape of two circles intersecting. Like the Olympic rings, with three of them missing.

"What are they?" I ask. "Some kind of charity thing?"

"Charity of *bullshit!*" she says so loudly that two girls move to the end of the room, glaring at us as they go. "It's for abstinence. Wearing it is, like . . . this promise to not have sex before marriage."

"Jesus Christ," I say, shaking my head. "So they're, like, wedding rings."

"Well, yeah, exactly." Fiona flops down and crosses her arms. "Can you believe this? Apparently those COB boys are holding, like, after-school clubs and people are *going*. Like, of their own free will. And getting these pins."

"Maybe some people don't want to do it before marriage," Lily says, docile.

"At this rate, I'll be married before I get to do anything again," I grumble. My parents are holding fast on the grounding. What we were previously referring to as "my life" is now being called "a distraction."

"It's not about, like, whether or not people want to do it on an individual level. It's that they're encouraging this whole *movement*, and . . . and . . ." Fiona starts to splutter and stumble, a rare occurrence for her. "This whole sense of honor around being a virgin that is completely bogus and sexist and is designed to control women."

"Hear, hear."

"We need to do something," Fiona says defiantly. "They should be banned in school."

124

"I'm not sure if that's really our, uh, remit."

"No," she says fiercely. "But I know what is."

What happens next is nothing short of genius. Fi becomes a one-woman guerrilla war. If she spots someone wearing a circle brooch, she goes over and starts talking to them. Then she pretends like there's a bit of dirt on their collar and acts like she's going to smudge it away. In that instant of her hand being on their collar, the tiny hole poked into the shirt by the pin heals itself, and the brooch falls out. Nine times out of ten, the girl doesn't even notice, and Fiona quickly snatches it away.

Soon, Fiona has a jacket pocket full of brooches, and she rattles them whenever she walks. Despite her joy, there's still an edge to our conversations, a loss of intimacy. She's sharper, spikier. It used to be that Lily didn't want to be left alone with me, and now it feels like Fiona doesn't. There's more Dublin talk than ever. Her audition for Trinity is in February, which will mark the beginning of her departure from Kilbeg and one whole year since she became my friend.

Detention doesn't quite go like I imagine it. Just when I think that I'll be allowed to do my homework for two hours, Miss Harris swoops in at the last minute.

"Detention is *not* study," she says. "Detention is when you reflect on what you've done."

Then she gives me a pile of bursting folders to sort out. They're mass sheets: the same yellowing A4 printouts that have been used and reused for every Christmas and Easter mass since I've been at this school. "They're all out of order. Sort, staple, and file."

Heather grimaces when she sees what I have to do, and suggests that we do it in her office over a cup of tea.

"What do you take?" she calls from the kitchen. "I have peppermint, ginger, chamomile, or breakfast."

I want breakfast, obviously, because all other teas are disgusting. Saying so would be unsophisticated, though. I have a weird urge to show Heather Banbury that I'm worldly, or want to be. "Chamomile, please."

I start sorting, and before long, I get that horrible dry sensation in my fingertips, the feeling of dust and paper. Heather doesn't talk to me at first. She tries to uphold detention as a serious thing. I sort page after page of prayers. For some reason the Ash Wednesday ones are the most mixed-up. The whole service seems extremely pagan: the black marks on the forehead, the burning of the palm fronds.

"Are you sorting?" Heather asks neutrally. "Or are you reading?"

"Sorting," I say, not very convincingly. She arches an eyebrow. "It's interesting, isn't it?" I continue. "That we just accept that millions of people all over the world smudge their foreheads with ash every year. It's so witchy. Yet people think Wicca and magic is, like, way out there."

"The difference," she says, "is that Wicca is very take-it-or-leave-it, but people wage war over the idea of God. And conveniently, one big male god who has very specific opinions on coveting your neighbor's wife and lands. It's like, hmmm, I wonder who came up with that ideology?"

"Men?"

"Men!"

There's a shift in the air, a slight warmth when she talks about magic. I remember that night on the hill with Aaron, the wind lifting behind her, the smell of copper. The sense that she knew.

"Are you . . ." I begin. "Are you like me?"

"Like you, how?"

"Are you . . . gifted?"

126

She pauses, presses her lips together. It's like she's trying to decide whether to laugh this off or take it seriously.

"I'm not sure what you mean, Maeve."

I go back to sorting the mass sheets, reading about the body and blood of Christ, and slowly try to peek into Heather Banbury's brain. I find her strand of light and try to follow it. I meet only resistance, the feeling of bumping into an invisible wall at the boundary of a video game.

"Stay focused on the task at hand, Maeve," she says, her tone chiding but not annoyed.

Oh, I think. *She knows.*

Roe texts me after detention to say that he can't drive me home tonight, that Small Private Ceremony has been asked to do a gig last minute at the student union bar. He asks if I can get the bus home instead.

But I'm still grounded. Now I won't see you all weekend?

He doesn't text back until midnight, when he tells me that he is sorry, and that he has only just seen his phone.

14

MUM AND DAD MIGHT HAVE THE BEST intentions about grounding me, but that doesn't change the fact that my weekend is their weekend, too, and they want to do things. It's a bright, warm Saturday, and they want to drive the dog to the beach, forty minutes away. That's another nice thing about Kilbeg. You're never far from the city or the sea.

"Will you come, Mae?" Dad says eagerly, putting his walking shoes on. "We'll go for a nice lunch afterward."

"No, thanks," I say mournfully, looking at my books. "I need to hunker down."

"All right. Well, we'll probably be back at about four."

"Cool. See you then."

Dad can't stand anyone fighting. Mum, however, is fine with it. The energy in the house is not great.

The minute they leave I call Roe, who is with Fiona and Lily, and they come over.

"Someone stuck this leaflet on the bulletin board by the music room," Lily says, unfolding a piece of paper from her pocket. "It has their logo on it." She taps at the St. Brigid's cross printed on the back.

I look at the leaflet. It's full of laughing young people, some of whom I dimly recognize as being Instagram and TikTok influencers. Not the fancy, international kind of influencer, but the more local ones. The kind of people who have French bulldogs and are always tagging themselves at free lunches.

EXAM STRESS?

POSITIVE THINKING CAN LEAD TOWARD FUTURE SUCCESS

CLARIFY YOUR VISION WITH A FREE PERSONALITY TEST

FIND YOUR PATH. TALK TO SOMEONE TODAY.

"They're in the Claringdon Hotel?" I say, peering at the address. "But that's like . . . fancy. Girls in *our school* are going to this?"

"I guess?" Lily shrugs. "It says here there's free food."

"I know," Roe says. "A big step up from that meeting in Aaron's weird apartment."

"Huge."

Lily and Fiona start examining it, and Roe puts his hand on the small of my back. "I'm sorry about last night," he whispers. "I couldn't say no."

"Couldn't, or wouldn't?" I reply, still mildly miffed.

"We're not in a position to turn gigs down," he says, a bit moodily. "We have a tour coming up."

"I know," I say, a little too fiercely.

"We should go," says Lily, tapping the leaflet again. I ignore her and plug quietly into Roe's thoughts.

She could ask me how the gig went.

"We should *go*," she says again, louder.

"To this?" I point to the leaflet. "Today? Wouldn't that be dangerous?"

Lily blinks at me, confused. "For *who*?"

We all look at one another, and a wave of confidence, silver and glittering, washes over all of us at once.

"Yeah," I say, tired of feeling like the bad guy, desperate to do some good. "Yeah, let's do it."

Fiona gets to her feet. "Come on, then, let's go."

I see Roe looking down, reviewing his outfit: black leggings and an embroidered tunic dress. I'm still tuned in to his thoughts, and I can feel him making a mental calculation about how he looks and where we're going. He considers going home to change, and then suddenly says: "Fuck it, let's go."

We don't really know why we're going, or what we plan to do. What we *can* do. We just know we're sick of doing nothing.

The Claringdon is a five-star hotel that sits on the Beg River in the middle of the city. They built it before the last recession, constructing a huge, expensive boardwalk outside, with a floating pontoon that you can walk down to in the summertime. My sister Abbie got married here when I was thirteen. I was allowed to bring Lily as my guest, and we ran up and down the pontoon during the speeches, jumping on it, making it shake. I slipped in the darkness and fell in the river. Lily had to pull me out.

I nudge her as we're walking toward the entrance. "Remember this, Lil?" I say, pointing to the pontoon. "Abbie's wedding? You pulled me out."

She lifts her eyes to it, scanning it slowly, trying to stir the memory. "Yes," she says finally, and a look of utter astonishment flowers in her face. "Your sister Abbie got married here."

"Yes," I agree as if I had not already said it.

She turns to me, a look of surprise and joy, but mostly surprise *at* the joy, blooming. "Maeve . . . that was *fun*?"

"Yeah." I nod. "Remember, Abbie murdered me? Then we were banished to her hotel room, and it was the bridal suite, and we . . ."

"Replaced all the minishampoo with tea! Tea we brewed with the tiny kettle!"

She starts to laugh, utterly unselfconscious, her mouth wide open, her lips peeled back. This is the first time in the many months since Lily has returned from the river that I have seen her take any joy in the past. I can't help but be delighted. Finally, Lily is feeling some kind of happiness about being human, and I got to be the one who let her see it.

We walk through the elegant double doors of the hotel, a blast of central heating coming down from the ceiling, and the people at reception immediately point us to the elevator. "Third-floor ballroom," they say without much enthusiasm. We take the elevator up, and the moment the doors open, we hear a hum of activity and pop music playing over a sound system. We follow the noise, our trainers hissing on the soft carpet.

"Hi, guys," says a cheerful girl at the door of the ballroom. "Can I stamp your hand?"

"Uh . . . no," says Fiona.

"You won't be able to get back in if you leave!"

"I think that's probably fine," Roe says as we file in.

There are about three hundred people in the ballroom, and most of them are about five years either side of our age. I actually recognize some girls from the year below us. For some reason, Katy Perry's "Firework" is playing. The energy is different from the apartment gathering we attended in February.

"These people . . . they can't all be here for the free food, can they?"

There are little stalls on the edge of the ballroom with dishes of snacks and ballpoint pens, like a career fair. I catch the ends of a conversation, one between a girl I recognize and another girl that I don't.

She's stunning, with those huge painted eyebrows that look great on camera and slightly odd in real life.

"I'm just so *stressed*," the girl I recognize says, picking at her face. "If I don't do well on my Junior Cert, I'm basically screwed for the Leaving."

The other girl nods, her eyes concerned. "This stress is a distraction," she says. "From bigger questions you're having about your life."

There's a sunny, party atmosphere. People are chatting, mingling, taking excited selfies with the influencers I presume are paid to be here. There's something else, too. A sense that everyone is lucky. A congratulatory kind of air, like an awards ceremony.

Immediately, there is no way to be inconspicuous. I'm so used to the way Roe dresses that I forget that other people find it unusual. Particularly *these* kinds of people. Within ten minutes, three young Children representatives have approached us to ask if we're OK, and all of them address Roe directly.

"Oh, hello," one woman says to him, and her tone is strange. "And who might *you* be?"

Even though she's standing upright, she sounds like she's crouching on her knees and talking to a child. Like she's asking, with the greatest of interest, what he is dressed as for Halloween. She's in her twenties, wearing a tight sapphire dress with capped sleeves, and looks vaguely like a flight attendant from the past.

"My name is . . . Barry."

Barry? I mouth at him. He shrugs, amused.

"Well, Barry! I'm Alice. I'm just so glad to see you here today. We're just such a fan of the arts and of creativity here."

"Creativity?" Roe looks puzzled.

"Oh, you know, freedom of expression. Like what you do. Dress however you want, y'know?"

"O . . . K."

"Sometimes"—she lowers her voice, like she's sharing a secret—"sometimes I wear cat ears to the supermarket, just to feel an extra sparkle!"

"That's . . . nice for you."

"But just so you know, we *will* expect you to use the gentlemen's loos."

He stops dead. His face blanches. We all look at her, shocked. Fiona seems to gather herself quickest.

"Alice, do you usually bring up someone's bodily functions the second you meet them?"

Alice doesn't even flinch. She looks at Fiona like she has simply misunderstood. "Oh, pet." She smiles. "I was only addressing the elephant in the room. I thought Barry would prefer that."

"Who is *Barry*?" Lily asks in wonder. Then she realizes. "Oh, right."

"Wait, who's the elephant?" Roe asks. "Me?"

Alice has had enough of this and moves away from us, giving us an *I'm sorry, I really must mingle* smile.

Roe still looks gobsmacked. He's only ever used the men's or the gender-neutral restrooms, but even so, it's a disgusting thing to say to someone. Particularly if you've just met them. *Hi, sorry, I don't know you, but where exactly are you planning to put your waste products? Just a ballpark answer will do.*

"Look," Lily says. "A drinks table."

She saunters over to a table where a tea and coffee urn sit, and pours herself a cup of hot water.

At that moment, a square-jawed guy who seems to be of Asian descent starts talking to Fiona. "You know, at first," he begins, "I didn't think this kind of thing would be for me, either."

"Uh-huh," she says, not missing a beat. "And what exactly is 'this kind of thing'?"

He doesn't answer the question. "Ireland likes to pretend that it's so liberal," he says. "Like, just because they don't have an empire, they can't be racist. But they can."

"Yeah?" she agrees, but slowly, as if waiting for the trapdoor to fall.

"I've lived here for five years. And I would say about *half* the people I meet act as if they're just so generous for 'letting' me live here, and that I should be grateful." He cocks his head to the side and puts on an old-lady accent. "They say, 'Aren't you glad you have a better life now?' Like I escaped some terrible trauma. I'm, like . . . I know ten people who could buy and sell your ass, and nine of them I went to high school with in Hong Kong."

And in spite of herself, Fiona laughs. Her orange light starts to warm up, a fire gently brightening.

"But the thing is, racism comes from greed, and a feeling that you need to defend your identity. And people only feel those feelings when they're not close to God. I used to be so angry. But now I feel like, when I talk to people about God, when I bring them back into the church . . . I'm really *doing* something. And I'm not angry anymore."

I'm expecting Fiona to say something snappy and clever, but it doesn't come. Instead, she just looks uneasy, nauseous. She moves away from him.

"Hey, what's your name?"

"Barry," she answers, and turns away.

"Beautiful name for a beautiful girl." He smiles, happy to play along, but then lets her go.

This was supposed to be fun. Wasn't it? Why did we come here again?

Someone gets onstage and starts talking about positive affirmations, positive thinking, and the destructive power of negative thoughts. It's all very general. Fiona is deep in thought. Without even meaning to, I pick up on her inner monologue.

He's right, though. Sometimes even Mum acts like we should be grateful to be here. And she spends all day looking after the sickest people in the country. Give me a break.

I want to talk to her, say that I would never think that about anyone, but then I realize that the only person that would make feel better would be me.

Roe puts his hand on my shoulder. "I'm going to make some trouble for old Alice," he whispers.

"Me too." Lily grins.

The woman onstage is still talking about negative thoughts. But then "negative thoughts" becomes interchangeable with "negative actions," and "negative actions" becomes "sin."

People are taking photos and then immediately posting them to their Instagram, so I know she's important in some kind of context. "In a world where you can be anything, be kind," she says. "And I think if Jesus were alive today, that's just what he'd say."

The nauseous look has started to clear from Fiona's face. "If Jesus were alive today," she says, "he'd be a judge on *Drag Race*."

I splutter with laughter. She goes on, doing a RuPaul voice. "In the challenge you performed miracles, but on the runway your daring 'supper' look was dead last. I'm sorry, my dear, you are up for elimination."

Someone turns around and shushes us, and Fiona makes a face. "Lily has been over there a suspiciously long time," she says. "And where's Roe gone?"

"Probably pissing in every bathroom he can find?"

We laugh, but then exchange a look. Where *is* Roe?

"I'll get Lily," she says. "You find Roe."

I nod and move toward the back of the room, where I see Aaron, standing with one of the few people here who is older, much older than the rest of us. She's middle-aged with a short, blond, feathery haircut. I immediately think of her as a *lady* rather than a woman. I don't know why. She has a gentle, old-fashioned kind of face, and her expression doesn't change the entire time she's speaking. A soft smile, a picnic smile. I cannot get out of the room without passing them, so I do, my head high.

"Is that *Maeve*?" the lady says, sounding a lot like Alice did on the way in. Like she's speaking to a child. If Alice's tone was *What are you dressed as?*, then this woman is more *Would you look how big Maeve has gotten!*

I have no choice but to face her. "Do I know you?"

She tilts her head toward Aaron, a square emerald in her ear. "Oh, darling, you're *famous* around here."

I look at Aaron, waiting for him to acknowledge me. He looks as though he's waiting to be introduced.

"Have you had anything to drink?" she asks. Her accent is not quite British, not quite American. She talks like people do in old films. A voice that sounds like garden parties and French windows being flung open. A voice you can imagine saying, *You simply* must.

"Who are you?"

"Isadora Manford," she says, stretching her hand out. "Everybody calls me Dorey, though."

I do not take her hand. She looks at me, perplexed but polite, as if I come from a strange culture that does not believe in these kinds of niceties.

"Well, Dorey, my friends and I were just leaving."

Aaron steps forward at last.

"I'm sorry," he says. "This is awkward, but I'm sure we've met. Your name is on the tip of my tongue. Is it Mary-Beth?"

I'm gobsmacked. I can't tell if this is an act or whether something has happened to his memories.

Dorey speaks again.

"I have a tip for you, Maeve, and it will put you in good stead: when you're speaking to someone, you really *must* look at the person you're *addressing*." Dorey's smile remains consistent. She comes from a generation of women who were always told to smile. She probably does it without even realizing now.

I feel uncomfortable, like I have disappointed her hugely, even though I have never met this woman before in my life. "I don't even *know* you."

My eyes flicker to Aaron again. Why doesn't he know who I am?

"No, you don't." Dorey sighs. "You burned through your three, didn't you? Was our boy so *very* unconvincing?"

I feel queasy, the conversation heavy and strange, like something in a dream. Dorey waves a long, slim hand in his direction. "Oh, don't worry, dear, he doesn't know it's you."

"He doesn't know *what*?"

"A little glamour never hurt anyone." She smiles. Then she looks at me, taking in my whole body. "Something you should know," she says coolly.

"What?"

At that moment, there's a blaze of light from the other side of the room and the fire alarm goes off. A small flame erupts in front of Lily, and someone goes to smother it with their jacket. She takes a step back, puts her hands to her face, seemingly amazed by what's happening. Then I see what she's really doing. She sinks back into the crowd, picks up another cup of water from the table, and spikes it like a volleyball across the room. A flash of white as her electricity surges through it, and then the rotten smell of burning, of the cup's melting plastic. The curtains at the back of the room are starting to smolder. There's a screech of panic, but no one seems to have realized that it's Lily who is causing this.

Someone grabs the mic. I see now that it's the guy who was talking to Fiona. "OK, everyone," he says calmly. "It looks like we're having a situation here. Can I please ask you to evacuate the room, single file? There are emergency exits to the left of the doorway."

The third cup Lily spikes bursts into flames, then hits the chandelier. It crashes to the ground. Thankfully, everyone has already cleared the center of the ballroom. I race toward her, completely forgetting Dorey and the silent Aaron.

"What are you doing?" I say, pulling her arm.

"Nothing they wouldn't do," she answers, and that forest fire is alight in her eyes again.

"Look," she says, pointing at the spotlights at the back of the room. "Look at them, Maeve."

"Why? Come on, Lily, let's get out of here before they . . ."

"Shh, shh. Focus on them. Hold my hand."

I feel her fingers tighten around mine like a vise. "Ow, Lily, let *go*."

"Just focus, come on."

And I do it. I focus on the lights, but I focus on Lily, too. I burrow into her sky-blue energy and follow it to the spotlights. They begin to burst, one after the other. My eyes start to water as hot pressure builds behind them, but as each bulb bursts, there's a feeling of release. The last few weeks of frustration, and cheating, and punishment, and loneliness, just swims away from me and into the warm, electric air.

"Maeve! Lily! Come on!" Fiona yells from the door. "We need to leave!"

We follow her out, our steps quick, but not so quick that we'll attract attention. There were so many people in there, how many people would have really noticed us, anyway? Or even comprehended what we did?

Roe is standing by the elevator, pushing the button frantically. "Come on," he says, voice full of mischief. "We need to get to the car."

As he's still jamming the button, we suddenly hear a "There he is!" followed by a "Stop!" Alice and another Children of Brigid person are coming down the hallway, practically running toward us. "You're disgusting," Alice spits. "You're disgusting, and what you did only proves it."

The doors open and we step in. "Roe, what did you *do*?" I ask.

"Tell you in a minute."

"You are perverse," Alice continues, still striding toward us. "You are perverse, and you will never know what it's like to be part of a *normal* society."

I look down and see that her shoes are wet, and that she's trailing watery footprints along the hotel carpet. The ends of her hair, I realize, are wet, too.

He presses the button for the ground floor, and the last word we hear is Alice screaming "Freak!" through the metal door.

"She means me," Roe says.

"She means all of us," I reply.

"She means me," Roe says again, in a voice so firm and strangely sad that I don't speak until we're safely out of the building.

15

WE END UP DRIVING TO AN EDDIE ROCKET'S
next to a petrol station on the motorway.

"What did you do?"

"I, uh . . ." He starts to smile. "I had a word with the pipes."

"The *pipes*?"

"Mmm." Roe bites into an onion ring. "They're copper. Old pipes. I could feel them in the walls when I walked in, sort of humming next to me. So I said—very politely, I might add—when our friend Alice went to the loo, 'Hey, pipes, how about bursting out of the wall and drenching our new pal?'"

My mouth falls open. "You did *not*. You can do that?"

"I can do anything," comes the response. "Within reason."

"And so, what? You flooded all the toilets? While old Alice was in there?"

"Mm-hm."

"Oh, that is *too* good. Did she know it was you?"

"I don't know. I think she suspected. She saw me hanging around outside."

We laugh and eat our burgers, but there's a strange taste in the air. Sharp and heavy, like storms. This is happening more and more with me. Maybe it's the telepathy, maybe it's the sensitivity, but moods and atmospheres have started to take on a color and smell. I watch Roe eat, and I start to fall into his mind.

Freak.

Disgusting.

Perverse.

Roe can't really still be bothered by that idiot woman. Can he?

"What an absolute wagon," I say, poking at my chili fries. "Those people were nuts, weren't they?"

"Yeah," says Fiona. "Find God, solve racism. Idiotic."

But she doesn't sound happy. "Are you OK, Fi?"

"Yeah."

"You haven't eaten any wings." We got wings for the table to share. I nudge the basket toward her.

"I don't want to eat meat anymore," she says. "In fact, I haven't eaten any meat in months."

"Really?" Then I think about it. All those fast-food trips where she just got chips and a milkshake. "Oh yeah, I guess you haven't."

"Well done, Fi," says Roe. "Better for the environment and all that."

"I saw fish bash each other to death when I was the river," Lily says. "The sick fish get bashed. It's horrible. So I don't feel guilty about eating animals. They would eat us if they could."

I wonder, idly, about putting the words SICK FISH GET BASHED on a tote bag.

"I just . . ." Fiona picks at her cheesy chips. "It reminds me of bodies."

We just ruined a Children of Brigid meeting. Why aren't we more triumphant?

"There were people there, people like us," Lily says. "People *our* age. Who are *from* here."

"Do you think maybe . . ." I try to puzzle it out. "They're bewitched or something?"

"I don't think people need to be bewitched in order to be transphobic," Roe says gloomily.

"No," I say. "Only . . . Aaron was there. And I think . . . I think he *was* bewitched."

I tell them the story of Isadora Manford, of the silent Aaron, of the three strikes. "I don't think he knew I was there," I say cautiously. "I don't think he could see me."

Fiona is immediately on her phone. "Isadora Manford," she says. "Oh fuck, she's, like . . . *a person.*"

She shows us the screen, and there's an array of images of her in brightly colored skirt suits. "What does it say about her?"

Fiona disappears into a research hole for a few minutes. "Kind of . . . nothing?"

"What do you mean, *nothing*?"

"It says she was born in England and now lives in Philadelphia. She's a pundit on 'the family,' whatever that means. She apparently coauthored a book in the eighties about 'the importance of family.' It's out of print. I think she's, like, some weird throwback lady who just wants women to stay at home. But that's it. She's, like, a right-wing person who is photographed at events and things, but there's not much actual *stuff* about her."

"Search her name and the Children of Brigid."

Another silence. "Nothing."

"But she knew me. She knew all about me. And she had Aaron . . . I don't know, it was weird. She was frightening."

I realize that all of us, in our own way, have found today uniquely disturbing. "Lily," I nudge. "Did anyone talk to you?"

"Yes," she says shortly, fiddling with the straw in her drink.

"What did they say?"

"Oh . . ." She tilts her head. "That as a person with a disability, I must never think that God has abandoned me. Then something about my ear being punishment for something my ancestors did? It was bananas."

"And after that, you threw the water?"

"Yeah. Because . . . screw him, right?"

I think about this. Lily's hearing aid is so small that most people don't even notice it. You'd have to be watching her for a long time to know she even has one. I don't remember it ever coming up, even in all the missing-girl reports last year. Then I remember Lily casually telling us that she was being watched. I took the bus with her to school every day after that and never noticed anything. But maybe we were all being watched. Maybe we were supposed to be at the hotel today.

"I think . . ." I begin hesitantly. "I think we did what they wanted us to do. They wanted to see our hand. Find out exactly what we're capable of."

"No." Roe.

"No." Fiona.

"Yes." Lily.

In the end, we draw cards to see whether I'm right or not. I split the deck. I hold up the picture of a full moon, with dogs howling at it.

"The Moon," I say. "Illusion."

"Cut them again," Roe says.

It's the Five of Swords.

"Betrayal."

"And again?"

Eight of Swords.

"Entrapment."

Roe squirms. "Once more."

Eight of Wands.

"Swiftness?" I look at it, confused. Then my phone buzzes. It's Dad.

On the way home.

And then:

Please make sure you're actually there or your mother will melt the skin from your body

16

ALL MY DREAMS HAVE AARON IN THEM after that. They're nothing like the old ones, where we were stuck at the river together. Now it's like I'm walking with him, doing his daily chores, except he doesn't see me. He posts a letter. He buys a new phone. It's all so ordinary, so boring. I wake up confused and tired, like I've done a full day of work.

Roe has a week off college, and the band is planning to go to Dublin. "Honor wants us to record some tracks in her home studio. So we'll have something slick on SoundCloud in time for the tour. Isn't that cool?"

"That is *so* cool!" I say as enthusiastically as possible. Roe hasn't been the same since that Saturday at the hotel. Despite his superb revenge with the toilets, the Children's words have stuck inside of him, like shrapnel. He drives me home a few nights in a row, less talkative every time.

One night, my mother calls me when we're in the car, and I try something out. Something I think will make Roe happy.

"I'm in the car with Roe," I say. "They're driving me home."

Mum balks a little, but then just says: "OK, see you later."

I hang up, and Roe smiles softly to the windshield. "See what you did there."

I smile back. "I thought . . . I don't know, I saw you look so happy when Honor used *they*, so I thought I'd wait for you to tell me. But then I thought . . . maybe you're nervous to ask or something. I don't know."

I really don't know. On the few occasions I've looked inside Roe's brain, there've been no clear thoughts on pronouns. Just lots of shifting little thoughts.

Roe plants a kiss on my forehead. "You're very sweet. But yeah, I don't know, either."

He lets out a sigh so long that it mists the windshield.

"It was cool when Honor said that, because it was like her acknowledging, oh, I see you. I'm trans, you're trans. You're not just in a costume. This isn't just a performance thing or whatever. But also, *he/him* still feels fine? It still feels like me, I suppose?"

"You're trans?" I ask, genuinely surprised by this. He's never referred to himself as trans before. "But I thought . . . sorry, I thought that meant that you're moving away from one gender and toward another. I thought you liked the genderless space."

"I do, but it's still . . . enby is still under the trans umbrella."

Roe suddenly rattles the steering wheel with both hands in frustration.

"I just . . . I feel like I'm bad at being cis and I'm bad at being trans. Miel is so great. So cool with *they/them*, so patient at explaining it to people. But the *amount* of explaining they have to do. I've known Miel for two years and basically every time we meet someone new, there's this big hand-holding moment. But it's worth it to Miel, because they love their pronouns. And I just feel like . . . I don't have the patience!" Roe slaps the steering wheel again. "I don't have the *time* to explain to cis people and talk about grammar every day. I just *don't*. I didn't almost die to then come back and *explain* things to people who don't care, anyway."

Tears fill his eyes. "I feel bad at this. Like, this is not the *correct* nonbinary feeling to have."

"Pull over."

Roe pulls over, and I throw my arms around him. "Listen. I don't know much about trans politics or whatever, but if *him* is fine for now . . . then *him* is fine for now. You can change your mind whenever you want."

"I just don't want to be inconsistent. I don't want people saying, 'Oh, he doesn't know what he is, he's always flip-flopping.' I don't want to be embarrassing."

I look at him. "Where is this coming from? And who are 'people'? Who on earth would you embarrass?"

I don't mean to look into his brain. Genuinely. But my gift has become taut and toned now.

Freak.

Disgusting.

Perverse.

"Is this about . . . the Children? What that idiot woman said to you in the hotel?"

"No."

Yes.

"The Children of Brigid are a hate group, remember? Their whole *thing* is to make people feel like freaks."

Roe doesn't say anything. He doesn't seem to think much, either. His mind is blank, bleached out by shame.

"I love you, and so does everyone else. You're a genius rock star. I hate that you were made to feel any other way." I bite my lip. "When you go up to Dublin," I continue, "you're going to have such an amazing time, because you're going to be with Honor, and with Miel, and you're going to be so surrounded by creativity and

150

brilliant people that you're going to completely forget about any of this."

And for the first time, I genuinely am excited for Roe to go away on tour. We are not enough, I realize. And that's OK.

Roe smiles weakly. "I know. Thank you. You're right. I love you, too."

We start driving. We turn the volume way up on the speaker, and we sing along to Honor's last album.

·)) ● ((·

At lunchtime in school the next day, the three of us girls are sitting around the break room table when I hear a voice behind me.

"You're that girl," it says. "The girl whose boyfriend is in the band."

I turn around and see two girls in the St. Bernadette's uniform. Idly, I wonder what they're doing in the sixth-year break room. I lift my head.

"Yeah," I reply. I recognize them as girls from the year below. Funny, how you always know the faces, but never the names, of the girls above and below you. "Are you fans or something?"

They scoff. "No," one of them says shrilly.

Fiona, Lily, and I look at one another in surprise.

". . . OK? Why are you here, then?"

They look at each other, each daring the other one to say something.

"Don't you know that your boyfriend is a big queer?"

They both scream with laughter and run out of the room. I'm so bamboozled that I don't know what to do or how to react. Fiona, however, does. She springs to her feet and disappears, and I hear a scuffle in the basement hallway. Fiona comes back, holding one by the collar.

"Do you have something you want to say about my fucking friend?" she says, and the girl looks so frightened that I think she's about to wet herself.

"Do you have something you want to say about my fucking sibling?" Lily says, getting to her feet.

I don't know where the other fifth-year has gone, but this one has adopted a kind of Joan of Arc expression, as if she's about to be burned at the stake for simply trying to save France.

"Well, isn't he?" she says piously.

"His name is Roe, and not that it's any of your friggin' business, he's nonbinary."

"Oh, and you like that, do you?"

"Yeah, actually," I say bitingly. Her face wrinkles in disgust. "I think he's *hot.*"

I begin the Process, trying to figure out, exactly, where this fifteen-year-old is getting off coming for Roe.

I get in quickly, and I am immediately treated to a vision of Roe as this random girl sees him. He looks fierce, demonic, his makeup applied in thick, clownish layers. She is watching me and Roe cross the street together, hand in hand. Judging by the weather, it's still the summer. He is kissing me goodbye as I enter Divination for an afternoon shift. Even at this, my heart throbs with a kind of loneliness for him. Already, something as simple as him walking me to work and kissing me goodbye feels like part of the past.

I take a closer look at what the girl is seeing as she watches us from across the street. The entire image is tinged with the ugliness of her memory: my skirt is shorter than it has ever been, my face a sneer, my boobs oddly enormous. My skin, which Mum describes as "kind of a pale olive," looks slightly jaundiced. Sickly. This is how she sees me, I realize. This is how she sees us.

"Freaks," she spits at me in the break room.

At that point, Lily loses her patience. She brings her face close to the girl's. "Just who in the hell do you think you're talking to?" she snaps.

The girl's memories start to swim into something new. Her at a COB meeting, looking adoringly at the Chastity Brothers. Ethan saying "It's all our jobs to bring our friends into the light." This girl raising her hand to ask "Do they have to be our *friends*?" Ethan shaking his head. "No, they don't have to be our friends to be brought into the light."

I stare harder. I start to hear "Firework." I start to see flooding hotel bathrooms. She was at the Claringdon over the weekend. She knows that we were there, too, causing trouble.

Lily starts to advance on her, and the girl's eyes widen in terror. Lily O'Callaghan, the girl who mysteriously disappeared last year, and reappeared just as mysteriously again. Lily, whose mystery was only emphasized by the cloud of magic and tarot cards that had immediately preceded her absence.

They think we're sinners.

No, not just that: they think we're *Satanists.*

I can see that Lily is itching to spark her.

"Lily." I tug on her arm. "Don't. She's just some poor idiot."

"Excuse me?" the girl interrupts, her fear turning once again to revulsion. Realizing she's outnumbered, she flounces out the door, but calls backward, "At least I'm not some devil-worshipping tramp."

The silence between the three of us only lasts a few seconds, but it is so dense that the air around us is almost humid.

Fiona is the first to speak.

"Did she just call you a devil worshipper?" she says quietly.

Despite everything, I laugh.

"Yeah, I think she did."

"Devil worshipper." She starts to smile.

"Yep." I'm almost giddy now, laughing from the back of my throat. I make a dry hacking sound, like a cat with a fur ball. At this, even Lily starts to giggle.

"Maeve, you're a devil worshipper," Lily splutters.

"And a tramp," I laugh. "A devil-worshipping tramp."

"Jesus Christ." Fiona is bent over now, holding on to her waist. "Devil-worshipping *tramp*?"

"Devil-worshipping tramp!"

And that's how the rest of the afternoon goes. Me, Lily, and Fiona whispering "devil-worshipping tramp" at one another and cracking up. I even pass Lily a note that says *devil-worshipping tramp* in biology, and I notice triumphantly when she smiles. She passes me a drawing back: it's a kind of super-sexy Jessica Rabbit sketch, only she's wearing horns on her head.

I smile, and despite the obvious worry that there's a girl in fifth year who apparently hates us so much that she's perfectly comfortable spitting at us in the break room, I can feel the beginnings of something with me and Lily. Some reawakening of an old dynamic. It's us, the weirdos, against them, the normals. It's a rhythm we know as well as our own breath.

The whole thing is extremely funny until the end of the day, when I go to my locker to dump my books. There, in permanent marker, a message has been scrawled.

EX. 22:18

Fiona and Lily look at it with me, utterly confused.

"Do you have to meet an ex at eighteen past ten?" asks Lily. "Do you even *have* an ex?"

Fiona traces her fingers on the stain. "I don't think it's ex like an ex-boyfriend," she says. "I think it's ex like Exodus. Exodus, chapter twenty-two, verse eighteen."

Sometimes I forget that, even though she's an atheist, Fiona's family is slightly more Catholic than mine. The Philippines is largely Catholic, and so, once, was Ireland, which means Fi was born—in her own words—a "double Catholic."

She takes out her phone and Googles the Bible verse. Her eyes, usually sparkling with jokes and fun, go dull and strange.

"What does it say, Fi?"

"It says . . ." She looks at her phone again, to make sure she's got it right. "Thou shalt not suffer a witch to live."

17

I HEAD TO DIVINATION AFTER SCHOOL.
There's so much to update Nuala on, and since my grounding, I've had no chance to tell her. Mum has sort of lost the will to keep track of me, meaning the grounding is now unofficially over.

Only when I get to Divination, she's not alone. There's a tall, pretty Black girl of about twenty by the counter, and they both stop speaking when I come through the door. I know immediately that she isn't a customer. I'm used to walking into Divination and finding Nuala with an old friend or a famous spiritualist, but there's something immediately unsettling between the two of them, a feeling that a great struggle is happening or is about to happen.

"Hey," I say. And then, because I don't want the girl to think that I'm just a random customer, "Hey, *Nuala.*"

The girl looks from me to Nuala, her eyebrows raised. She doesn't look very impressed.

"Fin, you said you would close the shop," she says, as if her presence in Divination was entirely dependent on this. She has a faintly European accent, a lilt that could be anything, but a dismissiveness that says French.

I remember then, the letter to France that Nuala sent weeks ago. This girl is, obviously, the recipient.

"I know," Nuala says, rubbing her temples. "Maeve, this is a bad time. Can we . . . ?"

"Sure," I say shortly.

"Is everything OK?"

"Yep," I reply quickly. "Is everything OK with *you*?"

Nuala waves her hand at me. "No, it's not that. This is just a private conversation."

"Extremely private," the girl adds, with a tone that says, *Were you born without manners?*

I want to dislike her, because she's being rude to me, but even through her unpleasantness I can sense a wary, tender anxiety. Her nails are bitten raw. My mind reaches out to hers, and I see something golden and pink, shimmering with hope and the fear of disappointment. But I can't go any further than that. I can't see what she's thinking or why she's thinking it. My head feels cloudy and hot.

"This is Manon," Nuala says apologetically. "She's . . ."

Manon shoots her a look.

"She's here from France," Nuala finishes.

"Sorry," I reply, because I'm not sure what else to say.

"Is everything OK, Maeve?" Nuala asks again. "You don't look well."

"I'm fine," I reassure her as I leave.

But I'm not well, it seems. It's one of those things that I only notice after Nuala points it out. My body feels heavy and sore, my skin too tight. I start to shiver at the bus shelter, sitting on the slanting red bench, my warm head against the plexiglass screen.

When I get home, Mum takes one look at me and her anger at the cheating finally melts away. "Pet, you look awful. Have you got the flu?"

"I don't know?" But it comes out "I guh go?"

Mum keeps me home from school until Friday. I'm not completely well, but she says it will be better for me to go back on a Friday, and then have a rest, and then start the week properly.

When I get back, the atmosphere has shifted, albeit subtly. The graffiti hasn't been cleaned from my locker and I see signs for an after-school club, the Future Girls, for GETTING REAL ABOUT ABSTINENCE & PREVENTION. But that's not all. There's a stiffness to everyone, a rigidity. People seem to talk less; the bright sound of hallway chatter—usually almost deafening—feels more like a soft hum. Their expressions are different, too. There's a glassy quality to everyone. A first-year drops her book in front of me, and when I bend down and give it to her, she takes a moment to reach out and take it. In fact, she gropes vaguely at the air next to it.

"Are you OK?" I say, wondering if the flu that has made me briefly dopey has made everyone else a bit slow, too.

"Your skirt," she says as if she's just seeing me. "Your skirt is extremely short." She says it like my skirt is something unpleasant in a dream.

I look down. I'm wearing an A-line skirt that stops just above my knees. *What?*

Has everyone gone weird since I took a few days off of school? Or has the atmosphere been slowly souring for weeks now, and the time away has only made me see it clearer?

"Everything has gone so weird," I say to Fiona at lunch. "I feel like the Children have got their hooks in the school somehow."

She picks at the dirt under her nails with a scalpel she stole from the art room. "Yeah, I don't know. This kind of crap, it's always more alive in small towns, isn't it? The fact that this crap is popular tells you everything you need to know about Kilbeg."

I shake my head. "No, that can't be. This isn't what it's like, Fiona. You know that. Kilbeg has always been really liberal."

She narrows her eyes at me. "If you're white, yeah, I can see why you'd probably think that."

My gut goes sour. "I'm sorry, I'm not trying to say it was perfect, but it wasn't like this. Like, didn't basically everyone in Kilbeg vote for marriage equality and for reproductive rights?"

She shrugs. "I don't know."

I take out my phone and start searching for the voter records. "Yeah, see: proportionally, Kilbeg had one of the highest amounts of yes votes for gay marriage. And for abortion rights." I show her my screen, but she doesn't look very interested.

"Backlash." She shrugs. "It always happens. Look at America: Obama, then Trump. It's just how it goes."

"It is *not* how it *goes*." I hear how shrill my voice sounds, see Fiona wince, and try to dial down the aggression. "OK, sometimes it goes like that, but something is happening here. The fact that the Children of Brigid are involved, that we *know* they have magic, that . . ."

"Why is that *my* problem, though?" she snaps. "Who cares *why* people are horrible? All I care about is getting out. And you should, too, Maeve."

I feel furious with her. You don't have to love your home. You don't have to think it's perfect. But you should at least want to protect it, right? What happens if everyone leaves? What happens when everyone goes to a big city? Do big cities just become the only real places in the world?

I watch Fiona dig under her nails with the scalpel, and then I see her hit the skin underneath. Blood starts to well up under the nail, and she watches it with interest. I feel queasy. She's still doing it, then. Still experimenting with her gift in the worst way I can think of. "Why do you do that?"

She shrugs again. "It's interesting."

We're silent. Finally, I can't take it anymore.

"Did you ever think," I begin, the tears already cracking at my throat, "that when you move to Dublin, you'll hardly see me anymore? Or Lily? Or Roe? Or your theater friends?"

Fiona frowns. "But even if I stayed in Kilbeg, I wouldn't see much more of Roe or Lily. Lily still wants to go to Galway, and Roe will be touring half the time." She pauses, digs the scalpel in farther. "My theater friends are all older and treat me . . . they treat me like a kid. I'm kind of done with them."

"You're done with them? Why?"

She shrugs. "They make me play all the kid roles. They're not even very good. The only person I would be staying for is you."

"Yeah," I say, pretending to yawn so she doesn't see the tears in my eyes. "Yeah, good point."

At detention that evening, Heather gives me a book to read. It's an old book, the spine rotting slightly under its brown leather binding. I hold it carefully, as if it might fall apart at any moment.

"*The Schools' Folklore Collection*," I read, confused. "Thanks."

"In 1937, the government did a project where it asked every child to record a story from the oldest person they knew, as a way of preserving Irish folklore," Heather explains. "It was all recorded here. Look at the table of contents."

I flip open the book. Witches (140 accounts), Hare-Hags (41 accounts), Banshees (367 accounts), Mermaids (311 accounts). I open to Hare-Hags and start reading aloud. "This old woman was supposed to be a witch. And she could turn herself into a hare. And

160

every year about the first of November the hunts would be out and they would have no trouble in rising her, but she was very swift and they could never take a wheel out of her."

"Cool, huh?"

"This was *homework*? For little *kids*?" I gaze at the pages, flicking through. "This is amazing. It must be so rare!"

"It is," she says simply.

"Why . . . why are you giving it to me to read?" I say carefully, hoping to learn more about her.

"I just think . . . Ireland has such a rich history of witches, doesn't it? And you're a witch, and you deserve to know it. This is your history, after all."

I study her expression, wondering whether she means Wiccan or *witch*.

"Are you a witch?" I ask plainly.

"In a way, all women are."

"But are you?"

She moves on and hands me some career pamphlets.

"There's a course you can do in media production," she says, sliding a brochure for a technical college over to me. "Audio, video, that kind of thing."

I peer at it, confused. She prods me again. "You love music, don't you? You could learn to produce it."

I brighten up. "I could produce Roe's music."

"Yeah," she agrees. "Although I would warn you against . . . you know. Basing your life decisions around a romantic relationship."

She goes out to the kitchen to make us some more tea, and I wander around to her side of the desk to grab a pamphlet on graphic design from the cubbyhole shelf on the back wall. I don't really know what graphic design is but it sounds interesting enough. The spots of mold are still coming through, stronger and darker, new black freckles springing through the paint.

Heather comes back into the room and tells me that I'll need to get at least a B in art if I want to do graphic design.

I sigh and take a long sip of my chamomile tea, which I'm sort of beginning to like, even though it's the color of wee. "I just feel," I say, and then swallow the hot liquid, "like I've failed at having a future before I've started."

"Oh, Maeve," she says. "When you tell me things like that, I wish I could just give you a hug. You have an absolutely enormous future ahead of you. It's perfectly fine to not know what it is yet. You can take a year off after school if you like. Travel abroad for a bit."

It's amazing to me that no one has even suggested the concept of a gap year. "Yeah," I say, cheering slightly. "Yeah, you know . . . maybe."

"It's the best thing I ever did."

"How do you sort that stuff, though?" I say nervously. "Do you just . . . buy a ticket to wherever?"

The idea is frightening to me. I just don't think I'm one of those people who can show up in a strange country and instantly make friends. My track record with friend making isn't that good even in my own language.

"I can look into some things for you," she says.

"Really?" I ask, and she nods. And for a few minutes at least, the future feels a tiny bit brighter.

The school is empty, and dark, by the time detention is over. As I'm leaving through the main entrance, I notice that the door to Sister Assumpta's office, for the first time in a long time, is ajar. She's still bustling around in there, and glimpsing her little hunched figure,

I realize that I haven't set eyes on her since school started. She's definitely been winding down her time spent in school over the last few years, but usually you catch sight of her at least once a week.

As I move closer to the door, I realize that she's not alone. There's someone sitting on the couch. I glimpse a woman's shoe.

"Henrietta," Sister Assumpta says. "You can't do this to me now. Or to the girls. They need you, particularly the sixth-year girls. You're their year head."

I hear a long sigh and the unmistakable sound of Miss Harris's voice. "I know, Sister, but I don't think I can stay. Not with this new program."

My first thought is: Miss Harris's first name is Henrietta? Her parents called her Henrietta Harris?

"It's morally not justifiable," Miss Harris continues. "It's poisonous. Usually I would say that the girls wouldn't take any notice, but they *are* noticing. Lots of them seem to actually *believe* this stuff."

Sister Assumpta clasps her hands, rubbing one thumb on top of the other. "I had no choice in this," she says, her voice heavy with regret. "This isn't my God at all, at all."

"I know, Sister," Miss Harris says. "I know."

This is confusing. If Miss Harris doesn't agree with this stuff, and Sister Assumpta doesn't, then how come they're allowing it?

I hear Miss Harris getting to her feet, and I back away from the door, rushing to the main exit, my head full of questions.

That night, the house phone rings, and my parents and I look around, amazed. No one calls the house phone. Sometimes I forget we have one. Dad picks it up.

"Maeve," he says eventually. "It's someone from the school. She wants to talk to you."

Mum looks angry already. "Maeve, what is it now?"

I freeze, assuming this is about the eavesdropping. Could Miss Harris really chew me out for that?

"I don't know!"

Dad passes the phone to me. I brace myself for Miss Harris's curt tone, but instead it's Miss Banbury's soft voice.

"Maeve," she says. "I'm so sorry to call your house. But I need a favor."

"What is it?" I ask.

"It's the book I let you borrow. I need it back. As soon as possible. I'm sorry." She sounds embarrassed. "I have a friend who is doing a PhD in this stuff, and she needs to borrow it urgently for a class. Apparently the copy at the university has been checked out. Can you bring it in tomorrow?"

"But tomorrow's Saturday."

A pause. "Jesus Christ. Of course it is. I'm an idiot." Another pause. "Um, I'll see if Monday is OK."

I'm not quite sure what to do. She seems stressed out. My parents are still looking at me, desperate to know if I've been expelled.

"I could meet you somewhere tomorrow and bring it."

"Oh, Maeve, would you do that?" she says, her voice flooding with relief. "I'd be so grateful."

It turns out we live pretty close to each other, so I arrange to stop by her house the next morning. I'm still supposed to be grounded, but as with all groundings, Mum has started to lose her grip on it and is only explicitly banning fun activities. Errands are largely fine.

"You're amazing, Maeve, thank you."

"It's no problem," I reply awkwardly. "Bye."

I hang up.

"What was that?" Mum asks suspiciously.

"A teacher lent me a book. I need to give it back to her."

"Oh." Mum begins to settle. "That's fine, then."

That night I call Roe, still in Dublin, and it rings, and rings, and rings.

18

THE ADDRESS HEATHER GIVES ME IS A BIG
Victorian house, a little like mine, but it sits directly on the river,
alongside others that sell for millions of euros. I wonder, as I walk
up to the house, how on earth Heather is living here. On a guidance
counselor's salary, no less. I start to lose a little of my faith in her as
a globe-trotting jewelry adventuress. Was she just from a wealthy
background and could afford to do these kinds of things? My parents
are comfortable, but they've made it clear that they're not squirrel-
ing money away for their adult children. "What we have, we spend,"
Mum said once, and meant it.

So my heart feels a little heavy when I knock on Miss Banbury's
door. I'm surprised, however, when a woman in her early forties
answers. She's in the middle of getting three young children ready for
what looks like a host of Saturday morning activities—I see a tutu,
a swimming bag, and a karate uniform—and hurriedly tells me that
Heather lives at "the lodge," and that I need to go through the side
garden gate to get to it.

I do as she says and find myself on a narrow stone path lined
with yellow honeysuckle and orange montbretia. It's a warm October morning. The path opens up to a large, wild garden that ends
in the twinkling Beg River. On the other side of the river is the city,

and the cathedral, and, if you squint, St. Bernadette's sitting on top of the hill.

I see immediately what must be "the lodge." It's a modern little cottage at the end of the garden, built with dark wood and glinting solar panels. I knock on the door, and despite the cottage's size, it takes Heather a few minutes to answer. When she does, she's on the phone.

"Hi, Maeve," she says, looking a little frustrated. "Sorry, I'm on hold with the bloody broadband people. They keep transferring me around to different robots. Come in, come in."

I follow her in as she continues cradling the phone to her ear. Then she spins around. "Sorry," she says, the tinny hold music playing out of the speaker. "Do you mind taking off your shoes? Her Highness at the Big House is very strict about it."

I'm wearing sandals. When I take them off, I have a weird, cringing realization that I am barefoot in a teacher's house.

"Why are you on hold with them?"

"Oh, there's absolutely no service down here. It's all landline." She gestures to her cordless phone. "Basically Stone Age."

I take out my own phone. I see that I have no internet, and my signal is down to a single bar. She gives me a cup of chamomile tea.

Despite her house obviously being a rental, it's the most Heather Banbury space I can possibly imagine. There are shelves of books on every wall, hanging plants, and a mixture of art from different cultures. There's a fair amount of Indian-looking stuff, but also South American. While she's on the phone, I inspect a black-and-white sketch of a naked woman, and then I'm embarrassed, because I think it might be her.

I'm on my own in her little sitting room for a few minutes, and I'm starting to think I should just leave the book on the coffee table and go. I reach into my bag and have it in my hands when she walks back into the room.

"I hung up." She shrugs. "Life's too short to talk to robots."

"I have the book," I say, holding it up. "For your friend."

"Great," she says, hardly looking at it. "Leave it down there."

"Anywhere?"

"Yeah, anywhere."

She starts telling me about the house and the good deal she got on it: how the owners use the cottage for Airbnb over the summer, but need someone to maintain it the rest of the time. "And I'm actually pretty good with DIY and stuff, so they're happy to have me. I only pay five hundred euros a month."

I have never had an adult talk about the infrastructure of their lives with me in this way. Even my siblings. They talk about rent and pay raises but never how much or why. I nod and try to think of something to say that makes me sound like a peer and not a student. "It's so beautiful here. What a great deal."

She nods. "Of course, I need to be out of here by summer, which suits me fine. I'll be gone, anyway."

"Where are you going?"

"Japan."

"*Japan?* Do you speak Japanese?"

"No." She shrugs. "But my friend works at a museum in Tokyo, and they have this big exhibition next year about all the Catholic priests who went over in the fifties and tried to convert everyone. They need someone who understands both Catholicism and stones to help with cataloging."

"That's so *cool*," I say, my voice cracking around the word. For some reason, I suddenly want to cry. "You have so many friends," I add uselessly.

She peers at me, looking a little concerned. "Why don't you come out into the garden?"

There are two plastic deck chairs set up outside, with two striped, nautical loungers across from them. I plop down into one, splashing my tea on me.

"Whoa, easy," she says. "Let me get you some more."

We sit and drink tea. She asks me questions about my family. But not teacher-y questions, like what they do for a living. She asks me how I feel about them, and who I'm closest to. She asks me about Lily.

"Your siblings are all so much older," she says finally. "I bet Lily felt like your sister, growing up. It sounds like she was the only person your own age you really spent time with."

"Well. There were people at school."

"It doesn't sound like you were much interested in them."

"No. I suppose not."

"It must have been awful when she went missing."

I sip from my cup. "It was."

There's a silence then, and my eyes rest on the water in front of me. The sun is warm on my face, and the last of my flu pushes to the front of my forehead, straining at the bridge of my nose.

"Funny," she says. "You always look at the water when you talk about Lily."

I shift in my seat. It's a weird observation, particularly for someone who has gone out of their way *not* to talk about magic with me.

"Do I? I don't mean to."

I don't want to accidentally confess that Lily and the water were once the same thing, so I close my eyes like I'm enjoying the sun. My flu is delighted at the rest, and I start to feel drowsy. I can feel my tired, sickly muscles giving in to the sun, knots unwinding as I sit in the lounger. My body still feels cramped and sullen, angry at me for being sick, sloppy after being in bed for three days.

"You're not so happy at school, are you, Maeve?"

I open my eyes. "Not especially, no." I fix my eyes on her. "I mean, are you? You must hate all this weird chastity stuff they're letting in."

She grimaces. "I know. I didn't realize it would be like that when I got the job."

"What's it all about?" I push.

"From what I can make out, they got a big cash injection from the government this year, like a grant. But the conditions of the grant are that they have to do this new horrible program."

"Why?"

Her eyes rest on me. "You know why."

"The Children? They have . . . they have *government* connections?"

"The government has contracts with lots of independent groups, particularly in education. The Children are just one of those contracts."

I look at her agog. "That's not right. That's *awful.*"

"Believe me, people are writing letters about it. Including me."

I pause. "Is that *all* you're doing?"

Heather says nothing, just the slightest nod to indicate her understanding. She coughs, clears her throat slightly.

"That night with Aaron," I say. "He left when you showed up."

She closes her eyes and basks in the golden stillness of the day.

"Is he . . . afraid of you?"

"He's not afraid of me," she finally says. "But you should be afraid of him."

Panic rises in me. "Why?"

"Pay attention to your body. To how you feel."

She keeps her eyes closed, soaking up the sunshine like a lizard on a rock. Sleep comes like I'm a silk scarf being twisted through its fingers. It wraps around me, cool and soft, and in muted, calming colors.

The dream is like a photograph found in a drawer. Everything is exactly the same, and we all look much younger.

There we are, the three of us, sitting and chanting, the air flecked with gold. I watch myself converse with thin air, air that, at the time, had looked a lot like the Housekeeper. I take the knife and turn it on myself, and watch Roe—his hair so much shorter then!—pounce on top of me, wrestling the blade from my hands, his strength no match for mine. He points it at himself. He lifts his shirt up to do it. Fiona's eyes open at exactly this moment, and I see what I could not have seen that night: her eyes filling with dread, her screams echoing out into the empty, moonless night.

And then the blood. And then the change.

The moon comes out, blinding us all. The warm river belches up a wet clot, a clot that is a girl.

I open my eyes and the air is cool. Heather is not in her chair, but under a tree. "Oh no," she says, her voice upset. "Poor babies."

For a second, I think she is talking about us. I get to my feet, my steps heavy, and see that she is talking about two baby birds that have fallen out of a tall tree. Their bodies are red, gray bits of downy fluff covering their shivering skin. Heather is wearing a pair of rubber gloves and standing on a kitchen chair.

"So their mother doesn't smell them on me," she says, putting them gently back into their nest.

"How long was I asleep?"

"An hour?"

"An *hour*?"

She shrugs, her expression saying, *Well, what did you expect me to do?*

"I have to go."

"Yes, I was about to say I have friends coming over for lunch so . . ." Her tone shifts slightly, and I feel deeply embarrassed, thinking about Heather looking at her watch and wondering how long this teenage student would stay sleeping on her lounger.

"I'm so sorry."

"No, not at all." She smiles. "It's just a work dinner thing. Priests in Japan."

"Right," I agree. "Priests in Japan."

She cocks her head and seems to consider me in a new light. "You know, I could always ask if they'll let me have an assistant. How would you feel about Tokyo for a summer?"

I laugh, but then her expression stays steady. "Are you serious?"

We had one conversation about spending time abroad after school, but I didn't think she was being serious. I thought she was just being nice.

"I don't see why not. What's the harm in asking?"

And there, in the sun-dappled garden, it all seems possible. I don't know very much about Japan, but then again, did Abbie know much about Belgium when she went to live there? I'm suddenly struck with an image of myself on a busy crosswalk in the middle of a Technicolor Tokyo, holding one of those plastic umbrellas with animal ears attached.

Have you heard about Maeve? She's in Japan now.

We walk back into her house, the soft green grass tickling my bare feet. "Of course, my contract with St. Bernadette's will be up then, so you wouldn't be my student, but more my employee."

"Of course," I agree.

"It'll be a long shot," she says, as if she regrets saying it out loud before checking with her friend. "So maybe keep it to yourself until there's some real news."

"I will." I beam, thinking of the moment I can unveil this to Roe and Fiona and Lily, and the look of utter shock on their faces. I think of living in a place where nobody knows me or who my siblings are, and of coming home to Kilbeg after three months with a suitcase full of cute gifts.

I walk home, my eyes glued to my phone, trying to keep the fantasy of an exciting life alive, if even just for myself.

19

"THERE'S SOMETHING I NEED TO TELL YOU,"
Lily says on Monday. "Actually, there's two things."

We're on the bus. The heat of Saturday fell, hungover, into a deep humidity that lasted all day on Sunday and has finally collapsed into rain this morning. Thick, warm splashes are assaulting the windowpane. I'm still feeling groggy, not much in the mood for chatting, and I don't know if I have the patience for one of Lily's obtuse declarations. I start flipping through my homework journal, making sure I have the right books for today.

"Go for it," I say, and a card falls out of my journal. The Chariot. Huh.

"The air around you isn't waving anymore."

I peer at the card. It doesn't look like it's from a deck that I own, but at this stage, Fiona, Lily, and I have so many that they sometimes get jumbled up.

"What?"

"The air around people goes all wavy," Lily continues. "Wavy, like how people are when you're looking at them through a fire. When their sparks are high it's almost like they're a blur."

"A blur?"

She nods eagerly. "So it's hard to tell people apart sometimes. But you're barely wavy at all."

"And Fiona?"

"Oh, she is the *waviest.*" Lily smiles. "But I always know it's Fiona."

"Am I wavy usually?"

"Yes. And not just wavy. Yours has a little bit of color in it. Like yellow and green."

I'm dumbfounded. It has never occurred to me that Lily might see things differently, the way I do with the lights. I had assumed her power was pretty one-dimensional: she saw things, she sparked them. She's never mentioned the electricity in *other people* before.

"But it's not there today?"

"It's been fading for a little while. But it's almost *gone* today."

The bus judders forward, and an announcement comes over the speaker that we will wait here for a few minutes while there's a change of driver.

I start examining the Chariot again, the two fierce-looking horses pulling a man to his destination. The longer I look at the card, the stranger I feel about it. A sense that I put it in my homework journal to remind me of something, but I don't know what that something is. If déjà vu is feeling like you've lived through a moment before, then this is double déjà vu. Like this particular Chariot has come up many times, and will keep coming up forever.

"What's the second thing?"

"The second thing is that the man who followed me is back."

"Back? Back where?"

"Here. On this bus."

I peer around. There are lots of men on the bus. "Who?"

"At the back of the bus. He's wearing a gray shirt."

I put my phone on portrait mode and we pretend to take selfies, craning my phone over our heads like we're trying to look big-eyed, when in fact I'm peering at the back of the bus. I snap a few photos. "I think there were some cute ones there," I say loudly. I start flipping through my camera roll, and I see him.

He's not much older than us, and he's dressed like he's about to start a day's work experience at his dad's office. A gray flannel shirt, black trousers. Darkish hair. I zoom in. He has tired, far-set eyes that pop out slightly, like a frog's, and a top lip so thin it's almost nonexistent.

"And you say you've seen him before?" I ask, a little doubtful. It's very possible he's just on the same route as Lily. "That he's followed you?"

"Yes," she says with certainty. "He always keeps a distance. He follows me when I go to music lessons. He stopped when you started taking the bus with me. But now he's back."

There's a light jingle of change, and I look up to see that the driver has arrived. He's a big man and takes a few moments to lock the change dispenser onto the ticket machine. His keys fall to the ground, he bends down to pick them up, and our eyes meet.

From the depths of my still-groggy, stuffed-nose, hot-eyed illness, I feel the zing of something sharp. Some kind of awareness that begins in my feet and is trying to push its way up to my brain but keeps getting diluted on the way. Something that is trying to yell *danger*.

"Lil," I whisper. "We have to get off."

"What? Why?"

"I don't know. We just do."

The bus lurches forward suddenly and then stalls. A baby with pigtails cries out in alarm. We accelerate again, far too quickly, and the handful of people standing up have to grab on to the guardrails for balance.

I hit the stop button and get to my feet.

"But we're still so far from school."

"It doesn't matter," I say, and jab the button a few more times.

The bus doesn't let anyone off at the next stop. Or the next one.

We speed through streets as passengers keep jamming on the stop button, the bell going every few seconds. People waiting at the bus stops peer at us, mystified.

"Lily, I don't even know if this man *knows* how to drive a bus."

"Driver!" a man calls, staggering his way down the aisle to knock on the glass partition around the driver. He starts swearing at him, and all I can see is the top of the driver's head through the mirrors that sit above the driver's seat. There is only one person on the bus who seems unconfused by this flurry of activity, and it's Frog Eyes, sitting perfectly still in his gray flannel shirt.

After a few moments of arguing, the driver slows to a stop, and the doors pull open. There's a rush of passengers struggling to get off, and somehow Lily and I find ourselves at the back of the queue.

Finally, when everyone else has stepped into the street, a strange tightening sensation starts curling its way around my elbows and knees. My shoulder blades press together, my back muscles sinking toward one another like an accordion.

"Lily," I whimper, my voice small. *"Lily."*

My eyes dart to the mirror again, where the driver is now staring at me, his gaze resting easily on my discomfort. He has put some kind of spell or enchantment on me, and now I can't move.

I try to fight, my power against his. I try to see his light, try to summon my sensitivity, but it seems to be missing. My mind is utterly blank, my body constricted and strange.

The bus drives on. Lily, Frog Eyes, and I are the only three people on it.

Frog Eyes begins to walk toward us, holding on to the top of each headrest to keep his balance. He sits on one of the flip-down chairs, his body angled toward us.

"Hello, girls," he says at last.

I cannot move or speak. The only parts of my body working properly are my brain and my eyes, so I absorb as much information about Frog Eyes as I can. Maybe this is why I notice that he's wearing something under his gray shirt. Something that looks curiously like a wet suit, but hardier. I follow my gaze down his arms and notice that it covers his whole body, gloving both hands.

"How are you today, Miss O'Callaghan?"

I peer harder. He is not so interested in me, anyway: a neutralized threat. I realize, then, that he is not wearing a wet suit. He is wearing rubber.

"Go on," he says, and he places his gloved hand on her knee. "You'll find I'm not so easy to shock."

I remember the hotel, and wonder if this is punishment for that. How, when Lily and I worked together, we could burst light fixtures halfway across a ballroom.

Lily looks at the gloved hand and seems to immediately calculate what it means. This person has made an estimation of Lily's power and seems pleased about it. But he has not made estimations about her character. And at the end of the day, it is *who* Lily is, and not what she is, that makes her special.

Her blue eyes widen, and despite my lack of power, I can tell that he thinks he has frightened her.

Lily lifts her hands and lays them on his chest. Crossed, like she might be about to give him CPR. He smiles mildly, as if he expected this and has done drills for it at home.

Instead, she uses the full force of her body to slam into his chest and pounces, like a cat, on top of him. He is suddenly sprawled on the floor of the bus, but there's no hope for Lily in a fistfight. All she had was the element of surprise. His arm starts to flail at her, but Lily holds firm on top of him. Then, without appearing to think about it, she bites down hard on his neck. I don't need to see what she's doing to know she has broken the skin, the bright blue voltage of her power coursing into his bloodstream, his fingers tweaking in shock.

Is he dead?

Do we care?

She gets off him, and there's a moment where we lock eyes and seem to both understand the enormity of what she has done. This is not a couple of light fixtures and some copper pipes in a hotel. This is not a magpie accidentally caught in the crossfire. This is violence. This is *hurting people.*

Lily spits on the floor of the bus, her saliva pink with his blood.

His arms start to move. *Not dead.* Just stunned.

The bus judders forward again, the driver accelerating and braking, trying to frighten us, to hurt us, to get us back. We're still stuck here, even if Frog Eyes is on the ground.

"Can you move?"

My bones still feel pressed together, my elbow glued to the top of my hips. I try to shake my head, my jaw feeling wired shut. I manage a stiff no.

"OK," she says, and grabs on to the yellow guardrail. A white volt of electricity blasts the red button off the rail, leaving a nest of smoke behind it. I hear a faint series of *pop* sounds and realize that every other stop button has suddenly burst away from its setting. Up and down the bus, the rails all have holes, little yellow mouths of missing teeth.

Each bell starts dinging to its own rhythm. *Ding! Ding! Ding!* And then, quickly, they run out of juice. The dings get longer, sludgier. *Drinnnng. Drinnnng. Drinnnng.*

The smoke alarm soon joins them, high and shrill, the alto to their soprano. The driver does not change his behavior, presumably because all his energy is focused on keeping this spell in place. His hands are still firmly on the wheel.

Lily loops an arm under my shoulders, knitting herself into me, and drags me to the middle exit doors. "Hold on," she whispers. "I think I have an idea."

She unzips her bag and digs around in it, finally producing her lunch.

"Jesus Christ," she mumbles, fixing her hands around her apple. "Well."

At that, Lily hurls the apple directly at the windshield, right into the driver's view. Finally, something seems to startle him. He brakes suddenly, and there's the familiar hissing sound coming from the belly of the bus.

She crouches down, and as a burst of air rushes toward her, her fingers splay out. A spark forms underneath her palm, reacting to the compressed air, and Lily starts to talk to it. "Come on," she urges, her voice barely audible above the continuing din. "Come *on*."

The spark has gathered and is now the size of a chicken's egg. The hissing sound has stopped.

"Now," Lily says, and I can't tell if it's to herself or me. With that, she hurls the egg-shaped ball of lightning at the middle exit, blowing it open. We're hurled onto the footpath, falling to our knees, the hot rubber sealant from the door's edge burning our skin.

We kneel there a moment, watching the bus move away, apparently undisturbed by the smoldering stop buttons, the fire alarm, or the exploding side. It trundles off into the distance, injured and heavy, not remotely perturbed by our existence. My shoulders begin to ease, and I start to feel the spell release itself as the bus disappears from view.

No one stops to look at the bus, or ask if we are OK, or observe the discarded door on the footpath. Commuters just walk on, skipping over the debris, their expressions curiously blank.

"Are you OK?" Lily asks, brushing herself off. "It's good that buses have that weird glass that doesn't shatter or else it could have gone into our eyes."

"I don't . . ." I'm trying to figure out my words again, trying to realign myself with the world. Lily just saved us. She saved *me*. "What was that? Where was he taking us?"

I roll my tongue over my teeth, the taste of pennies rotten in my mouth.

"It was him or me, wasn't it?" Lily says, and for the first time since she's come back from the river, there's a tinge of uncertainty in her voice.

"Yeah," I say, feeling my back muscles come alive again. "It was him or you."

A car beeps at us, and it occurs to me what we must look like: two girls sitting on a footpath, surrounded by the discarded remains of a bus door.

"How did you know what to do?" I say, gingerly getting off the ground. She reaches a hand out and pulls me up. "You were so in control."

I start gently patting my hair, feeling static strands sticking to my fingers.

"Your hair looks wild" she says, confirming my suspicions. "Do you want me to fix it?"

I nod, and we find a wall to sit on. Lily starts tightly plaiting my hair, a mimic of her long French braid. The skin on my temples starts to go taut with the strain. "Ow, be *careful*."

"Sorry."

She eases the pressure, if only slightly.

She finishes, wrapping an elastic band around the end of the braid. "What do you think their plan was?"

"I don't know. To take us somewhere? To kill us?" I rub my palms over my eyes, my skin still tight from the spell. "What do they *want*?"

Lily shrugs, and in the absence of better ideas, we walk the rest of the way to school.

20

THE BUS CHANGES EVERYTHING FOR ME.
Maybe it does for Lily, too. The line between theoretical threats and physical reality has been breached, and it radicalizes us in a way. We walk through town with a dual sense of predator and prey. A simultaneous notion of

We're not going to take this anymore

and

How much of this can we take?

We tell Fiona at lunch, and we expect the bus to be news. Not national news, of course, but local news. Twitter news. We search social media for pictures and reports, or at least broadcasts from Bus Éireann about a disrupted service. It was a busy bus, after all. At least fifty people must have had their morning commute disturbed, and that's not even to mention the people who must have noticed the bus with no door on it.

But it might as well have never happened. It might as well have been in our heads.

"Maeve," Lily prods. "I'm thinking of a number."

"I don't know if I have time for that now."

"No, go on. Try."

And I try. I clear my head. I sit in the blackness and wait for color. But the colors don't come. There's just a fug, a mist between myself and my own power.

"It's gone," I say at last, opening my eyes in terror. "How did you know?"

"I was trying to tell you. The waviness is gone. I think that's what magic is, you know. I think that's how I see it."

I am struck with a terrible panic, the feeling of being prey again. "No," I tell her. "No. Hold my hand."

Lily hesitates. "We're in school."

I am too frightened to care. "Hold it. Look at the lightbulb."

Fiona bites her lip. "Maeve, I don't know . . ."

I hold on to Lily's hand, and I focus my attention on the fluorescent lights in the canteen, the ones that flicker and buzz when you turn them on. "Come on." I try to burrow into her energy again, and although I can just about glimpse the edges of it when I'm holding her hand, I can't reach out to it with my mind the same way I could at the Claringdon.

Nothing happens, except the feeling of spark brewing in Lily's palm. I let it drop.

"It's gone," I realize. "It's all gone."

The moment I say it, I know that it's absolutely true. That there is a cavernous feeling at the root of myself, an empty echo that keeps repeating and repeating. How long has it been there? I haven't tried to use my magic for days, not since I got the flu and was too exhausted to do anything. I retrace my steps. When was the last time I used my magic?

Devil-worshipping tramp. I looked into the mind of the girl who had been brainwashed by the Children. Did I infect myself just by reading her?

"We need Nuala," I say.

At that moment, I get a message from Roe. My first in two days.

Back!!! Pick you and the girls up after school? Xx

I climb into the front seat and wrap my arms around Roe, breathing in his familiar smell, my body screaming to be held. I phoned him at the end of lunch, explained everything about the bus, everything about my magic. He didn't say much. He just said that he'd pick us all up after school, and we'd figure it out together.

"Are you OK?" he breathes into my hair. "Are you all right?"

I nod, my forehead nudging his cheek. I press my face deeper into him. I want to cry with the raw relief of being loved.

He holds me close.

"I love you," he says, his voice low. "I love you, and we're going to figure out what's happening. OK?"

"OK."

The girls are quiet in the back seat. They don't usually put up with me and Roe cooing at each other, but they're so shocked by the morning's events that they don't even bother to roll their eyes. I lean the full weight of my head against his shoulder as he reverses out of the school car park.

"What do we do, though?" I ask plaintively. "Honestly, I . . . I don't even feel like I know what's happening anymore."

"Do you think this is revenge?" Fi asks. "Do you feel like they're trying to get back at us for crashing the meetings?"

"Are you sure it was them? The Children?" Roe suddenly says. "It wasn't just, you know? A bad driver?"

We all look at him as if he's taking the piss. Oddly, though, Roe seems completely serious.

"The thing is," I say quietly, "something weird is happening to me. Inside. I feel so sick and tired all the time. And now my magic . . ."

I look to Roe for comfort, for him to tell me that it's going to be OK. But he just keeps drumming his fingers on the steering wheel in time to the music on the radio.

We take the car to Divination to find it closed.

"What?" Fiona says, peering through the windows. "But it's not even five."

It's strange. Nuala closes at six p.m. every day, even Sunday. I wonder if this has anything to do with the woman she was with the other evening, and decide that I don't have time to wonder anymore.

"I'm calling her," I say, and when I do, she invites us over without stopping to hear what I have to say.

"Come now," she says. "And come quickly."

We drive straight to Nuala's home, a surprisingly normal terraced house in the north of the city.

"*This* is where she lives?" asks Roe, pulling into the driveway. "I always assumed she'd be in some cottage with a thatch roof or something."

I've only been to Nuala's once before. She invited me over to learn about gardening, insisting that if I grew my own herbs, it would make all the difference to my magic. The lesson did not last long before I lost interest and started poking around in her tarot collection.

She opens the door to us, in her usual uniform of balloon pants and a silky wrap.

"The gang's all here," she proclaims as we file in. "Sit down now and I'll put the kettle on."

The kitchen is small and warm, with only a narrow strip of floor between the dining table and the laminated kitchen unit. It's definitely not a room that is used to hosting five people, and Nuala has to take a footrest from the living room and a garden stool from out-side so everyone has a place to sit down. The table is piled high with weathered papers, most of them handwritten, and crystals acting as paperweights.

We all sit down, and Lily starts curiously leafing through the handwritten pages. Some of the pages are parchment, some are torn-out sheets from a yellow legal pad, some are the double pages ripped from the center of a child's notebook. They seem to be organized by subject rather than material, elastic bands around the stacks. "Lil," Roe hisses. "Don't be nosy. That's not polite."

"Ah, not to worry, Roe," says Nuala, squeezing through us to put a loaf of cherry cake on the table. "It's all stuff you need to know."

We're all given a mug of tea and a thick slice of the sweet, sticky cake. Lily picks the glacé cherries out and leaves them on her china plate.

Nuala takes a long look at me. "You've been bound," she says. "Lily saved you."

"How can you tell?"

"There's a little glow, a little hint of someone else's magic. Changes the color on you."

I want to ask more about the colors. I've grown so used to view-ing such a wide palette in my brain that I am hungry to see them again. But I don't get a chance to, because Manon appears in the doorway wearing a long cardigan. Her arms are folded, and there's a silk scarf tied around her head.

"Oh," squeaks Fiona. "Hello."

"This is Manon," Nuala says with a great deal more warmth than she did when I met Manon for the first time.

Manon shimmies her fingers very softly, then rests them on her forearm again.

"She's my . . ."

"I'm her daughter," Manon finishes.

There's no use trying to act casual about this. It's all too shocking for us to properly grasp.

"Your *what*?" I say.

"You have a *daughter*?" Fiona.

"Since *when*?" Me again.

"You don't look alike." Lily.

"Hello," says Roe.

Nuala looks nervous, awkwardly averting her gaze, clearly wondering if Manon is offended that her name has never been brought up before.

"We don't have a relationship," Manon says, her French accent low and slightly detached. "Fin left when I was very, very young."

It seems strange that she would call Nuala that. I suppose it is short for Fionnuala, so it's as likely a nickname as any. Maybe it's because *Fin* is what they use in France to finish a movie. *The End.*

"Now, I think that's an unfair representation of the facts," Nuala says sharply.

"We don't have to discuss my childhood with these strangers," Manon replies, and picks a stray thread from her cardigan.

None of us knows where to look. There are simply too many questions, too many relationships, and not enough kitchen to hold them all.

"I called Manon because she's an expert," Nuala says finally. "What's been happening in Kilbeg is not normal. And it isn't something that will heal itself. We've been going through my archives to see what we can find."

She waves her hands at the stacks of paper secured with elastic bands. Her "archives," evidently.

Nuala sits down, places her hands on the archives, and closes her eyes.

"When poor Heaven passed away," she says, "I chucked school, and I went traveling. I've waitressed in every tourist trap in Europe, worked on every cruise ship between here and the South Pacific. I didn't know anything about magic up until that point. It was always her thing, and you know, with sisters, you always think that if they get to something first, you're not allowed to be interested in it."

She opens her eyes to meet mine.

"I wanted to understand what she did, how she did it, how she was able. I had found her drawings of the Housekeeper, and she had tried to tell me about being a sensitive, but . . . I was fifteen."

Nuala looks at us as though she is asking for forgiveness. "I didn't know what she was on about. I didn't understand what she was willing to do to get rid of our father. All to protect me and our mother. So, rightly or wrongly, I've dedicated my life to this. This is what you're looking at, my loves. My entire life."

Manon sighs loudly, as if she had thought that Nuala's entire life should really have included more of her. She pours herself a glass of water from the tap at the sink.

Each stack has a Post-it stuck to the top of it, categorizing it as a magical subject. There's *Runes* and *Revenge Spirits (A–J)* and *Gods: trickster, mischief, mayhem, etc.* There's a thin stack about banshees, and a much thicker one simply about hares. I remember the book Miss Banbury let me read, and realize how many similarities there are between Nuala and Heather. Young travelers with an interest in magic.

"Maeve's magic is fading," Lily volunteers. "We think that the Children have found a way to take it from her."

At this, Manon moves from the sink toward me. She glares at

Roe, who is sitting next to me, and he stands up and offers her his seat. She takes it.

Sitting down, Manon lifts my hand and places her thumb firmly in the center of my palm, pressing down. "Look at me, please," she says.

I meet her eyes, her gaze fixed steadily on me. The irises are a rich, deep brown, and so dark that it takes me a second to notice that her pupils are expanding and contracting rapidly. The pools of ink are so large that they look like they are about to break free and consume her entire face, and then they suddenly become the size of pinpricks again.

"Yes," she says gravely. "Yes, she has been bound. But more than this, she has been made into the channel."

"Into *what*?"

"You have become the channel for the well," Manon says, as if this clarifies everything.

"Sorry?"

Nuala gathers up the cups on the kitchen table.

"Right," she says, trying to sound pragmatic as a method of masking her awkwardness. "We need another pot of tea before we get into this. Maeve, do you remember when I tried to explain to you about the magic in Kilbeg, and about how your sensitivity works?"

I nod. "The thing about the supply chain. Yeah."

"Well, the supply chain, as we called it, is basically Manny's whole area of study. That's why I've been waiting for her. I didn't want to start sharing random theories that would confuse us all and send us down silly rabbit holes."

Roe gives an odd expression, as if he's not entirely convinced that this isn't a silly rabbit hole.

Nuala stands up and starts filling the kettle. "Let's see what Manny has to say."

Nuala does not let Manon talk until everyone has a fresh cup of tea. I drink it, the color deep and red, the china cups chipped but thin. At this point, I have no idea what I'm more curious about: who Manon's father is, or what on earth a "well" is in this context.

Once we are all drinking, Manon starts to speak.

"I don't expect any of you to understand this immediately," she begins. "But I will try?"

Her voice naturally goes up at the end, in a way that seems to imply she was asking a question. It's hard to know whether she is expecting an answer.

"Have any of you ever drawn a bucket from a well?"

We each exchange a look. This, apparently, requires an answer.

"No," Roe says slowly. "But I think we're all fairly . . . familiar with the concept."

"Bucket goes in, water comes . . . out?" Fiona ventures. "That's what having a well is . . . all about?"

"If you could please imagine a well," Manon continues. "But instead of water at the bottom, there is . . . magic? Or whatever it is you like to call it. Magic, energy, qi, the . . . the pure blood of the universe."

We all look a bit bemused. Particularly at "blood of the universe."

"There are these wells all over the world—far more, I think, than the scholars can hope to find."

Every so often, she looks away from us, as if delivering her speech to the dark evening outside and not to us at all.

"Some are little and shallow," she says, catching the gold chain from around her neck with her thumbnail and running it back and forth. "And some are big and deep."

This is twigging my memory. "All that stuff about the magic in Kilbeg going into me and then out into the world," I say slowly. "That's called a well? Kilbeg is a well?"

Nuala nods, picks up a bundle marked *Wells*, and hands it to Fiona.

"Lots of small Wells in South America. At least a couple in the Philippines, Fiona," Nuala suddenly volunteers, as if she's sharing a fact from a Snapple lid. "Plenty in China. Over a hundred scattered across mainland Europe. And a disproportionate amount, when you consider the size and population of this island, in Ireland."

Nuala's voice becomes grave on "Ireland," and we all know that this is the part we are meant to take seriously.

"When you say 'Wells,'" Fiona ventures, flipping through the pages, "you don't mean literal wells. Like, with a little stone wall and a bucket."

"No, not *literally* wells," Manon says shortly. "It's not something you can see with your eyes, or at least, not on this plane of reality. But if you know what to look for, you know when you are near a Well."

"Like what?"

"Moving statues," Nuala says. "A group of women who all have twins. Houses where things keep going missing, even when you *just* put your coat down, right *there*. Some cultures are better at recognizing these things than others. Most of them use religion as an explainer, which is fine, and healthy, if you like that sort of thing."

Nuala's tone implies that she, personally, does not like this sort of thing.

"And are you saying . . ." I say, trying to puzzle this out, "that there's a big one in Kilbeg? Under Kilbeg?"

"I've never been sure. It has always been one of . . . well, many theories as to why things happen here the way they do. And with you kids and your gifts, and these Children of Brigid lunatics . . . well, I wrote to Manny in France. She studies Wells exclusively."

"With your . . . father?" Fiona asks pleadingly, desperate for answers.

"That one thing that is common to all Well spots is sensitives," Manon says, ignoring the prying question. "I understand you are one?"

Everyone's gaze swivels toward me, and I suddenly feel very embarrassed.

"Yes."

"You are already this funnel for magic going into the world. You draw it up naturally. But when someone tries to make you into . . . into a super channel, taking up all the magic from the Well at once, it empties the Well and it empties you."

"And because the rest of you are now connected to the Well, you're in danger, too," Nuala says, smiling weakly. "Which is why, I imagine, Lily was being followed. Roe and Fiona are probably being monitored, too. They want to know how powerful you are, so they can assess how much they can stand to gain."

"My mother said that you summoned a revenge spirit," says Manon. "A revenge spirit? Yes? And then you banished her again?"

"The Housekeeper, yes," I say.

"Have you ever heard the expression . . ." She pauses. "When you catch a big fish, you make a big hole in the net?"

"No." Thinking: *SICK FISH GET BASHED*

"I think this city has been sitting on top of this Well for a long time. I think, maybe, nobody noticed. But when your revenge spirit was summoned, and when you beat her, it made the mouth of the Well bigger. You understand? Like a sinkhole that keeps spreading outward."

"Wells," Fiona says with disbelief. "Sinkholes."

"It's a metaphor," Nuala responds, trying to be soothing.

"Actually, it's two," Roe says, sounding a little unimpressed. "A sinkhole metaphor and a well metaphor."

Manon seems a little affronted, and continues her explanation sharply.

"Magic likes to be used, a little bit every time, by the people it has chosen. The more you use magic, the more magic there is, the more greedy people become to own it."

Nuala reaches over to the heavy teapot and tops up all of our china cups until they're steaming. Roe frowns slightly into his cup. At what exactly, I'm not sure.

"Where there is a Well, there is a sensitive to draw the magic," Manon continues. "If you can tap her, you can drain all of it for yourself."

"Tap me?" I interrupt, my voice so high it's near a screech. "*Tap* me?"

"I think Aaron was giving you three opportunities to become a channel willingly, Maeve," Nuala says, placing a hand on my shoulder. "And when you denied him, he—he and the Children, that is—decided to make you one by force. That's why you've been feeling unwell. That's why your magic is fading. All this stuff is moving through you like water, and your own essence is being washed away with it."

"Aaron." I say his name blithely, stupefied by all of this new information. It feels like the bones of my skull are stretching to make room for it. Then I remember what Heather said to me, that day in her back garden. *You should be afraid of him. Pay attention to your body. To how you feel.*

"I think he . . . I think that's why I've been sick. I think Aaron is the one doing the draining."

Nuala nods. "It makes sense. They would always use someone

194

who has a personal connection to you. Someone who knows how you work."

"He's been in my dreams lately, too," I say awkwardly, and everyone looks over at me. "Not, like, *interesting* dreams. It's always me with him on, like, errands."

Nuala frowns. "It could be that he has left a kind of fingerprint on your consciousness. If he's the one draining you."

"What I don't understand," Fiona interrupts, her brow furrowed, "is why bother with all the homophobic puritan bullshit if all they *really* want is to drain the magic away from Kilbeg?"

Manon and Nuala exchange a look, something between deep knowledge and deep concern, and for the first time, I understand how they are mother and daughter.

"It is, perhaps, a lot of information for one night," Manon suddenly says limply. "It is an extremely complicated area of study."

"Give us the short version," Roe says with an uncharacteristic rudeness.

"OK." She sighs. She drops the gold chain from her fingers, where it falls beneath her clothing. She folds her hands on the table in front of us, her nails perfectly trimmed pink ovals, cut short and painted with clear varnish. They were bitten and raw last time I saw them. She must heal quickly.

"So everyone in this room has some degree of magic?" Manon looks each of us in the eye, as if waiting for someone to opt out. "Whether they inherited it, or earned it, or *bought* it . . ."

At this, Nuala gives a small, nearly imperceptible flinch.

Manon looks, almost guiltily, at her hands.

Fiona and I quickly glance at each other and simply mouth, *What?*

"Well, we, all of us, have this power. But in a sense, everyone else does, too. It is free will, or consciousness, the ability to make up your mind, to be critical. This is all part of magic. That is what makes spells so powerful, not the words themselves but the focus and consciousness you put on them. You understand?"

I nod. This is what Nuala was trying to explain to me, but I was too distracted to listen. But I get it. Every spell I've done has not been about what's coming out of my mouth, but how the words are connecting to some deep, secret part of myself. A part I can touch but never fully see.

"When a Well spot is drained of magic, the people . . . they become soft. Like clay. They are easy to manipulate, easy to control, because they are lacking this substance. This magic has been taken from them."

"That's why people are acting so weird!" I announce, and I'm almost joyful at the discovery. It's not that Kilbeg is inherently small-town.

Roe and Fiona exchange a glance, as if they don't quite believe it. But then I remember that I actually have proof.

"It still doesn't explain why the conservative stuff would matter to them if all they care about is magic," Fiona says.

"It could be that they're working for someone else who wants magic," Nuala says. "Or it could be that it's a good distraction. Turning people against one another is a very good distraction technique while you accumulate power. Empires have been founded on less."

Roe isn't even paying attention anymore. He's on his phone. I nudge him and give him a look that says, *You're being rude.*

"It will keep getting worse, the longer it goes on," Manon says. "That's why we need to trap Aaron and bind his power. As soon as possible."

Nuala nods. "Bind Aaron, give Maeve a chance for her power to restore, and then once we're back to full confidence . . . we get rid of them. For good."

"Sorry if I'm being thick here," I say sheepishly. "But what is a bind?"

"It's a very old kind of spell. Probably one of the oldest there is. You prevent harm by binding someone's will. It's extremely powerful, and if done for the wrong reasons, very dangerous. By binding Aaron's will, we can prevent him from draining you any further."

Heather's words roll around my head like a stuck chorus.

You should be afraid of him. Pay attention to your body.

"What about Heather Banbury?" I ask. "She's part of this, too."

I tell them all about the conversation we had on Saturday, about the cash injection St. Bernadette's had taken from the Children, and Nuala's eyes widen in alarm.

"It makes sense," she says. "We know they have money and connections. And if they're so interested in magic, of course you'd take over the school where three young witches are."

She sighs, long and loud, as if she can't believe she has found herself in this situation.

"Watch her for another little while, and when you're ready, bring her in. We'll need all the power we can lay our hands on."

"And don't speak to her in school," Manon warns. "Walls have ears."

21

WHILE WE TALK ABOUT BINDING AARON, Nuala works on protection charms, sewing little leather bags by the light of an extending lamp that seems to have been fitted in her kitchen for exactly this purpose. Manon helps, cutting fresh herbs and blossoms with a big knife, as speedy and methodical as my dad when he dices mushrooms. She scrapes them into a mortar then grinds them hard with a pestle, taking her cardigan off so she can have full mobility.

"If we're going to bind Aaron," says Nuala, "we need to take something of his. Something personal."

"Like what?" I ask.

"Hair, teeth."

"Teeth?"

"How about I get us some pizzas?" Roe suddenly volunteers. "I'll head down to the big Dunnes and get the nice frozen ones."

I look up at him, bemused. He's already getting his jacket on, and starts asking if Nuala wants anything.

"Now feels like a weird time to go," I say, trying not to sound annoyed.

Roe kisses the top of my head on his way out the door, keys jangling. "Back soon."

"Or a scarf," Nuala says airily. "Whatever you can get, Maeve."

"How did they bind me, then? Did they have something that belonged to me?"

"Probably."

Lily picks a strand of long dark hair off her jumper. "Hair, probably. You *molt*."

"Girls"—Nuala motions to Fiona and me—"go into the garden and cut some fresh bay leaves for your protection charms. They'll keep you safe, I hope, until we can bind Aaron."

Manon quickly exits the kitchen for the living room, and comes back with a 1960s-style vanity case in shell pink. Fiona gasps involuntarily, completely stricken with longing for the thing.

Now Fiona is intent on watching Manon, who unzips the vanity case to reveal a supply of small brown bottles. Manon catches her eye and smiles. "All under one hundred milliliters," she says mischievously. "Ryanair doesn't rip *me* off."

Fiona laughs awkwardly and I nudge her. "Come on, let's get the bay leaves."

"Take your coats," Nuala calls.

I'm glad we do, because we step outside and are immediately bitten by a cold wind. "Jesus," I say, sucking in my breath. "Winter is on its way, hey."

We stamp our feet under the porch lights, gazing out at Nuala's garden, which is about three times the size of Nuala's house. It snakes on forever, getting thinner and steeper as it reaches a rickety chicken house at the top.

"Remind me what bay leaves are again?"

"Let me Google it."

We start looking around for the bay tree, and the farther we get from Nuala's kitchen door, the more comfortable we become in discussing what just happened inside of it.

"So," Fiona says. "I guess you didn't know she had a daughter, either."

"She's literally *never* mentioned it. To be honest, she's never told me anything about her private life apart from occasional bits about Heaven."

"It seems like they don't really talk," Fi says, shining her phone flashlight over some dark green bushes, peering into them. "This must be . . . a pretty big deal, for her to call Manon, and for Manon to come from France. How old do you think she is?"

"I don't know. Twenties?"

Fiona says nothing for a moment, and then pulls a bunch of leaves. "Do these look right?"

I smell them. "No, these are too . . . apple-y. Bay leaves smell a bit mustier, I think. Right shape, though."

We journey our way up the garden, the steepness increasing sharply in the dark. My breath starts coming hard. Fi holds on to me. "Are you feeling OK?"

"Yeah," I breathe. "Just . . . not all there."

This feels like the longest Fiona and I have been properly alone in ages. Really, since the day I came over to her house and she tried to tutor me for the test I eventually cheated on. We've never really discussed it. We just kind of . . . got over it. I thought that it was all water under the bridge, but so many of our interactions since then have come down to this fundamental divide: Kilbeg versus Dublin. Or really, Kilbeg versus the rest of the world.

But here, in the cold, damp dirt of Nuala's garden, in the wake of Manon and the Well, it feels like we're standing on neutral territory for the first time in weeks.

"How . . . how are you?" I ask. "We've never really talked . . ." I gesture at nothing. "About all of it."

We reach a greenhouse, its windows frosted up with condensation. Fiona stands on a few discarded stone slabs to try to see through the roof. "Do you think the bay leaves are in here?"

"No, she would have said if they were in the greenhouse," I reply. "Are you . . . are you still doing it, Fi?"

Her flashlight goes out, and for a moment, I don't know where she is. It's almost like she has disappeared into the inky blackness of the October night. Then, her voice.

"Doing what?"

"The . . . the hurting yourself."

"Why are you asking me that?"

"Because I'm worried, I guess. Turn your flashlight back on."

She says nothing, does nothing, so I reach into my pocket and get my phone out. When I shine my flashlight, she's already walking farther up the garden.

"Slow down!" I call.

"You think I'm one of those girls, don't you?"

"What?"

"One of those girls with *problems*."

"What does that even mean?"

"It's not the same for me as it is for other people," she says, hands jammed in her pockets, her back to me.

"Just because you can heal yourself doesn't mean I think you should . . ."

"Not just that," she says snippily. "I mean it's not the same. Everything is not the same. People want different things from me. Expect different things."

"Fiona, sit down."

And she does. She sits right down in the grass, even though what I really meant is that we should find a log or a bench or something. I sit down next to her, shivering when I feel the slight dampness of the earth.

"I'm not trying to judge you, Fi. I just want to understand what's going on. I feel like we've barely talked in ages."

She hunches her knees up to her chin.

"We shouldn't even be talking about this stuff," she says. "It's dumb. Not when there's literally, like, the fate of the world going on inside that kitchen."

"It's all the same thing." I shrug. "You, Lil, Roe . . . you basically are the world. You're my world."

"You always think," she says meditatively. "You always think that when really dangerous stuff starts happening, you'll just start acting really heroically. But it's never like that. The world could be burning and you would still be just . . . worrying about your own crap."

"You *do* act heroically, though. Remember the ritual? You saved our lives. You stopped the bleeding."

She shrugs. "You know what my first thought was, though?"

"What?"

She turns her cheek onto her knee, facing me. "My first thought was: I can't *believe* they're leaving me out of their suicide pact."

We're suddenly howling with laughter, realizing for the hundredth time how mad our lives are, and how the only thing that makes it bearable is that we're in it together.

I desperately want to ask her more. Why does she hurt herself, and why does she think it doesn't matter? And *does* it even matter?

She starts digging with a stick at the dirt in front of her.

"I'm going to stop doing it," she suddenly says.

"What?"

"Doing the . . . doing, you know. To myself."

"The cutting?"

"Don't say it like *that*."

"Like what?"

"Like I'm one of those girls."

"The ones with problems?"

"Yes."

Silence. She stands up again. "We should find those bay leaves."

We march through the muddy grass and hear the faint cluck-ing sound of chickens, flustered by the noise of our arrival. We're far from the lights of the city now, enough to see the stars and moon, the gleaming feathers of the chickens dimly visible in the silver light.

"Look at them," she coos. "Aren't they gorgeous?"

She starts poking her fingers through the wire, clicking her tongue for them to come near. Fiona laces the tip of each finger through the wire and pushes her face to it, like she's daring the chick-ens to bite her nose off.

"How does your mum feel about the meat thing? Being a veg-etarian and all that?"

"Hates it." She grimaces. "Thinks I'm being pretentious and rejecting, like, the entire Philippines because I don't want to eat meat."

"Heavy."

"Yeah," she says. "She hates that I want to go away. She's basically been in a mood with me since school started. I can't even mention Trinity at home."

I remember, suddenly, the hurt on her face when I said that she was perfect, and that everything usually went her way. Well, why wouldn't I think that? She *does* make things look easy. It strikes me that there's one thing that Fiona really can't do perfectly, and it's being imperfect. She wants people to know she has flaws, but she can't stand owning up to what they are.

Because Fiona isn't perfect. She's just a girl.

With problems.

We locate the bay leaves, eventually, and head back down to the house.

"What do you think about . . . all that stuff Nuala and Manon said?" I ask. "I mean, it explains a lot, right?"

"Right," Fiona says. "Like what?"

"Like why people are going crazy for Children of Brigid. It makes sense to me, y'know? It makes sense that the more magic that gets taken away, the less people are able to think for themselves."

Fiona doesn't look convinced. "I don't know. Seems a little easy."

"You think that Nuala and Manon are lying?"

"Lying? No." She looks down at her trainers, now caked in mud. "Look, it's a theory, isn't it? It's a pretty good theory."

The light of the kitchen draws closer, and Fiona takes a deep breath in, like it's her last moment to speak honestly. "Maybe people are awful because of the magic in Kilbeg. Or maybe some people are just shitty."

"It can be both, can't it?"

She shrugs. "Let's just go back inside."

Inside, Roe has returned with the pizzas. We watch them through the window, like we're watching a TV show about the people we love the most. Nuala tries to give him a tenner for the shopping and he pushes it away. She kisses him on the cheek. Lily takes the pizza out of the boxes, cuts off the plastic, and starts carefully rearranging the frozen pepperoni to one side.

We head back in, and Roe is already midflow, speaking combatively to Nuala.

"Are we sure, though, that this . . . this Wells thing is really *the* thing?"

"What do you mean?" I ask, fearful that his take on Manon and Nuala's explanation might be as questioning as Fiona's is.

"I've ruled out a lot, Roe," Nuala replies. "I've been going through my archives for weeks now."

"Your *archives*," Roe says, and there's something strange, something fundamentally un-Roe about the way he says it. Like the word *archive* is far too grand and important for someone like Nuala to use about a pile of papers tied together with elastic bands.

There's an awkward silence in the room. The only sound is Lily opening the oven and shoving the rearranged pizzas in.

"Look," Nuala says softly. "At the very least, you all need protection charms. And Aaron needs to be stopped. Do you think you can get something of his, Maeve?"

"I can try," I say limply, not quite sure how my friends became so cynical. It has knocked the spirit out of me somehow.

"Please," says Manon, who has been creating small piles of herbs cut so fine that they look like little pyramids of dust. "I have been studying this for a long time, and . . ."

"Yeah, but who *are* you?" Fiona suddenly says, and I can't believe how rude it comes out. Fiona, who is polite to everyone, and whom everyone loves.

Manon holds Fiona's gaze, studying her. Standing next to me, I can feel Fi's body almost contract with the intensity, her weight shifting back on her heels.

"This is a lot of information," Manon says. "Take some time to digest it."

Lily is still facing the oven, watching our reflections in the shiny black chrome.

After we've finished eating, the atmosphere in the kitchen feels a little less tense than it did a few minutes ago, although I can still feel something strange going on with Fiona and Roe. Like they're holding themselves apart from proceedings, not physically, but mentally.

Manon and Nuala finish the protection charms, and they are tied around our necks with great ceremony.

"Fiona, my strong bull: we have copper essence, honeysuckle, and thyme. Taurus rules over the throat, so there's a ground chicken neck in there."

Fiona's eyes go wide. "No. Not really?"

Nuala continues as though she hasn't heard. "Roe, my sharp Gemini: lavender, butterfly wings, and oleaster."

"From the chickens *outside*?" Fiona continues.

"Thanks, Nuala," Roe says, putting his on.

"Lily, the visionary Pisces!" Nuala is on a roll now, her gray eyes wild with excitement. I wonder again about Manon's comment about bought magic. Nuala always says she has no real magic of her own, but then the wind gathers around her and her eyes turn silver, and I know that something deep and cautious lives inside her. Something so wild and powerful that it frightens me. "Jasmine, cod liver, and plumbum candidum." She snaps her finger in my direction. "That's tin."

She hands me my charm, some combination of chili and feathers.

"I don't want to wear a chicken neck," says Fiona.

"And of course there's the usual bits in there, too," Nuala says briskly. "Hair, used tea bags."

"From *us*?" Roe asks, and even Lily looks shocked. "How?"

"It's good to save these things. Oh, don't look so appalled. I have to put my pickpocketing days to use somehow."

Something has changed about Nuala. Some mask, a mask that I never knew I was looking at, has been allowed to drop.

Manon is scribbling something down on baking paper, crossing out words and starting again. She opens one of her brown bottles of oil and beckons each one of us forward. "The sign of the goddess. For the spell."

"Which spell?"

"Not really a spell. More like a pact," Manon replies, tracing the sign in oil on my head.

"We are promising the Well that we'll protect it, but we're asking the Kilbeg Well to protect us from the people who threaten our lives. We're presenting a case to the Well."

She stands up and starts tearing the baking paper into scraps, passing us each a little bit. "It is only a very quick rhyme," she says, almost embarrassed. "But it should work OK."

Roe and Fiona shoot each other a look. And there, among the pizza crusts, we stand and join hands and begin to chant with this French stranger.

The Well is great and endless
Each day we draw once more
The Well is old and ageless
It is not mine or yours

After some time has passed, Nuala begins to bend and change the words.

The Well is ours to guard
As guardians we will stand
The Well is for Kilbeg alone
It protects us from your hand

If someone had told me a year ago that my friends and I would have magical powers by the time we were finishing school, I wouldn't have believed you. But if I had thought about it, here's what I would have imagined: balls of fire, ancient books, haunted amulets, and a cool, clean certainty that would drive our every action. We would always know what to do; we would follow an old scripture that pointed the way. I would not have predicted this.

We drive home, and I feel myself in the cradle of a spell that has not worked. Because half the people in the car didn't really believe in what they were doing, and were believing less and less the farther we got from Nuala's house.

22

THE DRIVE HOME IS STRANGE FROM THE
beginning. Fiona continues to hem and haw over the Well theory,
and keeps coming back to what she believes to be the central question of the evening: namely, who is Manon, and when, exactly, did
Nuala have a kid.

"Was she never going to *tell* us?" she exclaims. "Like, why now?"

"Because she's an expert in what's going on," Lily says. "In Wells."

"Lil," I turn around in my seat to face her. "You get it, right? You
believe her?"

A pause. "It makes sense to me."

"I think it makes sense, too."

"That's how it felt when I was the river," she suddenly says, her
face against the cold, rain-splattered pane of the car window. "Like
there was something underneath me. Something buzzing . . ."

Roe sighs loudly, and the wipers come on.

A silence falls on the four of us, the only sounds the swish of
the wipers and the dim smattering of loose, noncommittal rain. I
can't stop thinking about the draining. The sense that I am just a tool
for the Children. An organization for whom all people appear to be
just tools in getting what they want. Who was that bus driver? The

Chastity Brothers? The boy with the frog eyes? I think of the idiot girl at school. Are they all just conduits in the quest for more power, and what are they getting out of the deal if so?

How many of them even know what's going on?

Roe drops Fiona home first, then Lily. "I'm just going to drop Maeve off," he tells her. She nods and runs inside, coat pulled up over her head.

We drive the three minutes to my house and park outside. I ease into the driver's seat, sitting on his lap, my head on his chest.

"How are you feeling?" He murmurs the question in my hair, his breath warm, his neck smelling of heat and home and lavender.

"Weird," I respond, his heart beating against my ear. "The thought of Aaron just . . . taking stuff from me, without me even knowing. It's . . ."

"I mean, your flu."

I lift my head.

"My flu is fine," I say, puzzled. "It's fading."

"Good," he replies shortly.

There's a silence between us, and a faint chill. "Can you turn the heat on?"

"Heater's broken."

Now I'm truly confused. "Can't you just . . . ?"

But he looks at me blankly.

"Fix . . . it?"

"Oh," he replies. "That."

But he doesn't fix it. He doesn't really do anything. We just sit there, the cozy intimacy gone, and everything feels wooden and strained.

"How was Dublin?" I ask finally. "We hardly talked while you were there."

His smile comes easy, his tone lighter. "Honestly, it was awesome. I can't wait to play you the tracks. Honor is such a good producer. She taught me all these vocal exercises to protect my voice after recording so many takes. I can't believe how much I was just, y'know, screaming into the mic and hoping for the best."

"That's great." I smile and realize that this is the most committed to a sentence Roe has been all evening. Like this is what's real to him now, what's important, and not all this mad Well chat with his schoolgirl girlfriend.

"Does your gift help? When you're recording, I mean?"

He looks at me oddly. "I mean, I think I'm pretty talented?"

"No." Now I return the odd look. "I mean . . . your gift. Talking to the machines and all that."

Roe doesn't say anything, but instead just strokes my hair like I'm a cat.

"I need to go," he says. "I'm going to a party in Westcross."

"You're going out?"

"Yeah." He yawns. "I need a drink after all that."

I stiffen. "Wow."

"What?"

"It's just kind of amazing to me that you can go to a party after hearing all that."

"Jesus." He runs his hands through his hair, almost shoulder-length now. His fingernails are a bright violet, shining like gemstones through the darkness. "It's amazing to me that you can care about me going to a party after hearing all that. I would bring you if you were able to go."

I peer at him. "You really don't believe any of this matters, do you?"

"I don't know, Maeve," he mumbles. "It's all just a bit . . . much." He starts to fidget with the protection charm around his neck. "I hate this thing."

"They're draining my magic," I say. "I know they are. I know that's what's been happening to me, to . . . to everyone."

He scratches where the leather string is touching his collarbone, still tutting to himself. "Nuala, I know she means well, but god . . ."

"Roe!" I say sharply. "You're not even listening!"

"I am," he says, sounding exhausted.

"Right."

Why does he suddenly feel like a stranger to me? I don't fully understand what's happening, or how it happened so quickly. He sighs then, and I'm sure he's about to say sorry for being so dismissive.

"You know, I'm doing a psychology class. I needed to make up twenty credits with non-English stuff, so I chose psychology."

"OK," I reply, thinking that this is a strange time to discuss his academic career.

"I've been learning about post-traumatic stress disorder. Coping mechanisms."

"OK."

"Just . . . with everything we went through with Lily. Her going missing. We never . . . we never got any counseling, or therapy, or anything like that."

"No," I answer. "Because that would mean pretending it was a suicide-y thing, which it wasn't."

He clenches his hands on the top of the steering wheel, his knuckles whitening. He rests his forehead on it briefly, as if tired of discussing this, despite his being the one to bring it up.

"Whereas we know"—I can't believe I even have to say this—"that it was part of the *ritual*. Right?"

"Sometimes people create fantasies for themselves," he says quietly. "As a response to trauma."

I can't believe what I'm hearing. "You think *that's* what we're doing?" I respond, dumbfounded. "You think this is all a giant coping mechanism? That Nuala and her daughter are just . . . in on, for some reason?"

I remember Roe when he picked us up earlier this evening, and his weird joke about how maybe it was just a bad bus driver who was responsible for this morning's horror.

"What is going *on*, Roe? What are you thinking?"

"I think . . ." he begins tentatively. "I think my sister went missing for a month and then reappeared again, different."

His voice is so quiet now, so horribly quiet and still.

"I think we almost killed ourselves with knives."

I don't even know what to say. "Right."

"And I think we've only had ourselves to rely on, along with . . . an adult woman who runs a magic shop. And that maybe, we sequestered ourselves all summer, playing these mad games in the tennis court, to help us cope."

"Roe . . . what are you talking about?" I can feel panic rising in my chest, a sensation of everything around me being pretend, like painted scenery in a theater. "You think I invented reading people's minds?"

"But you can't read people's minds, can you, Maeve?"

"Not right now, no." I'm almost breathless with frustration, aware of how lame my own explanation sounds. He's making me feel absolutely insane. "Because of the draining of the Well."

"Or because," he says softly. "Because you don't need the fantasy anymore. Because we made up all this stuff to feel powerful during a time when we felt helpless, and . . ."

"Roe, *what?*"

"And now . . . it's run its course."

I suddenly remember the moment before he went to Dublin when, holding him tight, I instructed that he forget the ridiculous words that Alice from the Children said to him.

You're going to be so surrounded by creativity and brilliant people that you're going to completely forget about any of this.

"Roe," I say slowly. "I don't think it's me who is traumatized. I think . . . I think, maybe *you* were so upset about that horrible woman at the Claringdon that . . . that you forgot her, but you forgot everything else, too."

Roe doesn't even let me finish. "I just need to focus on the tour," he says. Then he looks at me mournfully, his eyes dark and shining. "I only have a few days at home before we head off. This is such a big deal for us, Maeve, and I know it's not easy for you, but . . ."

I nod slowly, wondering what on earth has happened, and how I can undo it.

"I better go," I say, because I don't want to burst into tears and make him feel worse than he does already.

"Maeve, don't. Let's talk. Just . . . not about magic, OK?"

We sit in silence. I'm about to say something when suddenly he cuts me off.

"I did it," he says. "I changed my name. Legally."

"Roe!" I can't believe he's only saying this now. Although, given everything we talked about today, it's hard to see when else he would have told me. He must feel like his thunder has been stolen. "You did it? In Dublin?"

"Miel and Honor were my witnesses," he says shyly. "We got champagne afterward."

I smile and, once again, try to suppress tears. I had thought that

216

I would be a part of his name change. That was how we had planned it, anyway. It makes sense that he did it with Honor and Miel, though, who are the right age to be witnesses. Now this is another part of Roe's life that I'm not a part of: another happy memory made without me, a living relic of his unhappiest ones.

"I'm so happy for you," I say, and I am, but it comes out sounding wooden and insincere. "I should go."

He can see right through me. "Mae, don't go."

But I've already stepped out into the chilly October night, the cold wind stinging at my wet eyes.

"The tour starts next week. Right?" I ask.

"Next Sunday."

"Maybe it's better that we don't see each other until then," I say, a statement I completely do not mean. "Or until you remember what happened to us, what has *been happening* to us, for almost a year."

"I'll call you tomorrow," he says, but he doesn't look at me when he says it. He stares straight at the steering wheel. "Take plenty of honey and lemon."

"Get a grip, Roe," I snap, and slam the door.

I sit on my bed, holding on to my own pillow. The soft covers and the smell of my own laundry feel reassuring and real, solid in a way that Roe no longer does.

When staring at the ceiling doesn't provide the answers I need, I call Fiona.

She picks up immediately.

"Yo."

"Fi, what happened to us?"

"Huh?"

"February. What happened?"

"Maeve, are you asking me to remind you of the thing we literally talk about nonstop?"

"Yes. Humor me." I start taking off my shoes, tugging at the laces, as she talks.

"Lily went missing because you summoned the Housekeeper card. Things went bad and then we brought her back in a ritual."

"And then what happened?" I ease off my shoe and hear the soft flap of cardboard as it hits the floor. I look down and see that there's been a tarot card stuck to the sole of my shoe.

"What?"

"I said, and then what happened?" I pick it up. The Five of Pentacles. Two poor people, bandaged and on crutches, walk past a church door. It's supposed to be a card about charity and accepting help.

"Um . . . we all got these weird powers."

"Right," I breathe out in relief. "OK."

"Why . . . why are you asking me this?"

"I think . . . I think a version of what's happening to me is happening to Roe. He's, like . . . forgetting. Forgetting what happened."

"I don't understand."

I start gnawing on a hangnail, tearing the skin, wincing at the pain. I look at the Five of Pentacles again, turning it upside down. The card isn't always about charity and accepting help, of course. There's a flip meaning. It can be about being locked out.

"He said that this is all a response to trauma from Lily going missing."

"What do you mean? *What* is a response to trauma?"

"Like we're inventing things. That we spent all summer in the tennis courts playing pretend because we needed to feel powerful. That we're all damaged and should have had counseling."

There's silence on Fiona's end of the line.

"Well, maybe we *should* have."

I don't know what to say. Because the truth is, Fiona probably *does* need to talk to someone.

"I need to go to bed," she says, suddenly sounding uncomfortable. "Are you OK?"

"Yeah," I lie, still turning the tarot card over. I don't think this belongs to any deck I own. "Talk to you tomorrow. Good night."

I fall asleep with the card on my chest.

23

IT'S SO EARLY WHEN I WAKE UP THAT IT'S dark outside. The Five of Pentacles is still on my chest, facedown on my breastbone, indicating that I haven't moved at all in my sleep. Like a corpse.

I grope for my dressing gown in the dark, trying to put my dream back together. It was another Aaron dream, another fly-on-the-wall moment from the incidental moments of his depressing life.

This time we were at an ATM. The machine kept saying that he had taken out the daily limit, and so he walked to another ATM and withdrew another hundred there.

I look at the tarot card again, the two beggars outside the church. *OK, moneybags*, I think. *You're certainly not relying on handouts.*

Lily and I don't take any chances on the bus anymore, so every day we walk the forty-five minutes to school.

"Hey," Lily says. She's found a winter wardrobe now. Powder-blue Doc Martens, blue jeans, a navy parka. Her hair is done in two long French braids. We trudge on, mostly in silence, until I can't stand not talking about Roe anymore.

"Has Roe spoken to you about . . . about his thoughts on all this?" I ask her.

For the first time since she came back from the river, a worried look crosses Lily's face. Her expressions in the last few months have usually stuck to bafflement, righteous indignation, and quiet reflection. Now there's something else. Something flush with anxiety, and for the first time in a long time, she looks like a teenage girl.

"A little," she says hesitantly. "It all seems to be . . . changing for him."

"Yes," I say, relieved she sees it, too. I explain to her about the day in the car before he went to Dublin, and how I told him to forget things.

Lily's eyes go wide, the blue irises so pale and clear that they look drinkable. She tilts her head upward, as if planning to negotiate with the sky.

"Maybe that's it," she begins nervously. "And maybe the Well is getting to him."

"Do you think? Is he wavy?"

"Sort of. But not as much. I don't think I noticed before, maybe because yours was *so* noticeable. But I don't know. I have thoughts, Maeve."

She looks at me sternly, like a drawing of a serious person, and if we weren't talking about Roe, I would laugh.

"Go on."

"When Nuala's daughter said that people go soft when a Well is drained, she meant, like . . . normal people. I don't think she knew that it affects people like us, too. The way *we* think."

"The non-normals?"

"Yes. Maybe, I don't know, maybe because Roe is older than us and away from us and . . . you know, more in the normal world, the grown-up world, than we are."

Lily continues, passionate, her eyes going from clear sky to electric blue.

"You, me, and Fiona, we all have each other, every day, to remind ourselves of . . . what happened to us. What we can do. But Roe is meeting new people all the time, and when you meet a new person, you have to try to forget who you are, don't you?"

She says this last part with great conviction, as if this is a known fact about meeting new people.

"You have to forget yourself a bit so you can make room for them. In your head."

"Right," I say, utterly perplexed. "Of course."

"And he's forgetting too much," she continues grimly. "He's forgetting."

"So what do we do? Spend more time with him?"

"But he doesn't want to spend time with us," she replies, and it's like being punched in the stomach. She glances over at me and seems to genuinely regret saying it like that. "Sorry."

As we walk the rest of the way to school, I realize that I can handle anything—any amount of crazy Children of Brigid antics, any amount of magic lost or gained—but this, this sense of Roe slipping away from me and from everything we went through, is too much. It's unbearable. I spent the month of August worrying that losing touch with Roe would mean having different schedules, or him being on tour while I'm at school. What I would have never expected was this, this forgetting.

And now he's going away.

"We need to get something of Aaron's," I say, my voice fierce. "We need to bind him so he can't drain any more magic, and we need to restore the Well so Roe can remember again. And so people will stop acting like it's the fifties."

"Yes," Lily agrees. "How are we going to do that?"

"We're going to go to Aaron's house."

"When? Now?"

"After school. If I miss another class, my mother is going to string me up."

We walk on, our steps together feeling, briefly, more like predator than prey.

·)）●（(·

When we get to the basement classrooms, Fiona is coming out of Miss Banbury's office. Looking, to my immense joy, happier than she has in weeks. I glance at the time. It's not even nine yet.

"Hey," she says brightly.

"Hey," I reply, cocking my head. "What were you . . . ?"

"I decided to take your advice. You know, about . . . talking to someone impartial."

"Oh, wow," I reply, even more surprised. "Let it not be said that Fiona Buttersfield does not take direction."

Fiona looks a little embarrassed, as if she is now admitting to being a girl with a problem. "I didn't talk about any . . . any big stuff. But she said that I should try journaling all the stuff I didn't want to say out loud."

"I think that's a great idea." I beam.

"Yeah, then I told her how nosy my mum is, and she said, well, just leave it in the locked drawer in my office. And she gave me this."

Fiona slides a black spiral-ring notebook out of her bag. "She said I can write in it in The Chokey and just leave it there, and that she won't read it or anything."

I look at her skeptically. I like Heather and everything, but even I don't trust a school employee not to read my journal, especially if it was locked in her office drawer.

"I know what you're thinking," she says, rolling her eyes. "But

I'm just going to put a few markers in, to make sure she's not turning the pages."

"How?" I ask her as we saunter into the canteen for our preclass cup of tea.

She lays the book down and closes her eyes. She plucks at her eyelashes, then lays one on the front page. "If she moves the journal, it will move, too."

"I'm sure she won't." I smile, happy that Fiona is finally getting help.

The first bell goes, so Lily and I file into our class while Fiona heads upstairs. School is getting slightly more manageable for me and Lily, especially since we no longer have to keep up with a huge class of girls who are achieving at a much higher level. The teacher goes slower, people are less ashamed of putting their hand up to say they don't quite understand something. Which is why it's so weird that this class doesn't start as it normally does, with us getting our homework back. Instead, it starts like this.

"For next week," Miss Marshall, the history teacher, begins, "I want an essay on US President Lyndon B. Johnson: his vision of the Great Society, and why it failed."

I look at Lily, wondering if I've missed a class somewhere. We've not done Lyndon B. Johnson yet, so it's weird to open the class telling us about an essay we're going to write about him.

"At the age of sixty-four," Miss Marshall continues, "former president Lyndon B. Johnson died at Stonewall, Texas, the same place he was born."

There's something a little odd about all of this, and maybe I'm only really recognizing it because history is my best subject and therefore tends to be the place where I pay the most attention. Miss

Marshall starts talking about Lyndon B. Johnson's death, and then his presidency, and then his hopes for the presidency, and then the Kennedy assassination. She then ends the lecture with the words "Lyndon B. Johnson was born in Stonewall, Texas, in 1908."

The class finishes like it should have begun, with her handing out last week's homework, graded.

"Is it just me"—I turn to Lily—"or was that class completely backward?"

"Hmm?" She looks up, and I realize she was barely paying attention, instead drawing pictures of great tidal waves of water bursting out of a little stone well.

I thought it was a fluke. That Miss Marshall was just having an off day, and that maybe she bumped her head before going to bed last night. But it keeps happening. It keeps happening all day.

In math, we have equations where we start with the answer and end with the problem. In Irish class, Miss Heaney begins with a discussion of the themes of a poem and ends with the poem itself. And the weirdest part is, no one finds any of this remotely strange. People are listening, or picking their nails, or taking notes. Lily is completely the wrong audience to ask if something is strange, because she thinks most of the pillars of the ordinary world—work, school, banks—are a bit weird, anyway.

At lunch, I tell Fiona about the plan to go to Aaron's apartment, and she's immediately game.

"Infiltrate the enemy," Fiona says with relish. "I've always wanted to go to that stupid apartment."

And for the first time, we don't call Roe to fill him in on the plan. We don't even discuss it. There seems to be an understanding that he is away from us now, at least for the time being, and that there is nothing to do but soldier on and hope he catches up.

At four p.m., the three of us set down the hill and over the bridge, heading to the south side where the Elysian Quarter apartments are. Fiona looks tired, and far less joyous than she did this morning.

"You OK, Fi?"

"Yeah," she chirps. "I don't know, weird day."

"Weird how?"

"Weird, like . . . I don't know, my classes were weird."

I slow down. "Like . . . backward?"

Fi's eyes widen. "Yes! All back to front!"

"Oh, my god, Fi." I shake my head. "I thought I was going nuts. Is this . . . is this part of it?" I say, hesitant, because I know that Fiona is still patchy on the Well theory. "Is this part of everyone going soft?"

"Soft and . . . backward?" She wrinkles her nose. "I don't know. It's just the teachers, though. My parents are still the same. Are yours?"

"Yes. Lil?"

"Same," she says. "Weird, but the same level of weird they always were."

The apartment is only a fifteen-minute amble from the city center, and the last gasp of autumn sunshine warms our hair as we walk through the riverside streets of Kilbeg. There's a freshness, a bright coolness in the air, and everything looks clean. One of the bakeries is starting to close for the day, and the cashier is shredding old donuts and scattering them to the seagulls that have come in from the riverbank. Lily clicks her tongue at them, like they're dogs.

I remember then Miss Banbury's idea about Japan. It all seems so distant, so like a pipe dream. I wonder if it will happen, and if Kilbeg will look different when I get back.

I find the address, still sitting in my Notes app, a whole other world ago. *Apartment 44, Floor 8, Elysian Quarter.*

A sudden painful crunch of memory, of Roe O'Callaghan

holding my hand as we bolted out of the apartment after Aaron's recruitment meeting, together in our hatred of the same thing.

When we get to the apartment complex, we spy the concierge still on duty through the glass double doors. We suddenly become very conscious of our lack of a plan, and then realize that the concierge himself presents an opportunity. He could have something that belongs to Aaron. My brother's concierge sorts everything out for him, even his dry-cleaned suits. It could be a perfect way of binding Aaron without endangering ourselves by actually going up to his flat.

Fiona and I decide to approach him together, while Lily stands guard.

"Hi," Fiona says, facing the concierge, a slight, bashful smile already forming on her face. "Aaron in apartment 44 was wondering if his package had come yet."

He blinks at her.

"He said you'd know all about it." She smiles, and her manner is exactly like someone who could either be a lowly assistant or a lowly girlfriend. It's impossible to tell which.

"Who?"

"Aaron," she says. "Apartment 44. The eighth floor."

She's keeping her tone bouncy and professional, if a little stupid, to cover for the fact that we do not know Aaron's last name. How on earth do we *not* know it? He's been on the radio enough times, but somehow it never comes up. He's always Aaron, from the Children of Brigid.

"American chap," he says.

"Yes!" she gushes.

"He's been gone weeks," the concierge says, confused. "Moved out in September."

"Yes, exactly," she almost squeals. "He sent me to pick up his package. He said you'd know all about it? He said, Peter will know."

He is wearing a PETER name tag, which clearly Fiona clocked the moment she came in, yet hearing his own name seems to convince him of her authenticity.

"Ah," he says, getting up reluctantly out of his chair. He starts poking at a row of letter boxes behind him. "No package, no idea what that's about, but I have his post all right. I thought he'd come to collect it when he didn't give a forwarding address."

"Yes!" she says excitedly. "He said it might be a package, or it might be a letter."

I am utterly dazzled when he falls for it, and even more dumbstruck when he hands her a stack of unopened letters from the postbox marked 44.

24

THERE ARE FIVE LETTERS. TWO OF THEM are from his cell phone provider: one confirming his request to end the contract, and one informing him the contract has ended. Two are from his bank: one that says he is thirteen hundred euros overdrawn, and the other that says he has been charged for the overdraft.

I stare at the letters, remembering those incredibly dull dreams I had. Are these the errands I was mindlessly accompanying Aaron on?

"Branum?" Fiona screeches. "Aaron's last name is *Branum*?"

I gaze at the address on the letters, absolutely stunned by this realization. *Aaron M. Branum, Apartment 44, Elysian Quarter, Denmark Street, Kilbeg.* Looking at it makes me sick, for reasons I can't fully explain but that Fiona can enunciate perfectly.

"Aaron's last name can't be *Branum*. It's too *normal*. His last name should be Hitler, or Satan. What does the *M* stand for? Mmmmm-assive douche?"

The last letter is the jackpot. In terms of the binding spell, and in the more traditional sense of the word.

The envelope has an American postmark, from California, and inside it is a smaller sealed envelope. The smaller envelope has an address, clearly written by Aaron, that ends *Yuba City, CA,* and when we open it, five one-hundred-dollar bills slide out.

Fiona lets out a long, low whistle. "Holy crap," she squeals. "He's overdrawn and canceling his phone contract, but he's sending away five *hundred* dollars?"

I shake my head, unable to put it together.

"Not five," Fiona continues. "Not fifty. Five *hundred*."

"Read the letter," Lily says.

We read the letter.

Dear Mr. & Mrs. Madison,

I write this in full expectation that you will burn this letter without reading it, and in your situation, perhaps I would do the same.

As you may know from my parents (who, I believe, still attend your church), I have been in Europe for the past few years, spreading the word of God and attempting to atone for my sins. While I know that I can never expect your forgiveness, I do hope that the enclosed will help express my continuing and most sincere regret for what occurred at Twin Pines. Not a day passes without my including Matthew in my prayers.

I realize that to hear from me now, after so many years of silence, must come as a surprise. But recent developments in my own life—and perhaps a maturing generally—have made me understand that we are in better control of our own destinies than I had thought.

Yours faithfully,

Aaron Michael Branum

"Why," says Fiona, who is the first person to finish reading, "do Americans always refer to any country over here as *Europe*, like it's one landmass? He's been in *Ireland*. Say *that*."

I look mutely at the letter, reading it again and again, trying to fit it with the Aaron I know. There's too much to take in. It seems obvious that this Matthew person has died and that Aaron was responsible. But there's more here, too—doors that open into whole worlds of impossible sadness.

Like, why isn't he *sure* his parents attend the same church as the Madisons? Someone who loves God this much would know that for a fact, wouldn't they? Clearly that relationship has also dissolved, and then there's Aaron, preaching about the importance of family.

"Twin Pines," Fiona says. "What's that?"

"It's a facility for weirdos," Lily answers.

We Google it. She's pretty much correct. It is a "center for troubled youth."

"How did you know that?" I ask Lily.

"Because that's what they all sound like. I found the brochures in my mum's glove box. Restful Pastures. Crystal Waters."

"Why does your mum . . ." But then I stop myself. "They wanted to send you somewhere?"

She shrugs. "They must have. They definitely sent away for brochures at some point."

I shudder at the thought. Lily locked away in some kind of institution. Imagine.

Then I realize that Aaron, at one time or another, must have been locked away in some kind of institution, and that is even harder to imagine.

"We need to take this to Nuala and Manon," Fiona says. "This has everything, right? It's a return to sender, so the envelope inside will be covered in his spit and things. And the money, which would have been riding around in his pocket for ages. The handwriting."

"His name," I join in. "His full name, in his own hand."

I'm suddenly transported back to February, when Roe almost

kissed me by the Beg River and told me his name instead. He said that real witches knew things by their true names.

"Why didn't they take the money?" Lily wonders aloud.

"They sent the whole thing back unopened. They didn't want to know."

"So he did something bad enough to go into an institution," Fi says. "And then he killed someone while he was there."

"He seems to feel quite bad about it," Lily counters.

"Well, yeah," I respond. "Thou shalt not kill, right? Pretty big deal if you're into God."

"And if you're not into God," says Lily, "it's still a pretty big deal."

"I had a dream," I suddenly remember.

"All right, Dr. King," Fiona says.

"No, I mean . . ." I rattle my brain, trying to remember. "He was getting hundreds out of the ATM. I was watching him. Like I was in his memories."

Lily examines the bills again. "It must have been a while ago. These have been across the Atlantic and back."

"Yeah," I murmur, not sure what this means.

Nuala is waiting outside school for us on Thursday. She's shut Divination early and has her sunglasses on. She doesn't look directly at the building, instead peers into the takeaway coffee in her hands, leaning against her hatchback.

We step out the main entrance, and suddenly Sister Assumpta is next to me, hunched and gripping the rail.

"Is that little Fionnuala Evans over there, Maeve?"

I look at her in shock. Since when does Sister Assumpta even know my name? Or Nuala's, for that matter?

"It is, Sister."

"She had a baby with a French man," Sister Assumpta says, and then disappears back inside.

"Did *everyone* know except us?" Fiona says.

We climb into Nuala's car, and she says nothing about the fact that Roe isn't with us. Something tells me that she could read between the lines the last night we were at her house and is sympathetic but unsurprised.

"Is Manon still staying at your house, Nuala?" Fiona asks searchingly.

"She is, love."

"And . . . and how old is Manon, Nuala?"

A brief pause as Nuala makes a turn. "She's twenty."

"Right, so . . ."

"I was twenty-five."

"And her fa—"

"That's all you're getting, Fiona." Nuala says it firmly, and Fiona doesn't say another thing.

I feel a bit guilty. I always thought Nuala was older. Midfifties, at least, but she's only forty-five. Maybe because my parents are that age and in my head that's just how old adults are. Maybe it's because Nuala always gives the impression of having lived several lives. Which, apparently, she has.

And so has Aaron. Aaron, whose shape in my head has already started to change. How old is he? Who was he when he was Aaron Michael Branum? Did he really feel bad about this Matthew kid, or is it just another one of his schemes?

When we get to Nuala's, Manon is sitting on the back porch, smoking a rolled cigarette. She nods when she sees us, and I can feel Fiona almost quaking with intrigue. Fiona, who feels so starved of glamour in Kilbeg, can't believe that a person so obviously glamorous has plopped down into it.

"We think we have what we need," Fiona volunteers. "To bind Aaron."

We lay everything out on the kitchen table. The hundred-dollar bills, the letters, the envelopes. Manon studies all of them in silence.

"I think what this requires," she says thoughtfully, "is a soft bind."

"Surely we want a *hard* bind?" I interject, despite not knowing the difference between one and the other. "One he can't break?"

"I think perhaps it will be dangerous for this person to be too hard bound. This letter was not written very long ago," she says. "And he is . . . clearly in great anguish."

"So?"

"A bind is a difficult thing. We are binding his will and that can be traumatic. He may be too fragile. If he finds his magic useless, he may take his own life."

The frankness with which she says this is dazzling.

"He's trying to destroy Kilbeg," says Fiona. "Surely whatever he gets . . ."

"We don't know what he is doing. We just know that he is involved." Manon sighs softly, turning over the American bills so the reverse sides are all faceup. "And people do things they regret."

Nuala places a pot of steaming tea on the table.

"They leave their children," Manon says, and then Nuala starts talking loudly about cherry cake. Manon doesn't seem to be listening, and falls into silence again as she studies Aaron's letters.

"He is on the run," she says finally. "He has cut off his phone, he has taken everything out of his bank in cash. See? It says here. Cash withdrawals."

"Oh," I respond. "So?"

"So if we leave him defenseless from whoever he is running from, it could be fatal. And whatever harm we inflict, it will return to us, times three."

"I thought that was an old wives' tale," says Fiona dismissively.

"The only people I listen to," Manon says, the hint of a smile on her face, "are old wives."

"We must bear in mind what happened to Heaven," Nuala says softly, and it takes a moment for me to understand what she means. Heaven killed her father with the Housekeeper, and died herself in the bargain. That, apparently, was a fair deal to her. I hate Aaron, but not enough to die myself.

The spell Manon comes up with is beautiful, and I can see why Nuala thinks so highly of her as a witch. She teaches us all to fold the hundred-dollar bills into origami sailboats.

"Fin, can you bring out the sugar water please?" Manon unzips her vanity case of oils. "The sugar water has been soaked in moon-light for two nights now. I think it will be strong enough." She peers into the case. "I think we will use lavender for this."

The idea is that every fold and crease is lined with a thin streak of lavender oil, daubed on by each of us with a cotton swab. The bills are then dunked in the sugar water, covered, and left overnight. "Sugar to sweeten, lavender to calm," she clarifies. The letter with his signed name is placed in the sugar water first, and I watch it wilt slowly to the bottom of the bowl.

Manon writes a chant out for us, Fiona watching her intently.

"It must be hard, rhyming in your second language," she says.

"Mmm," Manon murmurs in agreement.

"If it *is* your second language," she clarifies. "Is it?"

Manon doesn't say a thing, and as I watch Fiona watching her, I realize something. Something I might have realized much sooner if I had my gifts about me.

Fiona has a *crush* on Nuala's daughter.

"Here is the spell," Manon announces, and pushes it to the center of the table.

Aaron Michael Branum
We bind you with respect
From all the evil you may do
To pay for your regret
Aaron Michael Branum
We bind you but we bless
Your magic for escaping danger
Or those who are in distress
We ask for your understanding
We ask for your trust
Please know that in this binding
We do only what we must

"It's long," Manon says, semi-apologetically. "Take some time to memorize it."

"Manon, my magic is . . . still faded," I say, embarrassed. "Will I just sit the spell out?"

She shakes her head firmly. "No. As long as you have intention, intention and sensitivity, you are still an important part of the spell."

And so, we get to work. We cast a purified circle around the kitchen table in salt, and we start chanting and folding, daubing and singing. The lavender oil on the bills has to be done carefully, each of us with our own little brown bottle and swab, trying to keep up the chant as we sing Aaron's full name, over and over. With every verse, with every fold, I can feel the glimmer of my sensitivity still shining from the bottom of me. Tiny tendrils of my magic, faded but not yet invisible, start to unfurl themselves like a plant in morning sunlight. *Yes*, I coo, like I'm calling a frightened chicken. *Yes, come on. Come on out.*

For the first time in a long time, I feel the banded energy of a spell working, looping itself around all five of us. Five women to gently, diligently bind a toxic man. And as I say his name again and again—Aaron Michael Branum, Aaron Michael Branum, Aaron Michael Branum—the fragile strands of my magic start to conjure him. I see him as a baby, as a boy, as a teenager. They are brief visions, ghosts only, and I know I am not inventing them because I am surprised by how he looks. I am surprised that he was pudgy at fifteen. I am surprised by his glasses. He looks so ordinary, so untouched by the stains of hatred, and for the first time I get why my mother said that it was important to understand the people we hate. To understand that everyone was someone's child once, and that something dreadful must have happened to make them so sick.

Please know that in this binding
We do only what we must
Please know that in this binding
We do only what we must

Why is he on the run? Did he leave the Children? How, in such a short time, did he go from being their number-one spokesperson to fleeing the apartment they gave him?

We each finish our lavender boats at the same time, and we look at Manon for guidance.

"Set your spell out on a soft sea, and let sweet winds only blow your way," she says, and we each put our hundred-dollar bill on the surface of the sugar water. Lily can't help but zap the water lightly as she touches it, jolting each boat with a light ripple of power.

The spell is over, and I look at Fiona, Lily, Nuala, and Manon to see that a pinkish golden glow has come over all of them, each of them beautiful, each of them radiant. Immediately, I know that Manon was right. I know that spells cast in cruelty only pay in kind, and that every piece of magic you call on has to be done for the right reasons.

"Wait a second," I say, suddenly panicked. "We didn't sacrifice anything. You have to give big to get big, right?"

"Pet," Nuala says, chuckling. "We just bought ourselves five hundred dollars' worth of magic."

"I hope it works," Fiona says thoughtfully. "I could have really used that five hundred dollars."

25

AS WE PUT OUR COATS ON TO LEAVE, MANON says, "Wait!" and takes the sugar-water bowl full of money to the kitchen counter. She fumbles around under the sink and manages to find an old tea flask. She pours the water into it, the hundred-dollar bills sweeping along like twigs on a river, and seals it in.

"Here," she says, giving it to me. "Sleep with this near you. The bind is to stop him from harming people, and the person he is actively harming is you."

I pack it into my schoolbag, nauseous at the idea of carrying it around. It feels too personal, too intimate, like holding a vial of blood. Zipping my bag back up, I glimpse my schoolbooks and suddenly remember something.

"There's something else you should know, too," I say. "Our school has . . . gone weird. Not just with COB stuff. But in other ways."

Manon looks at me curiously. "How?"

"Like, the lessons are backward. They start at the end and work their way to the beginning. Nothing in school made sense today."

"For all of you?"

Fiona and Lily nod.

"I have not heard of this happening before," she ponders aloud. Then she looks at her mother. "I think I will have to stay longer."

Nuala looks strange, pleased and nervous at the same time. "Of course."

"This Well, it is not like the others," Manon continues. "Or maybe it is just different because I am here."

"What usually happens?" Lily asks.

"Usually when a Well is drained, a scholar will not find out until a long time later. There will be depressions, both economic and spiritual, that will last a long time. It is like a place folds in on itself, like the soul is gone. It is rare to be somewhere *while* it is happening."

"And what happens when you stop it?" Lily asks. "What then?"

"I don't know," Manon replies, then looks at her feet. "I don't think one has ever been . . . stopped."

A shadow of terror crawls over me, dampening the pinkish golden glow left from the spell. Manon, who evidently knows everything about Wells, can't even recall a single time one was saved successfully.

"Lily, I need to come home with you," I say once we're outside. "I need to talk to Roe. In person. I need him to remember."

She nods. "Sure. I don't know what time he'll be home, though."

I don't spend a lot of time in the O'Callaghan's house anymore. Rightly or wrongly, Mrs. O'Callaghan has been suspicious of me since I disappeared from Lily's life and then reappeared just after she went missing. I know she disapproves of me with Roe, and of Roe's gender expression generally, which she finds confusing in light of his having a girlfriend. To her, *girlfriend* is supposed to mean that you're definitely straight. It does *not* mean that you start doing your makeup together. It has only confirmed to her that I am some sort of perversion of the normal, and in some ways, she's not wrong.

Then there's Kilbeg University, which she also views as my fault.

Even though Roe's decision to attend college locally was because of the band, both his parents still think that he's pissed his chances away because of me.

And maybe now he agrees with them.

Perhaps this is why Lily's mum does not say very much to me when I come in the door. In fact, she does not say much to Lily, either. She was clearly relaxing before we walked in—there's a magazine on the kitchen table, and a steaming cup of tea—but as soon as we arrive, she scatters herself and makes a big production of folding tea towels. "You're home," she says. "I didn't know whether you'd be wanting dinner, so I just put some shepherd's pie in the fridge. You can heat it up, if you like."

"Thanks," Lily says. "How are you?"

"Good, now." She brushes her hands off her trousers. "All right."

It's so wooden, so awkward, that it almost breaks my heart. Mrs. O'Callaghan used to be confused by Lily. Now it's like she's frightened of her. "Your brother's upstairs," she says, and we take that as our cue to leave the room. Lily winces slightly. She doesn't use *brother* if she can help it.

We stomp up the narrow stairs and Roe's door is open. Lily and I exchange a look, and she disappears into her room.

I lean in the doorway, watching him. He sits on his bed with a long pendant necklace, diligently trying to pick a knot out of the chain. I smile, the way you smile when you're watching a person you love who thinks they are alone and, in that aloneness, being completely themselves.

But my eyes shift to Roe's hands, still fumbling with the knot in the chain. I furrow my brow. He picks his nails feebly at it, biting down on his bottom lip in frustration.

Why is it taking him so long?

"Hey," I say weakly.

He looks up, and his smile is almost guilty.

"Hey." He lets the chain drop in his lap and reaches his hand out to my waist, pulling me softly to the bed. I sit down, and we're immediately glued to each other, my hands around his shoulders, my lips to his neck.

"I'm sorry I didn't call," he says hoarsely. "I just . . ."

"It's fine," I say. "It's fine, it will be all right."

Will it, though?

Something wild inside tells me that I can simply kiss the disbelief out of Roe. That skin, so solid and real, so undeniably present, will clear the fog in his mind. Our lips meet and he pulls my face close, his thumbs on my jawline. I lean forward, and in one artful leg extension, he closes his bedroom door.

In these moments, it's easy to forget about what's real and what isn't. All that exists is heat and history, the memory of all the times we've been here, the knowledge of what the other person likes best. There are so few things that I feel like I'm good at, but I know that I am good at him. Good *with* him.

I wonder, as our clothes start to come off, whether his mum will purposefully interrupt. But I hear the soft slam of the front door, then the sound of a car outside, and she's gone. It's just him and me, and Lily across the hall, who wouldn't walk in if her life depended on it.

We've been here so many times before, but it feels heightened now. Warmer, more delicious. I wonder if it's the glow of Manon's spell that is making my skin dance or the fear of losing Roe forever. In the moment, I don't care. Neither, it seems, does he. He kisses my neck, my collarbone, my breasts, all while his thumb strokes at the thin cotton of my knickers, his hand slotted between my thighs.

It's too much, and it's not enough.

And then I glance over his shoulder, and I see the abandoned silver necklace on the floor. The knot still in the chain. The problem still unsolved.

"Roe," I say.

"Mmmmm?"

"Stop a second."

His eyes meet mine, and he stops. "Are you OK?"

"Yeah," I say softly, reaching out for him. My fingers stroke his scar, above his stomach and below his sternum, where the knife went in. Where he almost killed himself, trying to save me. "Roe, tell me how you got this."

The mood instantly changes. He looks at me, perplexed.

"From when I fell on the knife."

"Roe," I say, as gently as I can. "You never fell on a knife. You know that. I know you still know that."

He sits up and buries his face in his hands.

"I can't do this again."

I sit up, holding the pillow to my chest, and pick up the chain from the floor.

"Get the knot out," I say. "Try to get the knot out, and I'll talk to you while you do it."

He looks like he would rather do anything else. But he does it. He brings the necklace close, rolling the knot gently, trying to loosen the chain's hold.

"At the start of this year," I say softly. "You and I were getting the bus together, and we started talking. Didn't we?"

"Yes," he replies.

I decide to go on in this vein, starting with nonmagical things that definitely happened to lead us to the magical things that also did.

"Which was funny, because even though . . . even though we'd known each other forever, we hadn't actually chatted properly in a few years, had we?"

"No," he says. And then he smiles. "Still fancied you, though."

"Really?"

"I've fancied you since we were kids."

I laugh, extremely pleased with this. "Well, that's nice."

He picks again at the necklace, and I press on.

"And then Lily went missing, and . . . we didn't know what to do. We were lost. We crashed that COB meeting, didn't we?"

He nods. "Aaron and the horrible game."

"Aaron and the horrible game!" I agree, feeling as if I am leading someone blindfolded over a river. "And then we realized that . . . the Housekeeper card, the card that came up in my tarot, was actually a song, and Fiona's mum knew the song."

I can feel him pulling away, as though he's just heard the sound of rushing water underneath him and wants out.

"And then," I say quickly. "Then, we realized that the House-keeper . . . well, it had put the world out of balance, and the snow came, and . . ."

He closes his hand into a fist, the silver knot embedded in his knuckles. My speech comes fast and stuttered.

"So we decided we'd do this ritual, right? We tore up the white silk and we called Lily back to us, and right at the last moment . . ."

"Maeve, stop."

"You *have* to know what I'm talking about. You can't have just . . ."

He stands up, puts the silver chain on the dresser, and starts opening drawers. He takes out T-shirts, silk camisoles, a brides-maid's dress we found in a charity shop.

"I'm going in the morning," he says.

246

"In the *morning*?" I clutch the pillow closer to me, suddenly very conscious of being almost naked in his room.

"Which means I'll be back for your birthday," he says brightly.

Something inside me breaks. The feeling of levees bursting, of towns flooding. I start to cry. I don't even try to talk through the tears at first. I just sit there, soaked in them, holding the pillow like it is keeping the blood inside my body.

"Babe!" He sits down, all concern. "I thought you'd be *happy*. I'll be home when you turn seventeen, and I'll buy you something nice while I'm on tour, and we'll . . ."

"Roe," I croak. "It will be too late then. You won't even remember who I am."

These last four words unleash a fresh bout of tears, and I crumple further into myself. He puts his arms around me and starts to rock me back and forth.

"Maeve, Maeve, Maeve," he whispers. "I don't know what to do. Tell me. Tell me what I can do."

"Remember," I hiccup. "Just remember."

"I can't," he soothes. "I can't remember what isn't true."

"Then stay," I say, grabbing at him. "Stay. Don't forget anything else."

Roe pulls away from me, his expression turned to horror. He starts to pace the room, his shirt still off, his temper rising.

"You can't ask me to do that," he says. "You can't, Maeve, you can't."

I look at him blearily, still half blinded by tears. "I just think something terrible will happen if you go," I say desperately. "I know you think that I'm trying to keep you from being a musician or something, but I swear to God, Roe, that isn't it. I think we're in danger. You, me, all of us. I . . ."

"Next year," he replies. "Next year you can come on the road with me. Next year we can both be in KU together. We can even move in together, if you want! But this year, Maeve, we always knew that this year would be hard."

We go on like this. Talking past each other and never to each other. Eventually, it's almost nine o'clock, and we are exhausted. Bone weary from talking, mouths dry from explaining ourselves. We end up just holding each other in total silence. I start tracing his lip with my finger, pushing down on the berry plumpness, wishing that love could be just as simple as loving someone's mouth.

And for a few minutes, I convince myself it can be.

"Roe," I say, whispering. "Sleepover."

His eyes widen. "What? Really? Are you sure?"

"Yes," I say softly.

"Maeve . . . you know I have to leave in the morning? I don't want you to do this and then for you to feel alone."

"I know," I reply. "Don't worry. I know."

And to show I'm serious, I move on top of him. I twine my hands in his, kissing and moving against him, until eventually we're lost in each other again and the subject of magic feels wonderfully far away. Roe gets a condom out of his top drawer, and after a few moments of awkwardness and figuring out which way it goes on, he's inside me.

It hurts. Of course it does. I bite down on my lip and hold him close, and then the pain is too much, so we stop. He holds me, petting me like a spooked horse. I try to make sense of both the pain and the new reality I am in, the fact of no longer being a virgin. It was only a few seconds, no more than a minute, but I still need to process it.

"I love you," he whispers, looking half-dazed. "I love you, I love you, I . . ."

And we're there again, there and it feels real this time. Real like

248

how sex is supposed to feel. Real like I know magic is. There's an instant when we lock eyes, and we feel so joined together that I am sure we are the same thing. And I think: he remembers. He remembers it all. His gift, the ritual, everything. I'm so sure of it that, when it's all finished, I think that Roe is back.

"What time are you going tomorrow?" I ask. My insides are aching and my legs are tender, and for some reason I think his answer will be: *I'm not going. I'm staying. It's too dangerous for me to leave. I see everything now, everything for how it is, and I can't risk going away.*

"Eight a.m.," he answers, and his eyes are so full of love and blankness that I kiss him goodbye, leave the O'Callaghan house, and walk home. Trying, with deepest sincerity, not to fall apart.

26

THERE'S AN OLD IDEA ABOUT LOSING YOUR virginity.

Actually, there are lots of old ideas, but this is one of them: that people will be able to tell by *your face* when you've lost it.

It always seemed sketchy to me. Like a leftover from some long-gone scarlet-letter days, where women were ruined forever the moment they had sex. The kind of bullshit that the Children go on about; the kind of thing that keeps people feeling miserable and ashamed and insecure. Which, I'm learning, are very useful emotions if you want to distract people while you suck the magic from underneath their feet.

So when I walk through the living room door, newly relieved of my virginity, no one can tell by the look on my face.

Everyone, however, can tell by my hair.

"Maeve!" Mum says, and for the first time in a long time, she's saying my name in delight and not because I've disappointed her. "Your hair! It's *lovely!*"

At first, I think my hair has been so rumpled by the pillow that it's a dead giveaway. Then I take a strand and examine it, and I'm so shocked I yell, "Well, *shit!*" and my mum has to be disappointed in me all over again.

For the first time since I was a very small kid, I have curls. Dark, S-shaped curls have sprung into my hair and coiled the strands upward, so it almost looks like I've had a haircut. My hair used to go past my shoulders, and now it just tickles them.

I go to the mirror and examine myself, and it isn't just the shape of my hair that has changed: it's the color, the quality. The dark brown looks almost black, and it's shiny. Healthy looking.

"Did you get a perm?" Mum asks.

"Are perms back?" Dad adds, patting his own thinning curly hair. "Should I get one?"

"No," I say, too dazed to even come up with a lie. "No, I didn't get a perm."

Mum tilts her head. "I suppose your hair has always had a bit of a kink to it."

I go red at the word *kink* and don't say a thing.

Dad has already lost interest and gone back to channel-hopping. "Lots of horror movies on," he says. "That time of year, I suppose. Will you watch with us, Maeve?"

He looks so hopeful. So keen that I will wedge between the two of them and watch a movie with a bowl of popcorn on my lap, and I feel so tender and sore, so strange from the evening's events, that I want it just as badly.

"Yeah, OK."

I sit there, and we watch an old horror film from the eighties, one of those ones about teenagers who get gradually picked off by a masked killer who doesn't seem to have a very good reason for killing anyone except that a girl was once mean to him. The girls always die while having sex. The boys die in locker rooms or in cars, but the girls die on their backs. I sit there, watching the murders and touching my hair, wondering how the whole world got so obsessed with teenage girls and who we let inside us. I wonder if I will die for having sex, too. It's awkward, sitting there with Mum and Dad, feeling sore. I think about Roe and what having sex for the first time means for him. I didn't stick around long enough to find out.

At the end of the movie, I go upstairs and start typing messages to Roe, but I can't seem to find anything that works. It either sounds way too goofy (**how about that for a farewell eh?**) or way too sincere (**I want you to know that I am glad my first time was with someone who loves me and no matter what happens after this, I** . . .).

I've known for a long time that I would lose my virginity to Roe, but I always thought the moment that we did it, we'd be completely aligned. That there would be no doubt about who we were or what we could do. But now the sex feels more like a last-ditch attempt than a joyful celebration.

Nothing works. Nothing feels right. It's hard to say whether I regret it or not. I can't think of anything to text him so I wait until he texts me. I think: *As soon as he texts me, I'll start getting ready for bed. As soon as I get a sign that Roe still understands, even in a small way, I'll brush my teeth.*

And that's how I fall asleep: still in my clothes and holding my phone.

In a dream, a green light unfurls at the center of my chest and there's a sense of interior sunshine, of warmth from a new source.

Maybe it's wrong to call it a dream. It doesn't feel like one. It feels like a trance, a sensation of being both awake and asleep. A shallow kind of unconsciousness, like the half sleep of napping in a car.

I'm at the tennis courts this time. Rare enough for me to dream anywhere other than the river, but there you go. I'm not so much a person but a strand of green light, lined with gold, and my light stretches and covers the tennis courts as if I am giving the ground a hug. Under the rubber are small flowers, like buttercups, but black in the center instead of pure yellow at their heart. The flowers are trying to push up, arching their necks toward the green light, but the rubbery tennis court won't let them.

And then I'm deep in the earth, plunged in something damp and wild, and the earth smells good until it doesn't. Until a sour smell touches my nose, my ball of green light that is a nose, and I am under the earth. I have something like an epiphany then. Or not quite that. It's a realization, but it's the kind of realization that you have and then immediately think, *Oh, but I knew that all along. I knew that always.*

That in the earth there is soil and seeds and insects, but under that, there is something else. There is magic. Just as the clouds supposedly contain both vapor and heaven, the earth contains both the soil and the Well. The Well is no longer just an abstract construct now. It is a trickling line of silver water, and it is everywhere, reflecting rainbow light. It's something I'm part of, and something that is part of me.

And it's rotting.

The sour smell pinches at me, and the big green light starts to shrink, like the heat reducing on a gas stove. I realize that the trickle of silver is supposed to be a great, gushing river, but it's being starved. The yellow flowers start to give up on sunlight and die. The smell becomes too much. Like dried blood, like old bread, like boiling cabbage, like bad water.

And then I'm a person again, not green light after all. And the dried blood and old bread and boiling cabbage and bad water are all inside of me, and I'm on my knees and retching, trying to get the poison out.

I wake up with my mother holding my face.

"Maeve! Wake up, old beast," she says, her eyes wild.

My shoulders are convulsing, and every sound I make is like the strangled scream of a cornered animal.

"Maeve, you're still asleep." She shakes my shoulder. "Maeve, wake up *properly*."

"I'm awake," I breathe, and realize that I am still in my clothes. Still, in fact, in my jacket. My entire body is clammy with sweat, the underwire of my bra wedged into my bones, digging at the skin. My mouth is dry, my throat raw from trying to vomit in the dream. My crotch still pangs like a new bruise.

"Baby, you were screaming," she says. "What was happening?"

"Drink," I say, now shivering. "Water."

Mum pushes something to my mouth and I drink it down thirstily.

It's only as I'm swallowing down the third gulp of liquid that I notice the clean, fresh lavender smell filling up the room. I look down and see my poor, frightened mother holding the top of the tea thermos to my face.

I scream, bashing it out of her hands, letting the liquid soak through the rug.

"Maeve!" She jumps up, confused and horrified. "What are you doing?"

"I can't drink that!" I shriek again and again. "I can't drink that!"

I start to hyperventilate, my body stricken with panic. What does this mean? What have I just accidentally done?

"Oh, my god." She gets up, inspecting the tea flask. "Is this . . . Maeve, what's in this? Do you have to go to the hospital? You had it next to your bed, so I thought it was . . . tea . . ."

She sniffs the air, and in the half darkness I see her face sour.

"Maeve . . . is this gin?"

Even through my panic, I can tell why she thinks it's gin. In the hours the lavender and sugar water have been inside the tea flask, some kind of magic has already started to work. There's a sting in the air, something faintly like rubbing alcohol, and mixed with the floral, sweet fragrance it smells like fancy gin.

"Yes," I say, trying to calm down. "It's gin. Uh . . . sorry."

"I can't believe this." She starts to shake her head, her anger growing steadily. "Maeve, what has happened to you?"

Oh, god. I don't have time for this. I may just have swallowed half a binding spell. I need Nuala. I need Manon. I need to know what this means.

"I . . . I don't know."

"You used to be such a great girl," she says, her voice mixed with pity and fury. "And now I feel like I have no idea who's in my house. Ever since that business back in February, you've gone so . . . secretive, so shifty. You don't ever want to talk to us. You don't even talk to Jo anymore. Pat says he never hears from you. And now you're drinking *gin*? In your *room*?"

I scoop up the tea flask from the floor, empty now, except for the hundred-dollar bills stuck to the inside. I screw the cap on.

"Maeve, I've had four teenagers come through this house before you. There's nothing you could say that would surprise me. Really. But lately, I'm going through all the usual things in my head and I still can't explain what's going on. I'm thinking . . . it's not some kind of eating disorder. I don't think she's pregnant. Even her schoolwork is improving, albeit slightly. So what *is* it? Please, Maeve. Please."

How can I talk to her? How can I possibly begin to explain everything I've been through, and everything I'm afraid of?

"Mum . . ." I begin gently, groping at the air for something that is at least a little true. "I just . . . it's hard, y'know? I just feel like Roe and I are drifting apart, and Fiona's got all these big dreams, and . . . I don't know. I don't really know what there is left for me. I just want things to be good, like they were in the summer."

"That's when you were happy?" she says, raising her eyebrows. "The summer?"

She fingers the curls of my hair, trying to puzzle this out.

"Only you seemed so sad during the summer," she says thoughtfully. "But what would I know, I suppose."

"What should I do, Mum?" And it's only when I say it that I realize I want an answer. "Like . . . what is there *for* me?"

"Oh, darling," she says, putting her arms around me, rocking me like I'm a toddler. "There's so much you can do. You've got everything ahead of you. You don't need to decide at sixteen. You can take as much time as you want. I was in my late *thirties* before I found something that suited me, and that was after I had raised four children. Don't mind all this Leaving Cert stuff."

"But Fiona and Roe . . ."

"Fiona and Roe have chosen extremely difficult professions that will take them years and years to break into, love. Even *if* they're successful at them."

"He's already getting successful," I say grimly. "And it's so hard to be happy for him because I feel like . . . like he's leaving me behind. He's forgotten."

"I'm sure he hasn't forgotten. It's just, your relationship isn't his first priority right now."

"He has forgotten, though, Mum," I say desperately. "Soon he'll forget I exist."

I'm almost thankful that it comes out sounding like teenage melodrama, rather than an actual, literal concern. It relaxes my mum. Puts her firmly back in a world of adolescent problems that she understands.

"Darling, there's no good way to say this, but . . ." She pauses, strokes my hair. "If you and Roe are meant to be together, you'll be together. You'll make it work. But if you're not, that's OK, too. Almost no one ends up marrying their first love. I didn't."

The thought is so dismal that I fake a yawn and tell her I need to go to sleep. She gets me a glass of water from the kitchen. As I put my head on the pillow, my mouth still tasting of lavender, I convince myself that the power of the spell was entirely localized to Nuala's kitchen and swallowing a few gulps of sugar water won't do a thing.

I keep believing that when I wake up in the morning. I believe it in the shower. I believe it eating breakfast. I believe it when I'm walking to the end of the driveway.

I stop believing it when I see Aaron, curled into a ball, asleep on the road.

27

"HOW. . ." I WHISPER. "HOW DID YOU GET HERE?"

He unfurls himself slowly, his body creaking. He stands up, stooping slightly, one shoulder lifting toward his ear.

"Maeve?" he asks, equally as mystified. "Is it *actually* you?"

"What do you mean?"

"They made you look like other people," he says, his face full of terror. "And they made other people look like you."

The fear in his face puts me on edge. That was what was happening at the hotel? He really *did* think I was called Mary-Beth?

In the early morning sunlight I can see just how disheveled Aaron has become. His clothes are faded and gray, his skin pallid. His blond hair, usually kept short and tidy, has grown out to look fuzzy and unkempt. His face is covered in rusty stubble, with crops of acne and ingrown hairs festering underneath it.

"You look different," he says. His right eye, which I had noticed a brief squint in before, is trembling and weeping slightly, one eyelid puffy. "Your hair. No, your face, too. Something changed. What changed?"

"I'm not the one who looks different," I counter. "*You* look like crap. What's going on? What are you doing here? And what are you *talking* about?"

Aaron looks as though he's finally noticed his surroundings. He turns around, looking at the sky, the tops of houses, scrutinizing trees. "Where am I?"

"You're outside my house."

"Why?"

The logic of the situation seems clear, if slightly awkward. I drank the binding spell, and instead of binding Aaron from doing harm, I have bound him to me.

I'm not going to tell *him* that, though.

He's rubbing his eyes. He looks like a dirty toddler. He's still disoriented, confused by where he is. Now is not the time for a show-down, I realize. Now is the time for answers.

Behind me, I can hear the slam of my dad's car door, and I know that he's about to reverse out of the driveway. He *cannot* see me talking to Aaron.

"Come on," I say. "Let's go."

We walk, in bemused silence, down to the river.

"We went to your house," I say at last. "You left."

"My house? What house?" he asks confusedly. "Oh, the apartment. That was never mine. It was theirs. *Is* theirs."

"And you're not with them anymore?"

The sun bounces off the water, and a quad of ducks glide past us. You can already tell it's going to be a beautiful day. The kind of day that people talk about when they talk about autumn being their favorite season.

Aaron, bizarrely, pulls out a battered-looking box of cigarettes and starts smoking. Smoking and not answering my questions.

"I said, you're not with them anymore? The Children?"

"No. I'm not. Is there anywhere we can get coffee?"

"Why aren't you with them? What happened?"

He doesn't answer.

"Come on," I bark. "I'm not doing this. I'm not doing the moody-boy thing. You're not my friend. Either tell me what I want to know or piss off."

Nothing.

"There's coffee at the other side of the park," I grumble, and we march across the damp grass to a wooden coffee kiosk with two picnic tables outside.

The whole time, I wonder what I'm doing, and why I'm doing this. I hate everything about this man, about what he does and what he stands for. And yet here we are, stirring sugar into our coffees.

"Why did you leave them?" I ask. "When?"

"What date is it today?"

"October thirty-first," I reply, thinking: *As a witch, I should probably have something planned for Halloween.*

"A month ago."

"Why?"

"Because I found out what happens after three." He gives me a grim, tired smile.

"The draining."

"Yes."

"The Well."

"Yes. I see you've figured it all out."

"We're a clever bunch."

"Well, bully for you."

"So, what, you found out they were using me as a magic funnel and you thought, whoa, no, too far, torment the gays, but not this?"

A pause while we blow and sip on our coffees.

"Why the change of heart?" I press. "Why did you suddenly care about what they were doing to us? To Kilbeg?"

260

"Because it has to be a *choice*. You can't force people into believing things. You can't take away . . . take away their ability to reason."

"What would have happened if I had agreed to join, then?"

He shrugs. "They would have given you anything you wanted. And then they would have turned you into me."

Aaron looks so filled with misery at this idea, of anyone being like him, that I am convinced this is a trap again. No one can turn around their entire personality like this.

"I started . . ." He hesitates. "Asking questions. Questions that, to them, sounded suspiciously like I was arguing on your behalf. Like I wanted to save you."

"So they threw you out?"

"No. They did stuff first. They were suspicious of me, so they took away some of my power, tricked me with glamours, made me believe I was talking to you. They thought I was handling the job badly. And the less they trusted me, the less I trusted them."

"And then you left?"

"And then I left."

"So you left because they demoted you."

"I left because I found out the truth."

"And what's that?"

"That they don't give a damn about God or salvation. It's just power they want." He looks at his hands. "And they have so much of it.

"That's why I was so surprised this morning," he continues. "When you could see me. They . . . they suspected that I was too interested in you, too protective or something. That's why they wouldn't let me see you. So I sent the cards, spirited them to you. I needed something that you would understand but they wouldn't."

"The cards?"

"The Five of Pentacles. The Chariot."

"That was you?" I put my head in my hands, trying to make sense of this. "The Five of Pentacles," I repeat.

"Suffering outside the church walls. Locked out."

I nod. It's weird how I had the same interpretation, but I made it about me and Roe.

"And the Chariot?" I continue.

"I knew that they would try something on the bus. They always talked about how you all got the bus."

I can't believe this. I shudder at the idea of being spoken about, schemed against, our movements followed and exploited.

"Aaron, why were you *warning* me? You hate me."

"No, I don't." He shakes his head. "You always thought that. I never did. John 12:40."

"What?" I say.

"What?" he counters.

"What is John 12:40?"

"He has blinded their eyes and hardened their hearts, so they can neither see with their eyes, nor understand with their hearts, nor turn—and I would heal them."

"Why are you quoting Bible verse at me?"

"I don't know. Habit."

"It was never a habit before."

"It was, long before I met you. I just learned to cover it when I was . . . when I was powerful."

"Is this a trick?"

I so badly want this to be a trick. I don't want a pitiable Aaron. I don't want any kind of Aaron at all, but I especially don't want one I have to feel sorry for.

"What do you mean?"

262

"Are you trying to trap me by making me feel sorry for you?"

He laughs then, and sips at his coffee. "I'm flattered to be credited with that much genius."

Finally, a glimmer of the old him. The him I can comfortably despise instead of being confused by.

"Please tell me," I say slowly. "Please tell me what's going on. And try . . . try not to quote any Bible verse."

"Sorry." He smiles weakly. "It's the old Evangelical coming out in me."

"What does that mean?"

"I grew up Evangelical. Did you know that about me?"

"I don't think I understand what Evangelical means, exactly."

"Oh." He starts stirring the wooden stick in his cup, creating a vortex of coffee. "Well, it's like Protestants, but very strict Protestants. Very literal. Evangelicals tend to read the Bible a lot and take it at face value, but Catholics sort of let the priest interpret it for them. But the *main* difference is that Evangelicals are called to God. You're baptized when you get the call. I got the call *early*."

"That doesn't surprise me."

"No, it didn't surprise anyone else, either." He is talking quite casually now, as if we are old friends. "My uncle was the pastor of this megachurch out in Yuba City, and we would head out there every week, two hours in the car, to worship. I was only five and I walked up to the stage, and everyone was so proud of me, and I was baptized. And for years after that, I'm like . . . did I actually get the call from God, or was I just, y'know . . . five?"

"It sounded like you were probably just being five. But I don't know, I wasn't there."

I look at my phone. It's just gone nine o'clock.

"I was like, oh, wow, my call to God was completely fake, I made it up, everyone thinks I'm this child wunderkind and I'm just a liar."

He starts to laugh, as if this is an extremely charming story about believing in the tooth fairy.

"So I start cramming hard on being a good Christian, to keep up the lie, y'know? And, like, this whole narrative of me being this good Christly child keeps growing and growing, and now it feels like it's getting out of hand."

"You sound like . . ." I keep trying to seem diplomatic, to pretend as if this isn't the same Aaron that has helped make my life miserable. "Like you've had a lot of time to think about this."

"Oh-ho." He takes another sip. "Years. Years of therapy."

"*You* went to therapy?"

"I mean, I went to *our* version of therapy," he says. "I don't know if any of them were, you know, licensed therapists. But my parents didn't want to send me to a modern place where they would tell me that I was paranoid for following scripture."

"Why did they send you to therapy?"

"Oh, you know. Hell."

"Hell?"

"I saw Hell. All the time. Everywhere."

"What do you mean by that?"

"I don't know if I can be more clear." He pauses and coughs. "The land of gloom and utter darkness, of deepest night, of utter darkness and disorder, where even the light is like darkness. Job, chapter ten."

We are both silent for a moment.

"And when you say you saw Hell . . ."

"Suffering, fire, people screaming. People all crooked and small, like . . . like little maggot versions of themselves. I was fourteen, and it was when I started realizing that I was, you know. Like you. Like us."

"A sensitive?"

"Yeah."

"How did you find out?"

"Um . . . metal? Metal went weird? Did you get that? Did that happen to you? I would drop my fork, like, five times in every meal. And every time it would fall on the floor, it would get louder. Like a church bell. My dad would get so mad. He knew. All his belt buckles started veering away from me, and he knew that there was something wrong with me."

I am quiet for a moment.

"No, I didn't have the thing with the metal."

He looks disappointed.

"Do you see . . ." I can't believe I'm about to ask this. "The lights?"

"What do you mean?"

"I can look inside people. Or, I usually can. In their heads, I mean. I see a colored light, like a comet's tail, and I follow the light until I'm in their brain, looking out."

He looks down suddenly, breaking his fixed concentration on my face. Aaron starts to examine his nail beds. "No," he replies quietly. "That sounds very beautiful."

"What do you see?"

He looks at me, and for some reason I know exactly what he is going to say. And so, we say it together.

"Holes."

His eyes widen in shock. "How did you know?"

"It's the first thing I thought, when we met at that horrible apartment. You could see the holes in people."

He nods. A breeze rustles through the trees, and the sharp yelp of winter passes through me. And him. The wind whistles through

Aaron, carrying his smell on the air. A stale, sickly, yellow smell, of old sweat, and damp, and clothes that have been slept in for too long. I remember the phone bill, the overdraft.

"Where do you live?" I ask suddenly. "Where do you sleep?"

"Uh . . . well. Usually in a hostel. But last night, I just . . . I just walked and walked and walked until I fell down outside your house. Which I'm struggling to understand."

I am still uncomfortable with the truth and the prospect of telling him, *Sorry, dude, I drank your essence.*

"Who is Matthew Madison?" I ask.

He takes the name like a stab to the chest.

"I saw the letter," I continue. "The letter with the money."

"Matthew Madison," he says slowly, "was my Housekeeper victim."

28

WHETHER IT'S THE POWER OF MATTHEW
Madison's name or just the Irish weather, at that moment the sun
goes behind the clouds and a heavy wind starts to pick up. Five seconds later, it's hailing hard. We abandon our picnic table and hide
under the flat corrugated roof of the coffee place, the hail loud and
pelting.

We stand there awkwardly, unable to hear our own voices over
the sound of frozen rock on tin. Standing so close to him, I can smell
the damp, yellow smell even more strongly. The smell of filth and decay.

I look at my watch. My parents have both left for work by now.

"I'm not trying to be . . ." But I don't even bother trying to couch
my words. "Dude, you stink. Let's go back, you can shower, and we
can . . . I don't know. Talk about Matthew."

He looks alarmed. "You want *me* in your *house*?"

"I don't want you there, no. But you probably need to be clean
and we need to talk about the Housekeeper."

I realize this is trusting. Too trusting. Absurdly trusting. But
when someone has been pursued by the same revenge demon that
you have, it briefly transcends your personal history.

We run most of the way back, the hail not letting up for a second. I wonder if this is a coincidence or yet another flex from the

Children of Brigid; can they see us, even now? Is their magic that powerful that they can change the weather on a whim?

I look sidelong at Aaron, wondering if I can really let him into my house, after everything. After the gig last year, after everything with Jo, after the hauntings and the stalkings and the threats on my life. *This is going to be so interesting, if you live.*

Aaron is my enemy. But the Children of Brigid are, too, even more so. And if he hates them now, too, does that mean that my enemy's enemy is my friend? Can I afford *not* to know what Aaron has to say?

I unlock the door, and I let him in. The first rule of witchcraft, broken: *never invite a demon into your home.*

Mum and Dad are both gone, thank god. The dog walker will be here at noon to take Tutu for a big jaunt around the river. He shuffles out of his bed in the kitchen, tail wagging in gentle surprise, happy to have someone home again. For some reason, I wait to see how he reacts to Aaron. I tell myself that if the dog yelps and growls, I will use that as a sign that I should throw Aaron out. But he doesn't. Tutu just sniffs at him and jumps up to say hello. The same as he treats anyone else.

I shake my head, scolding myself. Why am I giving my dog's judgment more weight than my own?

Instinctively, I bring Aaron to the attic bathroom that only I really use. I don't want him near my parents' things: my mum's makeup, my dad's vitamin supplements. I don't want him to know anything about them. I keep behind him when we're in the house, not wanting to have my back to him at any point. He doesn't comment on the house. Most people comment on the house. It's big and old and my parents have done a lot to it over the years. Aaron doesn't. He keeps silent.

As I let him into the attic bathroom, he inhales sharply, like he's been winded.

My eyes dart to him, wondering what he's going to pull next.

"What?" I ask, slightly panicked. "What's wrong?"

"You've hot-spotted this place, haven't you?"

"Uh . . . like . . . Wi-Fi?"

He walks over to the tub. "You've done magic in here."

"Yes. Spells. Quite a few of them." It comes out like a brag. "Not all of them worked."

"It's in the walls now," he says, sucking his teeth. He sounds a bit like a plumber who is here to tell me that there's a dead rat in my drain. "In the tiles. That's here forever now. Good luck to the next people who live in this house. Let's hope they have a witch in the family."

"How do you know this? How can you tell?"

"They taught me."

"Who?"

"*Them*."

"The Children?"

He gives a strange kind of yes, a sort of weary finger gun with a badly administered wink.

"I don't get it. Are they religious *and* magic?"

He leans his weight on the edge of the tub and looks mournfully at his hands.

"They're anything that means power. They don't even really care about God or scripture, really. They just use it because it's convenient. The Church has a good infrastructure to control people. Lots of buildings, lots of community groups. And so many people have left the Catholic Church, priests leaving the seminary and so on, that the last few years have really opened up an opportunity for them."

He is much taller than me usually, but the way he's leaning on the bathtub means that we're at eye level. I've never had an interaction with him that went on this long before. It's starting to make me itch.

"There are towels in that cupboard," I say. "Knock yourself out. I'll be downstairs."

I leave.

I sit at the kitchen table, Tutu's head in my lap, and I wait. I wait and I wonder what I'm doing, far too aware of the danger of talking to Aaron. Not just on a literal, physical level. But emotionally, too: already I can feel my hatred eroding into a kind of pity, edged with disgust, edged with . . . well, fascination.

Aaron finally emerges from the bathroom and appears in the kitchen looking slightly less deranged than he did twenty minutes ago. The old yellow smell has gone and replacing it is the faint odor of . . . well, me. He's used my shampoo, my body wash, and, I think, even my moisturizer. Well, what did I expect?

"Do you want tea?"

"Please."

"Milk, sugar . . . ?"

"Milk, no sugar, thank you."

This is too bizarre.

"So," I say when both teas are ready. "You're going to tell me about the Housekeeper. And . . . everything else."

"It's hard to know where to start," he says meekly. "Some of it has gone scrambled."

"I don't know. Start where it's easiest."

So he goes back to the beginning. He tells me about California, and the peach orchards, and the smell of the peaches when they fell to the ground and rotted. "Rats would get into the orchards. Sometimes we would go in and shoot them with our BB guns."

"We?"

"My brothers. Samuel, Noah, and Jesse. I'm the second oldest. After Samuel."

The problem with Hell started when he was twelve, when "I found this verse in Revelations," he says, "where Jesus says, 'So then because thou art lukewarm, and neither cold nor hot, I will spew thee out of my mouth.' And, I don't know. It probably sounds funny to you. But the word *lukewarm* made me so scared because I knew that I was only keeping up this God thing because of my parents and, really, for my own vanity because I was supposed to be this holy kid, that was my *thing*, and when I read that quote, all I could think of was . . . oh, it's me. God knows I'm faking. God's going to spit me out of his mouth and send me to Hell. And that's when it started. I couldn't stop seeing Hell everywhere. In everything."

"What did your parents say?" I ask, still astounded by the image of being spit out of God's mouth.

"They were so . . . embarrassed. I think it was cute when I was a little kid quoting verse, but having this hysterical teenager always ranting about sin was just . . . too much. And then when my sensitivity came along, I figured I was being punished. I thought that was God saying, 'OK, kid, the jig is up. You were right all along. You are made wrong.'"

"It sounds like you were . . ." What I want to say is, *It sounds like you were mentally ill and badly needed help*, but I don't finish the sentence. Because that's the kind of thing you say to someone you're on the same side as. Someone you have compassion for. A memory from Roe's gig flashes before me: the kid in the makeup, who couldn't have been much older than twelve, getting soaked by a Children of Brigid member while Aaron impassively looked on. *That* kid needed compassion. They needed help.

But Aaron, whether through intuition or sensitivity, just nods, as if he has heard me. "I know," he says. "I know. So they send me away."

"Twin Pines," I answer automatically.

"Yes—how . . . ?" But then he remembers. "You read my letter."

"Yes."

"Well. Yeah. I was fifteen when I first went."

"First?"

"Yeah, and then again at the end of that year, and then again at sixteen and seventeen. That's when I met Matthew, and Alexander, and Ria. We always seemed to be in and out at the same time, so we were the crew. The gang."

"Riri . . . Ria. She was in for sex," he recounts, a tinge of laughter in his voice. "Couldn't stop. Wouldn't stop. Alex and Matt were in for ungodly desires."

My eyes flit to his at this term. "They were gay," he clarifies. "And I was in for being crazy. Or, I guess, obsessive-compulsive disorder."

I'm so confused by this. Everyone's heard of OCD, of course. It's one of those mental illnesses you see a lot on TV, usually accompanied by a lot of cleaning.

"I don't clean," he says sharply. "The obsession was intrusive thoughts about Hell, and the compulsion was, like, trying to do these wildly inappropriate things from the Old Testament to make them go away. Self-flagellation and all that."

It suddenly occurs to me that this might all be a trap. An elegant story to get me to feel sorry for Aaron, using exactly the kind of characters that I would feel empathy for. Self-flagellation. Isn't that just a fancy word for self-harm? Which, in essence, is what my best friend is going through? I feel myself straining against the story, turning it upside down, looking for the wires.

"You think I'm making it up," he says grimly. "You think I was just born awful and I try to convert gay kids for a hobby. You don't think there's anyone in my life who I loved, who I cared about, who mattered to me like your friends matter to you."

His voice starts to strain, like he is trying to fight a cry. He stops for a second, wrestles his sadness into anger. To him, a more acceptable emotion. "Well, I did," he snaps. "We loved one another and we were going to get out. Together."

There's a change in the room, a feeling of his words being sieved through air, of the atmosphere becoming thicker and filled with struggle.

"They were going to move Matthew," he says coldly. "Twin Pines was bad, but it was like . . . it was like maximum-security rehab. But his parents wanted to send him to this place, this conversion therapy place, where they . . . Anyway, he didn't want to go."

"So, the Housekeeper."

"So," he repeats, "the Housekeeper. I don't remember how we got the cards. But I could read them. I don't know why, but I could read them. I summoned her."

"Did it work?"

"In a way. Everyone knew I was the only one with real magic, so Matthew convinced me to do it. To summon her. He read about it somehow. I don't know. I was the only one who saw her. In person, I mean. They all saw the card, but she started coming to me. Visiting me. Looking at me. *She* was what I saw instead of Hell. And anyway . . . five nights later, there was a fire. That was her. She made it so that we could get out, and we did. All together. We got our money together and we got on a bus. We were going to head to San Francisco. Riri had an uncle there who she thought would put us up."

"And then what?"

"I fell asleep next to Matthew on that bus just as we left Sacramento. When I woke up, we were pulling into San Francisco, and he was dead."

Even though I knew this was coming—that this was, in essence, the point of the story—I'm still shocked. People don't die sitting up in a bus seat. They just don't. Not when the Housekeeper is involved. She's more blood and water, pomp and ceremony. Not a young man quietly fading as his friend sleeps next to him.

"After that . . . everything was wrong. Stayed wrong. We took Matthew home to his parents. They called us Satanists. And y'know . . . they weren't wrong. We had literally . . . we had worshipped the occult, we had done the number-one thing that Christian kids aren't supposed to do. And all I could think was . . . is Matthew in Hell now? Was he damned now, forever?"

"What about the others?"

"Riri disappeared. I tried to get in touch with her a few years ago. I think she heard that I was working for, uh, 'the enemy' and didn't want to hear from me. Alex got married at nineteen." Aaron bites at his thumbnail. "To a woman.

"My parents didn't want anything to do with me, so I thought the best idea was to, y'know, devote my life to God and make sure nothing like that ever happened again. And that's when I found the Children of Brigid. Or, I guess, when they found me."

"They found you?"

"They have people whose job it is just to find people like us, Maeve. Sensitives or people who have magic for whatever reason. They told me that I wasn't damned just because I was born this way. With power, I mean. They said there was a way of channeling my power so that I could serve God. And two months later, I was on a plane to Europe."

274

"When *was* this?"

"I was eighteen, so . . . three years ago?"

There's a pause as I consider all of this, the enormity of both Aaron's story and the Children of Brigid operation. The order, the structure, the scale. The idea that someone like Aaron could quickly be scooped up in the wake of a tragedy.

"The irony of all this," he says softly, "is that I was supposed to be the person who brought *you* in."

"If they need a sensitive to draw up the Well, why didn't they just use you?"

"It doesn't work that way. You have to drain through the sensitive that is connected to the Kilbeg Well. I'm not connected."

"And what about your Well? The one in California?"

He looks glumly at the ground.

"It was drained. They drained it through me. That's why they recruited me. Then they moved me on. That's what they'll do to you, too, if they can. Send you somewhere. Cut you off from your source so you can't get too powerful for them again."

Tutu's head goes up, and he looks at me with interest. A head tilt. A *You OK, hun?* expression. It's too much information, too much to calculate. I feel like the walls of my brain are starting to cave in, and I start rubbing at my skull, as if trying to prevent it.

"I was up north when I got the call about Kilbeg. They had noticed an energy shift, they wanted me to go down and figure out what was happening. It was either you or Rory." He stops, corrects himself. "Roe. I couldn't figure it out. *Someone* had *something* and both of you were so . . . I don't know. You were exactly how we used to be, back in Twin Pines. Fiona, too. That's when I started seeing the Housekeeper again. And then I heard about Lily, and it all made sense."

"This is going to be so interesting," I say, recalling his words. "If you live."

"Well, it *was* interesting," he says with genuine astonishment in his voice. "It was! And then Lily *comes back*, and the four of you are . . . the four of you . . ."

He starts to stutter, stumble, repeat.

"Th-the f-f-f-our . . . of you arr-eh . . . *alive*."

He spits out the *alive* like it's a pit in the middle of a cherry. And for the first time, I really see him.

No, that's not right. I've been seeing him this whole time, sitting here with my tea going cold. A more correct assertion would be that I see myself *in* him. I understand how it must be when your friends die or desert you, to blame yourself, to find comfort in something stronger and larger than you. Something that doesn't *seem* like a cult because you are promoted to middle management as soon as you join.

"We almost weren't," I say by way of comfort. "It was a fluke, really, that we're alive."

"Th-they always told me," he says, gulping back tears, "that Matthew died because . . . because we used our magic for evil. That by summoning the Housekeeper, we were all . . . cavorting. With Satan. But that I could repent by using my magic for good. That I could be saved. From . . . from . . ."

"From Hell?"

And it's the word that breaks him. The word *Hell*, which we have said dozens of times over the course of this long conversation, severs a link between emotion and propriety. Aaron Michael Branum folds in on himself and starts to heave quietly, his shoulders rising and falling, his cries the sound of air sucked in too sharply.

"But then all of you . . . you all *lived*," he spits out finally. "You're *fine*? You're *thriving*?"

276

I don't know what to do. I know what I *would* do, normally. If this were anyone else, even some random girl in the year below me, I would put my arm around her shoulders and try to comfort her, or ask her if I can find someone who can. But this isn't just any old person. This is someone dangerous, and powerful, and, despite his apparent epiphany that he's a dickhead, *still* a dickhead.

"If you were supposed to bring me in," I say instead, "you were very bad at it."

The shuddering, heaving sobs slow down and then stop. He starts to laugh. Not the sniggers or dry laughs I've heard before. But a real, human, grateful laugh.

"Yeah," he agrees, wiping his face with the heel of his hand. "Really bad."

He looks at me semi-apologetically. "When I was . . . they gave me a lot of extra power, you know. They do that. Gift it to people they like, take it away from people who have upset them. With their power fueling my gift, I could make anyone do anything. By the time you came along, I was . . . I was so arrogant I didn't think I'd really have to try."

"And now all that is gone?" I ask. "They took it away, because you upset them?"

"They store power in people, creatures, and things. But people most of all. People they trust. It's like a bank that is always moving its money around, making it grow. It's a reward system for their followers, as well as being a kind of . . . I don't know. Offshore account."

"*You* were one of their offshore accounts?"

"Yeah, for a while. Then they took it away." He pauses. "And I'm learning that without it, I'm just . . . I'm just some asshole."

"Correct. You are. You've done things," I say, wanting to spit the words. "You've done horrible things. You've made already vulnerable people *even more* vulnerable. You've made the world a worse place for people, queer people especially. You've gone on television, Aaron. You've gone on the radio to say that birth control is bad for women. You've promoted celibacy and misogyny and homophobia."

I'm channeling my best Fiona now. I'm pretending she's here and this is her talking.

"I know," he says. "I know, but you have to understand, I thought, I thought I was helping. I thought I was saving pe—"

I stand up and start clearing away the cups aggressively, dunking them in the sink with a clatter.

"It doesn't matter," I snap. "It's not enough. Put your coat on. We're going to Nuala's."

"Why?"

For the first time in a long time, I feel powerful again. I feel like fire could shoot out of my eyes if I willed it to.

"You're going to help us stop this."

29

WHEN WE GET TO DIVINATION, I ALREADY have two texts from Fiona and Lily, asking where I am. How on earth do I answer that question?

I'm with that guy we hate.

The shop is empty, and Nuala is doing a stock check, scratching her hairline with a pen as she consults her list. She looks up when the bell over the door sounds, and her warm smile at seeing me quickly dissolves into confusion when she sees who I'm with.

"He's here to help us," I say quickly.

Aaron just nods in confirmation.

"He's going to tell us everything he knows about the Children of Brigid," I go on. "He's told me a lot already. We're going to stop the Well drain. We're going to get rid of them."

Aaron shrugs, as if he agrees with this in theory but doubts it in practice.

Nuala clocks his expression right away.

"*Are* you, Aaron?"

"I . . . I'll do my best."

I cough loudly, aggressively.

"I'll do better than that," he clarifies.

Nuala's eyes slide from me to him, adding something up.

"Maeve," she says. "Where is the flask?"

"I have it in my bag," I reply hesitantly. "I, uh . . . I drank it. By mistake."

Nuala puts her head in her hands.

"What are you talking about?" Aaron asks tentatively.

"Maeve, I can't take anything he says seriously if you *drank* the bind."

"Why?"

"Because he's obsessed with you. It will wear off. You can't trust him like this. You can't trust him regardless, but you especially can't trust him now."

I had not considered this. I thought Aaron was bound to me physically. I hadn't considered at all whether he was emotionally, too.

Aaron coughs. "Excuse me," he says, louder this time. "What are you talking about?"

I feel better, somehow, about telling him this now that we're in front of Nuala.

"We put a bind on you yesterday, and, uh . . . I accidentally drank it. That's why you woke up outside my house. You're . . . bound to me for a bit, I think."

Aaron looks horrified. "I need to go," he says.

"Where?"

"Anywhere," he snaps. Aaron storms out, and we watch him through the window, attempting to cross the street. He's halfway over the pedestrian crossing when his neck snaps back, like a dog being pulled on a leash. We watch silently as he flails at the air, the invisible string buckling his shoulders together, the leash becoming an invisible lasso. The struggle continues, pathetically, for a full minute, until he is back on our side of the road again, looking terrified and embarrassed at once. He is, I can tell, too mortified to come back in the shop or even look through the glass at our pitying expressions.

"Maeve," Nuala says softly. "Has anything else changed in the last twenty-four hours?"

I hesitate. "What do you mean?"

She takes a length of my hair in her hands. "This, I mean."

I blush. "Does this happen, then? When you . . ."

Nuala looks somewhere between amused and concerned. She can't decide which.

"With witches, sometimes, yes."

"Why?"

She shrugs and says something so utterly surprising that I have to immediately make her repeat it. I have to make sure I've heard it correctly.

"Magic loves sex," she says.

"What? Why?"

"Because it's natural. Because it's the opposite of control. Because it drives men crazy. Because it gives women an income. Because everything that hates magic also hates sex."

"Wow."

"It was . . ." she begins, then casts her eyes outside. "It *was* Roe, wasn't it?"

"What?" I ask, dumbfounded. Then I realize who she's looking at. "You think that . . . ? With him?!"

She looks tensely from me to the window. "Well, you turn up in the morning with a boy, I don't know!"

It has barely been twelve hours since I lost my virginity to Roe, but for the first time, the fact that I did doesn't feel weighty or serious. It's actually extremely funny. Funny that I'm having the best hair day of my life. Funny that you can let people into your body. Funny that people get so obsessed with it. And funny, above all, that I am talking to my forty-five-year-old friend about it. And despite everything, we start to laugh.

Aaron walks back into the shop, seemingly ready to simmer down from his tantrum, ready for everyone to focus on him again, and Nuala and I are quaking and shaking with laughter. I'm holding on to her shoulder, realizing that the more I laugh, the more my muscles tense and the more I can still feel that slightly bruised feeling between my legs.

I had sex yesterday! I want to sing. *I had sex yesterday and I feel fine about it!*

"What are you two laughing about?" he says, the implication being: *I'm experiencing some trauma, you know.*

I look at Aaron's empty face and realize that, despite him being older than me, no one has ever loved him before. Not the way Roe loves me, or even the way Nuala and Fiona and Lily love me. I feel a magnitude of love for the people in my life so powerful that the only feeling I can summon for Aaron is the sense that he is very, very small. Wilted, like an undernourished plant.

Aaron watches us, confused, and then Nuala turns back to him. She scans him and seems to realize that even if he cannot be trusted, he is still powerless enough to not be feared.

"You didn't have him in your *house*, did you?" she asks finally.

"Uh . . ."

"I'm sorry," he interrupts. "Nuala, is it? We've not, uh, met, officially."

Nuala eyes him suspiciously, and Aaron doesn't seem to have the strength for the charm offensive. Is this really the same guy who made a room full of people confess their deepest secrets to him? The guy who had everyone hanging on his every word?

"I quit the Children," he says. "That's one thing. What they're doing isn't . . . it isn't *Christian*. It has nothing to do with Christian values. It's just coercion and greed and them trying to swallow up as much of the map as they can. Once they drain everything out of Kilbeg, they'll just leave, and all their new followers will be left completely radicalized. It will just run on and on."

"But why bother with the radicalization to begin with?" I ask. It's a part of the puzzle I've never understood. I can grasp Wells and magical greed. But hate for the sake of hate?

"Look," he answers. "Let's say they want to gain a foothold in Ireland. They know it has Wells, and they want magic, right? But this business is expensive, and it relies on connections. And there are all these Catholic groups that want to see Ireland become this beacon for Christian values again, and they've got money to spend, they've got the right connections in the government, they can help get us in the right rooms. That stuff with your school, Maeve? Two phone calls. Two phone calls is all it took to get the Children a major contract with the Department of Education. They couldn't do that on their own. It's like this spiderweb that goes out and out forever. And the right-wing religious thing is handy because it's distracting. It gets everyone looking at the left hand while they pickpocket with the right."

He pauses and rubs his eyes, exhausted from the burden of his own knowledge.

"As soon as they've got what they want, they move on. They plant the ideas and just let them fester."

"Festering," Nuala says sternly, "that *you* helped contribute to."

He burrows his head in his hands. "I know," he says. "I'm sorry."

Nuala considers this, narrowing her eyes at him.

"I lost someone to the Housekeeper," he says bleakly. "And when

I did, the Children were there. They told me that my friends and I were sinful, and that we had used power in a sinful way, and that the only way to find grace was to save as many people from the same . . . fate, I suppose. You asked me once why I hate gay people, Maeve, and I don't. I didn't, even then. I said *God* does."

I feel rage rising up through my gut. "How can a loving God—"

"But my God was *not* a loving God," he says, exhausted. "He just wasn't. And when people like *me* hear people like *you*, people who think God just . . . *loves* everyone, regardless of what they do, even if it's against the Bible . . . we think you're just naive. That you're purposefully denying the word of God."

"You don't need to tell me what people like you think," Nuala replies bitingly. "Ireland was built on people like you. People were imprisoned all their lives because of that kind of bigotry."

"I'm not saying I don't deserve punishment," Aaron says. "I'm not trying to deny that I got caught up in . . . the power, I guess. But all my life I've been hearing from people like you who want me to change my mind. And now that I have, now that I'm trying to make things *right*, you don't want to hear it."

I look to Aaron and Nuala and notice that they have fallen into a staring competition. There's a feeling of two invisible forces in close, silent combat. This is probably what it looked like last year when Nuala and I briefly occupied each other's thoughts. I've never been on the outside of one of these interactions, always in the middle. They are both utterly still, the stillness of a wild animal meeting a human.

Then, Nuala's muscles relax, and the feeling of struggle evaporates.

"All right, Aaron," she says, sighing. "I suppose we get to work."

And I wonder if I'll ever find out what went on in there. What happened, exactly, between Aaron and Nuala in that moment.

Manon arrives, holding two takeaway coffees from Bridey's, and takes in the scene.

"You drank the bind," she says, her tone annoyed.

"I didn't *mean* to."

Manon closes the door behind her and a gust of sharp, cold air is trapped in the shop. Nuala, Aaron, and I shiver and rearrange our clothes, and for the smallest second, I see Manon watching us all. Not even watching. Scanning. Noting. Observing. The steaming coffee sits in her hands comfortably, the thin, hot paper cups against her palms.

As if picking up the thread left by Aaron and Nuala's psychic conversation, Manon's energy seems to knit us all into a bond. It's hard to explain. Some invisible transference of information seems to happen between Manon and her mother, between Manon and Aaron, and—I think—between Manon and myself.

Our eyes meet briefly, and some part of me—the sensitive part, the part that will never go away, regardless of what Well I happen to be sitting on—realizes that Manon is something else. A witch, but something more than a witch. She's *like* me, but not the same as me. Not the same the way Aaron is the same. She is something more than human. Something extra. I try to dig at the truth, summoning the fragments of magic still left inside me.

What are you, Manon?

She breaks eye contact, and it's gone. Whatever glimmer of the true Manon that I almost witnessed becomes buried under an elegant French woman whom my best friend has a crush on. Good luck, Fiona. Not only is she too old for you, she's also deeply enchanted, a secret and possibly ancient thing. A secret and possibly ancient thing that still resents her mother for leaving her.

"We need all of us together. You, Fiona, Lily, Roe, Aaron. Manny. At my house. This evening."

"Roe is gone," I say. "He left on tour this morning."

"He left you?" Nuala says, disgusted. "In the middle of every-thing? That doesn't sound like Roe. Well, we can figure all of this out tonight. Come to my house later. Right now I need you two to leave."

"To leave? Why?"

"Because it's my busiest day of the year, and I have about seventy-five orders to fill, as well as the usual idiots who will come in here looking for tarot cards for their Halloween decorations."

And just like that, we're on the street again.

"I guess I could go to school," I say helplessly.

Aaron looks very worried. "I don't think you can do that."

"Why not?" I remember, then, what it looked like when Aaron tried to cross the street. I revise my question. "What does it feel like?"

"I don't know. Painful." He shuffles his hands inside his pockets. "I think if you were in a different building, it would be . . ."

"Fine," I snap. "Fine."

"You were the one who *drank*—"

"I know!"

"We could wait in a pub, or a cafe, or something."

The thought of that much time alone with Aaron, having to hear his carefully articulated tragic backstory, is too much. It's not that I don't necessarily believe him. I don't think he would lie about The Housekeeper. But I also know what a politician he is, how good at arranging a story.

"Fine," I tell him. "But I need to get some homework out of my locker. Let's head up there, you can wait while I get it."

I don't really think I could focus on class, anyway. But then I think about someone at school I would like to see, someone who could help me deal with Aaron. "Come on," I tell him. "We'll sneak in and meet with a friend of mine."

286 .

We walk toward school, mostly silent. I think we are both exhausted with talking to each other. I look at my phone, refreshing Small Private Ceremony's Instagram feed. Dee posted a selfie of them on the train this morning, with a simple "On the road!" caption. Roe has his jumper rolled into a pillow and is attempting to sleep.

"Roe is on tour, then," Aaron says.

"Yes."

A pause. "That's cool."

I glare at him, the full force of my hatred coming back again, teeming through me. "Oh, you're a fan now, are you? You don't think he's against God? You're not going to throw anything?"

"I never threw anything."

We get to school. The late-morning classes are in session, and the building is still. A blinding beam of white sunshine comes out from behind the clouds, not warm but bright, and small rocks of hailstone begin to melt beneath our feet.

The street gate leading down to the sixth-year terrace is padlocked, so we have to jump over it. I feel a pang of sadness for Roe, who would have sprung the lock open in a second. He'll be in Dublin now, getting ready for the show, thinking . . . thinking what? Thinking that his teenage girlfriend is mentally deranged, and she'll snap out of it with time? Does any part of him still believe in what happened to us?

The door downstairs leading into the canteen is, thankfully, unlocked.

"Wait here," I say to Aaron quietly. "I'm just going to grab some stuff. I'll be five minutes."

I clock Aaron looking around, seemingly fascinated and confused by the random assortment of abandoned lip balms, old magazines, and dirty tea mugs. I suppose he is used to American high schools, which seem to have the population of small towns. "I'm going to wait outside the door and smoke."

He steps into the stairwell leading to the street and closes the door.

As I move through the corridor, I can hear class happening in the adjoining room. I stop for a moment. Listen. The teacher's voice is too muffled to make out words, but she's in full flow, in what sounds like German.

Heather's door is ajar. It suddenly occurs to me that now would be a good time to bring her in. She knows about Aaron, and I trust her to know whether or not he can now be trusted. I peek into the room, and it's empty. By the looks of her handbag on the desk, she's in the building.

I find myself drawn to the same spot that always confuses me about this room: the molding paint just behind Miss Banbury's desk, which is getting worse with each passing week. Freckles of gray-green rot are moving up the wall, and the paint has completely buckled inward. The center of the rot, which began as a little vein of faint blue, has now turned to a circle of deep black. The whole wall looks like a diagram of the inner earth: a molten black core, then a mantle of brown-green surrounding it. It smells of wetness and old potatoes, the kind that take root in the cupboard and become alien.

There's a stir in me then. A stir and the beginnings of a memory. The dream from last night, the feeling of being a layer of green light and the smell of rot that seemed to pinch at me, dwindle my flame down to nothing.

"Maeve!" Heather's voice comes from behind me, and she's filled with delight at my presence. "Funny time to see you here."

I turn from the wall, the smell still lingering in my nose. "Hey," I say.

"I have some amazing news, Maeve." She grins. "I wasn't going to tell you until I was absolutely sure, but I've just gotten off the phone with the museum, and, well . . . you're here! So!"

"What museum?"

"The one in Japan. Where I'm going this summer? To help catalog it?"

"Oh," I reply. "Sure."

She seems almost hyper now, her smile almost too wide.

"Well, listen—they said I can bring you with me. The pay would be next to nothing, but it's a summer in Tokyo for free. Can you believe it, Maeve? You'll finish school and, bam, you'll be off to Japan."

"Oh," I say, sitting down in Miss Banbury's chair. "Wow."

The smell of rot from the back wall tickles at me again, and I feel a thrum of something within. Something like the green light that I felt last night.

"I need to talk to you," I say. "It's about the Children. They're draining the Well, which I guess you probably knew already, but now Aaron has left them and is helping us. He's going to help us take them down."

Heather looks a bit taken aback, but not really as shocked as I would have expected. "Well, gosh. Did he tell you that? You know, I wouldn't necessarily . . ."

"I know, I know, I don't trust him, either," I say hurriedly. "But in this case . . . I believe him. And I don't think we can take them down without his help."

She nods, thoughtful. "The thing is, I do need to call the museum today with a decision."

I feel like I've misheard her. I blink. Stare at her. "What?"

Heather shakes her head. "Never mind. If you don't want to go, that's fine, too."

"To Tokyo? Of course I want to go."

"No, no." She shrugs. "It's the kind of thing you need to be sure about."

I'm so confused. The whole conversation feels like it's taking place in a dream, where all the logic is backward yet is supposed to make an unspoken kind of sense. Only I don't feel quite so comfortable going along with the dream logic.

"Can we talk about Aaron first?" I press. "I just don't think . . ."

"Sure, sure," she says. She sounds kind of flustered and disappointed, like she's just brought me a birthday present and hasn't quite had the thanks she thinks she deserves. "Why don't I just make a tea and we'll talk about it, then? Properly, I mean."

"Yeah. And, uh, we can definitely discuss the Japan stuff, too, right?"

She raises her eyebrows slightly as she turns to the door. "Well, we'll see," she replies, her voice still disappointed.

I sit there and wait for her to come back. Feeling uncomfortable. Feeling like something isn't right. I hear the click of the kettle in the next room and the slow gurgle of boiling water. She starts to hum softly, and the smell from the walls seems to get stronger.

Where in the hell did this Japan thing come from? Why would she bring that up now, of all times?

I imagine myself riding the subway in Tokyo, having the kind of cool life that naturally unfolds, event by event, rather than one dictated by college or a vocation. I imagine my parents talking about me the way they talk about my siblings: *Abbie's in Belgium still, but Maeve, our youngest, is in Japan. Yes,* Japan.

It's a nice fantasy, and one I could indulge in more if the green light wasn't now swimming at the corner of my eye. The smell hits my nose again, and I turn to press my thumb against the damp wall, snagging my tights on Heather's desk drawer as I do. I look down.

In the drawer is a small gold key sticking out of the keyhole. With one small turn, I could see inside her desk. Which is a sneaky thing to do.

Which is a thing I would only do, really, if I didn't trust Heather.

The green light gets stronger and I realize that I am being told something by my body. I sit, listen for a second. I've spent so long listening to other people's thoughts. It's time to listen to my own.

Open the drawer, it says. *Now.*

I pull out the drawer, my heart so loud that there's a thump in my eardrum.

It takes me a moment to understand what I'm looking at. At first, I think they are dead mice. Little gray wet bodies, all sitting neatly in a line.

They are tea bags.

Rows and rows of used tea bags, arranged like rows of soldiers. Two inches between each. Each one sits on a little cotton pad, the kind for removing eye makeup with, apparently to stop it leaking through to the wood of the desk. I pick one up and smell it.

Chamomile.

These are not just any old used tea bags.

These are *my* old tea bags.

My spine goes cold, like a jagged metal rod rattling through my body. Miss Banbury has kept every tea bag I have ever brewed in her office. A wave of nausea descends over me as I realize that the teas were also hers. She had brought them from home.

I hear her step in the hallway and I close the drawer, my heart pounding. Somehow, I manage to get back to my seat.

"Tea," she says simply, passing me a steaming mug. I gaze into it, the bag bobbing around innocently. Oh, god.

The day I refused Aaron for the third time, Heather had appeared, dismissing him. I thought she was protecting me, when what she was really doing was taking over the case.

She is what happens after three.

I hold the mug in my hands, each palm clamped to the side as though it were the only thing holding me to the earth. This can't be real.

"You're such a bright girl, Maeve," she says softly. "So full of potential."

All my life, I've been hearing about my potential. *Potential*, always said like it's a huge treasure chest that I just need to find the key for. Now the word sounds different. Like a fruit going soft.

She runs her hand along the desk, stopping briefly at the drawer with the tea bags.

"If we're going to work together in Japan," she says, smiling still, "we need to be aligned on everything."

I suddenly remember Aaron's words about how he was brought back to his town in California, where he drained the Well, and then was quickly moved on again. Is this what the Japan stuff is all about? Are they just gently laying down train tracks to drain me and then get me out of Kilbeg?

The green light in my head surges again, starts to climb around this thought and reject it. I am starting to appreciate the green light. All the months of me following the tails of other people's light, and I never even thought to question what my own might look like.

"Now," she says primly. "What is it you wanted to say about Aaron?"

The flowering of the green light is so beautiful that it takes me a moment to realize that I can't move.

30

HEATHER GETS UP FROM HER SEAT AND comes around to my side. She leans her weight against the edge of the desk.

"You changed your hair," she says softly, taking a length of it in her hands. My muscles are still locked, my body holding firm, just like it did on the bus. "Or . . . ha. You changed *something*, anyway."

She moves her thumb up, feeling the silken weight of the new curl. Her fingers graze against my face, and I can't even flinch.

Heather whispers something, and the lock of curls she is holding lies straight. There's a feeling of shoulders buckling, of bones crunching together.

She looks me in the eyes, locking my gaze. Her hand travels up my arm, squeezing very gently where my forearm meets my elbow, and I feel as though I am a horse being looked over for sale.

Her hand is on my shoulder. Now my neck. Her hand is too warm to be filled with simply blood. Her other hand is flat to the wall, pushing against The Chokey's boundaries, tensing on the plaster.

The green light overwhelms me now, illuminating each corner of my paralyzed body. Without movement to work with, to worry about, the green light is able to settle in my mind and become the voice of ultimate clarity.

Listen, it says. *Listen.*

What? I ask. *What is it?*

St. Bernadette's is the Well.

The realization rolls over me in thick waves. That's why The Chokey door closed on me that day last winter. That's why the tarot cards brought to the school by Harriet Evans became bewitched. That's why two sensitives in the space of thirty years have gone to school here, despite the rarity of sensitives and the fact that there was no precedent in either of our families to send their daughters to fee-paying schools. I wasn't *supposed* to go to St. Bernadette's, after all. I was supposed to go to the same non-fee-paying school as my sisters. But my grades were too poor, and they were afraid that I would get lost in the muddle of a bigger school. Harriet, too: she had won a scholarship. The first scholarships ever given out by Sister Assumpta. And what about before that? Were there more of us?

There is a reason Miss Banbury is a teacher here, and it isn't just to get closer to me.

Although she is, right now, getting closer to me.

Her fingers are climbing up my neck, so hot now that they feel like batteries, something meant to power something else.

"So much potential," she says again, and I feel that same rotten fruit in my body again. The feeling of being a wilting, dying thing.

I think, for a second, that she is going to choke me. That she will kill me now, where I stand, and that will be the end of it. I consider that maybe I should have just taken the Japan offer, if that was ever real. I think about my body when it falls to the floor, how the last cough of magic will come out of me, and it will be hers, and it will be done.

But she does not choke me. Instead she touches my lips, and then hooks her fingertips around my teeth. *Oh,* I think from the bottom of my numbness. *Maybe I won't die. Maybe whatever she needs from me she can summon out through my throat.*

As I become aware of my own teeth, I begin to notice hers. She is smiling now, baring them, and I dimly remember hearing about President Lyndon B. Johnson's life in reverse. Being born and dying in the same town. Maybe that will be me, too.

It's funny, the things you think about when a woman's fingers are in your mouth.

Then, she stops. Her eyes are confused, her nostrils flaring. I can feel her hold on me start to loosen, feel the blood coming back into my arms. Feel the rage inside start to build again. I wrench away from her, moving so quickly that little purple and black spots start crowding the front of my vision, the kind that happen when a light is turned on and off too quickly.

But then the spots don't go away. They stay on her, moving around her face, spots of darkness sticking to her and growing larger.

No, not spots.

Holes.

Miss Banbury starts to claw at her face, letting go of me entirely. The holes move around, opening and shrinking. Pinpricks, then the size of a cat's eye.

My muscles loosen, her hold on me interrupted by whatever . . . this is. I bolt from the room, and Aaron is in the corridor, his hand on the other side of the wall. His palms pressed against The Chokey's boundaries.

This is his gift, I remember. I see the light in people. And he sees the holes.

"Maeve, get out," he says, breaking his reverie. "I can't hold her like this for long."

But I don't get out. At least, not right away.

"What are you *doing*?"

Aaron doesn't answer. He's too focused on her, his fingers pressed firmly to the wall, like he's about to climb it.

Miss Banbury sinks to the floor, clawing at her skin, yowling like an animal.

"Maeve, *leave.*"

The black spots are still erupting on Miss Banbury, moving around and scattering, like insects made from shadow. But they don't seem to be bothering her so much anymore. It looks like she is, at least mentally, fighting them. It strikes me then that whatever Aaron is doing is not a physical torture so much as it is a psychological one. She is not in pain, not on a skin level. It *looks* external, the shadow bugs moving around, but it's happening entirely within her own head.

Aaron starts to walk down the corridor, keeping his hand to the wall, his eyes closed in effort. He is still mumbling, and for a brief second, I feel something like . . . *something.* A dark resentment that Aaron and I were born with similar amounts of power, but that he has managed to hone and master his sensitivity over his years with the Children of Brigid. The way he was able to walk into the attic bathroom and feel the residual magic in the room. The way he can manifest his power in such a visual, dramatic, devastating way on Heather Banbury. He understands on a technical level what I only occasionally grasp with instinct.

And I'm jealous. And in that jealousy, I begin to see what it might feel like to be addicted to that kind of power. That kind of control, over yourself and over others. To stick with it, even if it violated every moral code imaginable.

No, I think. No, I would never do that. I would never trade decency for power. Then a snide voice from within me starts to beckon.

But you have, Maeve. You sold out your best friend for popularity.

That wasn't the same, I reason.

Yes, in some ways it's worse. Aaron actually got what he wanted. You couldn't even impress the popular girls.

"Maeve!" Aaron calls, his voice starting to tremble under the strain of his spell. "Run. Run for the stairs."

Aaron wanted grand cosmic power. That's reasonable. You just wanted to impress a few girls in your class.

There's a sense that something is about to break, and that I will be crushed under it. I lift my legs, still pained from Heather's spell, and try to make for the exit.

Think how much better off everyone would be without you. No Maeve, no Housekeeper. No Children of Brigid. No putting the people you love in danger constantly. Do you think Fiona is ever going to be OK again? Or Lily? No, Maeve. You ruined them. You ruined everyone.

I am behind Aaron's back, walking out backward as he does, closing my eyes to stop the voice. The terrible voice that is just like mine. That *is* me.

And then we're in the kitchen. And then the basement terrace. And then the street. It all seems to happen so slowly, my body feeble and confused, like a horse just born. The bell goes, the sound just barely audible when we're standing on the pavement outside. Class is over.

"We need to go," he says. I look at him and am taken aback by the change. He doesn't seem so washed-out anymore. His skin is golden, his acne and ingrown hairs disappeared, the squint in his eye barely visible. His entire being is pumped with magic, gleaming with the molten essence of the earth.

We leave the same way we came in, but we are not, in any sense, the same way we came in.

31

ONCE WE'RE ON THE STREET, MY ENTIRE body starts shaking. Aaron's not saying anything, but his face is tied up in worry, wondering whether what just happened has damaged me irreparably or whether it's a get-over-it-in-an-afternoon kind of thing. He's curious, too, I think. He's wondering whether I'm used to this sort of magic. The kind that is visible, fearsome, vicious. And I'm not, not really. My hands are still shaking, my knees knocking.

"Come on," he says. "We're going in here."

I look up and see that "here" is Shanty's, an old-man pub on the hill leading from St. Bernadette's and into town. Inside, everything is dark mahogany and green cushioned chairs. There's a fire in the grate, and two plush armchairs facing it. He sits me down in one and goes to the bar.

A few minutes later, he's back with two pints of Guinness and a packet of Scampi Fries. If the circumstances—and the company— were different, I think I would find this quite exciting. Drinking in a cozy pub on a school day.

"I don't like Guinness" is all I can say. And I don't. It's for old men and tourists.

"Just drink it," he says shortly. "It's got iron."

So I take a sip and find that I'm actually grateful for it. It's thick and creamy, sharp and dark. I slug it down, then wipe at my top lip for foam.

"What were you doing back there?" I ask eventually.

Aaron tears open the packet of Scampi Fries, sniffs them cautiously, and then starts to eat.

"Ew, are these *fish*?" he says disgustedly. Then he puts them to one side. "Back there was . . . well, that was my gift. My gift, with the volume turned way up because of that room. That awful room."

"It's the Well, isn't it? The Well is St. Bernadette's."

This clearly had not occurred to him.

"Oh . . . *OK*." Then, a tinge of excitement. "Jesus. OK. OK. Wow."

"What did you think was happening?"

"Just, like . . . a very strong hot spot. But you're right. I've never had a hot spot that strong. It must be the center of the Kilbeg Well."

I eye him suspiciously. "Why don't you *know* any of this? You were, like, the Children of Brigid poster boy here for years."

"Less than *one* year." He's gone back to the Scampi Fries again, still curious. He takes one out, examines it, eats it. "Everything changed for me when I came to Kilbeg. They were very pleased with me. Like, the minute I come down here, this big current of power starts flowing through, and I've got a connection to the little teenagers who are generating it all. Before that, I was nobody. Just another master manipulator in their ranks."

He crunches the Scampi Fry, decides he does like it, and eats another. "That thing you said," he continues. "About the holes. I can see the holes. It's more than that. I can make *other* people see their holes. Like, if someone has a bad memory, or a thing they hate about themselves, I can focus their mind so that's all they see. And with her just now, your Miss Banbury, that's what I was doing."

"I don't understand," I say, although I do, kind of. That voice in my head, telling me that life would be better if I wasn't in it—that was Aaron making that happen. That was being inside The Chokey at that moment in time, when his gift was in full flow.

"You know that stomachache you get when you remember a time when you were selfish, or mean, or stupid? It feels physical, doesn't it? It feels like food poisoning. That's what was happening to her, all over her body. Every horrible thing she's ashamed of, every evil thing she's done that she can normally convince herself was fine because . . . oh, I don't know, people always find a way to convince themselves that their terrible actions were actually fine and justified."

"Yeah," I snip. "Look who I'm talking to."

He ignores this. "All that came to her, at the same time. No defenses. Just the pure crushing weight of it."

I am floored by this. There's nothing I can do except drink my Guinness and try to wrap my head around it. Suddenly, everything that Fiona, Roe, Lily, and I can do seems like nothing. To make people feel accountable for their actions? To the point that it's *painful* for them? I remember the kids at the apartment when Roe and I went to the Children of Brigid meeting. How they opened their guts to Aaron, crying about the most minor moral infractions. It was so confusing to me then, but it makes utter sense now.

And even though I'm grateful to Aaron for getting me out of The Chokey alive, and even though I do sort of believe that he sincerely regrets his actions, I find myself burning with rage all over again.

"You could do *anything* with that gift," I say, spitting out the words. "You could, I don't know . . . you could make Jeff Bezos pay his taxes with that gift. You could end wars, if you got in the right room. You should be in government with a gift like that. Not wasting your time and your brain and your life going around to provincial Irish cities making vulnerable people feel *horrible* about themselves."

He is still looking at me, unmoved, eating Scampi Fries.

"These are pretty good actually," he says. "Once you get used to the fishiness."

"How are you going to palm me off like that?" I rage. "This is serious. You should be *helping* people."

"Look, Maeve, I'm willing to work with you. I'm willing to put the hours in to make things right with me and . . . with me and the world. But I'm not going to sit here and be lectured by a sixteen-year-old who doesn't know a hot spot from a hole in the ground."

"I'll say whatever I *want* to you," I snap, not backing down. "We're the same. I'm a sensitive, too. I should be able to hold you accountable, if anyone can. Like doctors."

"And is that what you plan to do with your gift, then? Save the world? Run for taoiseach?"

I cross my arms. "Maybe."

"I'll alert the Dáil."

"Shut up."

He sits back, dropping the empty bag on the table next to him. He dusts his fingers off on the palms of his hands and then folds them on his lap.

"Number one," he says in an irritated tone, "you have to understand that up until about, oh, six weeks ago, I thought I *was* saving people. The Bible is firm on gay sex. The Bible is firm on profligate behavior. The Bible is firm on abortion."

I roll my eyes. "If the Bible told you to jump off a—"

"A month ago, Maeve? Probably. Because that's what being a certain kind of Christian *is*. You don't have to understand that, but what you *do* have to understand is I *truly* thought I was saving people. With my whole heart."

"Well, you were wrong."

"Yes, I suspect now that I was," he snaps. "Number two, my gift doesn't work any differently than your gift or the gifts of the Best Friends Gang."

He says it with such exhaustion, and like he's said it before. *The Best Friends Gang.*

"What I do to people isn't permanent and, often, isn't very strong. The only reason it was strong a minute ago was because of the hot spot. The room was pouring out magic, and I've learned how to focus and ride the wave of energy when I sense it. I have a little more technique than you do, but I have the same amount of power. So even if I *did* get in a room with Jeff Bezos, he'd only decide to treat warehouse workers fairly for five minutes. Right now, Miss Banbury is getting up off the floor and planning her next move."

·)) ● ((·

When I'm in the restroom, I have a gross yet enlightening thought: What if the bind only lasts as long as the spell is in my system? Can I get rid of Aaron through peeing?

It seems simple enough that it might work, so I start ordering pints of water and chugging them.

We get to Nuala's house early in the evening. Manon is there already and lets us in. I'm halfway through the story of what happened to us at school when Nuala appears, and I have to start again.

"The mouth of the Well is the school," Manon marvels. "Merde."

"I thought that sort of made sense," I say limply. "Because me and . . . me and Heaven, Nuala, neither of us were meant to go to St. Bernadette's, were we?"

Nuala picks up on my train of thought right away. "No," she says, her eyes like saucers. "No, you weren't."

"Does anyone mind if I smoke?" Manon says, already taking out her tobacco pouch.

302 .

"No," Nuala replies, leaning against the kitchen counter. She looks in utter shock. "Roll me one, won't you?"

Manon does so and hands the cigarette to her mother. Nuala crouches down and lights it off the gas stove. Manon's face is full of concern as she holds back Nuala's platinum-blond hair while the blue fire flickers.

Nuala takes a long drag and leans against the counter again.

"All my life," Nuala murmurs as she exhales, "I've been angry at that school."

Somehow, I hadn't bargained for how this information would impact Nuala. I'm used to treating her like my problem solver. I often just spill information on her, and I rarely think about what it does to her, what it triggers.

"Everything bad that happened to us started with St. Bernadette's," she says tensely. "My father got worse after Heaven got in. Worse on her for thinking she was better than him, he had to leave school at twelve, didn't even have a Junior Cert—and worse on my mother for filling out the paperwork. And you know? I almost agreed with him. She never had time for me after St. Bernadette's. Always stayed late, planning for her supposedly bright future. She said it was the only place she felt *safe*."

Nuala's voice cracks on the word *safe*, and she takes another drag, as if bandaging the wound with a ribbon of smoke. She inhales sharply, her teeth hissing.

"She did her ritual at the school, you know. That's where she saw the Housekeeper first."

Manon nods silently, as if adding this information to her mental folder on Wells rather than registering that Nuala is talking about the death of her aunt.

"I always thought it was a mistake that she ever went there,"

Nuala says, tipping her ash into the sink. "But . . . it wasn't. It was . . . well. It was destiny, I suppose."

Manon takes a pen from the bun in her hair and tears the cardboard off a nearby cereal box. She starts to write.

Aaron is looking at his hands, together again on the kitchen table with the crossed thumbs. I don't know why, but I find this an infuriating way to sit still. His hands just clasped, like a 1950s schoolboy waiting for an apple from Teacher.

"Do you think destiny is real, Ms. Evans?"

For a second I wonder who he is talking to. I think even Nuala does.

"Oh, me," she says, slightly dazed. "Well."

I expect her to have a ready answer for this.

"I'm afraid I don't quite know, Aaron. In this case, it seems destiny has been at work. Destiny or divine coincidence."

He nods and looks at his hands again. "I thought I knew my destiny," he says. "Saving people from Hell was a good, solid destiny."

Then there is nothing but the scratch of Manon's pen. A minute later, the doorbell rings.

"It's the girls," I say, getting up. "I'll get it."

I meet them at the door. The evening is cold, their breath visible in the air.

"Where *were* you today?" Fiona says, bursting in the door. "Everything was weird again. Did you change your hair?"

"Weird how?"

"Weird, like backward classes. Weird, like people holding their books upside down. Does Nuala have any food? I'm starv—oh."

I'm behind her, still in the hallway, but I know what she's reacting to.

Who she's reacting to.

"What the *fuck* is he doing here?"

32

THE NEXT HOUR IS A BLUR OF QUESTIONS
and answers. Most of them asked by Fiona. Most of them answered,
in turn, by Nuala or Aaron or me.

Fiona is—quite fairly—not convinced.

"Are we all just forgetting what this prick put us through?"

"No," Nuala and I say at once.

Aaron looks at his hands again.

"Aaron has agreed that he needs to be held accountable for his
actions," Nuala says. "And that accountability begins with his helping to bring this terrible organization to its knees. Starting with that
Miss Banbury woman."

"Wait." Fiona pauses. "What about Miss Banbury?"

I realize that she's been so distracted by Aaron's presence that
she isn't even prepared for the real bombshell.

"Miss Banbury is Children of Brigid," I tell her. "She's been taking my . . ."

I feel a chill down my spine, thinking about it. I've managed
to avoid dwelling on the experience too much all afternoon, but
the memory of those tea bags, those little gray mice on the cotton pads, makes me feel nauseous. Her hands in my mouth, gently
hooking her fingers on the backs of my teeth. My shoulders buckle

together, frozen with the horror of it. Everyone looks at me, their eyes worried.

I stop.

Start again.

"She's been draining my magic with these teas," I say as evenly as I can. "It wasn't Aaron."

Fiona's face has completely paled, her eyes hollow.

"Fi?" I nudge.

She tries to say something, I think, but her mouth just opens mutely. She stops. Tries again.

"My . . . journal."

Oh, god.

"My . . . she's . . . to *me*."

Fiona starts to paw at her chest, her throat. For a second I think she's been bewitched by some silencing spell. Then I realize that it's shock that's keeping her from speaking, not magic.

"Your journal," I say. "Does she still have it?"

Fiona merely nods, and for the first time since I've known her, she looks small. She's two inches shorter than me, and about five below Lily, but I've never noticed it before. She's always had the loudest voice out of the four of us, and that usually makes her the biggest person in the room.

Aaron gets out of his chair and tries to guide her into it.

"Don't *touch* me," she snaps. "Don't *ever* touch me."

Fiona stands still, clenching and unclenching her fists, her knuckles going white.

"Maeve," she finally says. "Lily. Can you come to the bathroom with me?"

"Oh. Yes," I say.

Lily looks dazed by the request, but she follows. We never were "go to the bathroom together" girls, even in our old life.

"The upstairs loo is bigger," Nuala offers. "And has more privacy."

I mouth a *thank you* to Nuala and take Fiona by the hand, leading her up the stairs.

It's an old-fashioned sort of bathroom, all pale pink, the color of cough syrup. It smells like powder and flowers. The second I close the door, Fiona sinks down onto the fluffy white bath mat. She hugs her knees, her face full of terror.

There isn't enough room for us all to sit on the floor, so I sit next to her and Lily gets in the empty bath.

"What is it, Fi?" I say softly. "Because we know what we're doing now. We know what we're dealing with. We can fix it, whatever it is."

Fiona doesn't respond. Instead, she unfurls her limbs and reaches under her skirt. It's a corduroy miniskirt in dark red, and she has thick black tights on underneath it. She peels down her tights, and for a second I think she's about to strip off and have a bath. Lily clearly thinks so, too, and we look to each other in surprise.

But that's not what Fi is doing. She rolls the fabric down to just above her knees and stops, burying her face in her hands. I look down, and I understand.

Cuts.

Shallow red cuts, streaked across both thighs. Cuts that haven't healed. Cuts she thought *would* heal.

"Oh, Fi," I say, putting my arm around her. She leans her head on my shoulder. I don't know what else to say, so I just repeat her name. "Fiona, Fiona."

Tears start to scatter onto the bath mat.

"It stopped working," she says, her voice choked by sobs.

"When?" I say gently.

She bites down on her lip before she answers, her eyes red-rimmed and brimming. "A few days ago."

"Why did you do it if your gift wasn't working?" Lily asks, and I wonder how much she knows about Fiona's habit already.

"I don't *know*," Fiona cries. "It's just . . . it's just a thing I do. It's in my routine. I forgot. And then I couldn't say anything because you guys would know that I'm still . . . *doing* it."

She breaks off again, hiding her face.

"You don't have to worry about us," I say, holding her. "We just love you and want you to get better."

"*She* said she wanted me to get better," Fiona says furiously. "*She* said talking would help."

"It does help," I say, stroking her hair. "Talking *does* help."

"Not to her, though." The tears are coming fresh again, hot and anxious and deadly. She starts to claw at her hair, her throat. "You can't trust them," she spits. "You can't trust any of them."

"You weren't to know," I say, trying to soothe her. "You didn't know she was working for them."

"I mean you can't trust *anyone*," she snaps. "No one."

Despite her obvious trauma, I feel mildly hurt at this. I exchange a glance with Lily. "You can trust us. You can always trust us."

She ignores me. "People always do this to me," she goes on. "People think they can just take stuff from me, Maeve. Whatever they want. Even you, when you cheated off me. What do you think it is? Is it, like, an Asian girl thing?" Fiona lets out a hollow, empty laugh. "Or do you think it's just because I'm so pathetically eager to please?"

I feel a stab of guilt over the cheating, but still find it unusual that Fiona is bringing it up now. They say that it takes three incidents of something for it to be a trend, and I start to wonder if there is a third, unspoken thing that Lily and I don't know about.

"My *gift*," she spits. "My gift is *healing*. What a joke. It's like the universe is screaming at me, *Your job is to make sure other people are OK*."

She holds her legs again, her eye sockets resting on her knee-caps. I don't know what to say. What to do. Should I apologize for the cheating again, or would that just take the focus away and put it back on me? Lily doesn't seem to have any ideas. She just clutches the rim of the bath, looking upset. Fiona has stopped crying now. She's just holding herself tightly.

"Don't you mind it, Maeve?" she says finally, the words catching in the machinery of her throat. "She did it to you, too."

"I feel like . . ." I pause and try to answer truthfully and not how I think a Good Friend should react. I think of Heather's hands on my teeth. Her whispering about my *potential*. "I feel like I have no words for what she did to me."

Lily rests her cheek on the cool edge of the tub. "There are no proper words for the stuff we're able to do, and all the existing ones sound stupid and made-up."

Fiona and I let out a small, grateful laugh from the bath mat.

"True," I reply.

"We do magic. And that sounds made-up and weird, and we joke about it, and we use weird words like *gifts*. But it's not made-up. It's real. What happened to me, when I was the river, *that* was real. I know you guys don't understand it, but it was real. And what she did . . . *that* wasn't made-up. *That* was real. She did something to you."

Fiona rests her head on my shoulder and I slip my hand into hers.

"I just feel like I'm never going to be the same again," I say, my voice choked. "I never wanted to be this way, but now I can't imagine a different way of being. And now she's ruined it. She's ruined me."

"Oh, Maeve. I'm sorry."

There's a small window in the bathroom, a tiny square showing us that it's dark outside now. Black with a wink of the orange streetlamps, buzzing at the corner of the darkness.

There's some movement from Fiona, some internal sense of gathering herself.

"I used to feel the same way. Like I was ruined," she says in the smallest voice imaginable. "That guy I was with, when we first met?"

I haven't heard her bring up the older boyfriend since the week we started doing tarot together, way back in February. My eyes widen as I stop and look at her.

"The guy who wanted to have sex?" I ask. "Did you . . . ?"

"No," she answers sharply. "We didn't."

So this is it, I think. This is the third thing that makes a trend. Of people using Fiona. Of people thinking it's OK.

"But he made me do stuff," she says in a voice so thin it's almost a squeak. "Stuff to him."

"What happened?" Lily asks, her voice so gentle, gentle in a way I haven't heard in years.

"It was ages ago," she replies. "Honestly, I don't even know why it's come up now, I haven't thought about it in so long."

I don't need telepathy to know that this is a lie.

"Your cards when I met you were so sad," I say. "I should have known that something else was going on. I just didn't know you that well then."

"I felt horrible," she says, a slow tear gliding down her cheek. "I had put all this energy in trying to be friends with this group, and I still am friends with them, I guess. I mean, we did *Othello* together, but he just . . . he sort of ruined the whole thing for me. And by then I hadn't even bothered to make any real friends at school, so I just felt like a nothing."

Her voice breaks on *nothing*. She starts brushing back new tears with the heel of her hand.

"Do you want to tell me what happened?"

"Not really," she sniffs. "It was awkward and embarrassing, and the worst thing—the *worst* thing, Maeve—was what he said afterward. He said that . . . he said that . . ."

The words are stuck, a boulder that she is trying to push out with her tongue. For a moment I think she's choking.

"Fi . . ."

"He said it was a good thing I was a *fast learner*," she says, the words cracking out of her like thunder. "And that I would be much better *next time*."

Fiona dissolves into tears, fully pledging herself to the act of crying. I tighten my arms around her, trying to give her the solace that Heather Banbury pretended to give. Fiona weeps, hiccuping on her own sorrow, and I think about how Heather is a demon succubus and Fiona's ex-boyfriend was just a twenty-year-old guy but, really, there isn't much difference between them. Between what they were able to do and how they were able to make us feel.

"People think I'm so perfect," she sniffs, wiping her nose with her sleeve. "But they don't know what a trap that is. Like, there's actually no difference between being perfect and being desperate to please. Perfect *student*, perfect *daughter*, perfect little actress. And he was just there, smiling at me, as if my job was now also to be perfect at blow jobs. I wanted to die."

Lily's arms spread around us, her face between our faces. Our arms are wrapped together now, a many-legged amoeba of a teen girl, crying in a bathroom. It feels like a great emptying, a boil that needed to be lanced.

"I don't know why I'm crying about *that*," Fiona says eventually. "This was ages ago. Like, January."

"Because it's sad," Lily replies. "Because it's really sad."

And for a minute it's like all three of us are seeing the same thing. Like we're looking at the rest of our lives and wondering how on earth we're going to survive it.

"I had sex," I say. "I had sex last night."

Both of them look at me, astonished.

"With Roe?" Fiona asks. "How was it?"

"While I was in the next *room*?" says Lily, aghast.

"Yeah, sorry." I let out a long, loud sigh. "It was fine, y'know, but it wasn't fair. I was only doing it because I thought it would make him remember."

They nod. And I put my head in my hands. "It didn't work."

"I'm never going to have sex," I hear Lily's voice say. "Never ever."

"Don't say that, Lil," I respond. "It's actually nice."

Both girls look at me, astonished.

"I didn't say anything, Maeve." Lily stares at me.

In a haze of green light and curls, my gift has come back.

33

"MAEVE'S PSYCHIC AGAIN." FIONA BURSTS back into the kitchen to announce it. "She's gone and shagged herself psychic."

"FIONA!"

"Well, you *have*."

Manon is still writing on cereal cardboard and Nuala has taken down a wicker basket full of jars from the top of her cupboards. They both stop what they're doing and look at us. Aaron is nowhere to be seen.

"Is this true, Maeve?"

"I think so," I say, and I look at Nuala and receive three thoughts at once, each whacked on top of one another.

Of course, if magic loves sex, then two witches having sex was going to do something to her.

And

God, how did I end up in a world of teenagers' sex lives?

And

It's bad that I am here for Maeve and I wasn't there for Manny.

Nuala gazes back at me, shocked and flustered, like she could feel the intrusion into her brain. "Well," she says, ruffling herself like a hen. "Well, that's good."

"Very good," Manon says. "Power is everything right now. Read my mind and I will cut your throat."

"Understood," I say, wondering if I even have a choice in reading Manon's mind or not. "Where's Aaron?"

"He's on the back steps," Nuala says, still examining the jars. "I think it's bearing down on him. Realizing the damage he's done."

"Call him in, Lily," Manon says, still not looking up from her writing.

Lily heads out the back door.

"Fiona," Nuala calls. "Chop up this."

Nuala hands her a chopping board, a huge root that I'm not able to identify, and a sharp knife. I wince when I see Fiona take the knife, her gaze lingering on it, a flush rising to her cheeks.

"Maeve." Nuala touches me on the shoulder. "Drink this."

She hands me a steaming cup of tea. I shudder. The idea of tea is a little revolting to me now.

"What is it?" I ask suspiciously, clearly carrying some residual suspicion about tea of all kinds.

"Corn silk tea. It will help release the bind. I think it's easing already, but it needs to be gone by the time you leave. Aaron is going to stay here tonight."

"Here?" Fiona and I exclaim.

"Well, I can't send him back to that hostel. He's too exposed. Remember, Maeve, he was the one who attacked Miss Banbury."

"They don't know it was him, though. They didn't see him."

"True," she says. "But I'd rather not risk it. I want to keep an eye on him."

"Oh." I had not thought of this. Apparently you could fill a barn with the things I have not thought of.

Aaron and Lily appear in the doorway, Aaron looking slightly green. From this angle, with both their blond hair shining under the patio light, they look more like siblings than Roe and Lily ever have.

Roe.

I check my phone. There's one message from him, and I feel a surge of hope when I see it. Hoping that intimacy will have done for his magic what it has done for mine.

Hey, just checking you're OK. At the venue now. Let me know if you want to talk about last night: I know it was sooner than we planned but I love you and can't wait to see you when I get back xxxx

I sigh. It's a completely decent message, the message any normal romantic partner should send. But I don't *have* a normal romantic partner. I have a magic one. Only he doesn't seem to know that.

I remember what Lily said, about having to forget things to let new people in. I look to Aaron, who is now in the process of grinding something for Nuala. "No, don't smash," she instructs, her hand on his shoulder, trying to guide the movement of the pestle. *"Grind."*

Aaron is willfully forgetting part of himself to fit with us. He's trying to stuff twenty years of strict Christian teachings to the bottom of himself, and it's starting to work. That's what's so frightening about Aaron's supposed change of heart. If someone like that can change their heart entirely, then surely someone like Roe can, too. Except Roe is changing in the wrong direction. Or maybe it's the right one. Maybe Roe is better off this way.

I close my eyes, try to blink away the pain of it. *Not Roe.* I remember his hands on my body last night, his palms between my thighs, his curly hair resting on my bare chest. *Not Roe.* The knotted necklace on the floor. *Not Roe.*

I open my eyes and find that Aaron is staring at me, his expression drawn. He has stopped grinding.

"Maeve," Nuala snaps. "Drink your tea."

I drink the steaming mug of corn silk, quickly, and wonder if the bind means that Aaron can feel what I'm feeling. I am beginning to realize why Manon was so careful when she created the binding spell.

Manon has stopped writing and her gaze is firmly on me. Her eyes intense and feline, her irises golden.

"H . . . hello?" I say nervously. She merely tilts her head.

"Yes," she says thoughtfully. She looks at her cardboard workings again, smothering her mouth with her hand. "Yes," she repeats.

Manon stands up and paces the small area of the kitchen that doesn't have people in it.

"The job we must do," she begins, "is twofold."

Everyone drops what they're doing and listens.

"First of all, we must seal the Well from being drained and prevent it from being tampered with any further. For this, we need to send back the magic that was stolen from it. There must be no deficit."

I love the way she says deficit, Fiona thinks. *Why does that word sound so good in a French accent?*

I nod. If there's one thing I've learned about magic, it's that it works more like a bank than a bank does. If the ledger is even a little unbalanced, the system goes out of control.

"We must send the stolen magic back through the channel it came," Manon continues.

"So . . . me? Aren't I the channel?"

"Yes. Through you, Maeve. After that, we can seal the Well. But Miss Banbury must be willing to give it back. She took the magic through you; now you must take it through her and put it back where it belongs."

Aaron snorts. "No one at the Children gives anything back," he says.

316

"They will," Nuala says, as if grasping Manon's idea before she's articulated it. "Or at least she will."

Manon nods, a glimmer of excitement coming into her golden eyes. "Maeve, it's you who gave me this idea. I always thought that the power from drinking binds was an unfortunate side effect but I see now that it has untapped potential. We must create a new bind, a more powerful one, and whoever drinks it will be able to control her, and her magic," she says. "We bind her, and then we trick her into a sealing spell."

Nuala's eyebrows shoot up on the word *trick*.

"I don't see how that would work." Aaron frowns. "The bind you guys gave me . . ."

"Ah, but that was a *sweet* bind. We did it softly-softly. A more powerful bind will do more powerful things."

"Who drinks the bind, though?"

"I will," Manon says smoothly.

"Manny." Nuala is concerned. "Can't we just bind the woman and be done with it? I don't want you drinking something like that."

Manon shakes her head. "The magic *must* be returned, and she will never give it up willingly. I am the only one powerful enough."

She pauses, breathes in deeply, preparing herself for something.

"I must do it."

"God, you're cool," Fiona says, and then looks around like someone else said it.

Manon doesn't even register the statement. "I'll need something of hers. Teeth, hair, you know," she says thoughtfully. "Maeve, you know this woman the best. How can we do this?"

I think about it. "Her house," I say slowly. "We can go to her house."

"You know where she *lives*?" Fiona says, shocked.

"I . . . I went there. A few Saturdays ago." The memory feels hazy to me, like a fever dream. "She lives in a rented cottage at the back of one of the big houses near the river."

Nuala looks at me sharply. "Could you find it again?"

I shrug. "Sure."

"On a Saturday?" Fiona continues, still alarmed. *"Why?"*

"She . . ." I feel so unbelievably stupid. To have played into her hands so easily. I remember taking my shoes off, feeling the velvet grass underneath my feet, falling asleep in a garden chair. A queasy feeling comes over me. The nude sketch in the frame, which I realized was her after I looked at it for a fraction too long. "She was trying to get me to trust her," I finish weakly. "It worked."

"Everyone, in the car," Nuala says, and we follow her into the driveway and make our way across town, to where Miss Banbury lives.

It doesn't take long to drive across town, although with the car so cramped, it's not exactly comfortable. Aaron sits in the front seat with Nuala, and I'm annoyed again at men for having the de facto shotgun by virtue of their long legs. Fiona is perched on my lap, Lily in the middle, Manon on the other side.

"The cops better not be out," Nuala says, checking her mirrors. "I can't afford to have any more points on my license."

Manon snorts.

"Yes, I know, Manny, but even *so.*"

Fiona, her head touching the roof of the car, spies Manon's mischievous expression. From her vantage point, she can see everyone in the car, and is taking in the vibe forensically.

"OK," she says. "I've been patient enough. Someone tell me what the hell is going on."

"What do you mean, Fiona?" Nuala says coolly.

"I mean," she replies, not even bothering to hide her frustration, "why is it funny to Manon that we might get caught by the cops? What's the friggin' subtext here, lads? I feel like I'm watching a play and I missed the first act."

There's a silence, but Fiona refuses to be shamed.

"*OK*. Well. Anyone who is sick of all the weird mother-daughter mysteries, please raise your hand."

Aaron raises his hand. Lily raises her hand. Slowly, I also raise my hand. Manon, for the first time since I met her, starts to laugh. Her laugh is one of the most unusually out-of-character laughs I've ever heard, a high, inward giggle, like a dolphin somersaulting backward. We all turn to look at her.

"Sorry," she says, still laughing. "My laugh, it is terrible."

"It's not terrible," Fiona says.

Nuala sighs. "The reason Manny doesn't care about the Gardaí," she says, "is that she can trick the law. In most cases, anyway."

"What?"

"Manon isn't . . ." Nuala begins. Then she stops, hesitates. "Manon is special," she clarifies.

"I'm not *ashamed*," Manon snaps at her mother. Then she levels her gaze, steely, at the headrest.

"My name is Manon Renard," she says. "My family are the Renard trickster gods."

There is absolute silence in the car while each of us tries to grasp even a tiny piece of what this means.

"Trickster gods," Fiona repeats.

"Trickster *gods*," I repeat, with emphasis.

"You're . . . a god?" Aaron says, looking like someone just spat in his chips.

"Like . . . *Greek* gods?" Lily offers.

"Not quite so powerful," Manon says modestly. "But we are very remote descendants."

"Trickster gods are one of the last few god lineages left in the modern world," Nuala says self-consciously as we all try to imagine our much older friend having sex with a literal god. "They have quite a mild power but it's very hardy. Survives through . . ." She pauses awkwardly. "Mixed bloodlines."

As usual, Lily has almost no problem accepting this fact as the rest of us continue gaping in shock. "So what can a trickster god do?" she asks, fascinated.

"Well, Lily, they can imitate for a short time," Nuala says. "They can make money disappear and reappear. They can turn your tea into a mild poison: not something that will kill you, but something that will have you on the toilet for hours. They can do . . . well, lots of silly things, really."

"We trick," Manon responds, a glimmer of pride in her voice, "to humble people when they become too close to material things or social constructs."

"Social constructs?" I ask, bewildered.

"Like monogamy. An old trickster god would lure a new bride away from her husband to show them the silliness of trying to keep yourself to one person."

"That is so *French*," Fiona says in amazement while Nuala coughs loudly.

Manon shrugs. "We exist to remind people not to take life too seriously."

We each share a confused look, wondering how this applies to Manon, an extremely serious person. As if trying to prove us wrong, Manon rolls down the window, takes her chewing gum out of her mouth, and balls it in her fingers.

"I became a scholar," she says, throwing the gum out, "because I didn't want to spend my life on the Riviera making children drop their ice-cream cones."

Fiona nods. "Like me," she says, seemingly without even meaning to.

Manon cocks her head, confused.

Fiona flushes. "Well, my gift is healing people. And my family is full of healers. Well. Nurses and doctors. But I want to be an actor. It's all I've ever wanted. So . . . we both have things that are the opposite of the life we want."

Manon laughs, rolling the window back up. "Yes, maybe we are the same."

It takes me a minute to find the house. Not because I can't remember where it is, but because there are no lights on. It's so dark now that the house is almost invisible.

"You're sure this is it?" Nuala says to me, craning her head around.

"Yes," I say uncertainly.

"There are no cars," Aaron says.

"Yeah, I know."

"Are you sure . . . ?"

"Yes," I snap.

No lights. No cars. What happened to the busy little family I saw that Saturday morning?

"Look," Lily says. "It's for sale."

And she's right. There's a realty sign barely visible, threatening to sink into a hedge.

"It doesn't look like anyone lives here, Maeve."

"She lives around the back," I reply. "Maybe they're gone, but . . ."

Aaron suddenly gets out, closing the door softly behind him. A *ding-ding-ding* starts politely chirping, the car trying to remind us she's still open. He walks up to the house, half disappearing into the shadows.

After a few seconds of us watching in silence, Manon gets out, too, and walks into the night.

"Should . . . should we all get out?" I say.

"I'm getting out," says Lily, unbuckling her belt.

"It might not be safe!"

But at that moment, Aaron and Manon get back into the car and the dinging ceases.

"It's hot-spotted," Aaron says. "There's been some magic done to that house, and recently."

"I think what you saw, Maeve," Manon murmurs, "was a glamour."

"People keep using that word with me," I say, remembering Dorey at the hotel. "And I feel like . . . I don't know what it means."

"Like a temporary illusion," Aaron said. "Like when you were Mary-Beth."

"A glamour," I repeat. "That family was a glamour? So Heather was never actually here?"

"No, she would have been here. Just a lot of the things surrounding her were fake."

"A lot of things? Or everything?" I attempt to clarify.

Manon thinks about it. "A lot of things. It would have been too difficult for them to glamour *everything*."

We sit in silence for a second, not sure what to do next.

"Well," I say, "surely if we go to the back, the garden, where her house was . . . maybe she didn't live there, but something of hers might be . . . ?"

"This may be a trap also," Manon says. "Perhaps they would like us to go back there."

"Oh, let's just *go*," Lily says, impatient and ready to get out.

"Hang along," Manon says, and I presume she means *hang on*. She puts her hand on Lily's sleeve, and as she does, her own sleeve begins to turn the cobalt blue of Lily's jumper. Slowly, the whole arm starts to change, and the color runs out of Manon's eyes like the irises have been bleached. A swirl of blue starts to spin and settle, like a pipette of ink has been released into the back of her head. The alteration is so rapid that it's hard to keep up with what is changing and when. Skin lightens and Manon's curvier frame flattens slightly. Within a few seconds, I am sitting next to two Lilys.

"Jesus," Fiona breathes. "You weren't kidding."

"They will be focused on Lily," Manon says. "She is the one they are most afraid of, and who they have not latched on to yet. I will walk down with Maeve, and Lily, you will follow close behind. Ready to shock if anyone comes near us."

"What about the rest of us?" Fiona asks.

"Stay here."

"What?"

"You are still weak, Fiona. You have been drained, too. We need to keep you safe."

Fiona shifts in her seat, sounding miffed. "OK."

We make our way down, me and the decoy Lily. The real Lily follows quietly behind. It's so strange, walking with Manon-as-Lily after a lifetime of walking places with the real one. Manon takes long, light strides, her chin pointed up, her shoulders squared like a dancer's. Lily has a kind of heavier walk, throwing her weight into each step with hunched shoulders. It's funny how there are a myriad of things that make someone themselves other than how they look or talk.

"Maeve," Manon says as we walk down the dark driveway. Her

voice is Lily's Irish accent, but her cadence is all Manon. "How is it that you see people's minds?"

I talk, haltingly, about the lights. I never do a good job of explaining it, but Manon seems to grasp it quickly.

"I see. Now, when you enter into this Process stage, when you can see the lights—how about the lights of others? Of creatures, trees? Lives you cannot see but know are there?"

"They show up, too," I reply, thinking of the twinkling blips of light I used to see at the tennis courts, the lights of birds and bugs and rabbits.

"What about . . . what about if there was someone in hiding down there? Could you use your lights like, I don't know, a radar? For example, you cannot see Lily right now, but can you feel her light?"

I close my eyes. Center myself. "Yes," I reply, seeing Lily's cerulean glimmer.

"What about someone you don't know? Perhaps someone from . . ."

I nod, knowing exactly what she means. I try to push my power outward, the green light within me spreading out and out, tickling the trees and the night air. I feel a big fat joyful hunger in my chest, and I can't believe how much I missed my magic, missed training it and challenging it. A little shoot of hope springs up: If this is what sex has done for me, maybe it has done something amazing for Roe, too? Maybe he's on his way home right now, his senses sharpened?

I see a thousand glimmers, creatures and the beating hearts of trees, but I'm so focused on where I'm stepping that I can't keep the lights straight in my head.

Manon seems to know instinctively what I'm struggling with. "Hold my hand, I will guide you," she says. "First, tell me where we're going."

We're at the front of the house now, and I look for the side gate. "There," I say. "We have to go through there."

"Close your eyes. Focus on your vision."

I feel leaves tickling my face as we push through the side entrance, trip over uneven paving stones, and I scrape my sleeve against brick wall. All with my eyes closed, my palm sweating terribly in Manon's imitation of Lily's hand.

"Look for them," she instructs firmly. "This is a narrow passage; if they are on the other side, we do not want to be surprised."

I see blips and blips only. "No, nothing on the other side."

"OK."

Manon leads me through, and I open my eyes to see the moon lighting up the long grass and glimmering off the water of the Beg River. The little eco-cottage with the solar panel roof is gone. Instead there's a potting shed, a little run-down and just near the edge of the water.

I'm dazzled by the erasure of Miss Banbury's beautiful home. "*None* of it was real?" I say, the cold air sticking in my throat.

"None of it was," Manon says gently. Gentler than I've ever heard her. "This part can be hard, I know."

And I believe that she knows.

I hear Lily's faint steps trailing quietly behind us, feel her blue light edging closer. She knows instinctively to keep back. A train of her thought steams through my mind. *I'm like an assassin*, she thinks.

Without meaning to, I nod, and I can feel the message carrying itself back along the line. *Yes.*

A silence. *Is this you?*

Yes. It's Maeve.

How are you . . . ?

I don't know.

The thrill of it, the sensation of my gift being a phone call and not just a radio, lights me up from within. My hair seems to lift away from my scalp, springing slightly with joy. Can I do this with everyone now? Or just Lily?

Miss Banbury might not have been real. But *this* is. I am.

We stand in front of the shed that was briefly a cottage I once took my shoes off in.

"Even if it was fake," I say, "she was here. Surely there's *something*."

Manon nods and slides open the dead bolt on the shed door. Inside, there's a selection of long-abandoned tools, a rusty shovel, and a moldy bag of compost. It smells of earth and damp and the heavy latex of gardening gloves. It smells how all sheds smell.

I turn my phone light on to look around and manage to find the one thing that I do recognize from Heather's home. The striped loungers are bunched up at the back of the shed, mildewing.

"Here," I say, pulling them out. "We sat on these. These were here before."

Manon eyes them suspiciously with her phone light.

"Are you sure? She used these?"

We inspect the sun loungers closer, turning each one over and scanning it with our phones like a black light. "Ah!" Manon says, zeroing in on a long golden strand. "Is this her?"

She holds it up to the light. "Yes," I say.

"One strand," she tuts. "One strand will not be enough. Do you have a knife?"

"No."

"Keys?"

I hand her my house keys and she hacks away at the fabric, tearing strips off as carefully as she can. Cushion wadding starts to burst through and fall onto the floor.

As she cuts, two gray lights start to enter the corner of my consciousness. They are small and pearly, like buttons on a Victorian's sleeve. And they are coming closer. Moving quick.

"Manon," I whisper.

She stops immediately, her reflexes like a cat. "Qu'est-ce que c'est?"

"I think . . . someone . . ."

"Where?"

I burrow down into the light, frightened and new to the idea of using my magic as radar.

"They . . ." I whisper. "They're coming east and west. From the gardens."

There are no windows in the shed. No lookout points. Just the claustrophobic sense that someone or something is coming, and quickly. "We could run," Manon says, and for the first time in our short relationship, she sounds scared. I concentrate, try to pick up the tin-can phone line with Lily again.

Lily.

What?

I think there are two people, or things, coming for us.

Or things?

Left and right of this little shed, they're . . .

I break off, as the two pearls are so close now that my breath starts to come short. The dots begin to throb slightly, as if something within them is getting bolder.

Does Manon still look like me?

Yes.

Send her out.

Can you see them?

Yes.

What are they?

Two guys.

What are they going to do?

The shed suddenly gets darker, and I can't quite understand why, as it has no light source to begin with. I hear a rattling, a scraping sound, and I realize that the whole shed has been cloaked with . . . *something.*

Manon and I stay utterly silent, completely still. I tug on the thin line that connects me and Lily. *Lil, what's going on?*

"Come on out," I hear a male voice say. "The door's open."

"You know what I can do," Manon says. "I can put volts through your skin."

A laugh. "Like to see you *try*."

"What do you want?"

Another pause. Another laugh. "Just . . . a word with you."

"What are you doing here, Maeve Chambers?" says the other voice, and he says my name like it's the name of a famous person. "Back for more tea?"

Just send her out.

"Go on," I whisper to Manon. "Lily says it's safe."

Manon steps out and is immediately smothered with some kind of black tarp. She screams, and I see arms: arms wrapping around her, arms belting the tarp around her. She fights and claws against them, her mouth already struggling against the material. I remember the man in the rubbery suit on the bus, and how it had failed against the almighty power of Lily.

A leather strap secures the tarp around Manon like a straitjacket, and I cower against the back wall. *Come on, Lil. This is getting scary.*

I hear the cold sound of zips and metal, of something being placed either on or around Manon. I have no choice but to cower in the shed as Manon shrieks with a long string of French swear words.

I'm so frightened that I can't tap into my gift, can't think of anything other than how I don't want a rubber tarp belted around me.

Someone steps into the shed, and I'm astonished by my own helplessness. Why was Lily the only one who was granted destructive powers? What good is telepathy at a time like this?

The man is big, much bigger than me, his frame blocking out the moonlight. I grab at the only thing that resembles a weapon: the heavy, rusted garden shovel that I know I can barely lift over my head.

The frayed wooden handle leaves splinters in my hands, but I hold it in front of me anyway, the end of the shovel pointed at him like a sword.

He looks at me, looks at the shovel, and clearly finds something ridiculous about the two. "Now what," he says, his voice low and surprisingly rural, "do you think you're going to do with that?"

I jab at him, and he takes half a step backward, easily missing the hit.

"Right," he says. "That's enough messing around."

There's a flash of something in the distance, a great white, blinding light that catches the metal end of the shovel like a lightning rod. Time slows for a second, the way it did with Aaron in the café: where even though events are unfolding so quickly, I'm somehow able to take a brief second to analyze the situation like a photograph. Look for weaknesses. I see the man's face contort in surprise, the volt of Lily's electricity lighting him like flash photography. I'm able to see the volt touch the tip of the shovel, igniting it, sparking the old dull metal into a gleaming, spirited thing. I know now when my sensitivity is trying to tell me something. And right now it is trying to tell me, *This is your only chance.*

I jab at him, feeling the yield of his belly, the softness like sofa stuffing. He's instantly blown backward, and there's a dark, twitching smell, the smell of a hot iron being left on a shirt too long. The smell of clothes singeing.

There's a ringing in my ears, and I can do nothing but hold the shovel and step blearily out of the shed. Once my ears recover, I hear a vague sound of splashing. I get a good look at the unconscious men. Perhaps dead. I quickly unbuckle Manon from the tarp-cum-straitjacket that protected her from the blast.

"What happened?" I ask, as if she is supposed to know under a black rubber sheet.

And then I see her. Lily, naked and up to her waist in the Beg, looking like a river sprite.

"We better go quick," Lily says, her voice singing with barely suppressed joy. "They won't be out for long."

"Where are your clothes?"

"There," she says, pointing to a neat pile. The night is cold, but she doesn't so much as shiver. She's gleaming in the moonlight, sleek as an otter. I hand her the clothes, averting my eyes. We were never the sort of friends who were comfortable being undressed in front of each other, and now here she is with both her tits out.

"Are they dead?" Lily asks, stepping into her knickers and putting her jumper on over her shimmering wet frame.

"No," I say, and their lights start to throb a little. "But they're going to come around in about a minute."

Lily stuffs everything else under her arm. "All right," she says, squeezing out some river water from her hair. "Let's make a run for it."

And the three of us run across the moonlit garden: Manon first, then Lily, then me, the weakest runner of the three. As I follow Lily's steps, I feel the static glitching off the grass underfoot.

34

LILY STARTS TO SHIVER IN THE CAR, THE
adrenaline of her river display starting to wear off. Manon, her voice
high with trauma, starts explaining what happened, and why. She
talks fast, missing words, skipping tenses.

"Who did they send?" Aaron interjects. "What did they look like?"

"A big guy," I say. "Give me your coat."

Aaron throws his coat over the seat, and I wrap it around Lily's
shoulders, rubbing at her arms through the material, willing the
warmth back into her.

"What did he sound like? Look like?"

"I don't know." Lily is sitting on my lap now, Manon in the middle, Fiona at the window. The river water is soaking onto my clothes. I
wonder if Lily is updated on her tetanus shots. "He sounded a bit rural.
But he was big. And scary. I stunned him with the electric shovel."

"Pardon?" Nuala. "The electric *what*?"

"Manon." Fiona's voice is frightened. "There's something *on* you."

"What?" Manon says, still full of panic. "What is it?"

"On your . . . your *neck*?"

Manon starts to claw at her throat. "No, no," Fiona says. "Hold
still."

She peers at the back of Manon's neck, just below her left ear.

She moves in with her thumb and forefinger and removes something round and silver, like a strange coin. She plops it in Manon's open hand. Lily also stares at Manon's neck. "There's one on this side, too," she says, peeling it off. "What is it?"

Manon opens her hand again, and Lily gives her the coin. She stares at her new collection. Horrified, confused.

"Give them to me," Aaron says, holding his palm out. Manon fixes her gaze on him, as if she was considering giving him her life savings.

"Please," he says.

She nods slowly. The jury that lives in her brain has just decided that he's not guilty, and gives him the coins.

He examines them, turning them over under the roof light while Nuala drives. "I think . . ."

He scrutinizes them once more, and then holds one under the light again. He puts the coin right to the bulb, and it sticks fast, like a magnet. The light goes out instantly, and the whole car briefly stalls. We all let out a yelp. He yanks the coin off the light, and it flashes back on.

"These were meant for Lily," he says. "To contain her."

"I came back to my own form once they were on me," Manon says worriedly.

"Wow," I say, thinking of the rubber, belted straitjacket they brought with them. "They're *inventing* things for us now?"

Lily manages a weak smile. "Should we take it as a compliment?"

The enormity of this operation, this concentrated attack on Lily, makes me start rubbing at Aaron's coat around her again. Desperate to protect her.

"We need to corner Miss Banbury at school," Lily says decisively. "When there's no one else around."

"Will she still even be there?" Fiona asks. "After that run-in with Maeve?"

"She will stay until she's sure she has everything," Manon says. "You can count on this."

"At detention, it was always just me and her left in the building," I offer. "And sometimes Sister Assumpta."

We all look to Manon, desperate for her approval. "Yes. Perhaps." She roots in her pocket and takes out the strips of material from the sun loungers. "You are on vacation now?"

"Yeah. Half-term."

"Good. I can try to make a bind from this. It's a stronger bind, so will take some time. But by Friday after next, we will have to confront her, send the channel of magic back, and seal the Well on-site."

"Friday after next?" Fiona squeals. "We could be dead by then. Why?"

"The bind needs to mature, and that day is a new moon. Our power will be ripest."

"So that's it?" Fiona says. "Two weeks from today, the Well will be sealed and everything will go back to normal?"

It's incredible to me that we can do this in the time it takes Roe to do a tour. He is, technically, supposed to be back by my birthday. The twenty-third.

"For the love of god, keep a low profile over the next week," Nuala warns. "Don't leave the house unless absolutely necessary."

"That won't be hard," Fiona replies. "We've got our mocks the week after half-term. We're supposed to be studying all week."

Aaron, through all of this, says very little. I think he's wondering what he's supposed to do in the long week he avoids getting killed.

"You won't go idle, either," Nuala says firmly. "You're telling us everything you know. We're filling out the archives this week."

"You will sleep on the floor," Manon says sternly. "In the living room."

"Yes," Nuala agrees. "Manon's room is her own."

It strikes me that a witch, a minor god, and a former zealot all living together for two weeks is a reality show I would pay to watch.

Nuala drops us off outside my house. Lily wriggles her legs into her jeans as she hops out and slips her bare feet into her trainers. The ground is littered with broken eggshells and smashed yellow yolks. We each peer at them, wondering if this is some kind of spell or sign that things in Kilbeg have gone further awry.

"Oh," Fiona says after a minute of puzzling. "It's Halloween. People are egging."

"Ohhhh," Lily and I exclaim together, as if we are trying to remember a time before magic, when Halloween meant something. "Egging."

I'm so tired from the day, but I can't bear a night of sitting on my bed, looking at videos of Roe.

"Hey," I say, oddly sheepish. "Do you guys want to stay over? It's the first night of holidays, I'm sure no one will mind."

They are instantly on board. They text their parents, and we go inside and start melting cheese on toast under the grill. Mum comes downstairs in her dressing gown for a bit and seems relieved that we're acting like how a bunch of teenagers are supposed to act. I think we're relieved, too. For a few hours, it's like we're cosplaying at being regular. We laugh at stupid things. We feed the dog bits of cheese. And at around two, we all go into Jo's room, because it's the biggest and warmest. Fiona and I share the bed and Lily opts for an air mattress on the floor. We prop my laptop on some pillows and watch *Friends* until we start to doze off. By four, it's just me and

Fiona, hardly awake and watching Chandler tell Janice that he is moving to Yemen.

"Do you think he's serious?"

"Chandler?" she responds, sleepy but surprised.

"No, Aaron."

"Oh," she says. Then a pause. "I don't know. I was kind of hoping you were sure."

But am I sure?

The following Sunday night we meet at Nuala's to go over the plan. Nuala is so careful that she insists on paying one of her neighbors, a retired taxi driver, to pick us up and drop us off. Until the Well is sealed, she says, we have to behave like we're members of the Royal Family: no traveling together, no getting into a car with a stranger, no public transport. No enclosed spaces. No talking to people on the street.

I walk in the kitchen door and I'm hit with an almost overwhelming stench of grease. It smells, frankly, like KFC.

"What the hell is that?" I announce to the room.

Fiona's at the table, stirring something and looking green. "It's the sealing spell."

"Our sealing spell is chicken?"

Nuala swoops in with a boiling vat and tells me that for the sealing spell, we need candles and candle wax.

"Of course," I say. "Wicca, why you gotta be so literal?"

"So these are made from chicken fat. My chickens."

"All of them?" I'm shocked by this. Fiona looks nauseous again.

"Most of them," she sighs. "They've lived on my herbs, on my grass, on my small bit of magic. What else was there to do?"

I shudder, and the six of us spend the rest of the evening pouring vats of boiling chicken fat into mason jars filled with cut herbs, murmuring spells, laying out grease-spattered tarot cards as we go. Cards for power and victory, aces and queens and fiery wands. The room feels powerful and rancid. Of all the witchcraft I've done, this seems the most pagan, the most medieval, the most that could be associated with the down-home dirty Satanism that the Aarons of the world are so afraid of. I mean, it's not Satanism, but if I were a stranger looking through the window, I would *think* that it is.

I watch Aaron as we chant and pour and stir, and he doesn't look upset or bothered by any of it. He looks . . . not happy, but centered. Like this is natural for him.

The plan is this:

I need to get detention. It's the only time Heather Banbury and I are ever alone in the school. If she hasn't fled, that is. There's nothing to say she hasn't. She'll know something is up, and she'll come with her own firepower. But we have firepower, too: we have Lily and her electricity, Manon and her clever tricks, Aaron's emotional manipulation, my telepathy. Nuala doesn't have any outright gifts, and Fiona's power is still drained, but their job is more important than anyone's. As soon as darkness falls—which is early enough, now that it's November—they're to slip through to the tennis courts and set up the complicated process of the sealing spell. Aaron pushes the tennis courts as the spell's altar. He opens his wallet, takes out the little yellow flower he picked there, all those months ago. It's still gleaming with life.

"I think it's the deepest part of the Well," he says. "Why else would they go out of their way to buy that land behind the school?"

Fiona nods. "And build something big and flat and easy to access over it."

"Exactly," Aaron agrees. "They do that. If you ever see a cricket pitch or a tennis court in a weird place . . . that's someone trying to get at a Well."

At the corner of my eye, Manon starts writing this down.

"It says we're to slash the ground open," Nuala says, reading from the spell in her archives. "I don't know how we're going to do that."

"The court is rubber," Fiona says. "It shouldn't be too hard. Just bring a knife or something."

The way her voice curdles on the word *knife*, shaking slightly, makes me raise my eyes to her.

"Fiona, I—"

"No, it's OK," she says, cutting me off. "It won't be like last time."

I'll be in The Chokey distracting Miss Banbury, and Manon will drink the hard bind, spiritually strapping Heather to her like a grenade. Depending on the success of the bind, we'll either frog-march her out or drag her kicking and screaming. If the sealing goes to plan, then the magic will flow out of Miss Banbury, through me, and back into the Well. Then it will be sealed, like a letter, with the combined power of each of us.

"Except Roe," I say sadly, and no one says anything to contradict me.

35

WE GO BACK TO SCHOOL THE NEXT DAY
still stinking of chicken grease.

I would care, I think, if everything else about the school wasn't
so profoundly odd. From the moment I walk through the doors, the
whole building feels like it's buckling inward, the new parquet floor-
boards strangely warped. The diagonal pattern of the wood feels like
an arrow pointing down, and I feel my knees bending slightly, as if
the school itself is sinking into its foundations. The rot hits me again,
not just a smell but a feeling, something that grabs at my gums and
reverberates around my mouth. There's a strange pain, like wisdom
teeth coming up.

No one is talking to us, or to anyone else. The same sense of
floating, murmuring, of people speaking but not full sentences, and
not to one another.

"Everything is so . . . *wrong*." Fiona looks around, feeling the
chill, the dissonance. "Is it just exam stress, do you think?"

The last scraps of hope cling to her and then promptly fall away
as our gaze settles on a girl who has bent down to tie the laces on her
deck shoes. Only she's not tying the laces. She's tying the air next to
them.

"Jesus," Fi says, holding her own arms. "Should we even be here?"

"They won't try anything with this many witnesses," I say, only partially believing it. What else is there to do? We could run, but where would we run to? "Also, can you imagine what our parents would say if we skipped our mocks?"

How is this my life?

We file into the hall where our mocks are being held, the desks spaced apart, mimicking an exam situation. Girls here seem a little more normal. People are talking at least, although there's a deadness to it, not busy chatter. Maybe it's the hallway, the real heart of the school, that has warped the most.

"Everyone, we'll be starting the exam at nine fifteen sharp," Miss Harris calls authoritatively. "We will break at eleven fifteen for an hour, then resume again at one. At three, you'll be free to go home or study as you wish. The same schedule will resume tomorrow."

Quiet descends over the room and Miss Harris starts handing out papers, instructing us not to turn them over until she says so. Despite everything, I feel a little quaver of nerves come over me. I know the mocks don't technically count for anything, but it occurs to me that this is the first step toward the end of school. That pretty soon it will be Christmas holidays, and after that it's a short jump until our real exams and the rest of our lives.

"Turn over your papers," Miss Harris says. "And begin."

I turn over my paper.

I do not begin.

I do not begin because the paper looks like this.

Europe and the Wider World: Topic 6

The United States and the World, 1945–1989

Answer one of the following questions.

During the period of 1945–1989, what was the importance of US foreign policy on one of the following:

Berlin, Korea, Cuba?

I put my hand up. "Miss!" I say when Miss Harris doesn't see me right away. She frowns and walks over to my desk.

"What is it, Maeve?"

"I have the wrong paper. It's in Russian or something."

She peers at my paper, then frowns at me again. "Maeve, I really don't have time for you messing around on me today."

"I'm not messing around. But look, the paper is all wrong. Read it."

She glances down at it. "Maeve, this is your history paper. I'm sorry if you didn't study properly, but . . ."

"But I *did* study properly," I protest. "This isn't in *English*."

Other girls are starting to stare at me now.

"Maeve, you have the exact same paper as everyone else," Miss Harris says formidably. I glance over at Fiona, and she is still, watchful. I take it as a cue.

"It's fine," I say quickly, snatching the paper back. "I'm fine."

And it's only once I've studied it that I realize that the paper actually *is* in English. It's just backward. It's in mirror writing.

I look to Fiona and I see her realizing this, too, turning the paper on its side and squinting to read it. Lily, several desks away from us, hasn't even turned her exam over. She's just drawing on the blank space.

I'm not sure what to do. Seemingly, we are the only three people who have noticed something wrong. Everyone else is writing frantically, their heads bent over their papers. I look closer at Ciara

Connolly, who's sitting on the other side of me, and try to see what exactly she's writing. She lifts her head briefly to cough into her hand, and that's when I see it.

She is writing backward.

"Maeve!" Miss Harris snaps. "Eyes on your own paper."

"Sorry," I say, and go back to looking at my blank sheets of answer paper.

I try writing. Because I can't think of anything, I write my own name. But as I put pen to paper, I can feel my arm curling around the desk, my fingers morphing into a strange clawlike position around the pen. I can't help it, and I can't fight it. As the ink touches the paper, a blue ribbon of nonsense smooths out over the clean white page.

Maeve Chambers

"Jesus," I yelp, dropping my pen. "What the . . ."

"Maeve!" Miss Harris again. "I will remove you from this exam if I have to. You'll spend every Friday in detention for *another* term if you're not careful."

I catch Fiona's eye, and I realize this is exactly what we've been planning for.

I sit in my chair, and making perfect eye contact with Miss Harris, I place my hands on the edge of the desk.

And I simply

tip

the

desk

over.

Immediately, Miss Harris is pulling me out of my seat. I'm pretty sure that teachers aren't supposed to touch students, but Miss Harris and I have been through too much for that by now. She almost pulls

342

my arm out of its socket and drags me to the door, furiously telling me that I'm disrupting the exam for everyone else. I try to tell myself that Miss Harris would never be this harsh usually, that the Well is messing with everyone.

Lily smirks at me, and I give her an exaggerated shrug back. A *Well, what are you gonna do?* shrug. And as Miss Harris is shoving me out the door, I notice that Ciara Connolly's handwriting has now slid off the paper and is being engraved, rather heavily, into the bones of the desk.

I get Friday detention. I start to wonder how I'm going to explain this to my parents, and in particular, how I'm going to have to appear sorry for my actions when they were, in fact, planned. But explaining things to my parents already feels like an activity from a different lifetime. They'll just have to accept it and worry about me, as they always do, and wait for the day that they won't have to worry anymore.

The worst part is sitting in the office while she calls them.

"Purposefully disruptive," she says into the receiver. "With absolutely no regard for the well-being or concentration of the other girls. As you know, Mrs. Chambers, this is not the first run-in I've had with Maeve this school year, and it's one of many infractions committed at St. Bernadette's in her time here. One more strike and she's out, I'm afraid. I would never usually expel a girl during an exam year, but if she continues to be a distraction . . ."

I nod to myself, thinking, *Fair enough,* and hear the dim rattle of my mother's exasperated voice on the other end of the phone. I catch a few words now and then. The ones I pick up on are the ones I've heard before.

"*. . . used to be such a great girl . . . don't know what has gotten into her . . .*"

I wonder what would happen if I just told my parents every-thing. Would they believe me?

After she gets off the phone, Miss Harris frowns at me.

"Get out of here, Maeve. I'll allow you to study downstairs until your next exam. And I meant what I said: one more strike and you're out."

"I know you don't like how the school is being run," I say. I'm not sure why I say it. I just want to show Miss Harris that I'm not a delinquent, I think. "The . . . the new program."

She looks at me blankly. "I don't know what you're talking about."

"All this stuff about . . . chastity and all that. I know you hate it."

The blank stare continues, and as we hold each other's gaze, I begin to realize that the Miss Harris I overheard complaining to Sister Assumpta about the Children has changed. I concentrate and burrow into her mind, expecting a rich, dense landscape of ideas and thoughts and fed-up complaints about the ever-troublesome Maeve Chambers. But there's nothing. Or, not nothing, but a shallow, empty trench. A strangely two-dimensional space where all that exists are the words she's saying and how she is saying them.

"Maeve," she says impatiently. "I'll allow you to study downstairs until your next exam. And I meant what I said: one more strike and you're out."

Yes, you said that. You said exactly those words, in exactly that order, a minute ago.

A chill comes over me, and my eyes move to the window. It's a bright, cool November day, probably the last good day of the year. It's always grim by the time my birthday rolls around.

"Isn't it a nice day?" I say desperately. "Blue skies."

Miss Harris doesn't even turn her head.

"Look." I raise my hand, pointing at the autumn cherry trees at the edge of the school's property, their pink blossoms starting to float off into the sky with the wind's rustle. "They're lovely, aren't they?"

Miss Harris remains rooted, her expression unchanged. That feeling of shallowness seems to roll off her and into the room, and I feel as if I'm not standing in her familiar old office at all but on a soundstage. Finally, she opens her mouth to speak.

"And I mean what I said," she repeats. "One more strike and you're—"

THUNK.

The sound of something heavy and alive beats so hard against the window that I scream at the shock of it. A magpie, possibly blinded by the sunshine, has flown its body into the glass. The window—now double-glazed since the school's makeover—doesn't break, but a small hole opens up at the other side. I shriek as the bird hurls itself against the glass again.

Miss Harris does not react. She is stuck, like a spooked stage actor, on the same line.

"One more strike . . ."

"One more strike and the window is going to shatter," I yell, dashing past her and outside to the magpie.

By the time I've circled my way around, the bird has stunned itself into unconsciousness. It is lying on the pavement, it's creamy-white markings blood-spattered from effort. Or, no. Not blood-spattered.

I peer at its body and see that its white feathers are tipped with tangerine. Not rusty, like dirt, or crimson, like blood. But traffic-cone orange, Penguin Classics orange. Fiona orange. This, I realize, is the same magpie that Fiona healed all those weeks ago back at the tennis courts. A little bit of Fi is still in its system. Just like Nuala said. Someone else's magic changes the color on you.

Another chilly wind comes through the trees, and a haze of pink blossoms sweeps through the air. The bird comes to its senses, ruffles its feathers, and flies off. I tip my fingers to my forehead, not sure if a magic magpie still appreciates formality.

Through the bruised window, Miss Harris continues to stand perfectly still. My skin prickles with nausea and a sense that the adult woman who used to be inside there has been forced to vacate her own body. I look to the window of Sister Assumpta's office, on the opposite side of the main entrance, and it seems to be a hive of activity. The office that is so normally still in its pale lemon-yellow tranquility appears to be full of movement.

I make my way to the hexagonal hallway, staring at Sister Assumpta's office door. And for the first time in almost six years at St. Bernadette's, I knock on it.

There's no answer, so I press my ear to the door. There's the low, scurrying sound of life coming from inside. I push my way in and find . . .

Well, chaos.

There are towers of paper, like Nuala's archives gone completely mutant. There are stacks and stacks of manila folders, each bursting with documents. There are art projects, from the rudimentary still lifes of first-years to the complex machinations of sixth-year final exam pieces. There are glossy graduation photographs, the brown negatives paper-clipped to the side. There are hockey sticks, boxes for mouth guards, duffle bags that smell like grass.

And in the middle of the mess, there is Sister Assumpta. Standing at her desk, four foot eleven and sorting hymn sheets.

"Maeve," she says instantly. She doesn't look up. "I suppose you want to know how I let this happen."

She takes the hymn sheets and disappears, briefly, behind a column of paper.

"Let . . . what happen, Sister?"

"Let those louts in," she remarks disdainfully. "Took their money. Well, it wasn't my choice. We're part state-funded, you know. And when the government sold the contract on to those awful buggers, my hands were tied. All I could do was start moving things *out*."

She picks up another hymn sheet and starts to hum "O Come, All Ye Faithful." She begins to sing then, in her thin, reedy, old-lady voice.

"What . . . what can we do?"

"I own the building," she says. "But they, I'm afraid, have bought part of the contract."

I remember what Aaron said, about how the COB have the resources, the infrastructure. How they could afford to throw as many people—and apparently as much money—at a problem until they won.

"*Adéste, fidéles, laeti triumphántes*," she sings, and quite impulsively pushes some papers to the floor, a waft of dust and mildew releasing into the air. I immediately go to catch them, putting them back in a pile.

Sister Assumpta sits down on what I now see is a piano bench.

She flips the lid on an old upright piano, a big brown wooden thing that on first glance I thought was a cupboard. She settles her crooked hands on the old yellow keys and starts playing clean, chunky chords. She used to do this, back when I first started at St. Bernadette's. Play Christmas carols at the annual mass.

"*Veníte, veníte in Bethlehem*. Sing now, Maeve. It's almost Christmas."

I don't know the Latin words to "O Come, All Ye Faithful," so I murmur them in English. She keeps cocking her head upward, raising her eyebrows, shouting, "Come on now, more. More. Louder."

"O come, let us adore him," I sing, my cheeks burning red. *"O come, let us adore him, O come, let us adore him."*

Sister Assumpta keeps pushing down on the chords, over and over, even though I've run out of lyrics. "Isn't it beautiful, Maeve?" she says, her eyes shining. Her arms are bare. Skin thin, veins knotted but strong. "It can be this way, I think."

"What can?"

"Praising," she says, her hands slamming down even louder now. "Praising. And giving thanks."

She plays to the end of the song. "Sit down," she barks, scooting her body up the piano bench. "Sit down and turn the pages."

And so, we go through "O Little Town of Bethlehem," "The First Noël," and "Hark! The Herald Angels Sing." We're at least three weeks early for any of this, but something about sitting in this room with her, this terrible, untidy, mysterious room, gives me the sense that I am supposed to remember this.

That this is one of those memories that you know is a memory as you are making it, and that it will always be known to me as some kind of end, some kind of beginning.

She finishes, her breath short, her voice rasping. She is exhausted, but happily so, as if briefly distracted from the terror of life.

Sister Assumpta looks around at the mess all over her office, as if seeing it for the first time.

"I've been expecting this for some time." She sighs. "I wanted to move everything out . . . before. Before they could get their hands on it."

She presses just one key with her finger. A high one.

I am so shocked by this that I accidentally clatter my hands on top of the piano, a loud *FHWFIP!* sound emerging from the instrument.

"Sister . . . that's what . . . that's what moving all the stuff out of the school has been about? Since . . . ?"

She nods. "I knew they would come eventually."

"But *how*?"

"Because, Maeve." She starts tapping on the high key again. "My gift is sight."

"You . . ." I put my hand on my mouth, as if trying to catch my own shock.

"Maiden, mother, crone." She makes a chord again. Bangs it loudly. "You, Harriet, me."

"You founded this school . . ." I rack my brain, trying to remember school lore. "You were in a convent, and then you inherited, so you dropped out, and then . . . you founded it."

She shakes her head and starts to play "God Rest Ye Merry Gentlemen."

"This was my home," she says. "I was born here. And when my sensitivity started to show, my mother knew enough about the old ways to know that we were on top of a Well. That I was the Kilbeg sensitive for my generation. When I got the call to God, she said . . . she said, 'You belong back here. You'll have to come back here in the end. That's your service.' And she was right. She always was. So I inherited, and . . . I thought I'd just sit and wait for the next one."

"The next sensitive."

"Yes." She continues playing. "And I was an old woman by the time Harriet came along, you remember."

"Why did you make it a girls' school?" I push. "What if it was a boy sensitive?"

"Oh, it's always a girl."

"No," I correct her. "I know a boy."

"Hmm," she says dubiously. "Is he mad?"

I think about it. "Yes," I answer.

"Poor thing. Boys can be good witches, but never good sensitives."

"Do they know?" I ask. "Do the Children know what you are?"

"Ha!" she laughs, slamming down both hands on the keys, like Beethoven. "No. I've been in this game much longer than them. I'm clever as a fox."

I nod. She peers at me. "And do you know who else is?"

"Who?"

She looks up at the ceiling and I almost laugh.

"God?"

"God, Maeve." She smiles. "He's not fooled by any of this, either, you know."

I'm not sure what to say. I've never really thought much about God in any of this. It's always what people do with God that seems to be the sticking point. There isn't much room for God himself. Herself? Themself?

"When we willingly leave the church in the hands of thieves," she says, "we let them keep the faith."

I sit and watch her hands for a minute, wondering what she already knows, what I need to explain, what I need to ask.

"We're going to stop them," I say quietly.

"I know," she says approvingly.

"So you know everything?"

"Some things. My gift is that I can see things. My curse is that I am not allowed to interfere."

"Surely you can help?"

"No," she replies. "Except . . ."

She goes to her desk and takes out a long velvet box from her seemingly endless supply of velvet boxes.

"This one has something in it," she says. "Something for you."

I open it, hearing the soft hiss of hinges on plush material.

"It's a knife," I say. And it is. A long silver blade, like a dagger, with a heavy pearl handle. It looks like something for opening letters.

I feel bloodless looking at it. I don't have a great history with knives as it is.

"That was my mother's," she says. "It's been in this house much longer than me. Some old, old magic in that blade. Take it with you. You'll know when it's time to use it."

"Doesn't this count as you interfering?"

"No. It belongs to you, and you belong to it."

"Why?"

"Because you both belong to here," she says, and she raps her knuckles on the wall. She looks at me as if this is supposed to explain everything.

I nod, not quite understanding. And I leave, not quite knowing what to do with the knife.

36

I DON'T SEE MISS BANBURY ALL WEEK, BUT I feel her. I know she's in the building like you know a toothache is coming from the dull throb in your gums. I suspect she has some kind of protection spell over her, something that stops me from confronting her directly while she recovers from the incident with Aaron.

More than once, I walk down a corridor to find it extending on and on, so that I pass the same statue of Mary twice, the same framed photo of the fifth-year choir three times. There's a feeling of immense pressure: like turbulence, like a sinus infection. I know what is happening without having to say it out loud. I keep Sister Assumpta's pearl-handled letter opener close, not sure what it does, but comforted by its heft.

·) ☽ ● ☾ (·

On Wednesday I make one last-ditch attempt at getting through to Roe.

"Hey," he says, sounding grateful to hear my voice. He seems tired, like life on the road is starting to take it out of him. "It's good to hear your voice. Home on Monday!"

"Yup," I agree. Then I launch into it. "Listen, Roe. There's something you should know. Friday we're . . . we're doing a spell."

A long sigh on the other end of the line.

"It's an important one," I continue, trying not to let his embarrassment or exhaustion affect me. "We're sealing the Well. At St. Bernadette's."

Silence.

"The thing is," I go on, my voice warbling, "St. Bernadette's is actually the mouth of the Well, and . . ."

"I've got to go, Maeve," he says, and he hangs up.

And then it's Thursday night. The Eve of Destruction, as Fiona has started calling it. We gather at Nuala's and go through it all. Step by step. Beat for beat.

"After we seal the Well," Lily says tentatively, "what happens to us? Will our gifts . . . go away?"

Manon is holding a jam jar of Heather Banbury's binding spell up to the light. It is mossy green in color. "No," she says. "Or, I don't think so. What we are doing is sealing the hole the Housekeeper created, the one that made the Well so vulnerable. A normal flow of magic to Kilbeg will resume."

I tell them about Sister Assumpta and the knife, and we all agree that we should use it to expose the Well. I can see from Nuala's face, though, that she is thinking of her sister and how the knife could have been Heaven's to carry.

We eat dinner together. Nuala seems to think it's extremely important that we all sit down and break bread before we embark on our plan that is both wholly good and vastly imperfect. We know there could be variables we haven't counted on. We know that dealing with a human person is not the same thing as dealing with a spirit like the Housekeeper, that in many ways this is both easier and more difficult. People don't behave like demons do. Sometimes they behave worse.

Nuala's kitchen table is too small to seat all of us, so she brings in the plastic porch table and spreads a navy flowered cloth over both. She cooks the two chickens whose fat went into the candles, and serves them with salad and two sticks of French bread. Fiona has a little butternut squash pie in a white enamel dish, her initials pricked into the pastry.

Halfway through, there's a ring of the doorbell.

"It'll be that boy collecting money for the Guide Dogs again." Nuala frowns. "Honestly, he must know I'm a soft heart. He's come twice this week."

Aaron stands up. "I'll get it," he says. "I'll tell him to give it a rest."

He disappears to the hallway and I hear a murmur of voices, one of them getting loud quickly. We each drop our cutlery and look at one another. "I'll go," I say, standing up.

I get to the doorway and see that it isn't anyone collecting for Guide Dogs. It's Roe. Roe leveled up, Roe even more spectacular than I've seen him before. He must have gotten some clothes in Dublin, because what he's wearing outstrips anything I've seen in Kilbeg. High-waisted patent-leather trousers and a peep-toe heel, paired with a huge furry purple jacket. His hair curly, his eyebrows thick and painted. If Roe was a junior rock star before, it's fair to say he's graduated to the mid-leagues now. My heart leaps when I see him.

"Roe!" I squeal. But he doesn't hear it. Two sounds drown it out.

His fist hitting Aaron's face, and Aaron hitting the floor.

"Well, I guess that makes us even," Aaron says minutes later, holding a bag of frozen peas to his open lip.

"Even for *what*?" Roe hisses from across the kitchen. He hasn't sat down yet.

We have, in brief, explained Aaron's presence in the house. We tell Roe that he has left the Children of Brigid. Aaron, through the blood, explains himself. He talks Roe through the series of epiphanies that have led him to believe that perhaps the point of life is not, as he previously thought, to manipulate vulnerable people into believing outdated doctrine out of pure fear. He does not explain about Matthew. It doesn't feel like the right time.

This is not good enough for Roe. He is disgusted, perhaps rightfully, that it seems good enough for us.

"You were both there," he says to me and Fiona, bewildered hurt in his eyes. "You were there when he started the riot at the Cypress."

"I know," I say. "And I don't like it either, but . . . he knows too much for us not to use him."

"So, what? He's our friend now?"

"No," Lily, Fiona, and I all say at once.

"I can't believe this," Roe says, shaking his head.

Suddenly, a thought occurs to me.

"Wait . . . *what* don't you believe, Roe?"

His eyes widen, like he can't believe the person I've turned into. "That you would . . . you would even *entertain* the thought of sharing a *room* with him?"

He glances at the table of chicken and bread. "Or a fucking *meal*?"

"Why?" I prod, a theory starting to develop in my mind.

"Because he's a violent homophobe who manipulates people?" he says, narrowing his eyes at Aaron. "Because everything bad that's happened to this city in the last year in some way can be linked back to him?"

"How?" I jab again. "Tell me how he manipulates people."

"Because he's a fucking evil sensitive, Maeve. You *know* this."

I can't help it. A wide grin cracks over my face, like an egg spilling into a frying pan.

"A sensitive," I say, almost giddy. "What's that?"

Roe is so angry now that the words just spill out in one furious mess. "A person who is more connected to the magic of the earth, which is why you could summon the Housekeeper, and . . ."

He smacks a three-ringed hand over his mouth.

"Oh, my god," he gasps. "Oh my god, oh my god."

I go to where he's standing and wrap my arms around him, holding him tightly. Roe grabs my waist hard and holds on to me like he is about to drown, or has been drowning for some time.

"I'm sorry," he whispers, tears choking his throat. "I'm sorry, I'm sorry, I'm sorry."

For a few seconds, the rest of the room falls away and it's just me and him again. Two schoolkids in the underpass. Two children hiding under the bed. Two people who have literally taken a blade for each other.

"You came back," I mumble into his hair. "Did you remember?"

"Only just now," he says, untangling himself from me. "When I saw . . ." He gestures vaguely at Aaron.

"Then how come you're here?"

"I . . . I talked to Honor. About everything. About how I thought you were exaggerating or using this magic stuff as a coping mechanism for trauma. And . . . and she just looked at me and said it doesn't matter if it's a coping mechanism or it isn't. You need to be there for her. And I don't know. I just got a wake-up call. I realized it didn't matter what I believed. It mattered that you were safe."

"So . . . you left the tour?"

"Just one date." He smiles meekly. "And when you weren't at Fiona's house or your house or my house, I figured there was only one place you could be."

I throw my arms around Roe again, him feeling more solid and more real than he has in months. My mouth sinks onto his, and I feel like a person who has just eaten after weeks of starvation.

Nuala coughs. "Glad to have you back on the team, Roe."

37

FRIDAY ARRIVES IN A WHIRL OF UNSEASON-
able darkness. By three p.m., it's already pitch-dark outside, the birds
chirping manically, confused by the early roost. By four thirty, the
school is empty. I start emptying my locker, as if leaving for any other
normal weekend, each movement slow and deliberate.

Soon, my head throbs.

Soon.

"Maeve," Miss Banbury says, the voice coming from behind me.
"I believe I'm seeing you today."

I turn around. There she is. Same long skirt. Same combat
boots. Her face, though. Her face is different. Jaundiced and yellow
with puckered spots, like an overripe banana. Like the walls in her
office. Her cheekbones are sharp, or maybe they always were. Maybe
I couldn't tell when she was smiling softly at me.

"Lead the way," I say tersely. And for a moment, terror grips me.
This isn't how it should feel. It should feel like we're ambushing her.
She should be unaware. It should not feel like a boxing match that
has been on the calendar for months.

I follow her into The Chokey, close the door, and sit down.

Thinking:

Right now, Manon is drinking the bind.

Right now, Roe is breaking the lock on the main gate upstairs.

Right now, Lily is sparking the security system and the cameras.

Right now, Nuala is uttering incantations.

Right now, Aaron is . . .

And then I catch her eye and a dash of her inner monologue sprays across my mind. *I thought I was doing a good job, but if Branum can convince her he's some kind of reformed Christian, then she really must be an idiot.*

I stiffen. The word *idiot* dings off me like metal.

Right now he's probably coining those kids upstairs.

No, I think. She's bluffing. She's trying to trick me.

I want her to know that I know she's trying to trick me. "Coining?" I say.

She raises her eyebrow. She looks surprised. It's an act, I remind myself. Don't be taken in too easily.

"Your power is back," she says. "Congratulations."

"You know it's back. I'm not stupid," I say, and for once, I actually mean it. "What is coining?"

I remember, though, as I say the word. The silver coins on Manon's neck.

She shrugs. "This tea-bag-and-hair business. It's very . . . tawdry. Messy. Imprecise. The coins make it easier."

"You're making things for us now?"

"We make things for a lot of people," she says. "We even make people."

I try to remain calm. I remind myself that I am supposed to be here. I remind myself that Sister Assumpta built the very walls around me just so that I could one day be here, doing this.

"You," I reply. "They made you for me."

"I think 'made' me is rather strong. I would say they wrote a role and then cast me." She traces a line of dust on her desk. "Yes, they cast me for you."

"Why you?" I ask, and through my worry and fear there is genuine curiosity. Why this woman? Why these clothes?

"It's a very delicate art. They wanted me to remind you of your sisters. Right kind of age, you know. And they wanted me to offer you what no one else could."

"And what's that?"

She smiles at me. "Options."

"Options?"

"For the future. You were so convinced of your own failure. All you needed was someone to give you a little boost, a little attention. It wasn't hard, Maeve. You're so hungry for connection as it is. People will take advantage of a thing like that."

"That's what Japan was?" I say. "Options?"

"There are *still* options," Heather continues, and her tone seems to adjust back to her normal one, the one I've grown so comfortable with. "Listen. The religious stuff, I know it's not your thing. It's not my thing, either. But it's a very small part of the company."

The company?

She goes on. "There is, quite simply, a lot of money to be made in preserving old thought."

"Why do they need money?" I ask tightly through my teeth.

"Well, for all *this*. The more backers we have, the more Wells we can secure, which attracts more backers, and so on, and so on. There are huge opportunities here for young people with a bit of magic."

"Magic that *you* own," I counter. "That's not okay. You can't just own the world's magic."

She looks thoughtful. "The thing is, Maeve, if we *did* own it, then it couldn't be mishandled. Then your fight with Lily would have just stayed a silly little fight, wouldn't it? There would be no House-keepers, no ice and snow, no throwing the world out of balance. And that's just two teenage girls having a fight in an Irish backwater. Imagine what people are doing all over the world. People who *know* what they're doing."

Despite everything, this throws me. I find myself pausing to consider it.

"The Children," she continues, seeing my interest, "have ended civil wars before they became genocides. They've helped dissolve bad governments, ended corruption. There is no greater ally to global stability than us, and we've always been there, ticking away in the background. Helping."

"Draining," I correct her. "Hoarding."

She waves her hand as if this is all negligible, as if it's a matter of breaking eggs to make omelets.

"Maeve," she says. "You *know* me. This hasn't all been an act. Most of what I told you about my life was true. Do you really think I would be involved in this if it was an inherently bad thing? I mean, I don't *love* all of it. But I don't *love* Amazon either, or the fact that people die sourcing the material for iPhones. But it's life. It's the world. We do what we can."

I don't know how to take this. I'm supposed to be biding time until Manon drinks the bind and marches down here with Lily. If the bind is working, surely Heather Banbury should be feeling it? Aaron walked in his sleep to my house when I bound him, and that was just a light bind, a sweet bind.

"Enemies into allies, allies into enemies again," she continues. "It's all very circular, isn't it?"

My gums start to throb.

"Maeve . . . do you *really* think people can change their minds that easily? I'm curious. I *do* actually have an interest in the adolescent mind. That wasn't all a put-on. Do you think someone can override more than twenty years of God fearing and . . . change their mind in a couple of weeks?"

"You were in agony," I counter. "I saw the holes on your face."

She doesn't respond to this, but pulls open the top drawer of her desk and takes out one of the old tea bags. She holds it up, between her thumb and forefinger.

"Once they dry out, they lose their potency," she says. "But this one still has a little give in it."

The tea bag disappears into her palms and she squeezes on it, hard, like a stress ball. I immediately feel as though someone is trying to drill a hole at the bottom of me.

The lightbulb above us briefly flickers. Miss Banbury watches it carefully.

"I suppose that's your friend," she says. "Lily. Trying to shock her way inside."

I hear a scattering of footsteps on the basement steps, and I know they're here. But I suddenly feel weak, my green light fading, and my blood feels like cold pudding.

"This is your last chance, Maeve," she says. "We can leave together right now, and you can just have a short conversation with my manager. You don't have to commit to anything."

"Actually, it's your last chance," I say, standing up, every movement heavy and strange. The footsteps are coming closer. I'm just minutes away from Manon coming through the door. "We're going to end this now."

"Oh, Maeve," she tuts, disappointed. "We *own* the school. None of you are getting out of here alive."

How is she so sure of this? Where is her confidence coming from?

She opens her desk drawer and takes a coin out. "Binds are so messy," she says. "All that teeth and hair. And you can never quite tell who it belongs to."

And in that moment I know something has gone terribly wrong.

38

HEATHER'S MOVEMENTS ARE QUICK, VIO-
lent, and come with such unimaginable force that I briefly wonder if
she's human at all. She pounces on me, slams my shoulder against the
wall, and places two silver coins on my neck. They stick there, terrifying and cold. They look like metal. They are not metal. They are
something closer to a creature than an object, their underside reaching and suckering on to my skin like lizards' feet on a hot stone wall.
I scream at the feeling, the same scream of surprise and confusion
I heard Manon give at the cottage. There's a hand on my neck, and
then a sharp feeling at the back of my leg. For a moment, I don't know
what it is. I can't see anything except Heather's face, her teeth sharp,
her bitten lips. I think the sharpness is an insect, or a snakebite.

The bind didn't work, I think. We're fucked.

Then the blood comes, and I realize as I sink to the floor that
Heather Banbury has taken a knife to the skin behind my knee.

Blood. Again. Always blood.

There's the sound of leather and metal, and my hands are bound
behind my back with a belt. I am lying on my belly now, my leg cut,
my neck sticky with coins.

I think she's going to leave me to bleed out. There is nothing so brutal that I couldn't imagine her doing it at this point. But I feel probing, padding. I can't turn my head to look, but it feels like she's dressing the wound.

"Just collecting samples, my love," Heather says calmly, her voice nurturing.

The door swings open, and I think, finally, thank god. They're here. But there is no "they." It's just Aaron.

"Maeve," he says, and his tone is wrong. The quiet, punished-choirboy Aaron we've all grown used to in the last two weeks has disappeared, replaced by cold, mechanical speech and hard eyes. "Heather." He nods at Miss Banbury.

Then before anyone can react, he pushes his way into the room and pulls me, my arms still belted, off the floor.

"Against the wall," he says brutally. I'm so confused, peering at his face for the person I've gradually come to think of as . . . well, not a friend. A colleague. His expression is blank. His eye without twitch. He puts his hands under my shoulders and drags me over, bleeding, so I am propped against the wall like a hostage.

I can't get a grip on what's happening. This isn't in the plan.

"Listen, Maeve, I've got your friends rolling around upstairs. Roe—if that's what you're still calling him—is never going to be the same. Every sinful thought, every perverted action. Every terrible thing he's done to you—namely, I suppose, leaving you with only me to talk to. He really does blame himself for all this, you know."

Aaron touches the wall, and it glows a greenish color around his fingertips. "And I can keep this going, going as long as you want."

"What? What are you . . ."

Aaron puts his fingers to his lips. "Shhh, shhh," he says. "Ciúnas."

The Irish word for quiet. How did he learn that? I wonder. The very first word you learn at school, because it's the only way for a teacher to keep a room of five-year-olds quiet. The word Roe said to me, all those years ago, under the bed.

And I am quiet. Quiet in my confusion, my bafflement, my disbelief in what is going on. That's when I hear it.

The screams.

Something they don't tell you about a group of people screaming is how, unconsciously, they will find a kind of harmony together. Even among the chaos and pain, the screams will begin to blend, and that is how I am able to pick out Roe's: the bass note, the cello among violins. The sound tears through me and I realize this isn't a joke. This isn't a perversion of the plan. This is real. I leap from my seat, the screams worming their way into my inner ear, burrowing into my brain, becoming sounds I can never unhear.

I start to struggle, scream, my hands wrestling at the belt, trying to wriggle out. Aaron grips my head, hands on both ears, his fingers clawing at my face. "I could make this much worse if I wanted," he says. "You're taking forever with this, Heather. We don't have all day."

"I was waiting for *you*," she says. "Or for anyone. I was given instructions to hold her here."

The screaming sounds become weaker, choked, exhausted by themselves. They are dissolving into crying. I can hear Fiona in there, and remember the day I heard her sing for the first time. She and Roe in the living room, their voices matched so beautifully, his huskiness and her Disney princess sweetness. I remember Miss Banbury the day the black spots emerged on her face. That is happening, right now, to my friends. To Nuala. Nuala, whose guilt is already so primed from failing Heaven, from leaving her daughter in France. Fiona, who hates herself for people-pleasing. Lily . . . what is Lily being tortured with? With her desire to not be human, her one real desire that contradicts the wishes of everyone who loves her so madly?

"Give me everything you have," Aaron commands.

"Everything?"

"Tea bags, panty liners, whatever you witches use."

She looks at him, furious. "You had your three chances. You failed. This is my case now."

He goes to her desk and begins pulling out drawers and emptying them on the floor. The tea bags fall, but so do other things: papers, a hairbrush, brochures for college, half a roll of cough drops.

"Come on, Heather. Is this all you have?" He looks perplexed. "No clothes, no files on Fiona? Nothing on the O'Callaghans? This is poor work, Heath. You've been here for months."

"You *left*," she hisses. Then points to the floor. To me. "She's bleeding. Isn't that enough?"

He looks slightly disgusted. "You're a very coarse witch."

"You're the one who went AWOL," she yelps. "Do you think this is going to get you back in their good graces? Do you think they're just going to let you off the hook for this?"

He sighs, kicking at the pile on the floor.

"The right hand never talks to the left hand, Heather. And in this case, you're not even the left hand. You're the . . . left pinky finger."

The screaming goes on, and on, and on.

"You're not a sensitive, Heather," he says, still nudging at the heap with his foot. "You're just a cheap Walmart witch, and this job was always too big for you."

He puts his hand on the wall above my head and tears away the rotting paint, keeping up his lively brand of horrible conversation.

"What are you doing?" she snaps.

"I'm always fascinated with these old Wells. The house has

been on top of it so long. Tickle the paint and out it all comes," he says, peeling and tearing, tearing and peeling. "The thing with your Maeves of the world is that they get suspicious. Oh, you can trade on their loneliness, their trauma, their eagerness to trust someone older and wiser. But you can't bleed it out over months and months, Heath. They wise up. They talk. It has to be one swoop. One big leach."

He has made a hole as big as a fist, and to my surprise, some drops of water start to drip out of the wall. Like a leaky tap. There's the faint, muffled sound of water on carpet, and a few drops fall on my forehead.

Aaron looks down at me, smiles a happy smile, brimming with cruelty.

"We have to end this now, Heather. No open channels."

Then he turns to me. "Did you hear that, Maeve? No open channels," he says, as if he feels a little sorry for me. "Do you want to say anything? Once the last bit of sensitivity leaves your body, I don't know how long you'll be able to live. Ten minutes? Twenty?

"I know you've always had a bit of a thing for me," he says. "Do you maybe want a kiss goodbye? Completely on the house."

And he taps his lip.

His lip that Roe burst open last night.

That is perfectly healed.

Heather moves closer to me, seemingly fascinated by what is happening. Which is still . . . nothing. If anything, I'm recovering. My hands mobile, my chest less tight.

And I realize that he is biding time.

And I realize that he isn't Aaron at all.

39

I DON'T KNOW WHY THIS IS HAPPENING, OR what aspect of our plan had to go wrong in order for Manon to do this. She must have realized at some point that the bind was a dud. But what else have the Children planned? Was Aaron really a double agent, or is this just a distraction Manon has come up with?

I don't know.

But I do know that the only way to work with a trickster god is to keep the trick going.

I try to mimic how Heather responded when Aaron used his gift on her, the writhing with psychological torture. I make my breath short, labored, wheezing. It comes from deep in my belly and I sound like I'm choking on it. I sound like a vacuum cleaner stuck on a bit of rug. My leg is still bleeding, the shock of it wearing off and now falling into deep, abysmal pain. I channel the pain, scream it all out.

"Get behind her, Heather," Manon-as-Aaron snaps. "Hold on to her shoulders. Sometimes they have a last burst of energy."

Heather Banbury's hands clamp down on me, holding me in place.

"And make sure she doesn't vomit on the floor," Manon says, the emphasis on *floor*. "I don't want a stink down here."

Emphasis on *down here*.

I start to jerk uncontrollably and arch my back until I slide onto the carpeted floor, my head down. From this angle, I can see the drips from the wall, the pool of wetness gathering by Manon's feet.

"Well, don't just stand there, *restrain* her."

From my spot on the floor, I can see that Manon has taken a clump of hair from Heather's hairbrush and has soaked it in Well water. While Heather tries to restrain me, Manon is slipping the clump into Aaron's coat, deftly unscrewing something in the inside pocket. I feel a surge of respect for her tricky, tricky genius. She still has the bind. She's trying to modify it.

My hands free from the belt, I snatch a length of Heather's hair and yank it down, almost embarrassed by the childishness of the action. It works, though; she's caught off guard, yelps, and is on the floor.

"Maeve!" Manon hisses, still in Aaron's form, and there's a heavy sound of metal hitting the floor. I look around and see the silver coins. I take them into my hands and stick them quickly on Heather's skin: one on her arm, one on the base of her neck. Heather shudders, and I use the moment to pin her down, my knees to her shoulders.

"Manon, can you do this? Is it safe?"

Manon looks at me, and even though she is still using Aaron's face, she couldn't look more like a scared woman. She raises up the jam jar that holds the bind. "On verra bien," she says, and drinks the bind down, swallowing hard, the clump of hair sticking like a spider to the glass.

Manon steadies herself against the desk. It looks as though something small and alive, like a parasite, is rattling through her. The color drains from Heather's face, and her eyes shine pink, as if blood vessels have just burst inside them. She lies there, twitching slightly, staring dead ahead.

"Is she . . . ?"

"No," Manon says, sounding queasy.

"Are you OK?"

"Not really." She clutches her stomach. "But I had no choice."

"What happened?"

"Aaron, Lily, and Roe are upstairs. The Children have got people up there, they knew we were coming. It took the three of them to even let me slip through down here."

"And Nuala and Fiona?"

"At the court. We need to bring her there."

"To . . . carry her? Up the stairs?"

Manon shrugs.

And we do it somehow. I take the shoulders and Manon takes the legs. Even with me still bleeding. Even with Manon looking like she swallowed a swamp and it might come back up at any moment.

At the top of the stairs, Roe is there, standing outside one of the classrooms, his eye swollen and turning purple.

"Are you OK?" We both ask it at once, and then give each other a small, rueful smile. A smile that says, *No, but I'm here, aren't I?*

"How many?"

"Four. Lily stunned them and Aaron did his . . . thing. Seemed to almost finish them off."

"Where are they now?"

"Tied up. Locked in here," he says mischievously. He nods to the door handle. "I had a word with her."

I almost burst out laughing. "The door is a girl?"

"The door is a *woman*." He laughs, then a worried look crosses his face. "Let's move."

He takes over carrying Heather and I limp out to the tennis courts, where Fiona and Nuala are at the center in a cloud of candles. The smell is rancid, hitting our noses the second we step outside. The melting fat and burning sage choke me, the sharp wind blowing the smoke back toward the school. Lily is standing outside the wire fence, a bucket at her feet. The fence is dripping with water. I remember the day at the end of summer when Lily charged the fence, terrifying us all. We had all let ourselves become lazy with our gifts, but she seemed to know that something like this was coming.

Heather is still in some kind of trance, her skin bleached white, her eyes pink and staring. We lay her down and she's like a white rabbit on an operating table.

There is a brief second when we realize what we're doing, what we look like. Aaron, the real one, appears from the shadows. I feel a bubble of doubt, a sense of *Are we really doing this? Casting a spell over a woman's unconscious body?*

Around Nuala and Fiona are crystals acting as paperweights for cards arranged in a pentagram shape. Big cards. Major arcana, mostly. The World. The Empress. Judgment. *Judgment.* How would we be judged for this? How will we judge ourselves?

The candles have all melted down, the fatty liquid wax pooling onto plates.

"Maeve," Nuala says gently. "I need you to lie down by Fiona, if that's all right."

I see there is a little tartan blanket spread out next to Fi, precisely for this purpose. I lie there, looking up at the stars and into Fiona's face. "Hey, dude," she says, then looks to my blood-soaked trouser leg. "Rough night?"

"My leg is fucked."

"I can see that. After this I'll sort you out."

Nuala goes to Heather, and we are all in a circle now. Manon puts the sign of the goddess in oil on each of our foreheads, and there is no hailing to the watchtowers this time. Fiona has a sheet from the archives wedged under her knee, and she prepares to read aloud from it. She coughs, clears her throat slightly.

"OK, are we ready, everyone?"

We each nod.

"All right," she says, and takes a big breath. Then her voice comes out loud and booming, so full of brass and steel that I almost jump up. "We come to this Well today," she begins, "in the spirit of true heart and true service, in order to restore what is unbalanced, and to fix what is broken. We do not wish harm on anyone, and when we act, we do so only in defense. Maeve, do you come here in the spirit of true heart and true service?"

"I do."

"Roe, do you come here in the spirit of true heart and true service?"

"I do."

"Manon, do you . . ."

She goes around to everyone, asking with equal gravity every time, and power gathers around her like storm clouds. Nuala was right to get Fiona to do this. She's not just a great actress. She's a great witch. As if trying to prove my point, a magpie—white feathers tipped with orange—flies down to her side and watches her carefully, its head cocked to one side like a dog.

Fiona produces a length of black cotton; Nuala does the same. Fi places it gently over my eyes. She coughs again, consults the piece of paper wedged under her knee.

"I ask you to look inward, and to channel the greatest part of your power."

I hear Nuala say the same thing to Heather as she covers her eyes, and I feel another light drop of oil on my skin. Manon has begun to chant incantations, half in English and half in French, in some kind of conversation with the unconscious form of Heather Banbury. Commanding her to relinquish the stolen magic. Telling her that she will be forgiven once the wrong is righted. Fiona repeats her command again, and I do as she says, channeling the green light, the overwhelming warmth and honesty of it.

I hear Nuala's voice again. "Reverse the channel," she tells Heather. "Return what you have taken."

A surge of feeling comes through me, and it rises in my chest like an anxiety attack. I feel my lungs expand, my ribs stretch. I am getting bigger, bigger on the inside, as the power that was stolen from me and from the earth rushes back into my body. And for a few seconds, the life of Heather Banbury, or whatever her real name is, collapses into me.

And I see a frizzy-haired, skinny little girl who has contracted blood poisoning from untreated head lice.

And I see her on a children's hospital ward, alone.

And I see a series of professionals asking one another why certain people are allowed to have children, and isn't it funny that you need a license for a dog and not for a child. A statement a young Heather takes to mean *You matter less than a dog.*

And even as the magic flows out of me and into the ground, I realize that everyone who craves power once had none. That maybe Heather actually believes the thing she said about stopping a civil war before it becomes a genocide.

And it's gone. The magic passes through me and into the earth below.

"Are you OK?" Fiona whispers, and I realize that I am hyperventilating.

"Yes," I manage to say. "Is this the part . . . ?"

"Yes," she says softly, taking the black cotton away from my eyes. "This is the part."

It's time to send the magic back through to the Well, using the knife as the lightning rod. I take up the letter opener and jam it into the ground. I tense my arm, trying to get purchase in the rubbery material, feeling like the blade is going to come off the mother-of-pearl handle. I start to panic. It's not strong enough. The knife isn't moving.

I feel Roe's big hand on mine, stroking my fingers, and then his hand moves to the knife. The blade starts to tingle in my hand and I can tell that Roe is not just reassuring me, but speaking to the blade itself. He guides my hand, and we rip right through the court, sun-starved grass brushing against my wrist as we do.

Fiona's voice gets louder. "We have sealed this Well," she booms. "We have sealed this Well to prevent its draining, and to protect our lives and the lives of this community. We seal this Well."

Then everyone starts to say it, Lily and Aaron and Manon and Roe and Nuala.

"You can get up, Maeve," Fiona whispers to me.

I get up and we begin to pour the wax into the gash made in the earth. The wax disappears immediately, not settling for an instant on the grass or the delicate yellow flowers, but seems to be sucked straight into the ground. The wound of it, the ruptured court, seems to heal itself in front of us. *We're doing it*, we all think at once. *We've done it.*

"That's good," Nuala says shortly, her voice tense. "I think that's good. I think . . ."

There's the sound of footsteps, and we look up to see people approaching. Four, five, six. All in black, all with their faces covered.

They're coming from the alleyway that I once ran down to escape Aaron, when he offered the first of my three chances.

We see them only briefly, lit by the orange glow of the streetlamp.

"Lily," I say, reaching for her hand. We once exploded a lightbulb from halfway across a room. Could we do it outside, in the middle of the most powerful spell we've ever done?

She understands me immediately, and together we spark the streetlights, dazzling them with darkness. Then Lily gets to her feet, runs to the fence that she has already doused.

"Don't stop, everyone," Nuala says. "We need to fully seal it. No chancing."

We pour and pour, the wax and our magic, the wax *becoming* our magic. The fence around us hums with electricity. Roe gets up. He goes to Lily and takes her hand, and there's a surge, the hum so loud it becomes a din.

"Go ahead and try it!" he yells, and there's a yelp, a young person's yelp, and the hot, rotten smell of burnt fabric. I wince. Who *was* that we just electrocuted? Someone our age and accidentally on the wrong side of this war for magic?

There's a *clink* sound, and the hum of the fence has stopped. *Clink. Clink. Clink.*

"What was that?"

A wind picks up, and the last of the chicken-fat candles blows out.

"They've put those coins on the fence," Aaron says, his voice streaked with terror. "They're coming in."

And they do come in. It's a blur of faces and violence, of pushing and grabbing, and I feel a hand around my mouth. Then my neck. My head is in an armlock, and I'm being dragged out of the court. My eyes dart around, trying to mark everyone's location in the near-blackness.

"Fiona!" I scream. I see her arms being pulled around her back. I catch a flash of a face, and it's a boy, the boy who was on the bus with me and Lily. Frog Eyes.

There's a flash, then a fire. Lily lights up. The hot liquid fat goes up in flames, and the tarot cards become kindling. Everyone is blown back, and I look around, not seeing Roe, Aaron, or Manon. Nuala is struggling with someone. And on the ground, the body of Heather Banbury is beginning to revive itself. She blinks, and someone in black pulls her up, tries to get her to walk. She looks pitifully weak, staggering, not seeming to know where she is.

The fire crackles and spreads, roaring so hard that I wonder if the Well is doing its bit to protect itself. This fire can't just be from candle grease. This is something screaming and defensive, something that has been waiting to fight back. A branch from a tree snaps off and falls to the ground, then another, and then another. Whoever is holding on to me suddenly lets go as Aaron shoulders them into the still-hot fence. There's another yelp and the smell of clothes burning.

Another branch falls into the flames. *What is happening?*

No one seems to understand what is going on: not our side, and not theirs. It's just chaos and struggle, the fire looping around us, the wind tickling the flames into a bigger laugh. There's a sudden gust that carries the fire to a border shrub next to the school, and within moments, the school catches fire.

I look up, and suddenly the question of the branches becomes clear. A sky of orange-tipped magpies are dropping them into the flames. The birds circle Fiona, protective as pack lions, beating their wings heavily against Frog Eyes. I don't understand anything I'm looking at: it's all too strange, too inexplicable. Are they biting him? No, not biting. *Pecking.*

The smoke becomes too thick for fighting. What was a battle is now a wreckage, and it's all anyone can do to get out alive. Eyes are lit up by the orange flames, and I suddenly see everyone in the tennis court for who they truly are: just another young person, fighting for something they believe to be the morally correct thing to do.

"We need to get out," I scream uselessly. "This isn't . . ."

The Children have begun to flee down the alleyway they came from. Roe, his face streaked with blood, grabs hold of me and drags me to the exit. You never think of a tennis court—a nice outdoor one, surrounded by pretty shrubs and leafy trees—as a fire hazard. But in this moment, I'm appalled that they're even allowed to exist, this beautiful, luxurious thing that is now just a fire cage, all wire and kindling and burning, melting rubber. And now, only one exit.

That exit is through the school, the alleyway already cut off by flames. The dumpster, still not collected by the council, has caught fire. We all manage to run out of the court, through fire or around it, holding our jumpers up to our mouths. I do a checklist, counting each of my people, each of my team. Roe. Fiona. Aaron. Manon. Nuala. Lily. As we run through the long hallway of the school, it's obvious that some of the back classrooms have started to smolder.

"Lil, Maeve," Roe says sharply. "Run ahead. Get out of here."

And when we get outside, there are Fiona, Nuala, and Manon. Fiona is crouching over something, someone. My first assumption is that it is Heather Banbury. I didn't notice her leave the tennis court before it became too awash with smoke and fire to see clearly, but it seems as if she must have staggered out. The closer I get, the faster I realize that I am wrong.

I close my eyes, feel for the lights of every creature present, and realize two things.

One, that the body on the street belongs to Sister Assumpta. And two, that Heather Banbury did not get out alive.

In that second, I can't focus on anything. I can't think. I can't engage with the fact that Heather, a woman who—up until two weeks ago—I had trusted enough to walk barefoot through her house, is now dead. That she is now dead because of me. That Sister Assumpta is also dead, and probably because of me. That we hurt people tonight. That we caused this. All of these facts bounce off me. All I can concentrate on is the radar of lights in my brain and the fact that Heather Banbury is no longer on it.

But someone new is. Something royal blue enters my field of energy, and I am aware that I am being watched.

I look up and see a well-dressed woman across the street staring at us with great interest. She wears a hat and is utterly unaffected by the smoke billowing out of the school. She stands in front of a long black car, her driver visible within.

Aaron is standing next to me and breathing heavily. "Is that who I think it is?" I say to him, pointing to her. Knowing she would think it was rude to point.

"Yep," he says. His voice is flat. "That's Dorey."

And we walk, with cold formality, across the street to meet her.

THE WORLD

THE EMPRESS

LATER

The funeral for Sister Assumpta is held on a Monday, the day after my seventeenth birthday. The whole school is there, or what used to be the whole school, before the concept of our school became loose and hard to define. There is nothing about St. Bernadette's that remains habitable, and it won't be for a long time. There have been a lot of conversations about lessons over Zoom, other schools taking students, and classes being conducted in various vacant sports halls. There is, naturally, a lot of concern over the Leaving Cert students, who will never return to St. Bernadette's as students again and will complete the rest of their coursework at home.

It is, apparently, one of the biggest funerals in Kilbeg since a certain local football player died back in the 1980s. All week, there are articles about her, outpourings of appreciation for the wonderful things she did for women's education, evidence of the numerous and surprisingly left-wing charities she secretly donated to that seemed to exist in conflict with her strong Catholic faith. Even RTÉ set up camp to do a news slot on her, talking to former famous students like Anthea Jackson, who travels back from London to attend the funeral. There is discussion of a statue in her honor. Then a street named after her. Then both conversations seem to fade entirely.

The official story is that I was at detention, and that the fire on the tennis courts was brought about by a combination of bad new wiring after a rushed refurbishment and an unemptied dumpster that the council should have taken months ago. Miss Banbury, who had been supervising my detention, had unwisely attempted to put out the fire. There was a piece in the paper about how she had not been given proper fire safety training. There is no record of anyone else having been present at the St. Bernadette's fire, the security cameras having suspiciously short-circuited an hour beforehand.

No one can figure out what happened.

No one in my family can look me in the face.

The days crawl on, quiet and sullen, and I am gradually aware of the fact that my parents are afraid of me.

Roe tells me his side. The beatings from the Children of Brigid goons while I was in the basement, one of whom remembered him from the meeting back in February, and all of whom said things to Roe that he refuses to repeat. Things about how he looks. Things about who he is.

Fiona tells me hers. How the birds came from nowhere. How one bird, presumably the original one she healed, has not left. It perches on her garden wall every morning, waiting to see her. How she saw the flames engulf Miss Banbury, and how the image patrols her everywhere, appears to her in dreams.

Nuala tells me how Manon quickly changed her form to look like one of the Children, pretended to wrestle her mother, and then got her out of the court. They found Sister Assumpta collapsed by the door of the school.

Manon speaks to no one. She is at the funeral, holding her mother's hand, her head bent in prayer. It must be hard for her. She doesn't really know us, after all, and who knows what kind of connection she experienced when she was bound to Heather.

384

Lily kept hold of the knife. She wrestled it out of the ground, then gave it back to me later.

Aaron does not attend the funeral.

I do not see Aaron again, after the conversation with Dorey.

We stand outside the church, just the six of us. Unsure of who to look at, what to do. Two people are dead. One was elderly. The official cause of death for Sister Assumpta is that she fell trying to escape the smoke, and shortly after had a heart attack. An ordinary kind of old-person death for an extraordinary kind of day. An extraordinary kind of life.

From the corner of my eye, I can see a man approaching my dad. A man so upright and proper that I assume he is Children of Brigid, someone belonging to Dorey. I'm wrong though. He's just an ordinary lawyer, apparently.

"Maeve," my father says when we get in the car. "I've been asked to bring you to a solicitor's office tomorrow."

I look from my dad to my mum, wary. "Am I being sued?"

"No," Dad says, equally confused. "Quite the opposite."

The next day at the solicitor's office, with my dad sitting next to me, I am told that Sister Assumpta's will was recently changed to include me.

"Maeve," Dad stumbles. "I had no idea you were . . . close with Sister Assumpta?"

"I wasn't," I say limply. But I realize I will have to give them something. Both my father and the curious-looking solicitor who is trying his best to be professional about this. "We had a really nice afternoon a few weeks ago," I offer. "We played Christmas carols on her piano, and I've helped her clean a few times."

Still, there is a waspish silence in the air.

"I was punished quite a lot," I offer. "And she was often around after school, doing odd jobs, so we ran into each other."

The solicitor coughs, and then looks down at the paper in front of him.

"The building has been left to you, Maeve," he says simply.

"Excuse me?"

"The building has been left to you," he repeats. "It's yours. Or, it will be yours, once you turn eighteen. Until then it will be held in trust with your parents, but it specifically stipulates here that until then, you should be granted as much dominion over the building as possible."

I can't say anything. I just stare and stare.

"W-well," my dad splutters. "This is one of those things you hear about, isn't it? The urban myth of the old lady who leaves a stranger a fortune."

My dad is so nervous and overwhelmed that he can't do anything except make jokes. He can't look at the thing properly. Can't comprehend that his teenage daughter has been left property belonging to a person whose death she was present at. Even in my shock, I can see how bad this looks.

"How recently was the will amended?" I finally ask.

"A month ago."

I cringe deeper, darker, wondering whether this will get out. This new addition to my already terrible reputation.

Thou shalt not suffer a witch to live.

"Well, Maeve," my dad continues. "The building might be unsalvageable, but the land, I'm sure, is extremely valuable. I'm sure plenty of people will want a nice central location for a hotel or an office chain or something. We can sell it. The money would set you up for life."

I don't say anything. I just think about the letter opener with the pearl handle.

"No need to worry about college anymore," he says, his nervousness trembling in his throat. He tries desperately to convert it into a laugh. "You could travel the world until your thirties, if you like."

When I got the call to God, she said . . . she said, you belong back here.

The water gushing out of the wall. The glowing vein of power, hidden deep within it.

You'll have to come back here, in the end. That's your service.

"I'm not selling," I blurt out. "I'll never sell it."

"Maeve," Dad says steadily. "You have plenty of time to think about this. You don't even inherit for another year."

"The insurance is covering the repairs," the solicitor says helpfully. "So you can sell once it's good and ready."

You'll have to come back here, in the end. That's your service.

I shake my head. "Never," I repeat.

And I keep on repeating it until the solicitor gets tired of explaining things to me, until my dad stops making jokes, and until we get back into the car and drive home.

·)❯●❮(·

That night, I break into the old building. It isn't hard. There's police tape up everywhere, some barbed wire to protect against intruders, but if you've spent the last six years going in and out of a place, you know where the weak spots are.

The walls are streaked with smoke stains, the floor covered in ash. I run my hands along the walls, smudging my fingertips gray. For some reason, Sister Assumpta's office is untouched. The fire caught the first-floor classrooms, but not here, this lemon-yellow sanctum of everything she so desperately wanted to save. The hymn sheets, the photographs, the abandoned mouth guards. I sit at the piano bench.

I don't know how to play the piano. But I tap a key anyway.

I think, for the first time, about making a will myself. Who on earth would I leave this all to? Not my family, who would sell. What once felt like silly black-sheep loner instincts now feels like a chasm of difference. My life won't ever be like theirs.

My life. If there is one.

The conversation with Dorey was short. We crossed the road together to meet her.

Two sensitives together, Dorey said. *Now, there's something you don't see too often.*

Aaron spoke first. *What do you want, Dorey?*

Not a thing, she said. *Not a thing. I'm here as a courtesy. As a warning.*

We looked at each other, Aaron and I. Something like unity. Something like a team.

You know, Maeve, she continued. *Now that you've taken one of ours, this puts us back to square one.*

Square one, I said. *What's square one?*

I tap another key. I put my fingers together. I try to play "Chop-sticks." I forget how.

Now, she can be your downfall, or she can be your start.

That's what she said. She quoted the song and everything. The awful, terrible song. The song about revenge, and the revenge demon, and the desperate truth of our situation hit me and Aaron at exactly the same time. That the Children are willing to do anything but kill us outright. People who know magic really know it, understand that it is never worth it to kill someone in magic's name. The curse is too bad, the karma too toxic. But make them kill one of yours—well, then you're in revenge spirit territory. Then you get the big guns. Then you, the Children, get to call the Housekeeper.

I hit one of the sharp keys, the black ones, and marvel at the Children's cleverness. It's a catch-22: if they had successfully stopped us from sealing the Well, they could go on draining it indefinitely. If they couldn't stop us, they could at least let us win just enough to allow for the calling of the Housekeeper. The Housekeeper would reopen the Well and get rid of us. Either way, they do OK, aside from the loss of Heather Banbury.

And in the grand scheme of things, what's one Heather Banbury?

There is just one little tune I know how to play: a one-handed melody that sounds dimly like "The Way You Look Tonight" and can mostly be played by pressing three keys back and forth, back and forth, then moving up one note and repeating the same motion.

Then Aaron disappeared. Everyone wondered why. They asked me what happened at the other side of the road. He had finally found people, they said. Found a community. Found us. I don't tell them about the dreams I keep having, the little spyglasses into his day. The dreams where he's driving; the dreams where he's shaved his head; the dreams where he throws all his possessions into the sea.

He seems to think he can outrun this. This thing that's coming. That's already on its way.

I haven't said a word. How can I tell my best friends that they dodged death twice only to have the Housekeeper awoken again? How can I bring the burden of that knowledge to their door?

I play the notes, push the keys, roll my fingers, the same tune repeating again and again.

In this house that is mine, as long as I'm alive enough to keep it.

ACKNOWLEDGMENTS

This book was written when we were all locked indoors, and so I would like to spend this first bit of these acknowledgments thanking the people, places, and things that helped me survive.

To Ella Risbridger: God, what's left to say? We planned this whole book together on a napkin. You are the only person in the world who understands these characters the way that I do: if these are my kids, then you are their godmother.

To Gav: I was having a bad day once and you said, "Maybe you're afraid because you're trying to control your own excitement." I wrote it down, and it got me through the day. Thank you for saying things that get me through the day.

To Natasha Hodgson: an eternal Fiona, who had her theater run cancelled in 2020—allowing me to see her much more. I thank her for holding my hand and worshipping with me at the altar of Lisa Kudrow. Thank you, also, to Lisa Kudrow.

To Harry Harris: Someday we'll write another song and it will make you rich.

To Wren Dennehy: I almost feel like you should be put here

twice. Once for the rigorous work you did as my sensitivity reader, and once for keeping me sane with the hundreds of long phone calls you made as my friend. Thanks also to your lovely assistant, Dolores in accounts payable.

To Dolly Alderton: Because what's more teenage than spending a year on the phone with your big sister in the year above?

To Jennifer Cownie, you little green egg, you fireplace of angels, you wise freak.

To Sarah Maria Griffin, who upgrades my armor.

To Tom McInnes, my horrible son.

To my family—I didn't get to see you much during the writing of this book, and I missed you very badly.

To Sarah Savitt, who did not work on this book, but was very patient while my adult fiction deadlines got put off further and further.

To Vickie Maye at the *Irish Examiner*, who was EXTREMELY patient about my column deadlines.

Thank you as always to Bryony, my agent, and to the whole team at Walker Books. Thank you in particular to Gráinne Clear and Susan Van Metre for their editorial guidance, and to Rosi Crawley and Rebecca Oram for their publicity prowess.

Thank you to @ArcherofAnarchy for sharing your experience of the name-changing process!

Several books inspired and informed the writing of *The Gifts That Bind Us*, particularly when it came to the religious and queer narratives. I would like to both thank and recommend the following: *Unfollow* by Megan Phelps-Roper, *Sin Bravely* by Maggie Rowe, *Something That May Shock and Discredit You* by Daniel M. Ortberg, *Trusting Doubt* by Valerie Tarico, *My Life as a Goddess* by Guy Branum, *Against Memoir* by Michelle Tea, and *Are You There, God? It's Me, Ellen* by Ellen Coyne.

AUTHOR'S NOTE

This is a fictional work, but that doesn't mean some of the issues raised aren't very real. If you have concerns or questions about self-harm or other urgent health matters, please do not be afraid to consult the following resources.

National Alliance on Mental Illness (NAMI)
Crisis Text Line
National Suicide Prevention Lifeline
YouthLine
The Trevor Project
Trans Lifeline

ABOUT THE AUTHOR

CAROLINE O'DONOGHUE is an Irish author, journalist, and host of the acclaimed podcast *Sentimental Garbage*. Her book *All Our Hidden Gifts* has been translated into almost a dozen languages and is in development as a major television series. She lives in London.